THE BEST SHORT STORIES OF 1925

TO ROMER

BY WAY OF ACKNOWLEDGMENT AND REQUEST

Grateful acknowledgment for permission to include the stories and other material in this volume is made to the following authors and editors:

To the Editors of *The Boston Evening Transcript, The Reviewer, The Century Magazine, The Pictorial Review, Harper's Magazine, The Atlantic Monthly, Liberty, Collier's Weekly,* and *The Dial;* and to Messrs. Harcourt, Brace, and Company, Messrs. Boni and Liveright, Inc., Miss Sandra Alexander, Mr. Sherwood Anderson, Mr. Nathan Asch, Mr. Barry Benefield, Mr. Konrad Bercovici, Miss Bella Cohen, Mr. Charles Caldwell Dobie, Mr. Rudolph Fisher, Mrs. Katharine Fullerton Gerould, Mr. Walter Gilkyson, Mr. Manuel Komroff, Mr. Ring W. Lardner, Mr. Robert Robinson, Miss Evelyn Scott, Miss May Stanley, Mr. Wilbur Daniel Steele, Mr. Milton Waldman, Mr. Glenway Wescott, Miss Barrett Willoughby, and Mrs. Elinor Wylie.

I wish to make particular acknowledgments for editorial assistance to Mrs. W. J. Turner, Miss Katharine Macdonald, and Mr. Francis J. Hannigan.

In dedicating the present volume to my wife, I wish to record her invaluable coöperation in making this volume, as well as "The Best British Short Stories of 1925," less faulty than it otherwise might have been during my prolonged illness last summer.

I shall be grateful to my readers for corrections, and particularly for suggestions leading to the wider usefulness of these annual volumes. In particular, I shall welcome the receipt from authors, editors and publishers, of stories printed during the period between October, 1924, and September, 1925, inclusive, which have qualities of distinction and yet are not printed in periodicals falling under my regular attention.

Communications may be addressed to me *Care of Small, Maynard & Company, 41 Mount Vernon Street, Boston, Mass.*

E. J. O.

CONTENTS

INTRODUCTION

I

Is it, as Henry Adams suggests, a fiction that society educates itself or aims at a conscious purpose? In Europe at all events, as he points out, society has not done so. European society at the present time is old. Its youth was not more conscious than that of the average man whose character is formed by the blows and punches of fate. But in America society is young and at least self-conscious. Comparative peace surrounds it: experience of similarly thinking nations is at its service. With these advantages can it consciously form a new and finer civilization within itself, with new values from the experience of the old European civilization and values, now of doubtful worth? America, intellectually, is of European descent. Her language, her law, are not alien to those of the old world. When, therefore, one asks if her society can educate itself toward a conscious purpose, one must not answer that question with the experiences of Asiatic civilizations in mind.

Since 1914, it has been very clear that a new energy has begun to stir in America. It is as if the mass of the people has begun to realize itself not as a congregation of settlers, farmers and prospectors, but as a nation capable of an ideal somewhat different in spirit from those which, as it can perceive from its newspapers, animate the nations of Europe. In other words, America has begun to realize that she is capable of at any rate desiring an independent ideal worthy of attainment.

It is not in the works of such writers as Emerson, Whitman, Henry Adams, and Edwin Arlington Robinson, nor in the works of the younger writers who seek inspiration outside the sphere of American life, that one finds this realization actively leading American public thought. It is in such, at first sight, unusual forms of philosophical expression as acts of law, social customs, and even newspaper articles. There one hears the voice of the American nation beginning to assert that the old codes which it inherited from Europe have come under its criticism. This criticism, one feels, arises from a definite and conscious comparison of an inherited ideal with one which is being gradually formulated by the whole nation.

In order to follow an ideal of this particular and, one might say, personal kind, it is necessary that the nation which seeks after it should, in the first place, attempt to know itself. One sees that, in every way, America today tries by self-expression to realize her own character. In the East, in the West, particularly in the Middle West, every individual who is not wholly absorbed in making money or in furthering the material welfare of his country attempts at some time during his life to say what he thinks of the world as he sees it. His world is not an old world of traditions. There is no traditional way of expressing his thoughts about it ready to his hand, nor is every man a great literary artist. He has had, therefore, to invent a form of expression that is not too great a tax upon his powers.

Few men or women are capable of sustaining their energies through the length of a novel or of a work of philosophy, and fewer have the gift of poetry. It would seem, therefore, that almost of necessity the American people has adopted the short story as its particular form of art: not the sketch nor the episodic tale, but a fairly long and systematically constructed piece of writing in which primarily it liberates its own feelings, and by which secondarily it tells a tale. The American short story, therefore, has an immense and peculiar interest and value. One feels in it the striving of a nation to express itself, and thereby to come to a knowledge of its own character, in order completely and consciously to follow an ideal which it hopes to set before itself.

But whether through the evolutions of human life it is possible to follow a fixed ideal, whether it is possible for a whole nation consciously to mould its future, whether even it is possible for a people to realize its own character clearly enough to be able to impose a philosophy upon it, only the future can tell. One is inclined to think that it is impossible, but that does not detract from the extraordinary interest which the phenomenon of a nation seeking self-realization arouses.

Whatever the result of America's conscious attempt at self-education may be, the record of it, in the form at any rate of the short story, whether good or bad, will be of the greatest value to future generations.

II

To repeat what I have said in these pages in previous years, for the benefit of the reader as yet unacquainted with my standards and principles of selection, I shall point out that I have set myself the task of disengaging the essential human qualities in our contemporary fiction, which, when chronicled conscientiously by our literary artists, may fairly be called a criticism of life. I am not at all interested in formulæ, and organized criticism at its best would be nothing more than dead criticism, as all dogmatic interpretation of life is always dead. What has interested me, to the exclusion of other things, is the fresh, living current which flows through the best American work, and the psychological and imaginative reality which American writers have conferred upon it.

No substance is of importance in fiction, unless it is organic substance, that is to say, substance in which the pulse of life is beating. Inorganic fiction has been our curse in the past, and bids fair to remain so, unless we exercise much greater artistic discrimination than we display at present.

The present record covers the period from October, 1924, to September, 1925, inclusive. During this period I have sought to select from the stories published in American magazines those which have rendered life imaginatively in organic substance and artistic form. Substance is something achieved by the artist in every act of creation, rather than something already present, and accordingly a fact or group of facts in a story only attains substantial embodiment when the artist's power of compelling imaginative persuasion transforms them into a living truth. The first test of a short story, therefore, in any qualitative analysis, is to report upon how vitally compelling the writer makes his selected facts or incidents. This test may be conveniently called the test of substance.

But a second test is necessary if the story is to take rank above other stories. The true artist will seek to shape this living substance into the most beautiful and satisfying form by skilful selection and arrangement of his materials, and by the most direct and appealing presentation of it in portrayal and characterization.

The short stories which I have examined in this study, as in previous years, have fallen naturally into four groups. The first consists of those stories which fail, in my opinion, to survive either the test of substance or the test of form. These stories are listed in the yearbook without comment or qualifying asterisk.

The second group consists of those stories which may fairly claim that they survive either the test of substance or the test of form. Each of these stories may claim to possess either distinction of technique alone, or more frequently, I am glad to say, a persuasive sense of life in them to which a reader responds with some part of his own experience. Stories included in this group are indicated in the yearbook index by a single asterisk prefixed to the title.

The third group, which is composed of stories of still greater distinction, includes such narratives as may lay convincing claim to a second reading, because each of them has survived both tests, the test of substance and the test of form. Stories included in this group are indicated in the yearbook index by two asterisks prefixed to the title.

Finally, I have recorded the names of a small group of stories which possess, I believe, the even finer distinction of uniting genuine substance and artistic form in a closely woven pattern with such sincerity that these stories may fairly claim a position in American literature. If all of these stories by American authors were republished, they would not occupy more space than six or seven novels of average length. My selection of them does not imply the critical belief that they are great stories. A year which produced one great story would be an exceptional one. It is simply to be taken as meaning that I have found the equivalent of six or seven volumes worthy of republication among all the stories published during the period under consideration. These stories are indicated in the yearbook index by three asterisks prefixed to the title, and are listed in the special "Rolls of Honor." In compiling these lists, I have permitted no personal preference or prejudice to influence my judgment consciously. Several stories which I dislike personally are to be found on the "Rolls of Honor." The general and particular results of my study will be found explained and carefully detailed in the supplementary part of this volume.

EDWARD J. O'BRIEN.

London.
November 3, 1925.

THE BEST SHORT STORIES OF 1925

Note.—The order in which the stories in this volume are printed is not intended as an indication of their comparative excellence; the arrangement is alphabetical by authors.

THE GIFT[1]

By SANDRA ALEXANDER

(From *The Reviewer*)

THE sun came up around the bend of the river. The top of it, huge and misshapen, had just cleared the mass of juniper and swamp myrtle when Annie Sherrod opened the kitchen door and came down the rickety back steps into the yard. She carried in one hand a bucket of clabber for the pigs and in the other a tin pail full to the brim with a stirring of corn meal and sweet milk for the chickens. As she reached the chicken coop the sun shook away the dark myrtle and gave its red reflection to the river. The water tugged and pulled it out of shape as it flowed on by to the sound. The river and the dried mud along its banks shone brightly, but the woman noticed none of this red glory of sunrise. She scattered the meal and emptied the sour milk in the pig trough, and then filled the empty bucket with the dark water and gave it to the chickens to drink.

The sun had now risen so high that the reflection spread like burnished copper on the face of the water, and Annie shaded her eyes as she looked down at the fish trap anchored close to the bank. The fish trap was made of two hoops of seine and two dug-outs. The hoops were balanced upon a greased pole between the dugouts. The faintest puff of wind caused the top hoop to dip down until it was caught by the current and dragged under. As it came up the opposite hoop was pushed down. The hoops dipped and turned endlessly in the river current and sometimes brought up fish. When the hoops reached the top of their circle the fish fell out and down into the dugouts, sometimes to the right, sometimes to the left. "Lazy man fishin'" they called the trap on the river.

There were plenty of fish this morning, silver river herrings, and Annie gathered them up and carried them back to the house.

She busied herself with breakfast and when it stood smoking hot on the stove, she went down the hall to a room at the front of the house. "Henry," she called, outside the closed door, "it's time to get up—brekfast's ready." A voice answered her and she went on to the next room, opened the door and entered.

It was dark in there and the air smelled of stale bedding. Annie propped up a window and pushed open a broken shutter. The sun threw a broad streak of light across a bed in the corner which held a sleeping man. He roused himself, shivered, and threw one protecting arm across his eyes to shut out the sudden glare. "Can't you let me be?" he said. Annie did not look at him: "Brekfast's done," she said and went out.

The table stood under the window in the kitchen. She wiped the oilcloth top with a damp cloth and set it with thick china plates and cups. She "dished up" the smoking food, filled the cups with coffee and put the pot back on the stove. Then she sat down at one end of the table and stared in front of her.

Her brooding face was lifeless in its repose. There was no thought going on back of the woman's dulled eyes. She sat, heavy and relaxed, a little forward in the chair, and stared straight in front of her. Mechanically she lifted a hand now and then to frighten away the swarms of flies that hovered over the food before her. The sound of a tapping stick and carefully placed feet in the hall roused her. She sagged to her feet and went to the door. A man with a cane in one hand and the other spread out before him stopped beside her. "Annie," he said inquiringly.

"Here I be," she said, catching hold of his hand to guide him to the table.

"I smell fish this morning," the blind man said cheerfully, as he spread his hands to touch the knife and fork at his place.

"Yes, we got fish." Annie speared one with a fork and took out the backbone. She put milk and sugar in his coffee, cut up a piece of fat pork and put the plate down in front of him. "There you air!" She helped her own plate and sat down again.

They ate in silence.

Down the hall a door slammed. "Will's late," the blind man said.

"Yeah—he wuz drunk agin las' night!"

The blind man made soft clucking noises, his tongue against his closed teeth.

Will came through the kitchen, glancing at the table as he went by on his way to the back porch. There was a sound of water poured in a tin basin. "Ain't ther' a towel 'round here some place?" he called. Annie got up, took a towel from the cupboard drawer out to him, and came back to her breakfast. In a little while he came in, sat down between them and helped himself to food.

II

The two men were brothers, Henry and William Sherrod. The blind man was stout, his sandy hair thin on his round head. William was slim in build and the bones of his face prominent. His hair was thick and the color of Henry's. His eyes were blue and quick with impatience. Henry's were blue and flat with the vacancy of blindness.

Will leaned forward and took another fish from the heaped plate in front of him.

"Got in purtty late las' night, didn't you, Will?" Henry had finished his breakfast, and sat leaning back in his chair, his pale eyes staring in the direction of his brother.

Will did not lift his head from his plate. "Uh-huh," he said.

"Who'd you see up town?" Henry went on.

"Nobody much. I—" he cleared his mouth of the fish bones—"I went to the movin' picher place."

"Oh, you did, did you?" There was an eager interest in Henry's voice. He leaned forward and waited for Will to go on. Then he prompted him: "Ain't you goin' to tell us what you saw? Annie here wants to know—don't you, Annie?"

Annie roused herself from the stupor she had fallen into. "I ain't pertikler," she said.

Will suddenly scowled at the blind man. He paid no attention to Annie. "It warn't so much. Jest one o' them regler pichers. L's see—" he ran his hand through his thick hair in the effort to think. "Thar was a woman an' two men—an'—an' she liked purtty things an'—an' all. An' one man was poor an' tother was rich—so she runned away with him—an' then he did something crooked—bet on a horse or sumpin like that—an' so her husban' come an' got her. It was like that!"

Henry sighed when Will had finished. "It must er been a real good picher. Minds me er one I saw onct over to Adamton."

"Yeah! Everything 'minds you er somethin' you seen over to Adamton. It's right bad you cain't go back over there." Henry dropped his head at the sound of Will's voice.

Annie had not looked up from her plate or seemed to listen to Will's recital, but now she stared straight at him, and under the scorn in her gaze he hesitated. "You lay off'n Henry," she said.

"What you got to do with it? You better dry up yerself!" But as she still stared at him, his eyes wavered and he returned to his breakfast.

Almost paralyzed by this exchange between husband and wife, not because it was new or the first time he had heard it, but because he so keenly realized his helplessness, Henry's hands fumbled with his knife and fork. They made outlandish noises against his empty plate.

"Have some more fish, Henry?" Annie lowered her voice as she spoke to him.

"Believe I had a plenty, Annie."

"Gimme 'nother cup er coffee." Will held his cup back toward the stove without turning. Annie filled it for him. She had finished her breakfast and she went slowly about the kitchen, testing the water in the iron kettle and scraping the dishes clean. She gathered them into a pile and carried them to a table nearer the stove.

Henry tilted back his chair and lighted a pipe. Will

sucked noisily at his second cup of coffee, his arms propped on the table, one hand supporting his head.

"Going to do Four Acre?" Henry asked presently in a voice he meant to be conciliating.

"Yeah."

"It sure is goin' to be a hot day."

"You're dam' right!"

"Can't yer put it off?" Henry went on.

"Naw!" Will got up and stood with his hands on the back of his chair, looking down at him. "You got a purtty sof' snap sittin' 'round all day doin' nothin'."

"Trade you!" Henry said quickly.

"Like hell, you would!" He gave the chair a sudden push that sent it against the table. "Whar's them milk buckets?"

Annie pointed to them and he took the two empty pails and went out. There was a little space of silence as Annie poured the greasy dish water out through the open window on the ground, where it ran off in a rainbow streak down the slope of the yard. "Will oughter milk before brekfast," she said to Henry as she hung the pan on its nail.

"Well, it's purtty hard on him, doing all the work for bothen us." Henry shook his head solemnly.

"You can't help it!" Annie said fiercely. She went through the door carrying a bucket of scraps—more food for the pigs. When she came back she swept the kitchen, took the ashes from the cooling stove and covered the table with a cloth, then she darkened the room and went out. She swept the two bedrooms, beat the knobs out of the shuck mattresses and spread them with yellow sheets, yellow from having been washed in river water. When all this was done she returned to the kitchen, strained and set away the milk Will had left for her on the table. She carried it out to the wire-covered box nailed high up on the porch, to keep away the swarming flies. Then she put on a slat bonnet, took a knife and basket and went out into the garden.

III

The Sherrod house stood on a rise of ground above the river. The spring freshets never reached it, not even the

famous one of '98. The front of the house faced the long
red dirt track that led up to the crossroads, and the back
of it looked down on the river. The house had never been
painted, the clapboards had weathered an even gray, and
here and there patches of green moss clung to the roof and
the chimney bricks. Henry and William owned it jointly,
together with the sixty-acre farm on either side of it.

Henry knew nothing of farming. When he was in his
teens he had gone away to work on one of the river
steamers. In those days, twenty years ago, steamers ran
from across the sound, and up the river as far as Jamesville,
the town below the Sherrod place. There were no steam-
boats on the river now. The railroad had built a long
trestle across the sound and put them all out of business.
The old *Plymouth,* that Henry had gone out on, was lying,
a rotting hulk, at Adamton. The boat's trip from Adamton
across the sound and up the river to Jamesville had required
a day. Then she was tied up at the dock until next morning when her captain backed her around and headed her
downstream and again across the sound to Adamton. The
railroad now hauled the cotton and tobacco, and an occasional crop of peanuts from Jamesville to Adamton in three
hours.

Henry had been fat even as a young man. He had a jolly
laugh and took life pretty much as he found it. He knew
a lot of drummer jokes, collected from travelers on the
Plymouth. He told them to the old folks and to Will
whenever he came to the farm to spend a night. Will
listened to them with ill grace and Henry was forced to
believe Will jealous of him. He wooed Will with presents
bought in the superior stores of Adamton, and if he discovered Will was "courting" a town girl, he stopped going
to see her himself. He had a long talk with Will when the
old people died. He said if Will wanted him to he would
give up his job and come home, but Will said he didn't
need any river man around. So Henry had kept on with
the *Plymouth.*

The farm was a lonely place and Will's fine enthusiasm
for farming by himself soon wore itself out. He decided
to get married and went "courting" Annie Spruill, the

daughter of a neighboring farmer. He drove to her house in a shiny new buggy and a suit of clothes Henry had bought for him over in Adamton. Will had intended painting the house and making many improvements when he brought Annie home, but the spring freshet in the river ruined his corn that year, and afterwards he never seemed to get around to it.

Annie had been a pretty girl when Will married her. In those days she had bright brown eyes and black hair, but the eyes dimmed and ceased to sparkle after a few years on the farm with Will. The work was heavy, and Will, his disposition never good, fretted with his seeming ill-luck, rarely provided her with any of the things women like. He had drunk corn whiskey, and as Annie lost her good looks and became a drab creature who rarely spoke, he drank worse. His unfaithfulness to her was known throughout the county.

Annie's children died at birth. They were thin infants, old beyond the knowledge of mortals. She had wept noisily for the first and a little less for the second. She was carrying the third when Henry came home to stay. A doctor in Adamton had told him he was losing his eyesight. Will said he had been "kicked out of his job." Annie was glad to have him. He never lost his temper and he helped her around the house until the blindness was upon him. He was resigned and at first made a joke of his affliction. He sat in his rocking chair, never seeming to care whether he moved again or not. He told Annie all the drummer jokes and made her laugh long and loudly. He learned to knit and he sent away to a mail order house for a fiddle. He taught himself to play "Pop Goes the Weasel."

Annie's third child was born. Henry held it in his arms until the tiny overburdened heart ceased beating in thumps. He could not see the age-old little face, nor the coppery spots on its forehead, but he knew something was wrong.

Doctor White in Jamesville told Will that he and Annie must not have any more children, and that he was to come to town for treatment. Will listened to him in sulky silence—and never went.

Farm labor became harder to get. A great many farm

hands had gone north, lured by rumors of higher wages. Will rented out part of the farm to a negro tenant. This man had a still down in the hollow and Will bought molasses for him and sold the finished "monkey rum" in Jamesville. It was only a small business, for Will had no money to buy off the county officers and run the still on a large scale, but it was quite big enough to furnish him with all he and his town friends wanted to drink. Three or four times a week he drove into town with a jug under the seat of the buggy and, after he had disposed of it, spent the evening lounging around the drug store and talking to the girls from the tobacco stemmery. He spent his money buying them silk stockings and cheap perfume.

During all this time Henry sat on at the farm, moving only when necessity drove him. He grew stouter. He rarely told a drummer joke; Annie knew them all, so there was no need. His clothes were worn and shiny with grease from the food he spilled upon them. He had put his fiddle away. He told Annie he had heard that people born on the river came home to die on it.

IV

It was twelve o'clock and Will came in from the field. The perspiration streamed down his face and the top of his overalls was wet with it. Annie put dinner on the table. She had cooked a piece of smoked hog jowl and boiled some collards in the liquor, and there was a pudding of yellow corn. At Will's place stood a pitcher of milk, covered with a cloth to keep the flies out. Will washed his hands and sat down; Henry was already in his accustomed place. A cat came in and curled its sleek sides around the table leg. Will kicked at it and the cat jumped in a great arch through the kitchen door.

"I'm going to kill 'at cat," he said. No one answered him, no one spoke throughout the meal.

The kitchen was stifling hot. When Will had finished he carried his chair out on the porch. A little breeze was stirring, he propped the chair against the side of the house, sat down and closed his eyes. In a minute more he was

fast asleep. Annie washed the dishes and set the kitchen
to rights. As she crossed the porch on her way to the
house she leaned over and shook him awake: "Ain't you
ever goin' to work?" she said.

He stretched himself and stood up: "Tain't none of yore
business, ifn't I don't!" he told her as he crammed his hat
on his head and went down the back steps to the field.

He came in early, long before sunset, and asked for a
towel and hot water. He took the bucket Annie gave him
to their bedroom and whistled as he washed and put on
clean clothes. He joined them at supper in his best suit of
clothes and ate his food in a great hurry.

"Goin' to town again tonight, Will?" Henry asked.

"None er yore business!"

"Well," Henry said mildly, "you needn't take a feller's
head off when he asks you a question."

Will's eyes were red as he looked up, "Who ast you to put
in? You mind your own business—if you don't, you know
what's good for you! I guess I got a right to go to town
when I dam' please! Who does all the work aroun' here—
you tell me that——"

"I didn't mean nothin'," Henry said.

"No, an' you better not neither!" Will got up from his
place. He turned toward Annie, "An' you needn't leave no
light burnin' for me!" Annie did not look at him. In a
minute or two they heard him drive out of the yard. He
would be gone all night and in the morning would appear,
sober and sleepy, to spend the whole day lying in a stupor
on a pallet at the end of the porch, sleeping away the
effects of the raw liquor he had drunk.

Henry tapped his way out to the porch and sat down in
a rocking chair. When Annie had put up the supper dishes
she came out and joined him. It was cooler out there. The
sun had long since gone down and the river had lost its
look of parchedness. The water was black as it hurried by
to the sound. There were black shadows under the myrtle
and willows on the opposite bank, but the trees waved
green higher up where the light struck them. The sky back
of them was soft with a scattering of white clouds. Night
flew close to the water. A crane's broad wings circled and

went on downstream. The frogs began their nightly
singing.

Henry's hands rested on his knees. Annie sat tense and
drawn in her chair, her hands on the arms and her head
back against the high, broad top of it. They were both
rocking. Suddenly Henry's chair ceased rocking and he
turned to Annie.

"You ain't right well, are you, Annie?'

Annie did not answer him at once and he went on: "Seems
to me like you been ailin' quite a spell. You don't never
say nothin', but I kin feel you moving 'round slow like.
What's the matter with you?" His slow tones were anxious.

Annie rocked all the harder. "Tain't nothin'," she said
briefly.

"Well, I'm right glad to hear it. Maybe you need a dost
of quinine—that'll put you right in a jiffy——"

"It'll be a long time afore I'm right agin!" Annie said
passionately.

The full meaning of it sank into Henry's mind in the
long pause that followed. He cleared his throat helplessly,
and his voice, as he questioned her, had a quaver in it:
"You don't mean you're goin' to—to have another young
'un?"

"Yes, I do, an' I wish I was dead! I been thinkin' I'd
better go down and jump in that river——"

"Now, Annie, don't talk like that!" Henry put out a
hand and felt for her in the dark. "That kind of talk
ain't right. You know what the Bible says about takin'
your own life. It ain't right. You ought not to even think
it——" he lapsed into silence.

"Maybe you made a mistake—maybe it ain't so," he said
after a little.

"Yes, maybe!" Annie's voice was bitter.

"Does—does Will know?"

"I ain't told him, but he knows well enough—" she broke
off and suddenly stood up. "I—I forgot, I ain't fed the
cat." She went swiftly into the house. Through the blinds
back of him Henry heard her fling herself down on the bed
and smother her sobs in the quilts. He rocked violently,
his fat, helpless hands around the knobs of the armchair.

"It ain't right! It ain't right!" He repeated it to himself over and over.

The stars were out when Annie stole back to her place beside him. The sky was powdery with them. Crickets chirped in the yard and the frogs cried loudly out of the swamp. Annie's chair began to move. At first it went slowly back and forth and then it struck its gait. Henry's rocker kept time to it.

"I been sittin' here thinkin' while you was gone, Annie. I been thinkin' somethin' mighty curious—about us—an' how things is fixed in this world. It ain't right, some of it. Now here's us—Will all time runnin' after them girls in town—an' drinkin'. An' then there's you—you has to work too hard. Will don't work hardly enough—he reely ain't able too—maybe if'n he was to stop drinkin' he might——"

"He won't!" Annie interrupted.

"No, I don't guess he will. It's a pity. I seen a lot of it up an' down the river in the old days—it don't never lead to no good end. If you was to have somebody to help do the cookin'—an' was to go to meetin' now and then—an' git some pretty clothes——"

"Huh!" Annie's rocker stopped. "Where you think we goin' to get all them things? I ain't been to meetin' in months—that's how I git to meetin'!"

"I wasn't sayin' you was goin' to git 'em. I was just thinkin'," Henry's voice rebuked her.

"Huh!" The rocking chair took up its accustomed gait again.

"Maybe—maybe when yore time come—" Henry's voice went on out of the darkness, "maybe yore baby would live —and you could raise it up to be a comfort to you."

Annie said nothing.

"Then ther's me. All my life long I took good care of myself. I never had nothin' much to do with girls—never drunk much—a toddy now an' then, that's all—but look at me?" There was no bitterness in Henry's voice. "But here I am—a big lump—good for nothin'—I jest sit aroun' an' make a lot of work for you."

"You're a sight o' company, Henry," Annie interrupted.

"Well, thank you, Annie, but I'll never be good for

nothin' again. An' what I got to look forward to—just tell
me that? Tain't like I got married an' had some children
—it wouldn't matter so much then—I wouldn't keer—I'd
be more resigned like——"

Annie stopped rocking.

Henry went on. "I sometimes sits an' thinks about it for
a good spell. We don't know if what the preacher says is
true. We ain't certain 'bout that kingdom up in the sky—
leastways I ain't——" Henry paused uncertainly. "It
may be agin' the Scripters, but sometimes I think all we
got is right here on the earth—an' it don't seem right that
some of us gits so little."

Annie sat still under the weight of it. "No, it don't,
Henry," she said at last.

"I lived pretty good. I didn't miss much when I was
on the river—but I wish I'd got married. I wish I'd got a
boy or girl to take keer of me now." He heaved a deep
sigh. "Well, it's like that—but don't guess it does any
good to talk about it much."

"I never knowed you cared nothin' 'bout children,"
Annie's voice held a wondering interest.

"No, I don't reckon you did. I ain't never talked about
it to nobody before."

There was a long pause broken only by the creak of the
boards under the two swaying chairs.

"Henry," Annie began again, and her voice was solemn,
"if 'n I was to take keer of myself—same as Doctor White
tole me last time—drink a lot of milk and let some of the
heavy work go—do you 'spose this baby what's comin'
would live?"

"Maybe it would, Annie——"

She leaned forward and touched him on the arm. "An'
if 'n it does live, Henry," she said in sudden excitement,
"it's goin' to *be yore chile*——"

Henry stopped rocking. "What you mean, Annie?"

"I mean I'm goin' to give it to you—to grow up an' be a
comfort to you. It's going to be named Henry Sherrod—
an' you is goin' to raise it——"

"But how can you do that, Annie—you can't give Will's
child away?"

"Can't I?" the same scornful laugh was in Annie's voice. "Will hadn't ought to have no children—the doctor done said so—an' anyway he shan't tech it——"

"But what'll he say?"

"He won't say noth'n—you leave that to me!"

"But look here, Annie," Henry leaned toward her in the darkness, his voice betraying his earnestness, "supposen you did—people would think it kinder queer——"

"Let 'em! Nobody never comes down here no more. When he gits big we'll go away——"

"Where'll we go?"

"I dunno—some place!" Annie leaned back, relaxed. Her voice was full of ease and happiness. "We'll go away all right. Some place where there's movin' pichers an' 'lectric lights. He kin go to school—pay school. I ain't goin' to sen' my chile to no free school! Maybe he'll have a tobacco warehouse when he gits grown——"

"Maybe he'll be captain of a steamboat——" Henry's voice took up the chant.

"Yes, an' we'll have a parlor an' a organ——"

"Maybe he'll read the newspaper to me——" Henry's voice was wistful.

Once more the rockers rocked in cadence. It was cooler now, a little wind blew from across the river and brought the steady "flop flop" of the fish trap as it dipped down in the current.

Henry loosed himself from the dream first. "It's gettin' kinder late," he said. "I reckon we all better be gettin' to bed."

Annie drew a long breath. "Maybe it won't live," she said.

"Maybe so," Henry too seemed to have lost interest. He shuffled across the porch and through the doorway, the tap of his stick preceding him down the hall to his room.

Annie sat on, her hands gripped tightly together in her lap. "Oh, God," she prayed, "I got to have somethin'—I got to have somethin'——"

V

October was on the river. Swamp maples flaunted a blare of color as far as eye could reach. The slim dagger leaves of the willows, already yellow, fell to eddy in the current before the river swept them away. Pokeberries were as black as ink. Green holly was swelling, turning red for winter. Up in the bare branches of the gum trees mistletoe, in round full bunches, swayed with every passing wind, the milky berries gleaming against gray-green leaves.

Annie Sherrod was jellying. She stood over the kitchen table pouring the crimson juice of wild grapes into tumblers and sealing them with round pieces of white paper dipped in rum and white of egg.

Propped against the door in a split bottom chair, Henry was skimping through the strains of "Pop Goes the Weasel," on his fiddle. His head was bent low, only the thin, reddish hair brushed carefully across the top was visible to Annie as she looked across at him.

"It sure is gran' jelly!" she told him.

Henry lowered the fiddle. "I can tell that jest by smellin'," he said.

Annie wiped her hands on her big checked apron. "I'm goin' to git you some in a saucer to taste in a minute. I never did see the beat of it for jellyin'. Most times you has to wait 'till it gits cole—or set it in the sun—but this here—" She dug her fingers in the cooling stuff and lifted a mass of it high. It dropped with a soft "slosh," heard plainly across the room. Annie laughed, "Did you hear it?" she said.

"Sure did!"

"I got nine glasses," Annie went on. "I aim to pick some more grapes next week an' do up a even dozen 'fore I stops."

Henry returned to his fiddling. The kitchen glowed in the afternoon light. The stove shone red through the cracks and the kettle on it poured out its song of steam. There was a red cloth on the eating table and a bunch of goldenrod stuck in a tumbler decorating the center of it. Over all, hung the rich, spicy aroma of the fox grapes.

Annie brought a saucer half full of jelly over to Henry.

"Here, taste it!" She filled a spoon and put it in his hand. She stood over him as he sampled it, her hands akimbo on her hips.

"Um——" Henry smacked his lips noisily. "It sure is good stuff!"

"Tomorro' is Sattiday. You an' me is goin' to hitch up and drive to town right after brekfast and do some tradin' at Latham's. I already done washed your other ves'—it was terrible greasy. You got to stop dribblin' things on yourself, Henry Sherrod. If n' you don't——" Annie's voice was mocking, she threatened him with a flourish of the now empty saucer, "if n' you don't I'm goin' to tie you up in one er my apruns!" She threw back her head and laughed.

"Huh! Huh!" Henry laughed with her.

"You all seem mighty happy in here." Will stood in the doorway. He carried his gun slung across his shoulder.

The laughter stopped in mid-air. Henry returned to fingering his fiddle. Annie picked up the tray of jelly glasses and carried them out on the back porch, passing Will in the doorway, where he grudgingly made way for her. Coming back she took off her apron and, smoothing her new calico dress down over her full hips, got out the big pasteboard box she used for sewing.

All this time Will stood glowering in the doorway. No one had spoken to him. He seemed uncertain what to do, but as Annie fitted on her thimble and lifted a tiny shirt from the garments in the box, and began to stitch with fine stitches upon it, he turned and banged the door behind him.

"Huh!" Annie laughed, "Will don't feel right comfortable 'roun' me no more. He ain't forgot that piece er my mind I give him——"

"You best not be too hard on him, Annie," Henry lowered his fiddle.

"If that ain't jes' like you, Henry Sherrod! Now you takin' up for Will!"

"No, I ain't," Henry protested.

"It'll do him good. I notice he's been stayin' home pretty regular nights lately."

"Yes, he has, an' it's a good sign——"

"Time'll tell."

Annie stitched on in silence. The needle moved method-

ically in and out. Presently she began to hum under her
breath. Then she interrupted herself: "Henry," she said,
"why is it ducks' eggs don't bring as much as hens' eggs,
can you tell me that?"

"Seems to me you ought to git more for 'em."

"Well, you don't! I got a lot of 'em, too, but they don't
bring much. I believe I'm goin' to do all my cookin' with
duck eggs and sell every one of them hen eggs——"

"That would be a good thing to do——"

"Tomorro' I aim to buy a cake of that pink soap to the
drug store. It's real pretty——"

Henry nodded his head at her. He was busy with the
fiddle again.

VI

The river was rising. Already the banks were lost by the
engulfing water. The fish trap had been hauled high up the
slope of the yard out of harm's way. Myrtle and sassafras
drowned, while the topmost branches of the willows, heavy
with raindrops, dipped in the ever rising flood. It was a
sign of spring. . . . The river roared through its channel
and every day a broader expanse of water covered the
swamp bottoms and flowed sullenly outward over the young
corn planted in the bottom lands. Wild things sought
higher land. The surface of the water bore strange fruit.
Here an old log, turning over and over, on its way downstream, and there a young tree, uprooted and swept along,
its faint green leaves half submerged in the red flood. A
chicken coop rode its strangely dignified way downstream.

Water cut off the Sherrod farm from the highroad. Will
had taken the horse and buggy and escaped to town. He
gave as his excuse that somebody had to tell Doctor White
to come out at the end of the week.

Rain set in again the night Annie's son was born. It
started at supper time. Cold fingers tapped on all the
windowpanes. Aunt Julia, the negro midwife, climbed the
attic stairs and stuffed rags in all the broken windowpanes.
In the intervals when she could draw her breath a little
more easily, Annie lay and listened to it. She was afraid.

She was horribly afraid the doctor wouldn't get there in time. She asked continually if they had not heard him drive into the yard. "Jes' de win', honey!" the old negro woman would reply, placing her wrinkled brown hand on Annie's tossed hair. "Yo' res' easy, he'll sho' be here bimeby."

Henry sat outside the door and heard her cries. He wrung his soft, helpless hands. Tears ran down and splashed on his clean coat front, the coat Annie had washed for him just a few days before.

The old woman moved about the room, placing basins and folding cloths, she trimmed the lamp and put it close beside the bed where it would be most needed. She tested the water in the big kettle on the hearth, brought in pine logs to feed the ravenous fire, and then eased her rheumatic old body into the low rocker beside Annie.

"Mammy," Annie reached out and clutched her with straining fingers, "don't you reckon the doctor will be gittin' here purtty soon now—Will must er told him how bad I needed him——"

"Yes, honey, he'll come. Jes' you res' easy now. Hole yore breaf when you feels the pains—hole yore breaf and bear down——"

"He ain't comin'—I know he ain't!" Annie wailed. "Will ain't never told him!"

This went on for hours, Annie wailing and begging for the doctor and the old woman comforting her as best she could. Henry alternately dozed and wrung his hands in the cold outside the door. Toward morning Annie suddenly lifted up her voice and called him:

"Yes, Annie. He's coming—Will sure told him——"

"Henry, you listen to me—I don't care no more. *I don't care if he gits here or not,* but I want you to promise me that if 'n' I dies Will don't lay hand on this child—you promise?"

"You ain't goin' die, Annie——"

"Promise!"

"I—I promise."

Annie lay down quietly. "I'm goin' to be all right now— I ain't goin' to holler no more——" But even as she spoke the final agony came. "Help!" she cried in a voice that brought Henry to his feet and the old woman scuffling across the room. . . .

VII

The river began to go down the third day after Annie's son was born. It was a good sign, the old colored woman said, and she said, too, that Annie's baby was the finest baby in the world. Annie lay and listened to her with a smile. She uncovered the plump little body and saw for herself that it was perfect. She lay smiling as she nursed it at her breast.

This child would live. . . . She had given it to Henry— God couldn't let it die like the others. . . .

Will was still in town, and the doctor had not come; there was no need now, Annie and the baby were both doing well. Henry tapped up and down with his stick, a smile always hovering about his soft lips.

"If I just could see him." He sat with the child in his lap. "If the Lord would just give in once and let me see him, I wouldn't never ask for nothin' else."

Annie raised herself in the bed on one elbow and lay looking at them.

"He's like you, Henry, mor'n he is like Will."

"He's goin' to be a big man," Henry said. The child's curling fingers clung tightly to his thumb. It was night. Aunt Julia nodded in the slat-bottomed rocker before the fireplace. . . .

"I'm goin' give him pot-licker an' black-eyed peas—make him grow——" Annie crooned, her fingers poking the baby under the arm. It gurgled and they both laughed. "He called yore name, Henry." Annie prepared to lie down again in bed.

"I'll betcher he's smilin', ain't he, Annie?"

"You know he ain't, he's too little yit—yessir, his mammy's goin' to give this baby pot-licker an' peas——"

"Hold the lamp here, Aunt Julia," Henry called. "We got to see what this baby's doin'."

The old woman came to herself with a start and rubbed her eyes, "Sho' is smilin'—it's de bes' young un——" She pattered over for the lamp, lifted off the shield of card-board and brought it close to the bed.

"Look, Annie, ain't I right?"

Annie raised herself once more. "Hold it closer, Mammy."

"Gwine burn my chile," the old woman grumbled as she obeyed.

"No, we ain't, the idea of such a thing," Annie half laughed, and then she drew herself quickly higher up in the bed and leaned closer to the baby. "Look, Mammy, what makes him do like that?"

"Do lak whut?"

Annie passed her hand rapidly across the child's face. "He don't close his eyes like he ought when I do like that!" There was the beginning of panic in Annie's voice.

"Bless God Almighty!" The woman put down the lamp and lifted the child from Henry's lap. It wailed feebly at being so suddenly disturbed.

"What's the matter with its eyes?" Annie's voice was shrill with fear. "Tell me! Make her tell—" she appealed to Henry.

Henry struggled to his feet, his knees grown suddenly weak and unresponsive. He clutched at the woman's shoulder. "What is it? What's wrong with that baby's eyes?" he demanded in a choked whisper.

The old colored woman held the child against her breast. She made no effort to avoid Henry's hand.

"What is it?" Annie cried again.

The woman shook off Henry's hand and drew herself upright. "Dis chile," she said with strange dignity, "is bline."

"Blind!" Annie screamed. "Tain't so—you're lying! 'Tain't so, Henry——"

"No, I ain't tellin' no lie. Dis chile is bline——"

As she spoke the child's thin wails filled the room. She clutched it again to her flat breast, hushing its cries against her.

"No! No! I won't have it blind——"

"Hush, honey, don't you carry on so. Yo' got to git yo'

stren'th back." She attempted to push Annie down upon the bed.

"I don't care! I don't care!" Annie evaded her. She struggled to her knees and sat swaying back and forth, her hands clutching in desperation at the mass of tangled hair that fell about her face.

Henry had fallen back into his chair and now he sat, his fat hands twisting and untwisting about the arms of it, his loose mouth uttering words that died away before they passed his lips. The old woman carried the child across the room. She wrapped it in a piece of blanket and seated herself in the slat-bottomed rocker as before. Slowly she rocked back and forth, patting the little round back with her skinny brown hand. "Hush, chile, go to sleep," she crooned to it.

Slower and slower went the rocker. Annie's cries had ceased. Henry's head had dropped upon his breast . . . his hands were still. A log fell apart on the hearth. The old woman did not get up to replace it. The tick of the clock on the mantelpiece was the only sound in the room. They slept. . . . They slept the peace of exhaustion . . . the peace of acceptance.

THE RETURN[1]

By SHERWOOD ANDERSON

(From *The Century Magazine*)

EIGHTEEN years. Well, he was driving a good car, an expensive roadster, he was well clad, a rather solid fine-looking man, not too heavy. When he had left the Middle-Western town to go live in New York City he was twenty-two, and now, on his way back there, he was forty. He drove toward the town from the east, stopping for lunch at another town ten miles away.

When he went away from Caxton, after his mother died, he used to write letters to friends at home, but after several months the replies began to come with less and less frequency. On the day when he sat eating his lunch at a small hotel in the town ten miles east of Caxton he suddenly thought of the reason, and was ashamed. "Am I going back there on this visit for the same reason I wrote the letters?" he asked himself. For a moment he thought he might not go on. There was still time to turn back.

Outside, in the principal business street of the town, people were walking about. The sun shone warmly. Although he had lived for so many years in New York, he had always kept, buried away in him somewhere, a hankering for his own country. All the day before he had been driving through the eastern Ohio country, crossing many small streams, running down through small valleys, seeing the white farmhouses set back from the road, and the big red barns.

The elders were still in bloom along the fences, boys were swimming in a creek, the wheat had been cut, and now the corn was shoulder-high. Everywhere the drone of bees; in patches of woodland along the road a heavy, mysterious silence.

Now, however, he began thinking of something else. Shame crept over him. "When I first left Caxton, I wrote letters back to my boyhood friends there, but I wrote always of myself. When I had written a letter telling what I was doing in the city, what friends I was making, what my prospects were, I put, at the very end of the letter, perhaps, a little inquiry. 'I hope you are well. How are things going with you?' Something of that sort."

The returning native—his name was John Holden—had grown very uneasy. After eighteen years it seemed to him he could see, lying before him, one of the letters written eighteen years before when he had first come into the strange Eastern city. His mother's brother, a successful architect in the city, had given him such and such an opportunity: he had been at the theater to see Mansfield as *Brutus*, he had taken the night boat upriver to Albany with his aunt; there were two very handsome girls on the boat.

Everything then must have been in the same tone. His uncle had given him a rare opportunity, and he had taken advantage of it. In time he had also become a successful architect. In New York City there were certain great buildings, two or three skyscrapers, several huge industrial plants, any number of handsome and expensive residences, that were the products of his brain.

When it came down to the scratch, John Holden had to admit that his uncle had not been excessively fond of him. It had just happened that his aunt and uncle had no children of their own. He did his work in the office well and carefully, had developed a certain rather striking knack for design. The aunt had liked him better. She had always tried to think of him as her own son, had treated him as a son. Sometimes she called him son. Once or twice, after his uncle died, he had a notion. His aunt was a good woman, but sometimes he thought she would rather have enjoyed having him, John Holden, go in a bit more for wickedness, go a little on the loose, now and then. He never did anything she had to forgive him for. Perhaps she hungered for the opportunity to forgive.

Odd thoughts, eh? Well, what was a fellow to do? One had but the one life to live. One had to think of oneself.

even though it was three o'clock in the morning. She had been rather like a person waiting at a railroad station for the coming of a train. There is a blackboard, and a strange man comes out and writes on it, "Train Number 287 has been discontinued"—something like that.

Well, it had been all right, everything had been all right.

Later, four years later, he had married a New York woman of good family. Even in a city like New York, where there are so many people, her family had been well known. They had connections.

After marriage, sometimes, it is true, he had wondered. Gertrude used to look at him sometimes with an odd light in her eyes. That boy he picked up in the road—once during the day when he said something to the boy, the same queer look came into his eyes. It would be rather upsetting if one knew that the boy had purposely avoided him next morning. There had been Gertrude's cousin. Once, after his marriage, John heard a rumor that Gertrude had wanted to marry that cousin, but of course he had said nothing to her. Why should he have? She was his wife. There had been, he had heard, a good deal of family objection to the cousin. He was reputed to be wild, a gambler and drinker.

Once the cousin came to the Holden apartment at two in the morning, drunk and demanding that he be allowed to see Gertrude, and she slipped on a dressing-gown and went down to him. That was in the hallway of the apartment, downstairs, where almost any one might have come in and seen her. As a matter of fact, the elevator boy and the janitor did see her. She had stood in the hallway below talking for nearly an hour. What about? He had never asked Gertrude directly, and she had never told him anything. When she came upstairs again and had got into her bed, he lay in his own bed trembling, but remained silent. He had been afraid that if he spoke he might say something rude; better keep still. The cousin had disappeared. John had a suspicion that Gertrude later supplied him with money. He went out West somewhere.

Now Gertrude was dead. She had always seemed very well, but suddenly she was attacked by a baffling kind of slow fever that lasted nearly a year. Sometimes she

seemed about to get better, and then suddenly the fever
grew worse. It might be that she did not want to live.
What a notion! John had been at the bedside with the
doctor when she died. It was at night, and as the boy was
asleep, he was not called. There was something of the
same feeling he had had that night of his youth when he
went with Lillian to the ball field, an odd sense of futility,
of inadequacy. There was no doubt that in some subtle
way both women had accused him.

Of what? There had always been, in some vague, inde-
finable way, a kind of accusation in the attitude toward
him of his uncle, the architect, and of his aunt. They had
left him their money, but—— It was as though the uncle
had said, as though Lillian during that night long ago had
said——

Had they all said the same thing, and was Gertrude his
wife saying it as she lay dying? A smile. "You have
always taken such good care of yourself, haven't you, John
dear? You have observed the rules. You have taken no
chances for yourself or the others." She had actually said
something of that sort to him once in a moment of anger.

II

In the small town ten miles from Caxton there wasn't any
park to which a man could go to sit. If one stayed about
the hotel, some one from Caxton might come in. "Hello,
what are you doing here?" It would be inconvenient to
explain: "I didn't want to go to Caxton in the daylight.
I want the kindliness of evening light for myself and the
people I may see there."

John Holden's boy—he was but twelve—one might say
his character had not begun to form yet. One felt in him
sometimes a sort of unconscious and casual selfishness, an
unwareness of others, a rather unhealthy sharpness about
getting the best of others. It was a thing that should be
corrected in him and at once. John Holden had got himself into a small panic. "I must write him a letter at once.
Such a habit gets fixed in a boy and then in the man, and it
cannot later be shaken off. There are such a lot of people

living in the world! Every man and woman has his own
point of view. To be civilized, really, is to be aware of the
others, their hopes, their gladnesses, their disillusionments
in life."

John Holden was now walking along a residence street of
a small Ohio town composing in fancy a letter to his son
in the boys' camp up in Vermont. He was a man who
wrote to his son every day. "I think a man should," he
told himself. "One should remember that now the boy has
no mother."

He had come to an outlying railroad station. It was
neat, with grass and flowers growing in a round bed in the
very center of a lawn. Some man, the station agent and
telegraph operator perhaps, passed him and went inside
the station. John followed him in. On the wall of the
waiting room there was a framed copy of the timetable,
and he stood studying it. A train went to Caxton at
five. Another train came from Caxton and passed through
the town he was now in at seven-forty-three, the seven-
nineteen out of Caxton. The man in the small business
section of the station opened a sliding panel and looked at
him. The two men just stared at each other without speaking, and then the panel was slid shut again.

John looked at his watch. Two-twenty-eight. At about
six he could drive over to Caxton and dine at the hotel
there. After he had dined, it would be evening, and
people would be coming into the main street.

The seven-nineteen would come in. When John was a
lad, sometimes, he, Joe, Herman, and often several other
lads climbed on the front of the baggage- or mail-car and
stole a ride to the very town he was now in. What a thrill,
crouched down in the gathering darkness on the platform
as the train ran the ten miles, the car rocking from side
to side! When it got a little dark, in the fall or spring,
the fields beside the track were lighted up when the fire-
man opened his fire-box to throw in coal. Once John saw
a rabbit running along in the glare of light beside the
track. He could have reached down and caught it with
his hand. In the neighboring town the boys went into
saloons and played pool and drank beer. They could

depend upon catching a ride back home on the local freight that got to Caxton at about ten-thirty. On one of the adventures John and Herman got drunk, and Joe had to help them into an empty coal car and later get them out at Caxton. Herman got sick, and when they were getting off the freight at Caxton, he stumbled and came very near falling under the wheels of the moving train. John wasn't as drunk as Herman. When the others weren't looking, he had poured several of the glasses of beer into a spittoon. In Caxton he and Joe had to walk about with Herman for several hours, and when John finally got home, his mother was still awake and was worried. He had to lie to her. "I drove out into the country with Herman, and a wheel broke. We had to walk home." The reason Joe could carry his beer so well was because he was German. His father owned the town meat market, and the family had beer on the table at home. No wonder it did not knock him out as it did Herman and John.

There was a bench at the side of the railroad station, in the shade, and John sat there for a long time—two hours, three hours. Why hadn't he brought a book? In fancy he composed a letter to his son and in it he spoke of the fields lying beside the road outside the town of Caxton, of his greeting old friends there, of things that had happened when he was a boy. He even spoke of his former sweetheart, of Lillian. If he now thought out just what he was going to say in the letter, he could write it in his room at the hotel over in Caxton in a few minutes without having to stop and think what he was going to say. You can't always be too fussy about what you say to a young boy. Really, sometimes, you should take him into your confidence, into your life, make him a part of your life.

It was six-twenty when John drove into Caxton and went to the hotel, where he registered, and was shown to a room. On the street as he drove into town he saw Billy Baker, who, when he was a young man, had a paralyzed leg that dragged along the sidewalk when he walked. Now he was getting old; his face seemed wrinkled and faded, like a dried lemon, and his clothes had spots down the front. People, even sick people, live a long time in small Ohio towns. It is surprising how they hang on.

John had put his car, of a rather expensive make, into a garage beside the hotel. Formerly, in his day, the building had been used as a livery-barn. There used to be pictures of famous trotting and pacing horses on the walls of the little office at the front. Old Dave Grey, who owned race-horses of his own, ran the livery-barn then, and John occasionally hired a rig there. He hired a rig and took Lillian for a ride into the country, along moonlit roads. By a lonely farmhouse a dog barked. Sometimes they drove along a little dirt road lined with elders and stopped the horse. How still everything was! What a queer feeling they had! They couldn't talk. Sometimes they sat in silence thus, very near each other, for a long, long time. Once they got out of the buggy, having tied the horse to the fence, and walked in a newly cut hayfield. The cut hay lay all about in little cocks. John wanted to lie on one of the hay-cocks with Lillian, but did not dare suggest it.

At the hotel John ate his dinner in silence. There wasn't even a traveling salesman in the dining room, and presently the proprietor's wife came and stood by his table to talk with him. They had a good many tourists, but this just happened to be a quiet day. Dull days came that way in the hotel business. The woman's husband was a traveling man and had bought the hotel to give his wife something to keep her interested while he was on the road. He was away from home so much! They had come to Caxton from Pittsburgh.

After he had dined, John went up to his room, and presently the woman followed. The door leading into the hall had been left open, and she came and stood in the doorway. Really, she was rather handsome. She only wanted to be sure that everything was all right, that he had towels and soap and everything he needed.

For a time she lingered by the door talking of the town.

"It's a good little town. General Hurst is buried here. You should drive out to the cemetery and see the statue." He wondered who General Hurst was. In what war had he fought? Odd that he hadn't remembered about him. The town had a piano factory, and there was a watch company from Cincinnati talking of putting up a plant. "They figure there is less chance of labor trouble in a small town like this."

The woman went, going reluctantly. As she was going along the hallway she stopped once and looked back. There was something a little queer. They were both self-conscious. "I hope you'll be comfortable," she said. At forty a man did not come home to his own home town to start—— A traveling man's wife, eh? Well! well!

At seven-forty-five John went out for a walk on Main Street and almost at once he met Tom Ballard, who at once recognized him, a fact that pleased Tom. He bragged about it. "Once I see a face, I never forget. Well! Well!" When John was twenty-two Tom must have been about fifteen. His father was the leading doctor of the town. He took John in tow, walked back with him toward the hotel. He kept exclaiming: "I knew you at once. You haven't changed much, really."

Tom was in his turn a doctor, and there was about him something—— Right away John guessed what it was. They went up into John's room, and John, having in his bag a bottle of whiskey, poured Tom a drink, which he took somewhat too eagerly, John thought. There was talk. After Tom had taken the drink he sat on the edge of the bed still holding the bottle John had passed to him. Herman was running a dray now. He had married Kit Small and had five kids. Joe was working for the International Harvester Company. "I don't know whether he's in town now or not. He's a trouble-shooter, a swell mechanic, a good fellow," Tom said. They drank again.

As for Lillian, mentioned with an air of being casual by John, he, John, knew of course that she had been married and divorced. There was some sort of trouble about another man. Her husband married again later, and now she lived with her mother, her father, the shoe merchant, having died. Tom spoke somewhat guardedly, as though protecting a friend.

"I guess she's all right now, going straight and all. Good thing she never had any kids. She's a little nervous and queer; has lost her looks a good deal."

The two men went downstairs and, walking along Main Street, got into a car belonging to the doctor.

"I'll take you for a little ride," Tom said; but as he was about to pull away from the curb where the car had been parked, he turned and smiled at his passenger. "We ought to celebrate a little, account of your coming back here," he said. "What do you say to a quart?"

John handed him a ten-dollar bill, and he disappeared into a near-by drug store. When he came back he laughed.

"I used your name all right. They didn't recognize it. In the prescription I wrote out I said you had a general breakdown, that you needed to be built up. I recommended that you take a teaspoonful three times a day. Lord! my prescription book is getting almost empty." The drug store belonged to a man named Will Bennett. "You remember him, maybe. He's Ed Bennett's son; married Carrie Wyatt." The names were but dim things in John's mind. "This man is going to get drunk. He is going to try to get me drunk, too," he thought.

When they had turned out of Main Street and into Walnut Street they stopped midway between two street lights and had another drink, John holding the bottle to his lips, but putting his tongue over the opening. He remembered the evenings with Joe and Herman when he had secretly poured his beer into a spittoon. He felt cold and lonely. Walnut Street was one along which he used to walk, coming home late at night from Lillian's house. He remembered people who then lived along the street, and a list of names began running through his head. Often the names remained, but did not call up images of people. They were just names. He hoped the doctor would not turn the car into the street in which the Holdens had lived. Lillian had lived over in another part of town, in what was called "the Red House District." Just why it had been called that John did not know.

III

They drove silently along, up a small hill, and came to the edge of town, going south. Stopping before a house

that had evidently been built since John's time, Tom
sounded his horn.

"Didn't the fair-ground use to stand about here?" John
asked. The doctor turned and nodded his head.

"Yes, just here," he said. He kept on sounding his horn,
and a man and woman came out of the house and stood in
the road beside the car.

"Let's get Maud and Alf and all go over to Lylse's
Point," Tom said. He had indeed taken John into tow.
For a time John wondered if he was to be introduced.
"We got some hooch. Meet John Holden; used to live
here years ago." At the fair-ground, when John was a lad,
Dave Grey, the livery-man, used to work out his race-
horses in the early morning. Herman, who was a horse
enthusiast, who then dreamed of some day becoming a
horseman, came often to John's house in the early morning,
and the two boys went off to the fair-ground without
breakfast. Herman had got some sandwiches made of
slices of bread and cold meat out of his mother's pantry.
They went 'cross-lots, climbing fences and eating the sandwiches. In a meadow they had to cross there was heavy
dew on the grass, and the meadow larks flew up before
them. Herman had at least come somewhere near expressing in his life his youthful passion: he still lived about
horses; he owned a dray. With a little inward qualm
John wondered. Perhaps Herman ran a motor truck.

The man and woman got into the car, the woman on the
back seat with John, the husband in front with Tom, and
they drove away to another house. John could not keep
track of the streets they passed through. Occasionally he
asked the woman, "What street are we in now?" They
were joined by Maud and Alf, who also crowded into the
back seat. Maud was a slender woman of twenty-eight or
thirty, with yellow hair and blue eyes, and at once she
seemed determined to make up to John. "I don't take more
than an inch of room," she said, laughing and squeezing
herself in between John and the first woman, whose name
he could not later remember.

He rather liked Maud. When the car had been driven
some eighteen miles along a gravel road, they came to

Lylse's farmhouse, which had been converted into a road-house, and got out. Maud had been silent most of the way, but she sat very close to John, and as he felt cold and lonely, he was grateful for the warmth of her slender body. Occasionally she spoke to him in a half-whisper. "Ain't the night swell! Gee! I like it out in the dark this way."

Lylse's Point was at a bend of the Samson River, a small stream to which John as a lad had occasionally gone on fishing excursions with his father. Later he went out there several times with crowds of young fellows and their girls. They drove out then in Grey's old bus, and the trip out and back took several hours. On the way home at night they had great fun singing at the top of their voices and waking sleeping farmers along the road. Occasionally some of the party got out and walked for a ways. It was a chance for a fellow to kiss his girl when the others could not see. By hurrying a little, they could later easily enough catch up with the bus.

A rather heavy-faced Italian named Francisco owned Lylse's, and it had a dance hall and dining room. Drinks could be had if you knew the ropes, and it was evident the doctor and his friends were old acquaintances. At once they declared John should not buy anything, the declaration, in fact, being made before he had offered. "You're our guest now; don't you forget that. When we come sometime to your town, then it will be all right," Tom said. He laughed. "And that makes me think. I forgot your change," he said, handing John a five-dollar bill. The whiskey got at the drug store had been consumed on the way out, all except John and Maud drinking heartily. "I don't like the stuff. Do you, Mr. Holden?" Maud said and giggled. Twice during the trip out her fingers had crept over and touched lightly his fingers, and each time she had apologized. "Oh, do excuse me!" she said. John felt a little as he had felt earlier in the evening when the woman of the hotel had come to stand at the door of his room and had seemed reluctant about going away.

After they got out of the car at Lylse's, he felt uncomfortably old and queer. "What am I doing here with these people?" he kept asking himself. When they had got into the light, he stole a look at his watch. It was not yet nine o'clock. Several other cars, most of them, the doctor explained, from Yerington, stood before the door, and when they had taken several drinks of rather mild Italian red wine, all of the party except Maud and John went into the dance hall to dance. The doctor took John aside and whispered to him. "Lay off Maud," he said. He explained hurriedly that Alf and Maud had been having a row and that for several days they had not spoken to each other, although they lived in the same house, ate at the same table, and slept in the same bed. "He thinks she gets too gay with men," Tom explained. "You better look out a little."

The woman and man sat on a bench under a tree on the lawn before the house, and when the others had danced, they came out, bringing more drinks. Tom had got some more whiskey. "It's moon, but pretty good stuff," he declared. In the clear sky overhead stars were shining, and when the others were dancing, John turned his head and saw across the road and between the trees that lined its banks the stars reflected in the water of the Samson. A light from the house fell on Maud's face, a rather strikingly lovely face in that light, but when looked at closely, rather petulant. "A good deal of the spoiled child in her," John thought.

She began asking him about life in the city of New York.

"I was there once, but for only three days. It was when I went to school in the East. A girl I knew lived there. She married a lawyer named Trigan, or something like that. You didn't know him, I guess."

And now there was a hungry, dissatisfied look on her face.

"God! I'd like to live in a place like that, not in this hole! There hadn't no man better tempt me." When she said that she giggled again. Once during the evening they walked across the dusty road and stood for a time by the river's edge, but got back to the bench before the others had finished their dance. Maud persistently refused to dance.

At ten-thirty, all of the others having got a little drunk, they drove back to town, Maud again sitting beside John. On the drive Alf went to sleep. Maud pressed her slender body against John's, and after two or three futile moves to which he made no special response, she boldly put her hand into his. The second woman and her husband talked with Tom of people they had seen at Lylse's. "Do you think there's anything up between Fanny and Joe? No; I think she's on the square."

They got to John's hotel at eleven-thirty, and bidding them all good night, he went upstairs. Alf had awakened. When they were parting, he leaned out of the car and looked closely at John. "What did you say your name was?" he asked.

John went up a dark stairway and sat on the bed in his room. Lillian had lost her looks. She had married, and her husband had divorced her. Joe was a trouble-shooter. He worked for the International Harvester Company, a swell mechanic. Herman was a drayman. He had five kids.

Three men in a room next John's were playing poker. They laughed and talked, and their voices came clearly to John. "You think so, do you? Well, I'll prove you're wrong." A mild quarrel began. As it was summer, the windows of John's room were open, and he went to one to stand, looking out. A moon had come up, and he could see down into an alleyway. Two men came out of a street and stood in the alleyway, whispering. After they left, two cats crept along a roof and began a love-making scene. The game in the next room broke up. John could hear voices in the hallway.

"Now, forget it. I tell you, you're both wrong." John thought of his son at the camp up in Vermont. "I haven't written him a letter today." He felt guilty.

Opening his bag, he took out paper and sat down to write; but after two or three attempts gave it up and put the paper away again. How fine the night had been as he sat on the bench beside the woman at Lylse's! Now the woman was in bed with her husband. They were not speaking to each other.

"Could I do it?" John asked himself, and then, for the first time that evening, a smile came to his lips.

"Why not?" he asked himself.

With his bag in his hand he went down the dark hallway and into the hotel office and began pounding on a desk. A fat old man with thin red hair and sleep-heavy eyes appeared from somewhere. John explained.

"I can't sleep. I think I'll drive on. I want to get to Pittsburgh and as I can't sleep, I might as well be driving." He paid his bill.

Then he asked the clerk to go and arouse the man in the garage, and gave him an extra dollar. "If I need gas, is there any place open?" he asked, but evidently the man did not hear. Perhaps he thought the question absurd.

He stood in the moonlight on the sidewalk before the door of the hotel and heard the clerk pounding on a door. Presently voices were heard, and the headlights of his car shone. The car appeared, driven by a boy. He seemed very alive and alert.

"I saw you out to Lylse's" he said, and, without being asked, went to look at the tank. "You're all right; you got 'most eight gallons," he assured John as he climbed into the driver's seat.

How friendly the car, how friendly the night! John was not one who enjoyed fast driving, but he went out of the town at very high speed. "You go down two blocks, turn to your right, and go three. There you hit the cement. Go right straight to the east. You can't miss it."

John was taking the turns at racing speed. At the edge of town some one shouted to him from the darkness, but he did not stop. He hungered to get into the road going east.

"I'll let her out," he thought. "Lord! It will be fun! I'll let her out."

GERTRUDE DONOVAN[1]

By NATHAN ASCH

(From *The Transatlantic Review*)

A SOUND of cutting reached her ears. She halted and listened. So they were ripping the ticker out, as Charlie said they would. Then it was all over. She didn't believe it yet. Failed. Bankrupt. She didn't understand it. What did it mean? Then she remembered what Charlie had further said: a new job. And she saw a picture of herself going downtown to the employment office early in the morning; filling out a blank; being told that she would be notified if an opening could be found. Then waiting; every morning waiting for the postman, and finding that there was nothing for her. Then the call at the office. The manager would first look at her legs, then at her neck.

He would measure her with his eyes. The old look. She tried to picture the new boss. Fat? Thin? Good looking? Will he try to get fresh? She'd put him in his place.

She became angry. They had no business hiring her, if they were going to fail. She wasn't working for love. It's no fun to be looking for a new job every day. Just as you get started, and the clerks stop looking at you as if you were lying naked on the bed waiting for them, you've got to give it all up and start all over again.

Her hands began automatically to hit the keys. And the Hudson Seal: she'd have to forget that, for this year. Mother would never let her off on the board. She'd start crying about the high prices, and the raise in rent, and a million and one other things. Then she'd look at her as if she were murdering her. No coat and no permanent wave next month.

[1] Copyright, 1925, by Harcourt, Brace, and Co. Reprinted by permission of the publishers.

Her hand momentarily stopped typing, and touched her hair; then opening a drawer in her desk, she took out a patent leather bag, from which she extracted a small mirror and examined her hair. It was getting loose. They charged you twenty dollars and it didn't last more than a month.

She took out a powder puff, and powdered herself, twisting her lower lip over the upper and blowing at her nose.

A pink light shone out of the call box, and taking a pad and a pencil, she walked out of her cubicle.

With Mr. Glymmer in the room were Mr. Reed and Harry Widener. They did not notice her entrance but kept on talking with gravity. She sat down in the soft chair that she always took, crossed her legs, and did not adjust her skirt as she always did when the junior partner was not there, and waited. Her hand went once again to her hair, lifting it near the temples.

He was nice. Much nicer than Jim Denby. He always looked at you nice, and his dark eyes looked into yours something personal. He was a man. And he didn't look as if he played servant girl to any woman, like Jim did. It was nice; it was equal, it was.

She caught a few words. Protective Committee and Supreme Court. Reed was as usual very cool, he sat on the edge of the desk, and his fingers played with a cigarette holder. Glymmer seemed more nervous. She didn't like him. Too anxious to please always. Not to her or to the other clerks, but to the customers, or to his partners. She didn't like his smile. She never had liked it. She wouldn't trust any man with a smile like that.

She looked again at Harry Widener. He seemed amused at the whole affair. He hardly said a word, just looked at them, the corners of his mouth curled up. Then he looked at her, and she stiffened up. But his gaze immediately dissolved.

Then Mr. Glymmer began to dictate. She copied his words, with concentration as always, forgetting everything else, even ignoring the meaning of what she wrote. When he had finished, she rose and prepared to leave. But she stopped and asked.

"Mr. Glymmer, will the office be open tomorrow?"

"Mr. Zuckor, when he returns, will have an announcement to make."

She became angry again, considered whether she should bang the door, became frightened, and then resolved that since she was losing her position she might as well bang it. So she did, and walked into the general office.

"Well, Cutie," said Charlie when he saw her, "it's up."

"Do we work tomorrow?" she asked.

"Not a chance. Better take a typewriter home with you. It'll be your pay." The other clerks laughed.

"If I don't get my pay," she said, "I'll have Mr. Glymmer arrested."

"Harry Widener, too?" asked Charlie.

She stiffened up and said:

"Mind your business." And walked back to her desk. She began to copy the letter Mr. Glymmer had dictated to her. In typing it was different than in shorthand taking: she could think as much as she wanted to; the eyes communicated to the fingers unconsciously.

Harry Widener arrested! Harry Widener arrested! Arrested! Arrested!

"I know one thing," she said nearly loud. "If Harry Widener asked me, I wouldn't care if he were married a million times; I'd go with him." She became frightened, and looked around to see if anybody were listening. Then she said in a high voice:

"I would!"

The telephone bell rang. Still repeating, "I would," she answered it. A familiar heavy voice came from the other end:

"That you, Gertie?"

Jim. Oh, bother. What did he want?

"Just heard the news," he said. "What are you going to do?"

She kept silent. In her mind she was comparing Harry Widener with Jim Denby. "He's got better eyes and a better figure; and he's nicer. Yes, he's lots nicer."

"Gertie," she heard.

"What?"

"I'm coming around tonight. I've got something to tell you."

She wished he wouldn't. She didn't want him around that night. And his hair was nicer. Straight and nice, not all curled up. And she'd bet he didn't look so foolish when he kissed somebody.

"I'm tired, Jim," she said,

And she thought, "I'd bet if he were asking me to see him tonight, he wouldn't ask like that: he'd say something."

"It's all right, Gert. I won't stay long."

She hung up. What did he want from her? He would come around tonight, pestering. Would she marry him? He had two thousand saved up. Live in the Bronx. Two rooms and a kitchen. Toilet on the floor. Bath in the wash bowl. Not she.

Then Miss James, the telephone girl, came in. They began talking. Miss James told Gertie where she might look for a job.

"He told me yesterday," she said. "Theatrical office. Twenty-two a week, and you don't get killed like here on the Street."

Theatrical office. Maybe she'd get a chance to go on the stage. She'd been quite good at it in school. And then Jim had taken her a few times to the theater. It was easy. All you needed was pull.

And then, maybe Harry Widener. If she'd be an actress, it would be all right. Actresses can do those things. Why, you read about them in the papers.

"I don't know," she said to Miss James. "A girl is taking an awful chance going to one of those theatrical offices. Why, the manager would want you to do all kinds of things for the job."

"What's the difference," said Miss James. "Twenty-two a week. Me for money. If I could take shorthand . . ."

The afternoon slowly wore on. At four Zuckor came into her office and dictated to her an announcement, that owing to the liquidation of the firm's assets the office would be closed. Gertrude copied what he said without hearing it. The office had stopped interesting her. She was leaving, and it already represented a forgotten past. And she would have completely ignored this fact of bankruptcy if not that it represented a parting from Harry Widener. In the few months that she had been with Glymmer, Reed the junior partner had become a part of her. True she knew that, while in the office, there was a gulf that divided them, a gulf that was insurmountable: the difference between employer and employee. Each one had his or her rights, which were not to be disregarded. And although at times she almost wished that the junior partner would tear that difference away, something within herself said, that if he did, he would not be Harry Widener, and she would cease being Gerty Donovan. She knew that although physically they would come nearer, there would be a complete divorce of their spirits. And she knew that now their spirits were near, that he noticed her, that when she passed he looked at her with eyes puzzled, and that whenever their eyes met, for however a fleeting moment, a union had been accomplished. And she had been satisfied, even gratified by this fleeting communion.

He had been her criterion. She had used him as a standard by which she measured all her acquaintances. She had never been dissatisfied with Jim Denby. She had known him for a long time, for so long that the beginning of their acquaintance was completely forgotten. She had taken for granted that some day she would marry him, she had been encouraged in this thought by her mother, by all who knew her. She had to get her man.

But when she had seen Harry Widener, she became doubtful. Intuitively she knew that he was a higher type of man than her accepted future husband. And although she could not define his finesse, nor possibly even locate it, she knew it existed. And she noticed that in all comparisons Jim failed and Widener triumphed.

And possibly she would have been satisfied with Jim if she could continue to see the other. Even to be near him. She somehow felt cleaner, more refined, in a higher world with the junior partner. She saw him rarely. He did not come into the office often, but stayed at his club, from where he sent in any new business he had secured. But sometimes he did come, and she knew he would, and it was enough. He was a rare drug, that she needed but seldom, but without which she felt she could not live.

And now it was over. Harry Widener was no more. She was to go home and stay with Jim Denby. She was made for such as he. For men with warm, moist palms, and warm, moist faces, and warm, moist looks. For men who do not take but beg. For sixty dollars a week, and a bookkeeper's household, and a bookkeeper's children, and a bookkeeper's life. Oh! Hell!

Absentmindedly she cleaned her typewriter, and was ready to place the cover, and then she remembered that it didn't matter, and left it where it always lay during the day, under her desk. Then she turned to the wall where her cloak and hat were hung. No, she should go into the general office and say goodbye. She didn't want to. But she might yet see Harry Widener. So she went in.

She was surprised to see the office as it had always been. It was not at all changed. You might come in tomorrow and begin to work again. Possibly it was all a lie. Or a joke. There was no failure. It would go on as before. And she would continue to see Harry Widener. Harry Widener. Harry Widener. Harry Widener, something shouted into her ear.

She saw him halfway across the general office. He was sitting on a desk, reading an evening paper, and smoking. The blue smoke twined itself about his manicured finger nails. Run over to him now, and . . . and what? Why, kiss him, of course, and tell him you want him, that he can do anything he wants to with you. He can walk over you, and spit on you. But quick, or it'll be too late. Hurry. Hurry. He's looking up. He's looking.

"I guess it's all over, Miss Donovan," he said with a smile.

"Yes, Mr. Widener," she answered.

"Too bad," he said, and returned to his paper.

Her knees weak, she passed him. It was too late. It was too late. Too late. What shall she do?

There was a little group near Mr. Zuckor's desk. He was paying off. He seemed very pale and very tired. He called her.

"Miss Donovan, here's your pay."

She came over. Took it. Signed the receipt. Too late. She rode home with her mind a blank. She did not even read the paper which she had automatically bought with her ticket. Somebody gave her his seat, and she did not thank him, but absentmindedly sat down, drew on her gloves, and sat. People jostled over her, pressed her knees, stepped on her pumps, but she ignored this. There was nothing she could do. Everything was over. And she was not given to brooding.

Then she came out of the train, walked to the street, and turned the corner grocery toward her home. This was her neighborhood, where she had been born, brought up. Here was the motion-picture house, "The Lakewood," where, when a little girl, she used to wait outside, for some one to take her in, children not being admitted without companions. Later, when she had entered high school, she used to come here every night, and in a corner, far away from even the dull light, she would sit with a neighborhood boy and mush: kiss, and soul kiss, and hold, and he would try to touch her not yet full grown breasts, and she would refuse and then unwillingly consent. There had been many couples in the corner, and they would all sit there, ignoring the picture; just sit in the dark and press one against the other.

And here was the ice cream parlor, "Gunn's," with its inviting display of sweets, and the little room in the back, with tables. After the movies she used to come here with her friends, and they would gorge themselves with the ice cream, ordering the most fancy concoctions, until their mouths would become like acid, from too many sweets.

Then she passed the "dark corner" of Harrigans's, the hardware man's. Here was the least light in the neighborhood. And into here, after the movies and the ice cream, her companion would pull her, and here they would stand in the shadow of the two glass cases, holding one another in their arms, and they would seek something which they did not understand, and did not know where to find it, until she, frightened at the lateness of the hour, would tear herself away and run home.

And finally just before her home, she passed the *Borough
News* printing works, above which was housed the Lakewood Business College, which she had entered after her
two years in high school. Here was where she had learned
stenography, and typing, and the little bookkeeping she
knew. Nearly all her friends had entered this school which
was their stepping-stone into the business world.

Mother was in the kitchen, and as she took off her coat
Gerty wondered when would be the best time to break
the news to her. Before dinner or after dinner? It would
be better to get it over with before, but then again, dinner
would be spoiled; there might even be no dinner at all.
Gerty had no appetite, but she reflected that anything,
even eating, was better than listening to her mother's
lamenting. So she decided to wait.

She walked into the dining room, took the doily off the
table, went to the sideboard, and took out the napkin.
Automatically she began to set the table.

Mother appeared, fat, satisfied, white aproned.

"That you, Gertie? Jim was here awhile ago. Said
he's coming after dinner."

Gerty said nothing. She placed on the table the salt
cellar, the knives and forks, the only really good things
they had in the house. Came from the family. Solid
silver.

"Would you believe it," continued her mother, "butter's
sixty cents a pound. And eggs a dollar a dozen. I gave
Strinelli a piece of my mind. Mrs. Brown told me he's
got no end of eggs in his cellar, and he's keeping them for
higher prices. I said to him: 'It would be a good thing
if they threw you foreigners out. Trying to live on us
poor people. A dollar a dozen for eggs. The idea.'"

Gerty kept on setting. Even after she had finished
placing on the table everything that apparently was necessary, she continued. She adjusted the position of the cutlery.
Brought water, something very rare. Dusted off the top
of the sideboard. Anything better than talking. An idea
was being born in her mind, and her mother was preventing
her from developing it.

Harry Widener would be with another firm, of that she

was sure. Why not try to get a job there? She would ask him to recommend her. He couldn't refuse her. She had been a good stenographer. Never late. No nonsense in the office. No peek-a-boo waists or transparent skirts. She didn't chew gum or anything. Why shouldn't she be able to get a job there? And then she would be with him.

Her mother fixed her nearsighted eyes on Gerty, followed her movements, and went on talking.

"Mrs. Denby's awfully low. They expect her to go any day. The doctor said it was cancer of the stomach. Incurable, he said. Lying in St. Mark's. Private room. A day nurse. A night nurse. It must be awful for Jim to pay all that. He's nice to come down to see us, and his mother almost dead."

Gerty understood her mother's weak tactics. At other times it amused her to hear the older woman talking, praising Jim. But now it only served to irritate her. It was none of Mother's business whom she was going to marry. She was free. Earning her own living. She could do as she pleased. She could even go to live by herself if she wanted to. She'd save money anyway. And time. With the subway, she was wasting two hours every day travelling. And if she went out in the evening it was two more hours lost. If this kept up, she'd do it. She wasn't going to listen to anybody's talking. She was a free and equal human being, she was.

"I'm hungry," she announced.

Dinner proceeded more or less quietly. The few attempts of the mother at conversation were promptly squelched by her daughter's silence. Only toward the end did Mrs. Donovan begin her attacks again.

"Jim told me, while he was here, he's getting a raise at the end of the month. Three hundred a month, and assistant teller. He might even get to be assistant cashier some day. One hundred dollars a week and a private room. He's a good boy, Jim is."

"If you're going to keep on like this," said Gerty silently to her mother, "I won't tell you about the failure."

"And he's got a flat at One Hundred and Fortieth Street. Two rooms and a kitchen. The landlord will paper the walls any way you'll want him to. Yes, and a bath tub, too. In the kitchen."

A few moments before, Harry Widener had been far away, almost imperceptible. Now he came quite near, and looked at Gerty with his nice black eyes, and said: "You're going to be an actress on One Hundred and Fortieth Street with two rooms and a kitchen. Bath tub in the kitchen. And you're going to take dictation on the walls he'll decorate for you because you don't chew gum."

She was going crazy. If she wasn't, her mother was making her. And she looked at her mother and with her eyes said: "I want Harry Widener, and I don't care who knows it. You or Jim Denby or anybody else. I don't give a good God damn who knows it." Like that.

And aloud she said.

"I am going to my room."

"Better get ready for Jim," her mother said. "Put on the mauve waist."

As she shut the door of her room Gerty reflected that she had not told her mother of the loss of her position. She didn't care. Let her mother worry later. With those dirty tricks. Trying to talk her into marrying Jim. She wouldn't have him if he were the last man on earth. Not if he had all of the world's gold. And all the diamonds. Not with a face like that. He'd have to have it made over again.

She sat down on her bed, adjusted her hair, and said:

"If he'll begin pestering me, I'll send him to hell, I will."

Charity. Trying to give her something. Protecting her from the terrible woild. She didn't want protecting. She wanted to be left alone. People shouldn't interfere into what she did. It was all their fault anyway. If they wouldn't have interfered, she. . . .

"Shut up," she said to herself, and began unbuttoning her waist.

"Mauve waist," she said. "I'll give him mauve waist. If he'd be a man, he wouldn't come around me. He'd stop bothering me. Can't he see I don't want him and his protecting."

She walked toward the closet, opened the door, and took off the hook the mauve waist. Absentmindedly she placed her arms through the sleeves and buttoned it. Then she sat on the chair before the mirror and began to powder herself.

She remembered that once, about two months before, a woman friend of Harry Widener had come into the office toward the end of an afternoon, and had waited for him. A woman of his kind. With hair that received the attention of a frisier, face that was massaged, and hands that were manicured every day. She had worn a dark tailor-made suit and a mauve waist with a lace collar cut so low that the upper parts of her white breasts could be seen in the opening. She was stunning, Gerty had admitted that to herself. This was class. And when Harry Widener had come in, she had held out her hand to him, a black kid gloved hand, in a manner that Gerty knew she could never have imitated. The hand had gone right out, accompanied by a smile, in which the teeth were shown, even teeth, and dazzlingly white. And one Saturday afternoon, walking up Fifth Avenue, Gerty had seen a waist like that: mauve, with a white lace collar, cut very low. She had bought it, although the price had been exorbitant and a large part of her salary had been spent in the purchase. She never dared to wear it in the office, it was cut so low, and she had been afraid that Widener would notice the resemblance. And even in the house she wore it only on rare moments. When she wanted to feel equal to him, to do something that she should want him to see her do, she dressed in the mauve waist.

Noticing that the ribbon of her chemise showed in the cut, she untied it and tucked it into her bosom. Her neck now looked similar to the neck of the woman in the office. A white triangle deep into her bosom, with the curve of a breast showing on each side. Her breasts were just as round as the other's, and just as white. It would be better to show a little more. She tucked aside the collar, and the curve became more pronounced. She sat at the mirror examining her face, fixing her hair. If he were to see her now, he would not be able to resist her. He would look at her with his black eyes, his brows would contract a little, and his nostrils puff out. And his arms would stretch out toward her, would envelop her, and she would lie in them quiet, unafraid.

She closed her eyes, and through the shimmering darkness of her lids she saw Harry Widener. He was looking at her. And she was looking at him. He was saying to her "You are with me now, and you are quiet." And she answered to him, "Yes, I am quiet." And they sat there in the darkness, she feeling his odour, and lulled to sleep by it.

She felt a draught of wind, heard the noise of a door opening, and saw Harry Widener tumble into the light. She opened her eyes. Her mother was standing in the doorway.

Mrs. Donovan was talking, but Gerty did not hear what she said. She could not orientate herself. She did not recognize her surroundings, nor the fat woman before her. This was strange to her. She had no place in the room where she was. She belonged somewhere else. In dazzling, flickering sunlight with Harry Widener. And peace.

"You're a nice one," her mother was saying. "It's got to be a stranger that gives me the news about my own child. Why didn't you tell me you were out of a job?"

Gerty did not answer. She heard somebody talking, felt she was being reproved, but it did not move her. She had been with him a moment before, and she still felt his presence.

Then she heard her mother say:

"Jim's in the front room. Better go out to him. And you'd better be nice to him. You won't find a better man."

Her mother was talking, but Gerty did not understand her words. But she felt that she was commanded to go, so she stood up and walked toward the front room. Her mother not understanding, placed herself out of her way, and let her pass.

She came into the front room, and looked at the figure sitting on the sofa, a figure that rose when she entered, and came toward her. She answered his hello, sat down on the sofa in the spot he had sat in. Felt him sitting down beside her, noticed her mother had not come in with her, and sat.

She tried to gather her thoughts together. Who was it who was sitting beside her on the sofa? It was Jim Denby.

No, it was Harry Widener. It was Harry Widener with eyes that were not so nice, and with a face that tried to be as expressionless as it could. But no, it could not have been Harry Widener. Harry Widener looked at you personal like, and decent. And Jim Denby didn't. He looked at you as if he wanted to eat you up. He was in love with you. And Harry wasn't. Why?

Further her mind refused to travel. A black cloud came into her brain and forbade all thought. And she surrendered to the cloud and sat motionless and thoughtless.

Then she heard Jim or Harry talking. He was asking her what she would do. And she did not know how to answer. Because she knew she had to give two different answers. If this were Jim, she'd have to tell him she would look for another job, and if this were Harry she'd have to say. . . . She could not decide which it was. So she kept quiet.

Then she heard:

"Gerty, I've got something to tell you."

He was speaking. At last he was speaking. This was the moment she had been waiting for. Now he would look at her with his black eyes, and fold her around. And peace.

"Gerty, what's the use of you looking for a job. You can't work all your life. You're not made for work. You've got to stay home and be taken care of."

He stopped, and she waited. Why was he talking? Why didn't he do it? She felt he was looking at her, but she did not dare to turn her eyes. He was gazing at her. His eyes travelled over the waist, went into the lace collar, and followed its contour to the breasts. Her heart stopped. Would he recognize it? Would he be angry because she imitated his lady friend?

He began speaking again:

"Gerty, let me take care of you. I can do it. I'll treat you like a queen. There won't be nothing too good for you. I'll love you, and I'll honor you. I'll be dirt under your feet. You ain't made for an office. I'll be good to you. Swear to God, I will."

What was he waiting for? What did he want? Why didn't he take her? She was his. She had always been his. Hadn't she waited for him all this time. Did she have to teach him how to make love?

He was evidently waiting for an answer, and while waiting, his gaze travelled on her breasts. He was looking at them. And involuntarily she wanted to screen them with her hands, but then remembered who he was, and felt ashamed. He could do with her what he wanted. He could take all she had.

She felt his breath on her face, and closed her unseeing eyes. The moment had come, and she was not surprised when she felt his arms around her, enveloping, and his lips on hers.

And she said: "Yes, I'll marry you."

And he kissed her again and again, and she was satisfied. Then she heard steps, and her mother came in. And she heard him say to her mother that he was going to marry her, and then her mother answered:

"Jim, I'm glad to hear it."

And she looked with her eyes. And she saw it wasn't Harry. It was Jim! Jim! Jim! Not Harry!

In one bound she jumped up, and rushed to her room. When she had banged the door shut, she threw herself on the bed, and moaned.

"What did I do? What did I do?"

GUARD OF HONOR[1]

By BARRY BENEFIELD

(From *The Pictorial Review*)

ONCE in Asphodel they had called him Willie when he
was a little boy, and then they called him Bill. There
came a time when, upon his occasional trips back to his
Arkansas home, his old friends ventured a little nervously
to call him Will, and the Asphodel *Argus* printed him as
"Mr. William P. Ott, sales-manager and treasurer of the
Apollo Clothing Co., of Chicago."

Somewhere somehow in the flat fields of northern France
he lost his richest worldly treasure—that part of his marvelous memory that covered the period between his six-
teenth and thirty-second years, that segment of his memory which had known not only all his war experiences up
to that moment, but also every garment manufactured by
his company down to the last button, every trade route
sold by the Apollo travelers, every customer's rating and
idiosyncrasies, every weak and strong point of the goods
and the salesmen of his company's chief competitors.

And so, having come home by way of three or four Government hospitals, he was, after a brief period of lionizing
that puzzled the pink-faced, snub-nosed, chubby little man,
once again to his friends of Asphodel, and as always to his
widowed mother, just Willie.

On that hot June morning Willie left his mother's house
and went down the red hill leading from the higher resi-
dential section to the six business streets, completing his
habitual morning round by ten o'clock: to the post-office,
where he received and read and shook his head over an
eagerly solicitous letter from the president of the Apollo
Clothing Co.; to Hampton's Furniture Store and Mortuary
Parlor, where he sat awhile in a cane-bottomed chair on

the sidewalk, apparently listening to other men of leisure
talk, though their words merely buzzed in his ears; to
Embree's Confectionery Store, where he bought a tinfoil
package of cigarettes; and finally to his real goal for the
morning, Zebedee Smith's Barber Shop, where he silently
submitted to shaving and shoe-shining, and then sat in front
of the big plate-glass window, staring, round-eyed, out
across the street, through an old brick building that had
lost everything in a fire except its side walls, out across the
depression in the earth, at the bottom of which Little Sandy
River slipped southward on its unquestioning way toward
the great gulf that would presently swallow it up.

As he stared and consciously saw nothing in detail, while
his mind continued its eternal reaching down for something
precious that it could almost but not quite touch, two figures in the street moved across his vision, and he sat up
suddenly and studied them. As well as he knew any one
he knew Goldie, once the owner of Asphodel's only candy
store and soda-water fountain, and Honey Boy, Asphodel's
best-known individual, the small town's huge, red-headed,
freckle-faced, obscenely dirty, half-witted son.

Goldie's infinitesimal figure, frail and stooping, was covered with an old and spotted and worn Confederate uniform, the gray coat hanging in a confusion of folds and
wrinkles from his narrow shoulders, the trousers turned up
at least two inches at the bottom. His black slouch hat
made his very thin, old face seem even thinner than it was.

Honey Boy had once owned a donkey, and it was one
of the few memories that lived in his cloudy mind. He
always carried a stout switch with which he belabored his
imaginary mount, while he frequently jumped up and
down as if he were being bounced by the donkey that was
no more. Now as he pranced along behind Goldie, Honey
Boy, between attacks upon his invisible donkey, mimicked
as nearly as he could every movement of the little old man
who marched along in front of him. Laughter was thrilling
to Honey Boy; he was accustomed to that reward for his
antics, and he kept opening his wide mouth, filled with
yellow stumps of teeth, in a leering grin as he looked from
right to left at chance passers-by for applause.

Goldie stopped in front of the red, square, brick county court-house, diagonally across the street from Smith's Barber Shop. He removed his hat and stood at attention, listening. Southern Arkansas architecture sometimes shows the influence of New Orleans, especially in narrow balconies jutting out under second-story windows. Goldie remained looking up at the empty balcony of the court-house, from which speeches were often delivered. Now and then he clapped his hands, nodding his head approvingly over eloquence that came back across the years only to him.

Everybody called Levi Goldbaum Goldie, almost entirely in affection. For a long time he had kept his candy store open, with occasional closures due to bankruptcies without a taint of fraud. Even in the full flush of his middle-aged manhood he had been a frail, haggard, stooped, feeble-looking, little man, the husband of an abnormally healthy and handsome wife, the father of a brood of unusually vigorous boys and girls, who grew up, married, and moved away from Asphodel, leaving him and his wife alone in their old age.

When Goldie had attended Confederate reunions—and he attended every one he could—or had marched with the diminishing group of old soldiers on great occasions in Asphodel, many people, especially boys and girls wondered if he really could have been a soldier. But there was no doubt in the minds of the comrades who had been with him at Shiloh.

Goldie's store having closed its doors five years before as the result of two new competitors and inevitably final bankruptcy proceedings, he had sadly retired. He was now over seventy, was considered a trifle queer, and spent most of his time pottering around at home. He owned his house, and his grown children sent him what little money he needed to pay the last penalties of existence.

After standing listening in front of the court-house for some thirty minutes Goldie, drawing himself as straight as he could, proceeded down Walnut Street, turned into Broadway, and marched up that main street, Honey Boy cavorting behind him. And there was that in Goldie's bearing and in his stride that drew Willie after him, and presently

the little soldier with the wounded memory got out in the
street and walked along by the side of the little soldier with
the wounded mind, keeping step, the dry dust dimming his
newly shined shoes and rising in small, lazy clouds around
his white-duck trousers.

Goldie's mind had gone back to other days when Asphodel's citizens had made much of June 3, Jefferson Davis's
birthday and Confederate Memorial Day, and now he was
celebrating it in his town alone, for Asphodel, like many
another Southern town, had neglected the day for many
years.

To most of those who saw the unmartial figure of Goldie
and Willie and Honey Boy marching slowly along the dusty
street it did not occur that this was the South's Memorial
Day. Goldie's wearing of his old uniform was not uncommon enough to be striking; many a time-beaten soldier,
reduced in circumstances, at last falls back on his most-
treasured suit for every-day wear.

But if those who saw Goldie had looked carefully they
might have noticed that, however slowly he moved, he
proceeded in a straight line, with regularly spaced steps,
and they might have suspected that Goldie was at the
corner of a company invisible to all except his fading,
sunken, black eyes, marching to music unheard except by
him. Most people, indeed, gave their attention to Honey
Boy, trailing directly behind and mocking the little gray
man who labored with difficulty through the deep white
sand.

It was eleven o'clock when Goldie and Willie and Honey
Boy passed Pinder's Marble Yard and its group of waiting
white angels with downcast eyes. Pinder's is just beyond
the business section of Asphodel, and after that the ground
rises to the north and east. The street leading to Highland
Cemetery begins there a long, tedious hill. The sun was
unclouded, the wind was still, and Goldie, his coat carefully buttoned to the throat, was panting hard and reeling
as he made Pinder's Marble Yard.

Wilted by the terrific heat and his violent exertions, and
no longer encouraged by laughing spectators, Honey Boy
now merely followed on behind the staggering figure march-

ing toward Highland Cemetery, a mile away. And Willie
stalked along by his side, seeing nothing, as if he were in a
dream deeper even than Goldie's. Now the Memorial Day
Parade was coming to the edge of Asphodel, to the section
of straggling houses. Belle Foscue, a negro washerwoman,
ran to her paling fence and asked the three chance comrades
to come in and rest awhile under the shade of her oak tree.

Goldie halted, bringing his feet together bravely. He
was moving his lips, but no words that could be heard a
foot away issued from them. Belle came out of the gate
to the soldier who could not leave his company. She bent
her head close to his lips, listened, and then ran to bring
him water.

"Thank you," he said in a whisper. "You're a good
girl." He waited patiently until she could bring Honey
Boy another dipper filled from the well. But when she
offered the freshly filled dipper to Willie he seemed not
to see, so she turned it upside down, rolled her eyes at
him, and went back into her yard.

After a while Goldie braced himself and marched on up
the red hill. At this point the red clay beneath the
cemetery road shows through the white sand, and rains
keep washed out deep and ever-deepening gullies on both
sides of it. About half-way up the hill Goldie, stubbornly
holding his position at the corner of the invisible company
in spite of the fact that the road had narrowed considerably, found himself on the edge of a gully; and presently
he lost his balance, and staggered over into it, and rolled
down to the bottom of it. Honey Boy crowed and chortled
and gurgled, and began frantically beating his unseen
donkey with the switch. Willie stood still, staring ahead,
waiting.

The fallen soldier, having made two or three desperate
attempts to rise, sank back into a crumpled sitting posture,
his head bent in shame. After a while Honey Boy got
down on his hands and knees in the bed of the gully. "Ride
Honey Boy," he stuttered. "Ride up-hill. Honey Boy
strong."

And Goldie, trying to sit astride the big boy's broad
back, fell forward and clasped his arms around his steed's

red, sweaty neck. Honey Boy crawled out of the gully and
slowly climbed the hill with his burden, occasionally buck-
ing like a horse and throwing the little man off on the road.
But then he would stand patiently until the fallen soldier
could crawl up on his back again.

At the top of the hill Goldie got to his feet once more,
and as the roadbed was now level as well as firm he walked
awhile and then rode awhile on Honey Boy, and so, riding
and walking, he finally marched, with Willie at his side,
through the arched gateway of Highland Cemetery as the
whistles were blowing for twelve o'clock. Old man Miller,
the sexton in charge there, and his two helpers were in a
far corner of the graveyard, so that none saw Asphodel's
Memorial Day parade enter to honor the men Lee had
loved and led.

The parade proceeded across the graveyard to a clump of
oak trees clustering about and almost hiding the grass-
grown plot that is called in Asphodel "The Confederate
Cemetery." The town had been headquarters for a rather
large body of Confederate troops during the Civil War,
and there are in the palinged enclosure nearly two hundred graves of the men in gray who had come to their end
far from their homes.

Opening the rotting gate of the paling fence, Goldie
stepped inside, Honey Boy and Willie close behind him.
Here again Goldie stood in rapt attention, his brown face
shining, his head bared, and his eyes lifted, listening to the
famous orators his imagination had brought there for this
day from out of the endearing past. Honey Boy sprawled
on a rickety old iron bench. Willie stood stiffly by Goldie's
side, looking straight ahead.

Honey Boy moved. "S-sh!" hissed Goldie in a whisper.
"Senator Collamore is speaking. Oh, he is good! I have
heard him speak twenty times before. He says this custom of setting aside a day especially to do honor to the soldier dead originated, in this country, in the South, though
now every little town as well as every big city in the North
celebrates its Memorial Day; and he says that as long as
memory lives we of the South shall continue to pay this
sincere tribute to our men encamped beneath the green

grass awaiting the bugles of a better day." Goldie nodded his head vigorously, softly patting his thin, little hands together in respectful applause—softly so that he should not disturb the speaker. "Yes, that's good and true," he whispered, "very true indeed."

"Did you hear that?" he whispered again enthusiastically after a while, turning first toward Willie and then to Honey Boy. "That is Governor Marcus speaking now. 'The South is loyal,' he says, 'and it never forgets.' Ah, yes, that is so true, too."

And so Goldie, as if some part of him sensed the fact that his two comrades were not getting all that he was getting, from time to time picked out and tossed to the tired and hungry boy and to his brother-in-arms whose mind was thousands of miles away some of the crumbs from the feast of oratory that only he could enjoy—gilded words and fancy phrases that the little soldier had hoarded lovingly in his memory for years.

Well, after a while the speeches were all made, but Goldie stayed on. In other times it had been a custom in Asphodel to guard the Confederate Cemetery the night of Memorial Day, and Goldie was certain that he had been ordered to do guard duty that night.

Weak and hungry though he was, Goldie had been heartened by what he had heard, and as he sat on the rusty-red old iron bench enthusiastically talking at Honey Boy and Willie his voice was almost loud.

"Look yonder!" he cried. "Every grave is a bank of flowers. And did you notice how many people were here? Every store and office in town must have closed up. It's a grand day. I'm a proud man this Memorial Day, I can tell you. If President Davis could only see all this—and Lee! But, there, I must not speak that last name again. If I do I'm bound to cry, and I'm too old for that. Two words can always make me cry—'mother' and 'Lee.' "

The mounds above most of the graves had been leveled by time, and over all of them was a rank growth of weeds and grass. Honey Boy stared hard at Goldie, then he began giggling. Suddenly his small gray eyes filled with tears; he twisted and wrung his hands, and began whimpering, "Honey Boy hungry. Honey Boy must go home right now."

"Hungry?" said Goldie, in high scorn. "Why, you poor little fool, you don't know what hunger is. A soldier often goes two or three days on a single meal. But wait; our ladies will presently bring a banquet for the guard of honor —chicken and cake, strawberries and cream, and coffee— oh, I don't know what all, but it will be splendid. When the South does a thing it does it splendidly."

But the hot, damp, still afternoon wore away and no feast appeared. The notion that he was to do guard duty that night finally drove Goldie to consider the wisdom of fortifying himself in advance with sleep.

"You know," he explained to the unheeding ears of Willie and Honey Boy, "it is a serious offense to go to sleep on picket duty. In war-time it means courtmartial. There is no punishment here and now except a man's conscience, but a conscience can be terrible sometimes. And do you boys know, ever since the war whenever I've been assigned to any duty at reunions or on Memorial Days I've had a feeling that if I didn't do it right *he* would know—General Lee."

Creeping off to a secluded, shady spot some distance from the Confederate Cemetery, Goldie took off his coat, rolled it into a sort of pillow, and lay down in the deep grass, now wilted by the shimmering, moist heat. "This is how a soldier often has to sleep," he said proudly, looking from one to the other of his comrades.

Honey Boy, now completely subdued by hunger and thirst and fatigue, but held by fear and perhaps also by some boyish emotion of loyalty from deserting the little brown man in gray, sat staring at him a few moments, and then he too sank back on the grass and closed his eyes. Willie, his immaculate white suit of the morning wrinkled and soiled, dropped his straw hat to the ground at his feet and sat leaning against a stump, studying Goldie's face intently. Except for picketing the graves that night, Asphodel's Memorial Day exercises in honor of its soldier dead were over.

In the great sweet-gum tree above the three odd companions a pair of bluejays brought frequent instalments of food to their young and feasted them with much excitement and noisy importance. Out in the well-kept sections of the graveyard six or seven women appeared at various times during the afternoon, pulled a weed or a blade of grass from a grave, put down fresh flowers, pottered lovingly about it for a while, and then went home. But no one came to the Confederate Cemetery, and Goldie was as still as his comrades who slept beneath the tangles of grass and that weed called bitter. Honey Boy, waking up from time to time, looked around hopelessly, then weepingly lay back down. Willie continued staring at Goldie's face, as calm as death and as sweet as life.

Late in the afternoon slim, dazzlingly white whips of lightning slashed about in the gray clouds that had been assembling above, thunder tumbled and mumbled and boomed, a quick shower of rain came sliding down the wind. It slipped under the waving branches of the tree above the sleepers and drenched them to the skin before they were fully awake. Willie now sat with his head leaning back against the stump, staring at the sky. He paid no attention to the rain or to his comrades.

Honey Boy began crying, his teeth chattering with cold, and he raised up and wrung his hands. "Oh, what is a little shower?" asked Goldie roughly, getting to his feet. "I have marched and slept a week in wet clothes." Moving closer to the trunk of the sweet-gum tree, where it was almost dry, he laid his body down again and drifted away to sleep as sweetly as a child. Honey Boy beat his hands together and sobbed bitterly, but finally he crept close to Goldie, rolled himself into a ball, and was once more quiet.

And while two of them slept and one of them prowled desperately in the darkness of his mind for a lost thread a search-party that had been started by Mrs. Goldbaum came to the Confederate Cemetery, looked in, called loudly Goldie's name, and went away.

When night, and it was a heavy, clouded night, came on, Goldie rose, put on his hat and coat, selected a fallen dead limb of a pine tree to serve as a gun, and proceeded to his post. Honey Boy stumbled along close behind him, now and then breaking out in a huge bellow of desperation. "Shut up!" hissed Goldie. "Have you no respect for the dead?"

But the frail, little, old soldier himself, reeling with weakness, often caught hold of the fence to steady his trembling legs. He was so tired that at the corners he sometimes stopped and rested his head against the flat-topped posts. But he had not been relieved of duty, so he kept on marching around the enclosure, often stumbling and falling in the dark, but always getting up and forcing himself along. Honey Boy flung himself into the deep grass near the paling fence and lay there moaning. Willie stood, a dozen yards away, against a tree intently studying Goldie.

Meanwhile searching parties were excitedly combing Asphodel and its environs for the missing men and Honey Boy; and some time after midnight a party made a second trip to the Confederate Cemetery. As the searchers approached, their lanterns and blazing pine-knots burning ragged yellow holes in the night, Goldie tried to shout and almost did shout, "Halt!"

"Is that you, Goldie?" some one called.

"This is Private Levi Goldbaum."

"What are you doing out here, man? Your wife is crazy; she thinks you're dead. Where have you been all day? You're wet to the skin now, I'll bet. You look like it, anyhow. What in the world are you doing here?"

"I took part in our Memorial Day exercises, of course. Now I am on picket duty, guarding the graves of my comrades. I should have been relieved at midnight, but I reckon something went wrong. Anyway, I couldn't go until I was relieved, could I? Answer me that, Mr. Smarty. Don't come any nearer. You can't get through unless you've got the password. It's a point of honor. I don't care a rap who you are. Halt, there, you!"

Goldie stood up straight now, his bayonet pointing at the imprudent person who had come too near. The lights flickered over his frail figure, touching with yellow, beneath his slouch hat, the lower half of his cleanly shaven face, revealing the pale, thin, old lips drawn tightly across his false teeth.

The invaders gathered to talk among themselves, and as they whispered Goldie's gun drooped slightly in his hands, dropped lower, and then the little old man moaned and crumpled stiffly to his knees.

He tried to rise and did, and fell again. He whispered, "Halt! You can't pass here. It's a point of honor, you see. If General Lee found out he would be—would be sorry for me."

But the guard of honor had been relieved.

In his tracks stood another little soldier, this one clothed in white and shining with strength and fire and authority.

"Take him home, boys, but don't step across the line he set. Don't, don't, I tell you! This is no joke. Lift him up gently now. He dropped just like my buddy over there —the picture, with the lights and everything, was just exactly the same. He has reminded me in a thousand ways all day of my buddy. But he's only cold and hungry; my buddy was warm and dead. Take him home now, and when he comes to tell him not to worry; another soldier who remembers is covering his post. And General Lee will never know."

THE BEGGAR OF ALCAZAR[1]

By KONRAD BERCOVICI

(From *The Century Magazine*)

EVERY Spaniard will tell you that Spain has the most beautiful women in the world. Every man from Andalusia, richly colored, sun-tinted, green-mountained Andalusia, will tell you that Andalusian women are the most beautiful of Spain; for have they not the smoothness and the hue of olive fruit and hair like black silk? And the men of Seville, the capital of Andalusia, old Seville with its crooked streets upon which abut blind walls, whitewashed and high-windowed—Seville, towered and domed by a thousand old churches and cathedrals and palaces built of huge stone mellowed and softened by biting time, Seville with its leisurely coursing river, the Guadalquivir, the great river, named so by the Moors in olden times, but which can be waded across at some times of the year; every Sevillan, prouder of the women of his town than of all the other marvels it contains, will tell you that the women of Seville are the most beautiful of the Province of Andalusia.

And Maria del Alcazar was the most beautiful woman of Seville.

She was the daughter of Don Hermanos, the head keeper of the Alcazar, the old palace of the Moors, planned and executed at the time when the Saracens had glided above the peak of virility and had become softened and fattened from tribute paid by vanquished nations, and effeminate from a long period of peace and the affluence come from plunder.

Maria's father, Don Hermanos, had obtained the post of keeper in lieu of compensation for injuries he had sustained while fighting the wild tribes of the Spanish possessions in Africa. She was only ten years old when the family moved into one of the little whitewashed huts within the inclosure of the palace destined for the keeper. Black-eyed, with lustrous black hair, fine and silky like ebony filaments falling over her ivory-white neck, full-lipped, with a delicate chin, she was the pride of the family. Her mother, who came from Granada, instilled into her daughter that love for beautiful things and soft colors which had come to her with the blood of Moors that flowed in her veins. And with that she had also given to Maria that sinuous, graceful gait which holds both of the tiger and the angel—an imperceptible glide with slightly bent knees, while the arms sway softly like movements of invisible wings.

The Hermanos family had come to live at the Alcazar from one of the houses in the Triana, the crowded, squalid section across the river, where the poor of Seville live. The hut in which they had lived there was one in an immense yard in which fifty more little houses, leaning one on another, formed an open square; a *Casa Vesinante* of the neighborhood. There was not much difference between the hut they were occupying in the Alcazar and it, and the mother and the father were frequently complaining about the uncomfortable and dilapidated condition of their new home. But not so Maria. She was not complaining, for she had the Alcazar all to herself. Daily, before the arrival of visitors from all over the world who came to see the old Moorish palace, and in the evenings after they had left, the big palace, with its jewel-studded, mosaic-wrought wings, with its stalactite ceilings, like frozen skies of crystal tears, and the ceramic walls, with the lemon alleys in the gardens and the intoxicating flowers and shrubs, with roses bigger than the full moon and redder than the reddest blood, with cypresses in pools of water and rose-veined marble colonnades and alleys, the whole palace belonged to her. It was hers to roam wherever she pleased, sit wherever she wanted, and dream her dreams. The very greatest treasure of the world was hers. For nowhere, nowhere she knew, was any other palace the like of that to be found in the universe. Roaming daily, she discovered for herself new treasures which were unknown to others. The beautiful marble columns that stuck out underneath the overlaid brick near the bathing-pool of the sultana, the paintings on the walls, which had stupidly been smeared over by careless repairers after the Moors had been driven out of Spain, the carved oak beams inlaid with mother-of-pearl mosaic in what was formerly the dressing room of the harem, and which had lain covered with cement. And panels of wood sawed so finely they were transparent when the light shone through them, and others cut so finely they were like spider-webs, and which had lain there perhaps for centuries unobserved by any one, were hers to look at, hers alone, undefiled by other eyes, hers to bathe in their lacy softness of color and line.

True, she had to come into the hut late in the night and lie down on the bed within the squalid hut. But long before sunrise she would take her blanket and run out into the palace to sleep on the marble couch of the sultana, which faced the fountain of the Room of the Ambassadors; where once the sultan of the Saracens received the representatives of other nations, dressed in glittering silken garments, while black, nude, oiled slaves piled soft cushions under the guests and offered them refreshments in golden trays and from long silver vases.

The family had not been there long before all the keepers and the people in the neighborhood loved Maria. Shortly after their instalment, their daughter became known as "Maria del Alcazar." Not because people felt that she belonged to the Alcazar, but that the Alcazar belonged to her. She could tell such beautiful stories of the things she saw. She kept them all entranced when she spoke of the palace and its beauties. No one referred to her as the daughter of Hermanos the keeper. She was Maria del Alcazar to the neighbors, Maria del Alcazar to the priest, as well as to the working-men continually busy restoring and fixing what should better be left as it was.

And after a few years the reputation of Maria's beauty spread far and wide, as spreads a river after it has gone out from its bed. And many were the young men who, dressed in their best velvet, pale blue and dark brown, costumes, with wide-brimmed *flamenco* hats in their hands, now came to visit the Alcazar after their afternoon siesta, paying their good *pesetas* for the hope of catching a glimpse of Maria. They loitered and looked interested in the walls and gardens and trees and pools and fountains, but their long-lashed eyes were continually watching for an apparition. And many of them carried their guitars under their coats to begin their courting then and there should occasion present itself. The whole young malehood of Triana, remembering her as a child, would come to bid *buenos dias* to her father, with the hope of catching a glimpse of his daughter.

But during the day Maria was busy helping her mother. She had no interest in the Alcazar during that time. It belonged to strangers who came from all the corners of the world, to tread with unsympathetic feet the ground she considered holy and defile with their eyes and harsh voices, whispering, and pointing to one another the walls and the gardens she loved so much. It was only after they had gone that the Alcazar belonged to Maria, and after they had gone, all had to go. And so, reluctantly, the young men of Triana turned their backs and slowly shuffled out of the palace after the keeper had called out the evening hour. They would then remain outside the gate, waiting yet, pining for a glimpse before sighing deeply and departing slowly to their homes. And the young women of Triana bitterly clamored that because of Maria they were themselves unsung and unwooed by the young men of the neighborhood.

All this was happening unknown to Maria, for she lived not in this world. And after the late autumn had shaken the leaves of the crooked, brown-trunked olive trees in the garden and made the ceramic walls colder than they had ever been, she was the undisputed owner, the only one to enjoy the marvels of the Alcazar all to herself. While the winter rains were beating down upon the town of Seville, thus keeping away the visitors, Maria was happy. She grew and developed very fast, looking more and more like one of the Moorish sultanas who had for centuries queened over the palace. She imagined herself to be one of them, never thinking of sultans; as if the place had never been peopled by any others but women. For there seemed to be no trace of any male residence there. The delicate tracery of the rooms and the alcoves, every nook and corner, seemed to her to have been erected by delicate and whimsical hands of angels who had first dreamed about all this on some huge canvas which they had embroidered upon.

And yet work was going on continually, repairing here and there, and reconstructing. It seemed to her outrageous that the hands of men should have any right to touch such divinely delicate dreams in wood and stone. More than once she spoke angrily to the architect who was directing the work, telling him again and again the old Moorish legend current to this day all through Andalusia, that the Alcazar was never built, but appeared one day, called thither by the magic wand of some great magician in the employ of the sultan.

II

One afternoon early in the spring, when the buds in the lemon trees had begun to burst and had spread their little sweet-sour blossoms all over the place, Jose, the bull-fighter, a lad who had already won his first spurs in the bull-ring of Seville—Jose who had been one of her neighbors while they were living in Triana, stopped on his way to the ring to see Don Hermanos. He had been attracted by tales of the beauty of Maria del Alcazar, and had for a long time tried to see her without succeeding. But dressed in the costume of the matador, with a gold-laced black cap on his head, and a colored, spangled coat over the narrow, red-velvet breeches, tightened at the knees over the white stockings with green tassels, Don Jose felt he could dare make the attempt to see her. He braved bulls; why should he step back from meeting a woman?

While the hundred and one urchins cried, "There goes Don Jose!" he crossed into the vaulted entrance of the Alcazar and was received at the gate by Don Hermanos, who had been attracted by the outside noise.

"What great honor!" bowed Maria's father, shaking the decoration dangling on his breast.

heard the cry of the barefoot boys in rags selling papers. Don Jose had been wounded severely by the first bull he had fought.

"Quick, Mother!" Maria begged, and dragging the old woman by the hand she began to run in the direction of her old home in the Triana, where she was certain Don Jose would be brought to his mother.

But on arriving there they were told that the Gitanas had moved out from the "Casa" to a more comfortable home, now that Jose was earning so much money. And when the former neighbors heard about the accident that had happened, they left their cooking-pots, and the children left their play in the mud, and howling and running they followed the two women to the home of the matador.

Jose's face was white from the loss of blood. He was lying stretched out on a white bed. A number of friends and the priest and a doctor crowded the room.

"Will he die?" Maria screamed, looking up at the physician.

The man shook his head and put a finger to his mouth. "No noise, please."

And then Jose opened his eyes and saw Maria; and his faint lips murmured her name.

Jose did get better; he had not been wounded in any vital part of his body. He was only weak because of the blood he had lost before they had succeeded in driving away the bull that had gored him. Daily, Maria and her mother would come to sit at his bedside and care for him. When the wounds in his upper thighs had healed, it was upon Maria's shoulder that he first left the bed to sun himself on the balcony. And with that marvelous recuperating power of youth he was able before the summer to appear again in the ring.

Maria sat in a box with her mother watching the first appearance. And the cheering of the crowd as he bowed before the balcony of the queen was deafening. Maria, paler than usual, was not interested in the bull-fight as such. To her it was merely the man she loved who was now facing a formidable brute. It was her man that was in danger—in danger of that black bull, snorting and running

wildly about the arena. She could not appreciate the cheers
that came, round after round, as Don Jose with graceful
fleetness avoided the charging animal by fooling him with
the red *capa* that he held in his hand. She could not
understand why he did not use the spade and kill the brute.
To her mind every bull was the same that had wounded the
man she loved.

The crowd cheered and yelled in appreciation of their
idol's dangerous play. Suddenly there was a great silence.
The *banderilleros* had done their work and distanced themselves from the animal. The matador alone faced him now.
He played and enraged the bull for a few minutes, then he
poised himself with his spade for the final thrust. But
when the bull made a movement, courage failed him, and
he stepped aside. And the same crowd that had been cheering so wildly now began to hoot him. The other matadors
sprang to his help and began to throw their red *capas* over
the bull. Don Jose shook his head sorrowfully without
looking up, and waving his quadrilla aside, he again posed
himself before the bull, trying to get him to lower his head.
There was silence again. Maria's heart stood still. And
while the crowd was hooting again the matador, who had
side-stepped for a second time, her own heart was glad, for
he was there yet and alive. Her mother and the mother of
the matador were pale with anger and shame. What had
happened to Jose? The bugle gave a warning to the matador that he must be quick about his business. His time
was up. And this time the matador did not side-step. His
thrust was sure and deep, and the crowd cheered wildly,
although when the ring had been cleared, the *afficianadoes*
were looking at one another and shaking their heads, as if
saying, "The best days of the Gitana are over." Never
before in his short, but glorious, career had he been known
to side-step a charging bull.

He did not do much better with the second animal. And
it was only because they remembered how severely he had
been wounded before that the crowd did not do the usual
things on such occasions, throwing the hard cushions underneath them into the arena, and even empty bottles and
stones. Even Jose's mother looked coldly at her son when

he returned home with her in the waiting carriage, for the papers were sure to report his lack of courage. Only Maria was happy. He had come out of the fight alive and he had killed the bulls.

The next few weeks took the matador out of the city to fight in other *pueblos*. It was understood that he was going to marry Maria as soon as he returned from the season's activities. Left alone, Maria, now the acknowledged fiancée of Don Jose, again took possession of the Alcazar. But everything within it was now filled with Joses. Joses in silken garb. Joses in the center of bull-rings. Joses wounded, Joses side-stepping, and crowds upon tiers and tiers in a large circle. She tried to conjure again the old visions of sultanas and *bayaderes* dancing in the great halls and in the gardens. And when they did appear, Don Jose was somewhere about them. And she would harshly order her vision figures to disappear, for they all looked at him so longingly. And they were all so much more beautiful than she was.

She would wait trembling with fear the afternoons she knew he had appeared in the distant bull-rings for a telegram that he sent her at the end of every *corrida*. He gave no details, only telling her that all was well and that he loved her. But in reality things were not as well with him as they had been before. There was great doubt whether he would ever be engaged again to fight in the bull-ring after that season. There was great dissatisfaction with his work. He still gave them great thrills in playing with the bull, but courage generally failed him when he faced the animal with spade in hand. He could not forget that he had been wounded. And he played longer with the animals than he should have done to avoid as long as possible the last moment. And again and again the warning bugle had sounded, the papers reported. Don Hermanos was far from being satisfied with his future son-in-law. Yet all Maria cared was that Jose was alive and untouched by the brutal beasts.

She rejoiced to the fullest of her soul when he returned. Only Don Hermanos was not satisfied to see him walk about in street clothes instead of the matador uniform, like the others of his profession. Every day after sundown Jose would come to the Alcazar, and Maria would show him the great halls and the gardens and tell him the legends of the place. She had found again the Alcazar now that he was near her. Speaking to him, all the old charm of the palace had returned. She was not even jealous of the sultanas she now conjured from the ceramic walls and from behind the balconies overhead.

As the day of her wedding approached, Don Jose spoke to her.

"How will you ever be able to live within the poor walls of your home after having lived here amid such great beauties?"

Maria laughed and laughed. Don Jose intended to leave Seville and go elsewhere. He had saved quite a goodly amount of money. He had premonitions about his being killed in the ring if he should continue to fight next season. An old sorceress had told him so also. He had different plans. He thought sheep-raising upon the Saragoza Hills pleased him best. He owned there quite a good stretch of land. And there was an old adobe house on top of the hill. He thought it was better to live in seclusion for the next year or so than being hooted and reviled in the bull-ring. Maria was willing to follow him anywhere.

And he told her: "When my feelings change, I will return to the ring."

"Which I hope you will never do!" Maria exclaimed.

She had no desire to see her husband glorified by the multitude after he had been gored to death in the ring.

IV

It was a great affair, the wedding of Don Jose with Maria del Alcazar. All the retired and active matadors of Seville came to the wedding in their bespangled clothes, for they understood what the populace refused to understand. They knew what premonitions were and how they acted on a matador in the ring. It was easy to cheer and easier to hoot, but bulls carried death on the tips of their horns.

A week later the two newly married were in the Saragoza

adobe. It was not much better than the home in which
their people had lived in the Triana. Still, Maria thought
it was very beautiful. The bare mud walls she decorated
with her eyes, which reflected all the beauties they had
absorbed. And through them she projected her dreams,
the delicate traceries and colorings, and the mosaic and the
stalactite of the ceilings. And she was happy. For there
were no working-men tearing down and repairing and touching with brutal hands what was about her. And from the
top of the hill the olive groves and vineyards and the tall
cypress trees that stretched below her were even more beautiful than the gardens in which she had roamed. And the
serpentining, snaking river below, shimmering with the blue
of the sky in the sunlight, was like the limpid water pools
and bathing places of the Alcazar. Indeed, it was more
the Alcazar than anything else. And it was hers. No
working-men, no visitors, disturbed her.

Jose was busy building sheds for the sheep. And evenings his powerful arms were delicately wrapped about
her. He appreciated her love and was flattered that she
could be so happy in such poor surroundings. And he wondered what there was in him that she, the most beautiful
woman in the world, should be able to stay with him in so
desolate a place, away from all the things she had been
accustomed to. In his eyes she was not a poor girl, the
daughter of a keeper, that he had married. She was Maria
del Alcazar, the one raised in surroundings so beautiful
there was none the like of them in the world. Evenings,
when the work was done, the two lovers would face each
other, sitting outside their hut.

And one evening Don Jose said:

"There never happened a better thing to me than to have
been gored by a bull."

To which Maria quietly answered, seizing the hands of
the man near her:

"And yet I hate bulls."

But the courage did not return to Don Jose. Month
succeeded month. And after the long winter was over, the
first winter they had passed together, he was approached to
appear again in the ring. Refusing, he wondered whether

the courage would ever return to him again. He hung his head when the man tried to convince him by saying:

"You, who have received the applause of thousands and thousands while so young, should now live in the company of sheep and mules on the top of a hill! You who have received thousands of *pesetas* for one hour of work, and been glorified by the whole of Spain, should now work so hard with the hope of getting a pittance at the end of the year! And your wife, Don Jose. Don't forget your wife."

But Don Jose shook his head and answered:

"Not this year."

And when the men who had come to engage him left his house, they said to each other: "Many a good matador has become better and more courageous to win the woman he loved, only to become a coward for fear of losing her."

Maria was happy that he refused. She did not understand why every time these men returned Jose should be so sullen and dark. Oh, were they not happy there on top of the mountain? And were they not living in the most beautiful palace that man had ever built? If it was true the Alcazar had never been built, but had been conjured up by the wand of some great magician, an even greater magician had conjured the greater Alcazar she was living in now. She had always, she realized now, missed something when she had been living in the Alcazar of Seville. Now she knew what she had missed. There were only walls and ceilings. Even the phantoms she conjured were cold despite all the warm colors about them. But there on the Saragoza Hills she had realized and filled out her dream. Draperies, heavy silks came down, called by the magic of her love, and covered everything, and uncovered greater beauties on softer backgrounds.

But Jose walked about sullenly, muttering to himself:

"It was a bad day for me when that bull gored me. It was a bad day for me when that bull gored me." He missed the applause, the cheering, the excitement. And yet he did not have the courage.

And one day, when he had returned from the village at the foot of the hill, instead of recalling as he had frequently done the beautiful days during which Maria had sat at his

bedside, he spoke angrily to her, and she could recognize
the smell of *aguardiente*, burning water, on his breath.

"It was because of you that I was gored by the bull! I
was thinking of you instead of the beast before me! You
are the cause of my misfortune!"

And suddenly, when she reëntered the hut, the walls
appeared as they really were, dirty mud walls. The ceilings which she had enlarged and domed with her eyes, and
beamed and wrought with mosaics, appeared to her as they
really were, cracked, low, and ugly. The rickety bed which
stood in the corner, which had been to her like the richest
couch of the most beautiful sultana, was nothing but a
squalid heap of rusty iron, rags, and mattresses. The low-
burning lamp had lost its mystic quality. It was but an ill-
smelling kerosene lamp. All the riches of the adobe were
gone. It had been conjured by the magic wand of a sorcerer, and been dispelled by a few ugly words. And so she
lay down and wept.

When she awoke in the morning, the squalor of her surroundings was even more appalling. The sheep, which had
been so beautiful, were now ugly. And the mountain and
the river and the olive groves and the vineyards were nothing but ugly, brown, crooked cripples scorching in the hot
sun. It was worse than the Triana mud huts in which she
had lived. And Jose himself, Jose himself, what a different
man he was! An unwashed, unkempt, rag-clothed stranger,
with a hard voice and an evil odor.

A few months later, another group of men came to induce
Don Jose to appear again in the bull-ring. He assured them
he would do so the following spring.

"But where is Doña Maria, his wife, of whose beauty we
have heard so much? The woman we have seen could not
have been she, for she looked so much older and anything
but beautiful." The men looked at one another outside.

Indeed, where was she?

For none of them realized that a single year could have
changed a woman so much. She wandered about mute, list-
less. Her eyes were lusterless and her gaze vacant.

And he did get back his courage the following spring.
And he again became the favorite of the people. There

were pictures of him hanging in every store and every home from one end of Spain to the other. He was piling up great wealth and had furnished a beautiful apartment, more beautiful than he had ever expected to live in, with a profusion of silks and carpets and silver vases and copper urns. He thought Maria had been made unhappy by the poverty of her surroundings, the fool.

It was all in vain. He could not make it as beautiful as the Alcazar. It was squalid, poor, ugly, decrepit tinsel compared with the gold of the palace, and more so when compared with the gold of her dreams, which he had destroyed once forever.

When he had withdrawn from the ring rich and honored, she returned to her father's home. And before she was thirty, when her father died, unable to leave the Alcazar, she sat outside its gates. Her face withered. The skin of her hands dried up like parchment. She still sits there, wrapped in rags, begging from the tourists.

But after sundown the Alcazar is hers.

THE LAUGH[1]

By BELLA COHEN

(From *The Calendar of Modern Letters*)

MEYER lay on the bed, the covers drawn up over his mouth. His thin, long nose projected over the quilt seemed very long and wax-like; and his eyes were closed. His feet stuck out beyond the edge of the bed, for Meyer was a tall man, and illness seemed to have stretched him out.

Hannah, his wife, stood near the bed, looking down upon him sorrowfully, her fingers patching her mouth.

"A man who has never been sick in his life to fall so sick. And he only fifty years old—the best years," she thought.

She turned from the bed and silently began to clean the rooms she and Meyer had lived in for the last eight years. Every now and then she stopped to look at the man in the bed.

"It seems so strange for him to be in the house with me and yet not say a word to me." Hannah spoke to herself. "I don't like that white sheet over the quilt."

Hannah carefully placed the broom in the corner near the stove and pattered over to the wooden trunk where she kept her red shawl. A close, layer-like smell of moth balls and unaired clothing lifted itself sluggishly and receded. The red shawl was near the top. It had white stripes and was made of sheep's fleece. Hannah had knitted and dyed the shawl when she was still young and wore a black plait down her back.

She placed the red shawl over the sick man's feet, but they persisted in sticking out—their long, misshapen toes digging into each other with soles as hard as leather. They stood up stiffly perpendicular.

Hannah looked at them and a strange terror gripped her.

[1] Copyright, 1926, by Bella Cohen.

Her Meyer was sick. Her Meyer was very sick! Desperately, she thought of the House. Perhaps she had better call Mrs. Brandt. Some one. . . .

A knock sounded.

Hannah hurried to the door and opening it softly, looked up into the ruddy, round face of her sister Brahne.

"You!" she cried delightedly. For a moment, the sadness left her eyes. She was no longer alone—all alone—for now, if only for a few moments, she had her sister with her. Some one of her own blood.

"Yes, here I am!" And Brahne stepped into the room. Everything in it became dwarfed, for Brahne was large, large of feet, hands, head, mouth, teeth, and voice. By lifting her hand she could have flattened its palm on the ceiling as easily as she carried her twins on each hip.

The two looked at each other, for they had not seen each other for a year. Brahne had moved her bakery, her husband and children into a suburb, and Hannah, who could not ride in cars because it made her dizzy, did not visit her.

"Meyer is sick, very sick," Hannah finally said. Her hand went up to her mouth again.

Brahne turned to the bed and looked at the man.

"He doesn't seem so bad," she decided. "What is it, a cold?"

"No, it's something more. The doctor wouldn't tell me. I think it's his heart."

"Heart! That's how much you know about men."

Brahne seated herself and discoursed in bellows.

"Men are children. They don't know how to bear even a scratch on the finger. They get a little cold and right away they want to go to Coloraydo and get consumption. They want to be petted and fondled like a month-old baby. The more attention you give them the more they want. Many times I think to myself, why do they send men to fight in the wars when they are such weaklings!"

Hannah listened meekly, her hand on her mouth.

"Maybe that's true what you say, Brahne," she offered timidly, "but Meyer is now laying like this the third week. And, you know, he's never been sick since we've been married."

THE HANDS OF THE ENEMY[1]

By CHARLES CALDWELL DOBIE

(From *Harper's Magazine*)

WITHIN a hundred yards of the hill's crest Walton Pringle's pocket flash winked spasmodically and died. He paused a moment to catch his breath; the pull up from the creek bed had winded him and the sting of cold rain in his face added a further discomfort. If he hadn't dawdled at Preston's Flat, hoping for the rain to cease or abate, he would have made his objective before nightfall. But since he had elected to wait so long it would have been much better to continue there until next morning. As it was, he felt sure that he had strayed from the trail—a particularly unhappy thought to a man who could claim only a speaking acquaintance with the wilderness. And this too under the pall of a stormy night without the slightest ray of light to guide him. Well, the best he could do was to stumble on: it was far better to keep moving in circles than to resign himself to inactivity and chills.

He was glad now that he had been persuaded to take a pistol when he came away from Walden's Glen. If he were lost, at least he could provide himself with game, and in the mountains one could never tell how long one might wander aimlessly along false paths once the proper trail was abandoned. At first this pistol business had seemed absurd: California was no longer a bandit country, and even if it were he had nothing worth stealing. A jack-knife, a pocket-flash, two bars of chocolate, and a sheaf of notes on "Itinerant and Rural Labor and Its Relation to Crime" were poor pickings for a hold-up man. His notes especially were valueless to any one save himself, and even their loss would not have been irreparable. He was still near enough to

his investigations to have the material for his book clearly
fixed in his mind and, once back at his desk in San Francisco, he would be able to recall every detail of the last two
weeks spent among the economic nomads of the mountains.
But in spite of all these obvious guarantees against violence,
it appeared that there *were* reasons for being forearmed.
. . . It was Lem Thatcher, one of the oldtimers, who had
put him straight on this point.

"Bandits be damned!" Thatcher had exclaimed. "But
how about a stray bobcat? Or a crazy man? Or a lost
trail? . . . A man who goes into the open with nuthin' but
a jack-knife and a couple o' bars o' chocolate is a fool. . . .
Give a man a gun and you give him the next thing to a
pardner."

Under the depression of the moment he felt that his original stupidity lay not so much in failing to realize the needs
of such a trip as in essaying the venture at all. Why hadn't
he been sensible and taken the stage as far as Rock Point
and swung on from there to Marchel Duplin's cabin? He
had no time to waste, and had there been no other reason
this alternative would have given him several additional
hours with a man who, everybody conceded, knew more
about sheep herding than any other within a hundred miles.
He had talked to a Basque shepherd near Compton's and to
a Mexican herder just the other side of Willow Creek,
attempting to get sidelights on their profession, but they
had been taciturn and he without the proper moisture for
limbering their tongues. Duplin, everybody conceded, was
exceptionally garrulous for a sheep herder even when he
had not the help of thin wine. It seemed expedient, then,
to go to Duplin if he wished properly to complete the picture of rural economy whose drawing he contemplated.
But for an untrained mountaineer—a tenderfoot, in fact—
it was nothing save a whimsical extravagance to plunge
along a fifteen-mile trail through forest and shifting granite
when an easier course was open. Being valley bred he
hadn't expected rain in August, but if he had stopped to
think he might have known that anything was climatically
possible in the mountains.

Stumbling, crawling, cursing, somehow in spite of the

blackness he felt himself making progress uphill. Presently his feet touched level ground. This in itself was reassuring. He raised his eyes in a desperate effort to pierce the gloom, took a few steps forward—and suddenly, miraculously, found himself in a clearing from which beckoned the friendly light of a cabin. With a smothered exclamation of joy he quickened his gait, almost running forward, and the next instant he had gained the window, instinctively stopping to peer within.

The unreality of the scene which met his eye gave Walton Pringle a feeling that he was either dreaming or gazing down on a stage set for a play; only sleep or the theater seemed capable of a picture so filled with melodrama. But in the theater one was never at once spectator and participant, and in sleep one did not have the tangible physical discomfort which he felt. He drew his rain-soaked body closer against the cabin, raising himself on his toes so that he might get a better view of the interior. A man stood hovering over a table lighted by an anæmic candle, and through his fingers dripped a slow trickle of silver. In a corner, uncannily outlined by a steady gleam of light, was a crucifix nailed to the wall and below it lay a couch piled with disordered bed clothing. On the floor, midway between table and couch, was sprawled the figure of a man—arms flung wide, his black-bearded face upturned—a startling inanimate thing that made Walton Pringle turn away with a shudder. The man at the table undoubtedly was a thief. Was he also a murderer?

For the second time that night Pringle was glad that he was provided with a pistol, and yet in spite of his preparedness he had a momentary misgiving, an indecision: to be secured against an unavoidable contingency was one thing; to push deliberately into trouble was quite another. Pringle was no coward, but he knew his limitations; he was not trained in any superlative skill with firearms. Was it discreet, then, to thrust oneself across the path of a desperate man?

He continued to gaze through the window with morbid fascination and uncertainty: the picture was too revealing —violence had been done, that was obvious; plunder was

"Is this Marchel Duplin's cabin?"

The youth stared, then nodded.

"And is this Marchel Duplin?"

"Yes."

Almost with the same movement Pringle and the youth turned away, the lad dropping into a chair before the table.

Pringle drew a bench from the wall and straddled it. "What's your name?" he demanded.

"Sam—Sam Allen."

"Where do you come from?"

"Down—down by Walden's Glen."

"Ah! . . . And what are you doing here?"

"Gettin' out o' the wet, mostly."

Pringle pointed to the heap of coins on the table. "And making a little clean-up on the side, eh? . . . Well, what have you got to say for yourself?"

Sam Allen dropped his ineffectual blue eyes. "Nuthin' much . . . I come here to get outa the rain, like I said before. He was layin' on the bed there, mutterin' to hisself, and burning up with fever. I went up to him and I says, 'Marchel, don't yer know me?' With that he grabs me by the throat. I never *did* see anybody get such a stranglehold on a man. . . . I jest couldn't pry him loose. He went down like a chunk o' lead. And when his head struck the ground"—Sam Allen shuddered—"It was jest like a rotten watermelon went squash. . . . I didn't dare look fer a minute, and when I did he was dead!"

"And then you proceeded to rob him, eh? Without even waiting to lift his dead body from the floor . . . or seeing what you could do to help him?"

Sam Allen shook his head. "I know when a man's dead . . . and I don't like to touch 'em, somehow—that is—not all by myself. It was different when you come. Besides, I've heerd tell that the law likes things left in a case like this—that it's better not to touch nuthin'."

Pringle could not forego a sneer; really, the youth was too ineffectual! "Nothing except money, I suppose!"

Sam Allen ignored the sarcasm; it is doubtful if it really made an impression. "It musta got kicked out from under his pillow in the scuffle. . . . Anyway, I seen it layin' there

on the floor, jest where his head struck, almost. Of course
I was curious." He turned a childishly eager face toward
Pringle. "Do you know, he had nigh onto fifty dollars in
that there bag."

"Indeed!"

But again Pringle's sarcasm rebounded and fell flat.
Apparently Sam Allen was not quick witted. He mistook
irony for interest. Without further urging the youth began
to tell about himself. His father had a hog ranch just this
side of Walden's Glen—a drab, filthy spot. This father
kept drunk most of the time on a potent brand of moonshine which he himself distilled. The whole drudgery of
the place had fallen on the boy. "Cows, I wouldn't have
minded so much—they ain't dirty like pigs—leastways what
they eat ain't!" He breathed hard when he spoke and his
clipped words took on descriptive vehemence. The whole
atmosphere of the Allen ranch rose in a fetid mist before
Walton Pringle: hog wallow, sour swill, obscene grunts and
squealings, the beastly drunkenness of Allen senior. Since
no mention was made of a woman's presence, Pringle
divined that there was none. Sam Allen had grown sick to
death of it all and had run away: without money, provisions, or proper clothing—even lacking decent footgear—
without plans. It was a pitiful story and yet it damned him
superlatively; gave point to the situation in which he had
been found. Listening to him Pringle lost the conviction
that he was a premeditated murderer, but there seemed no
reasonable doubt that he was an accidental one. It seemed
he knew well the Duplin cabin; used to steal up there on
rare occasions, when Marchel was out shepherding, to
share the Frenchman's dribbles of thin wine. He liked
wine. One mouthful and your heart felt freer, more gay.
Why, one could sing then— almost. At least Marchel
Duplin could. Moonshine never gave a man a singing
mood—only a nasty one. At this point Pringle could not
forego a question: Did he know that Duplin had money?
. . . Allen hesitated and Pringle had an impulse to warn
him against answering; it didn't seem fair to let the boy
unwittingly incriminate himself. But before Pringle could
caution him the youth blurted out the truth: he had heard

something of it. Pringle felt his heart contract in a rush of
pity: the whole situation was so obvious—a desperate,
weak, perhaps degenerate boy rushing blindly toward freedom and disaster. Had Duplin's wine jug been part of the
youth's hapless plan? Had he attempted to get the shepherd drunk before he despoiled him?

At all events he hadn't managed skillfully and the Frenchman had put up a fight. The results spoke for themselves.
Well, it all came back to heredity and environment. He'd
have an interesting lot of notes to make on this case. No
theorizing this time, but something at first hand, alive and
palpitating. Quite suddenly he found his pity receding,
submerged by his scientific desire for truth. The youth
before him was like a moth pinned to the wall, before which
the investigator lost all sentimental interest in his eagerness
to measure the duration of the death agony. Now was
the time to get data, before fear or caution stepped in to
dam up Sam Allen's naïve garrulity. Pringle was interested in the youth's mother. But Sam Allen couldn't
remember much: Lizzie Evans, that had been her name—
a girl who "worked out." Yet the very economy of this
picture was illuminating. Lizzie Evans, a girl who "worked
out." It was perfect! A girl who doubtless had been
ruined, to use the phrase of unemancipated women. She
probably had had just such a pinched, yellow, wistful face
as the son she had borne to feed the hangman's noose.
Pringle had a fad for reconstructing the faces of mothers
from the bolder outlines of their male offspring. He usually found the test successful even with the most rugged
material; he had a feeling that in this case his imagination
did not need to overleap any confines whatsoever to achieve
its goal. Lizzie Allen, born Evans, had died: a futile, weak
anæmic slip of a girl, stifled by the nauseous vapors of the
hog pens. Not that Sam Allen put it so, but Pringle could
read a shorthand of life almost as skillfully as a complete
script. He swung the conversation back to Allen senior.
The son embellished the portrait with a wealth of sinister
details, finishing with a malicious little chuckle.

"An' he's deputy sheriff for the district, too, moonshinin'
an' all. . . . Oh, I've seen him track fellars down an'

shoot 'em when they had the goods on him. Didn't matter whether they was guilty or not. . . . I've seen him beat 'em, too—over the head—with the butt of a pistol—or anything else that came handy!"

Pringle turned his eyes to the inanimate figure on the bed. How completely everything was dovetailing! *"I've seen him beat 'em, too, over the head."* Precisely. For all the youth's inadequacy he had absorbed some of the inhumanities from his sire.

A strange exalted cruelty began to stir in Walton Pringle, the cruelty of an animal on the scene of some furtive thing pitifully intent on escape. His mood must have communicated itself, for suddenly Sam Allen fell into a silence that no amount of prodding could shatter. Well, there could be little more that bore upon the particular issue. Pringle began to think of the most expedient move. He found himself shivering. Naturally, since he had been wet to the skin. . . . A rusty stove huddled itself just below one of the windows, sending its pipe crazily through a shattered pane. Pringle suggested a fire; dumbly the youth assented. Together they began to collect débris from the cabin floor: crumpled newspapers, empty cartons, a handful of pine cones. Soon a cheerful blaze crackled and roared. Even Sam Allen found its warmth agreeable, but its cheer did not serve to melt his sudden reticence.

Presently for lack of fuel the fire began to spend itself and its snap and roar sank to a faint hiss. The night too seemed to have grown miraculously silent. Pringle rose and threw open the cabin door. The rain had stopped, even the wind had fallen, and through a rent in the storm clouds far to the east a faint glow gave promise of a rising moon.

Pringle closed the door and went back to his place before the stove. The situation in which he found himself made him suddenly restive. It seemed as if he could not possibly wait until morning to settle the issue that must ultimately be settled.

Walden's Glen lay a good fifteen miles to the east, but at least it was for the most part down grade. His exhaustion of the previous hour had been swallowed up in the absorbing shock of drama. He felt like making a decisive move and yet a certain pity for Sam Allen, shrinking visibly before his questioning gaze, made him resolve to give the youth a meager choice in the matter. He sauntered casually to the table. The candle was guttering to a feeble decline, and it threw out a flickering light that touched with spasmodic fire the coins lying in a disorderly heap where Sam Allen had abandoned them. Pringle ran his hand nervously through the silver pile.

"What do you think," he asked abruptly, "shall we strike out for Walden's Glen now, or wait till morning?"

Sam Allen gave a gasp. Then recovering himself, he returned with slow drawling defiance, "If you're headed that way, suit yourself. . . . But I set out to leave Walden's Glen and I don't see no reason why I should go back."

Pringle felt himself grow ominously cool. "I dare say you don't. But, unfortunately for you, there *are* reasons. . . . In a way I'm sorry I walked into this mess. But I did walk in and I can't shirk my responsibility. There's the law to reckon with, you know!"

Sam Allen's lips began to tremble. "I tell you it was an accident. Don't you believe me?"

"No."

"And you mean to give me up—to—to—my father?"

Deputy sheriff for the district! For a moment even Pringle trembled: the picture which the youth had drawn of his sire had been too vivid. And besides, the bare situation was pregnant with disaster.

"I'm afraid there's no help for it," Pringle returned, trying to check any show of emotion. Sam Allen crept nearer to the table like a whipped dog. Pringle was stirred to a profound pity. "Besides," he went on more softly, "your father can't really touch you. You'll have all the law on your side."

Even in his terror the youth could not check a sneer. "Much you know about it!" he cried passionately.

"But I'll go with you—don't you understand—every step of the way . . . I mean, I'll stand by you till everything's put straight." Pringle broke off suddenly. Sam Allen's white face seemed to draw closer to the table and

his two eyes were fixed craftily upon the gun which Pringle
had neglected to restore to his hip pocket.

An intense nervous silence followed; Pringle made a
swift movement toward the pistol, and the next moment the
candle was violently extinguished.

Pringle stood momentarily inactive under the shock of
surprise. The slam of the door roused him. He went
stumbling through the gloom, knocking down impediments
in his path until he gained the open. The moon was still
hidden by the thick clouds in the east, but directly overhead a few stars showed dimly through thin vapors rising
from the drenched hills.

Almost at once he realized the futility of pursuit. He
knew nothing about the country, and besides, the greatest
service he could render was to report the situation promptly.
An aroused community would deal effectively with the murderer—he wouldn't get very far with his lack of resources
and wit.

Pringle went back into the cabin and lighted the candle,
forcing the stub out of the candlestick to prolong its life.
The pile of silver had been scattered about by the impact
of stumbling fingers but it appeared otherwise intact; the
pistol, however, had disappeared. Pringle laughed to himself, shrugging his shoulders. It was plain that he had
much to learn about the custody of prisoners. Urged by
the expediency of taking stock of all emphatic details connected with the situation, he raised the candle and swept
the interior with its faint radiance. This was the first com-
prehensive view he had taken of the room. But there was
really little of fresh significance: the cot on which lay the
body of Marchel Duplin, the rusting stove, the table, the
one chair, the bench; and over in a corner—back of the
door when it swung open—a burlap curtain screening a
shallow triangle. This last item was the only detail which
had previously escaped him, partly because of its neutral
color and partly because it hung in the shadow. A faint
suspicion crossed him as he caught the movement of the
curtain. He put the light down on the table. Could it
be that the slammed door following on Allen's apparent

exit had been a clever ruse? He took a quick gliding step forward and thrust the curtain dramatically aside, almost expecting to find Sam Allen cowering behind it. But the space revealed nothing except a muddle of clothes and discarded boots, and a sharp current of air drifting through a wide crevice in the floor.

The reaction from the tenseness of expectation left him shivering. An impatience for the whole situation swept over him. He felt relieved that young Allen had fled, eluded him. It lifted an unpleasant duty from his shoulders and at the same time confirmed the youth's guilt. He would have hated, now that he considered it, to be the instrument for turning an uncertain situation into an inevitable one. His testimony might have damned an innocent man—that he was now willing to concede. But Allen's escape immeasurably cleared the issue: innocent people were never fearful. How many, *many* times, in divers forms, had this truism been brought home to him!

Yet in spite of the emphatic case against young Allen, Pringle felt the necessity of having his own movements clear in his mind. He'd be questioned, naturally; that went without saying. Quite rapidly he recapitulated the events of the day: the start from Walden's Glen at sunrise, the untoward rain at noon, his dawdling in the shelter of a redwood hollow against a sudden clearing; his resolve to push on when he saw no prospect of the storm's abatement. . . . It all sounded so clear and simple. Once he explained his mission, any testimony he might give must gather added weight. And his credentials would render his testimony doubly valuable. His book on *Radical Movements in Relation to Post-war Problems* would carry him past any reasonable skepticism, and then a B.A. from Yale and the prospects of a Ph.D. from Columbia ought to impress even a rural magistrate.

He decided to count the money and take it with him to Walden's Glen. It wasn't safe to leave it in the cabin, and besides, it had a significant bearing on the case. In a half hour, he figured, the moon would be fully risen and if the sky continued to clear he would have a brilliantly lighted path to travel back.

He drew the single chair up to the table and fell to his task. The money was in all denominations of silver, but mostly quarters and halves. He began to group them into systematic piles. A faint scraping sound made him pause. . . . A twig, probably, brushing against the house. . . . He continued counting the money. Again the sound came. This time a tremor ran through him as he stopped his task. He kept his eye straight ahead as if fearing to turn to the right or left. Then slowly, fearfully, with the inevitability of one who feels other eyes fixed ironically upon him, he turned and looked up at the window, very much as Sam Allen had done less than an hour before. . . . A man's face answered his startled gaze and the next instant the door flew open.

Walton Pringle rose in his seat, again repeating the gesture of Sam Allen in a like situation. A faint, almost imperceptible sense of this analogy crept over him; he felt his heart suddenly contract.

The man in the doorway had an impressive bulk, a swaggering, insolent grossness that must once have been robustly virile. His coarse underlip had sufficient force to crowd upward a ragged mustache, and as he stepped heavily into the circle of light, Walton Pringle felt a glint of sardonic and unpropitiable humor leap at him from two piglike eyes.

"Where's Duplin?" the stranger demanded.

Pringle pointed to the cot. The visitor strode up to it and drew down the quilt. "Dead, eh!" He bent over closer. "Ah, a tolerable blow on the head. . . . Neat job, I'd say." He flung back the quilt over the face of the corpse with a gesture that showed an absolute indifference, a contempt even for the presence of death. "Well, stranger, suppose you tell me who you are?" There was an authority in his drawling suaveness which brought a quick answer. "Pringle, eh? . . . And just what are you doing here?"

Pringle stiffened with a rallied dignity. "I might ask you the same question. And I might ask your name, too, if I felt at all curious. As a matter of fact, I'm not, but I must decline to be cross-examined by a man I don't know."

A grim humor played about the protruding under-lip. "Correct, stranger, correct as hell! My name happens to be Allen—Hank Allen. That don't mean nuthin' to yer, does it? Well, I'll go further. I'm deputy sheriff for this county and I've got a right to question any man I take a notion to question. It ain't exactly a right I work over-time, but when I come into a man's cabin and find that man dead and a stranger pawin' over his money, I guess I just naturally calc'late that I'd better get on the job." He threw a pair of handcuffs on the table. "Why I happen to be here don't matter much, I guess. A man sometimes goes hunting for jack rabbit and brings home venison. You get me, don't yer?"

Walton Pringle stood motionless, trying to still the beating of his heart. He understood something now of Sam Allen's terror, Sam Allen's fear of being turned over to his father. But he knew also that a betrayal of fear would be one of the worst moves he could make.

"You don't have to tell me why you're here," he said quietly, "now that I know your name. There's a runaway lad mixed up in it somewhere, if I'm not mistaken."

The barest possible flash of surprise lighted up the features of Hank Allen, destroying for a moment their brutal immobility. "I ain't saying 'yes' or 'no' to that," he half laughed, recovering his careless manner. "But I don't figger how that answers the question at hand."

Pringle smiled a superior smile. "Perhaps you're not the only one to look through the window at a stranger sitting before this table *pawin'* over a dead man's money. Perhaps I wasn't the first in the field. Perhaps there is more than you fancy to connect up a runaway lad with the question at hand. Who knows?"

Hank Allen's shoulders drooped forward with almost impalpable menace and his brows drew down tightly. "Look here, Pringle, I ain't accustomed to movin' in circles. When I shoot, I shoot straight. What's more, I usually set the pace. In other words, let's have no more riddles. Good plain language suits me. What's on your mind?"

Pringle shrugged his shoulders with a hint of triumph and proceeded to tell his adversary just what was on his mind in good plain language that he felt would suit Hank Allen down to the ground. But as he progressed he found an uneasiness halting the glibness with which he had opened fire: Hank Allen's impassivity became as inscrutable and sinister as a tragic mask whose inflexible outlines concealed a surface animate with fly-blown depravity. He finished upon a note of pity for the youth and rested his case with a tremulousness of spirit which disclosed that he was pleading his cause rather than Sam Allen's; and pleading, as Sam Allen himself had done, to a tribunal that had already reached its verdict.

"I'm not saying the boy meant to do it, mind you," he repeated, stung to a reiteration by Allen's ominous silence. "And I'm right here to do all I can to pull him out of a hole. *My* testimony ought to have some weight."

Allen ignored Pringle's egotistic flourish. "Let's see," he mused coldly, "what time did you strike out from Walden's Glen?"

"At seven this morning."

"And it took you until nearly nine at night to make this cabin? . . . You're a mighty slow walker, if you ask me."

"The rain came on shortly after one o'clock. I thought it might let up, so I dodged into the shelter of a redwood stump near Preston's Flat. But it only grew worse. At five I decided to push on."

Suddenly Pringle stopped, chilled by the fact that Hank Allen's air of sneering incredulity was rendering devoid of substance the simplest and most truthful statements. Even in his own ears they rang out falsely. He desperately recovered himself and again took up his defense. It was terrifying how hollow even his credentials sounded, let alone the story of the day's events: a Yale B.A., a Ph.D. from Columbia, the author of *Radical Movements in Relation to Post-war Problems*—every statement he made grew more incredible, more fictitious, more hopeless. It was as if the monumental skepticism of Hank Allen were capable of destroying all reality. When he had finished, Hank Allen cleared his throat significantly.

"You'll have a mighty interesting story to tell the judge," he half-sneered, half-chuckled.

The brevity of Hank Allen's comment was packed with presage, and yet for a fleeting moment Walton Pringle took courage. A judge—precisely! A judge would be quite a different matter. Really, the situation was little short of absurd! In answer Hank Allen merely turned his gaze toward the disheveled cot, and he continued to tap the table significantly with the empty handcuffs.

In the portentous silence which followed Walton Pringle's thoughts leaped to Sam Allen. Had his own skepticism of the previous hour also flattened the youth's defense? If he had listened with an open mind would the boy's far-fetched statements have held germs of reasonability? After all, what was there so extravagant in Sam Allen's tale? It could have happened just as he had said. But there was the youth's absurd escape. What point did any man have in damning himself with any move so suspicious—so futile?

As for Allen senior, what did he really think? It was almost incredible to imagine that he fancied Walton Pringle guilty. Then why the pose? Did some smoldering clan spirit in him rouse instinctively to his own flesh and blood in its extremity? Or would his son's disgrace expose his own delinquencies? The story that Pringle had listened to must merely have scratched the surface of his father's infamies. No, it was patent that Allen senior was in no position to invite the law to review his private record. . . . Yet he must know that he could but postpone the inevitable. What would happen tomorrow when the proper magistrate heard the real truth? The thought, spinning through Walton Pringle's brain, gave him a sudden feeling of boldness. After all, what had *he* to fear? He rose in his seat, all his confidence recaptured.

"Mr. Allen," he said clearly, "you are quite right. I *have* an interesting story to tell the judge. Therefore, I think the sooner I tell it the better. Shall we start back to Walden's Glen at once?"

A sardonic smile fastened itself on Pringle. He picked up the handcuffs. "If you will oblige me—" he nodded toward Pringle's folded arms.

The faint suggestion of a chill crept over Pringle. "Do I understand, Mr. Allen, that you intend to put me to the indignity of handcuffs?" Allen shrugged. "No, I won't have it! I'll be damned if I will!"

"You won't have it? Come now, that ain't pretty talk. And it ain't reasonable talk, neither." He narrowed his eyes. "Resisting an officer of the law is sometimes a messy job, stranger."

Pringle's resistance died before the covert snarl in Allen's voice. He put out his wrists and in the next instant he felt a cold clasp of steel encircling them and heard the click of the lock. At the moment he remembered the words of Sam Allen: *"I've seen him beat 'em, too, over the head, with the butt end of a pistol—or anything else that came handy."*

And in a swift, terrible moment of revelation he knew that that was just what Hank Allen intended to do.

He fell back on the bench utterly helpless and without defense. Every story of the law's brutality that had ever reached his ears seemed to beat mockingly about him. He remembered now that not one of these tales had ever concerned an unshackled victim. No, what petty tyrants liked best was something prostrate which they could kick and trample with impunity. That was always the normal complement of bullying, but in this case corruption gave the hand of authority an added incentive. Hank Allen would murder him not only for the pleasure of the performance but to save his own hide. A man struck down for resisting an officer would tell no tales. And how neatly the situation would be cleared up: a suspected murderer paying the penalty of his crime without process or expense of law. A bit of sound judicial economy, to tell the truth, in a community not given to rating life too dearly. And he thought that he had managed it all so cleverly!

At this point he noticed that Hank Allen was intent on investigating a menacing six-shooter and his mind moved alertly past all the futile movements he could make toward defense. Where was Hank Allen planning his latest atrocity—here in Marchel Duplin's cabin or somewhere on the trail to Walden's Glen? Here in the cabin—or he missed his guess—with a litter of broken furniture to add confirmation to a tale of resistance.

His gaze swept the room with a sudden hunger for even a drab background to life, as if his soul longed to carry a homely memory with it into the impending darkness. He saw the tumbled cot, the rusting stove, the table before him with a sudden passionate sense of their rude symbolism. Even the guttering candle, almost spent, took on significance. It was the candle, blown into untimely darkness, that had paved the way for his predicament. If only his pocket flash had worked! Upon such trivialities did life itself depend! A flickering candle . . . a flickering candle . . . a flickering— The rhythmic beat of this reiteration snapped. Unconsciously he had looked past the gleam of light to the closed door and the burlap curtain, screening its shallow triangle, swaying gently in the half darkness. Abruptly candlelight, doorway, and curtain became fused into a unit—startling and lucid. Would it be possible? The prospect left him as breathless as a dash of cold water; he could hear himself gasp. Hank Allen fixed him with a suspicious glance.

"What's the matter?" he demanded brutally.

Pringle's mind cleared to a point of supreme intuition. "I'm—I'm ill!" he gasped. "Would—would you mind opening the door—it's suffocating in here."

Hank Allen hesitated, then a diabolic humor seemed to move him to compliance. He threw back the door with a chuckle and resumed his seat. It was as if he had said, "Try it, my friend, if it amuses you!"

For a brief moment Walton Pringle closed his eyes; then quite suddenly opened them, took in a deep breath, and with a quick upward leap he blew out the candle.

Drawing himself flatly against the wall, Pringle felt the impact of the door swinging back before Allen's stumbling pursuit. It was inconceivable that a man on such good terms with subterfuge could have been tricked by anything so obvious as a slammed door. But how long would he remain tricked? He wouldn't search the hills all night, nor would he be likely to strike out for Walden's Glen without returning to the cabin. Pringle's first elation at the extraordinary success of his ruse fell before the realization of his plight. What chance had a handcuffed man in any case? And his attempt to escape—how beautifully that colored his guilt! *Innocent people were never fearful.* The memory of this mental deduction bit at him sharply. Yet with all the odds against him he felt that he must plan something and that quickly. Cautiously moving back the open door he peered over its rim. At first his vision could not pierce the gloom, but suddenly a flood of moonlight released from the imprisonment of dispersing clouds made a path of silver into the cabin. Pringle listened: everything was extraordinarily still.

All at once the silence was cracked by a keen report. A snapping fusillade answered Pringle's mental interrogation. . . . He heard a shrill cry, clipped and terrible. Then the silence fell again. . . . Presently the soft beat of cautious footfalls drifted toward the cabin. Pringle withdrew to the curtain's shelter. Something fluttered on the threshold. Then slowly, warily, the door was closed.

Pringle leaned sidewise, the tail of one eye thrust past the curtain's edge. Moonlight was flooding now even through the grimy windowpane. A shadowy form crept stealthily toward the table, halted as if sensing a living presence, turned sharply and revealed the unmistakable outlines of Sam Allen's ineffectual face.

Walton Pringle gave a cry of mingled relief and surprise and stepped from his hiding place.

The youth shrank back. "I—I wondered where you were," he gasped. He gave a little hysterical flourish with his right hand and Pringle saw that he held the stolen pistol. "Well, I'm a murderer *now!*" he spit out with quivering venom.

In a flash Pringle knew everything, and yet he could only stammer out in stupid conventional protest:

"You don't mean . . . *not your father!*"

The youth's face grew ashen. "Who else did you think?" He gave a scraping laugh. "Would *you* stand up and let him get you, if you had a chance to shoot first? I guess not. . . . Well, what are you going to do about it?"

Pringle brought his shackled wrists into the moonlight. "Damned little, I fancy."

Young Allen put an incredulous finger on the handcuffs. "What's the idea?"

Pringle smiled ironically. "Just a little joke of your father's. He pretended he thought I was the murderer. He was for taking me back to Walden's Glen." He stopped, overcome with a passion for self-accusation, self-abasement: "Just as I wanted to take you back. . . . Yes, on the surface he was as self-righteous and smug as I was. But he didn't fool me. I knew that he intended to murder me in cold blood—to save your hide and incidentally his. . . . Well, I blew out the candle as you did—to—to save myself."

A curious look came over Sam Allen's face. Walton Pringle had a feeling that for the second time that night he had delivered himself into the hands of the enemy.

"You were a fool to tell me that," Sam Allen drawled, with a hint of his father's biting irony in his voice. "I wouldn't have thought of such an easy way out—all by myself. . . . Yer know what I mean, don't yer?"

Pringle felt himself grow unnaturally calm. "You mean you could shoot me down and settle everything for yourself? . . . Yes, you could. Dead men tell no tales, and in this case three dead men would be even more silent than two. . . . I can't say that I blame you. I didn't give any quarter in your pinch; why should you spare me?"

Sam Allen gave an impatient cough and his words vibrated with sudden and strange maturity as he said coldly:

"I'm trying to figure it out. . . . It *would* be simpler to kill you." He held up the pistol, gazing at it with the tragic fascination of a stripling who has tasted his first victory—drawn his first blood. His whole body seemed animated with some strange new power that still struggled for foothold. Was the spirit of Hank Allen so soon fighting for a place in which to lodge its sinister corruption? . . . Suddenly he began to shiver violently. "No, it wouldn't be simpler," he half whispered—"not in the long run. . . . What do you say? Shall we go back to Walden's Glen—together?"

A faint blur dimmed Pringle's gaze. "I don't deserve it!" he cried with a vehement passion. "Upon my word, I don't!"

Sam Allen laid the pistol on the table. "Shucks!" he said simply, "everybody makes mistakes."

And at that moment Walton Pringle fancied that the pinched, yellow, wistful face before him re-created with a curiously poignant glory the face of Lizzie Allen, born Evans—the girl who had "worked out"!

THE CITY OF REFUGE[1]

By RUDOLPH FISHER

(From *The Atlantic Monthly*)

I

CONFRONTED suddenly by daylight, King Solomon Gillis stood dazed and blinking. The railroad station, the long, white-walled corridor, the impassible slot-machine, the terrifying subway train—he felt as if he had been caught up in the jaws of a steam-shovel, jammed together with other helpless lumps of dirt, swept blindly along for a time, and at last abruptly dumped.

There had been strange and terrible sounds: 'New York! Penn Terminal—all change!' 'Pohter, hyer, pohter, suh?' Shuffle of a thousand soles, clatter of a thousand heels, innumerable echoes. Cracking rifle-shots—no, snapping turnstiles. 'Put a nickel in!' 'Harlem? Sure. This side —next train.' Distant thunder, nearing. The screeching onslaught of the fiery hosts of hell, headlong, breath-taking. Car doors rattling, sliding, banging open. 'Say, wha' d'ye think this is, a baggage car?' Heat, oppression, suffocation —eternity—'Hundred 'n turdy-fif' next!' More turnstiles. Jonah emerging from the whale.

Clean air, blue sky, bright sunlight.

Gillis set down his tan-cardboard extension case and wiped his black, shining brow. Then slowly, spreadingly, he grinned at what he saw: Negroes at every turn; up and down Lenox Avenue, up and down One Hundred and Thirty-Fifth Street; big, lanky Negroes, short, squat Negroes; black ones, brown ones, yellow ones; men standing idle on the curb, women, bundle-laden, trudging reluctantly homeward, children rattle-trapping about the sidewalks; here and there a white face drifting along, but Negroes pre-

[1] Copyright, 1925, by The Atlantic Monthly Company.
Copyright, 1926, by Rudolph Fisher.

dominantly, overwhelmingly everywhere. There was assur-
edly no doubt of his whereabouts. This was Negro Harlem.

Back in North Carolina Gillis had shot a white man and,
with the aid of prayer and an automobile, probably escaped
a lynching. Carefully avoiding the railroads, he had
reached Washington in safety. For his car a Southwest
bootlegger had given him a hundred dollars and directions
to Harlem; and so he had come to Harlem.

Ever since a traveling preacher had first told him of the
place, King Solomon Gillis had longed to come to Harlem.
The Uggams were always talking about it; one of their
boys had gone to France in the draft and, returning, had
never got any nearer home than Harlem. And there were
occasional 'colored' newspapers from New York: newspapers that mentioned Negroes without comment, but always spoke of a white person as 'So-and-so, white.' That
was the point. In Harlem, black was white. You had
rights that could not be denied you; you had privileges,
protected by law. And you had money. Everybody in
Harlem had money. It was a land of plenty. Why, had
not Mouse Uggam sent back as much as fifty dollars at a
time to his people in Waxhaw?

The shooting, therefore, simply catalyzed whatever slug-
gish mental reaction had been already directing King Solomon's fortunes toward Harlem. The land of plenty was
more than that now: it was also the city of refuge.

Casting about for direction, the tall newcomer's glance
caught inevitably on the most conspicuous thing in sight,
a magnificent figure in blue that stood in the middle of the
crossing and blew a whistle and waved great white-gloved
hands. The Southern Negro's eyes opened wide; his mouth
opened wider. If the inside of New York had mystified
him, the outside was amazing him. For there stood a handsome, brass-buttoned giant directing the heaviest traffic
Gillis had ever seen; halting unnumbered tons of automobiles and trucks and wagons and pushcarts and street-cars;
holding them at bay with one hand while he swept similar
tons peremptorily on with the other; ruling the wide crossing with supreme self-assurance; and he, too, was a Negro!

Yet most of the vehicles that leaped or crouched at his

bidding carried white passengers. One of these overdrove bounds a few feet and Gillis heard the officer's shrill whistle and gruff reproof, saw the driver's face turn red and his car draw back like a threatened pup. It was beyond belief—impossible. Black might be white, but it couldn't be that white!

'Done died an' woke up in Heaven,' thought King Solomon, watching, fascinated; and after a while, as if the wonder of it were too great to believe simply by seeing, 'Cullud policemans!' he said, half aloud; then repeated over and over, with greater and greater conviction, 'Even got cullud policemans—even got cullud——'

'Where y' want to go, big boy?'

Gillis turned. A little, sharp-faced yellow man was addressing him.

"Saw you was a stranger. Thought maybe I could help y' out.'

King Solomon located and gratefully extended a slip of paper. 'Wha' dis hyeh at, please, suh?'

The other studied it a moment, pushing back his hat and scratching his head. The hat was a tall-crowned, unindented brown felt; the head was brown patent-leather, its glistening brush-back flawless save for a suspicious crimpiness near the clean-grazed edges.

'See that second corner? Turn to the left when you get there. Number forty-five's about half-way the block.'

'Thank y', suh.'

'You from—Massachusetts?'

'No, suh, Nawth Ca'lina.'

'Is 'at so? You look like a Northerner. Be with us long?'

'Till I die,' grinned the flattered King Solomon.

'Stoppin' there?'

'Reckon I is. Man in Washin'ton 'lowed I'd find lodgin' at dis ad-dress.'

'Good enough. If y' don't, maybe I can fix y' up. Harlem's pretty crowded. This is me.' He proffered a card.

"Thank y', suh,' said Gillis, and put the card in his pocket.

The little yellow man watched him plod flat-footedly on

down the street, long awkward legs never quite straightened, shouldered extension-case bending him sidewise, wonder upon wonder halting or turning him about. Presently,
as he proceeded, a pair of bright green stockings caught
and held his attention. Tony, the storekeeper, was crossing
the sidewalk with a bushel basket of apples. There was a
collision; the apples rolled; Tony exploded; King Solomon
apologized. The little yellow man laughed shortly, took
out a notebook, and put down the address he had seen on
King Solomon's slip of paper.

'Guess you're the shine I been waitin' for,' he surmised.

As Gillis, approaching his destination, stopped to rest,
a haunting notion grew into an insistent idea. 'Dat li'l
yaller nigger was a sho' 'nuff gen'man to show me de road.
Seem lak I knowed him befo'—' He pondered. That
receding brow, that sharp-ridged, spreading nose, that tight
upper lip over the two big front teeth, that chinless jaw—
He fumbled hurriedly for the card he had not looked at
and eagerly made out the name.

'Mouse Uggam, sho' 'nuff! Well, dog-gone!'

II

Uggam sought out Tom Edwards, once a Pullman porter, now prosperous proprietor of a cabaret, and told
him:—

'Chief, I got him: a baby jess in from the land o' cotton
and so dumb he thinks ante bellum 's an old woman.'

'Where 'd you find him?'

'Where you find all the jay birds when they first hit
Harlem—at the subway entrance. This one come up the
stairs, batted his eyes once or twice, an' froze to the spot
—with his mouth open. Sure sign he's from 'way down
behind the sun an' ripe f' the pluckin'.'

Edwards grinned a gold-studded, fat-jowled grin. 'Gave
him the usual line, I suppose?'

'Didn't miss. An' he fell like a ton o' bricks. 'Course
I've got him spotted, but damn 'f I know jess how to
switch 'em on to him.'

'Get him a job around a store somewhere. Make out
you're befriendin' him. Get his confidence.'

'Sounds good. Ought to be easy. He's from my State. Maybe I know him or some of his people.'

'Make out you do, anyhow. Then tell him some fairy tale that'll switch your trade to him. The cops'll follow the trade. We could even let Froggy flop into some dumb white cop's hands and "confess" where he got it. See?'

'Chief, you got a head, no lie.'

'Don't lose no time. And remember, hereafter, it's better to sacrifice a little than to get squealed on. Never refuse a customer. Give him a little credit. Humor him along till you can get rid of him safe. You don't know what that guy that died may have said; you don't know who's on to you now. And if they get you—I don't know you.'

'They won't get *me*,' said Uggam.

King Solomon Gillis sat meditating in a room half the size of his hencoop back home, with a single window opening into an airshaft.

An airshaft: cabbage and chitterlings cooking; liver and onions sizzling, sputtering; three player-pianos out-plunking each other; a man and a woman calling each other vile things; a sick, neglected baby wailing; a phono-graph broadcasting blues; dishes clacking; a girl crying heartbrokenly; waste noises, waste odors of a score of fam-ilies, seeking issue through a common channel; pollution from bottom to top—a sewer of sounds and smells.

Contemplating this, King Solomon grinned and breathed, 'Dog-gone!' A little later, still gazing into the sewer, he grinned again. 'Green stockin's,' he said; 'loud green!' The sewer gradually grew darker. A window lighted up opposite, revealing a woman in camisole and petticoat, arranging her hair. King Solomon, staring vacantly, shook his head and grinned yet again. 'Even got cullud police-mans!' he mumbled softly.

III

Uggam leaned out of the room's one window and spat maliciously into the dinginess of the airshaft. 'Damn glad you got him,' he commented, as Gillis finished his story. 'They's a thousand shines in Harlem would change places with you in a minute jess f' the honor of killin' a cracker.'

'But I didn't go to do it. 'T was a accident.'

'That's the only part to keep secret.'

'Know whut dey done? Dey killed five o' Mose Joplin's hawses 'fo he lef'. Put groun' glass in de feed-trough. Sam Cheevers come up on three of 'em one night pizenin' his well. Bleesom beat Crinshaw out o' sixty acres o' lan' an' a year's crops. Dass jess how 't is. Soon's a nigger make a li'l sump'n he better git to leavin'. An' 'fo long ev'ybody's goin' be lef'!'

'Hope to hell they don't all come here.'

The doorbell of the apartment rang. A crescendo of footfalls in the hallway culminated in a sharp rap on Gillis's door. Gillis jumped. Nobody but a policeman would rap like that. Maybe the landlady had been listening and had called in the law. It came again, loud, quick, angry. King Solomon prayed that the policeman would be a Negro.

Uggam stepped over and opened the door. King Solomon's apprehensive eyes saw framed therein, instead of a gigantic officer, calling for him, a little blot of a creature, quite black against even the darkness of the hallway, except for a dirty, wide-striped silk shirt, collarless, with the sleeves rolled up.

'Ah hahve bill fo' Mr. Gillis.' A high, strongly accented Jamaican voice, with its characteristic singsong intonation, interrupted King Solomon's sigh of relief.

'Bill? Bill fo' me? What kin' o' bill?'

'Wan bushel appels. T'ree seventy-fife.'

'Apples? I ain' bought no apples.' He took the paper and read aloud, laboriously, 'Antonio Gabrielli to K. S. Gillis, Doctor——'

'Mr. Gabrielli say, you not pays him, he send policemon.'

'What I had to do wid 'is apples?'

'You bumps into him yesterday, no? Scatter appels everywhere—on the sidewalk, in de gutter. Kids pick up an' run away. Others all spoil. So you pays.'

Gillis appealed to Uggam. 'How 'bout it, Mouse?'

'He's a damn liar. Tony picked up most of 'em; I seen him. Lemme look at that bill—Tony never wrote this thing. This baby's jess playin' you for a sucker.'

'Ain' had no apples, ain' payin' fo' none,' announced King Solomon, thus prompted. 'Didn't have to come to Harlem to git cheated. Plenty o' dat right wha' I come fum.'

But the West Indian warmly insisted. 'You cahn't do daht, mon. Whaht you t'ink, 'ey? Dis mon loose 'is appels an' 'is money too?'

'What diff'ence it make to you, nigger?"

'Who you call nigger, mon? Ah hahve you understahn'—'

'Oh, well, white folks, den. What all you got t' do wid dis hyeh, anyhow?'

'Mr. Gabrielli send me to collect bill!'

'How I know dat?'

'Do Ah not bring bill? You t'ink Ah steal t'ree dollar, 'ey?'

'Three dollars an' sebenty-fi' cent,' corrected Gillis. ''Nuther thing: wha' you ever see me befo'? How you know dis is me?'

'Ah see you, sure. Ah help Mr. Gabrielli in de store. When you knocks down de baskette appels, Ah see. Ah follow you. Ah know you comes in dis house.'

'Oh, you does? An' how come you know my name an' flat an' room so good? How come dat?'

'Ah fin' out. Sometime Ah brings up here vegetables from de store.'

'Humph! Mus' be workin' on shares.'

'You pays, 'ey? You pays me or de policemon?'

'Wait a minute,' broke in Uggam, who had been thoughtfully contemplating the bill. 'Now listen, big shorty. You haul hips on back to Tony. We got your menu all right'— he waved the bill—'but we don't eat your kind o' cookin', see?'

The West Indian flared. 'Whaht it is to you, 'ey? You can not mind your own business? Ah hahve not spik to you!'

'No, brother. But this is my friend, an' I'll be john-browned if there's a monkey-chaser in Harlem can gyp him if I know it, see? Bes' thing f' you to do is to catch air, toot sweet.'

Sensing frustration, the little islander demanded the bill back. Uggam figured he could use the bill himself, maybe. The West Indian hotly persisted; he even menaced. Uggam pocketed the paper and invited him to take it. Wisely enough, the caller preferred to catch air.

When he had gone, King Solomon sought words of thanks.

'Bottle it,' said Uggam. 'The point is this: I figger you got a job.'

'Job? No I ain't! Wha' at?'

'When you show Tony this bill, he'll hit the roof and fire that monk.'

'What ef he do?'

'Then you up 'n ask f' the job. He'll be too grateful to refuse. I know Tony some, an' I'll be there to put in a good word. See?'

King Solomon considered this. 'Sho' needs a job, but ain' after stealin' none.'

'Stealin'? 'T wouldn't be stealin'. Stealin' 's what that damn monkey-chaser tried to do from you. This would be doin' Tony a favor an' gettin' y'self out o' the barrel. What's the hold-back?'

'What make you keep callin' him monkey-chaser?'

'West Indian. That's another thing. Any time y' can knife a monk, do it. They's too damn many of 'em here. They're an achin' pain.'

'Jess de way white folks feels 'bout niggers.'

'Damn that. How 'bout it? Y' want the job?'

'Hm—well—I'd ruther be a policeman.'

'Policeman?' Uggam gasped.

'M–hm. Dass all I wants to be, a policeman, so I kin police all the white folks right plumb in jail!'

Uggam said seriously, 'Well, y' might work up to that. But it takes time. An' y've got to eat while y're waitin'.' He paused to let this penetrate. 'Now, how 'bout this job at Tony's in the meantime? I should think y'd jump at it.'

King Solomon was persuaded.

'Hm—well—reckon I does,' he said slowly.

'Now y're tootin'!' Uggam's two big front teeth popped out in a grin of genuine pleasure. 'Come on. Let's go.'

IV

Spitting blood and crying with rage, the West Indian scrambled to his feet. For a moment he stood in front of the store gesticulating furiously and jabbering shrill threats and unintelligible curses. Then abruptly he stopped and took himself off.

King Solomon Gillis, mildly puzzled, watched him from Tony's doorway. 'I jess give him a li'l shove,' he said to himself, 'an' he roll' clean 'cross de sidewalk.' And a little later, disgustedly, 'Monkey-chaser!' he grunted, and went back to his sweeping.

'Well, big boy, how y' comin' on?'

Gillis dropped his broom. 'Hay-o, Mouse. Wha' you been las' two-three days?'

'Oh, around. Gettin' on all right here? Had any trouble?'

'Deed I ain't—'ceptin' jess now I had to throw 'at li'l jigger out.'

'Who? The monk?'

'M–hm. He sho' Lawd doan like me in his job. Look like he think I stole it from him, stiddy him tryin' to steal from me. Had to push him down sho' 'nuff 'fo I could git rid of 'im. Den he run off talkin' Wes' Indi'man an' shakin' his fis' at me.'

'Ferget it.' Uggam glanced about. 'Where's Tony?'

'Boss man? He be back direckly.'

'Listen—like to make two or three bucks a day extra?'

'Huh?'

'Two or three dollars a day more'n what you're gettin' already?'

'Ain' I near 'nuff in jail now?'

'Listen.' King Solomon listened. Uggam hadn't been in France for nothing. Fact was, in France he'd learned about some valuable French medicine. He'd brought some back with him,—little white pills,—and while in Harlem had found a certain druggist who knew what they were and could supply all he could use. Now there were any number of people who would buy and pay well for as much of this French medicine as Uggam could get. It was good for what ailed them, and they didn't know how to get it except through him. But he had no store in which to set up an agency and hence no single place where his customers could go to get what they wanted. If he had, he could sell three or four times as much as he did.

King Solomon was in a position to help him now, same as he had helped King Solomon. He would leave a dozen packages of the medicine—just small envelopes that could all be carried in a coat pocket—with King Solomon every day. Then he could simply send his customers to King Solomon at Tony's store. They'd make some trifling purchase, slip him a certain coupon which Uggam had given them, and King Solomon would wrap the little envelope of medicine with their purchase. Mustn't let Tony catch on, because he might object, and then the whole scheme would go gaflooey. Of course it wouldn't really be hurting Tony any. Wouldn't it increase the number of his customers?

Finally, at the end of each day, Uggam would meet King Solomon some place and give him a quarter for each coupon he held. There'd be at least ten or twelve a day —two and a half or three dollars plumb extra! Eighteen or twenty dollars a week 'Dog-gone!' breathed Gillis.

'Does Tony ever leave you heer alone?'

'M–hm. Jess started dis mawnin'. Doan nobody much come round 'tween ten an' twelve, so he done took to doin' his buyin' right 'long 'bout dat time. Nobody hyeh but me fo' 'n hour or so.'

'Good. I'll try to get my folks to come 'round here mostly while Tony's out, see?'

'I doan miss.'

'Sure y' get the idea, now?' Uggam carefully explained it all again. By the time he had finished, King Solomon was wallowing in gratitude.

'Mouse, you sho' is been a friend to me. Why, 'f 't hadn' been fo' you—'

'Bottle it,' said Uggam. 'I'll be round to your room tonight with enough stuff for tomorrer, see? Be sure'n be there.'

'Won't be nowha' else.'

'An' remember, this is all jess between you 'n me,'

'Nobody else but,' vowed King Solomon.

Uggam grinned to himself as he went on his way. 'Dumb Oscar! Wonder how much can we make before the cops nab him? French medicine—Humph!'

V

Tony Gabrielli, an oblate Neapolitan of enormous equator, wabbled heavily out of his store and settled himself over a soap box.

Usually Tony enjoyed sitting out front thus in the evening, when his helper had gone home and his trade was slackest. He liked to watch the little Gabriellis playing over the sidewalk with the little Levys and Johnsons; the trios and quartettes of brightly dressed, dark-skinned girls merrily out for a stroll; the slovenly gaited, darker men, who eyed them up and down and commented to each other with an unsuppressed 'Hot damn!' or 'Oh no, now!'

But tonight Tony was troubled. Something was wrong in the store; something was different since the arrival of King Solomon Gillis. The new man had seemed to prove himself honest and trustworthy, it was true. Tony had tested him, as he always tested a new man, by apparently leaving him alone in charge for two or three mornings. As a matter of fact, the new man was never under more vigilant observation than during these two or three mornings. Tony's store was a modification of the front rooms of his flat and was in direct communication with it by way of a glass-windowed door in the rear. Tony always managed to get back into his flat via the side street entrance and watch the new man through this unobtrusive glass-windowed door. If anything excited his suspicion,

like unwarranted interest in the cash register, he walked
unexpectedly out of this door to surprise the offender in
the act. Thereafter he would have no more such trouble.
But he had not succeeded in seeing King Solomon steal even
an apple.

What he had observed, however, was that the number
of customers that came into the store during the morning's
slack hour had pronouncedly increased in the last few
days. Before, there had been three or four. Now there
were twelve or fifteen. The mysterious thing about it was
that their purchases totaled little more than those of the
original three or four.

Yesterday and today Tony had elected to be in the
store at the time when, on the other days, he had been
out. But Gillis had not been overcharging or short-chang-
ing; for when Tony waited on the customers himself—
strange faces all—he found that they bought something
like a yeast cake or a five-cent loaf of bread. It was
puzzling. Why should strangers leave their own neigh-
borhoods and repeatedly come to him for a yeast cake or
a loaf of bread? They were not new neighbors. New
neighbors would have bought more variously and extensively and at different times of day. Living near by, they
would have come in, the men often in shirtsleeves and
slippers, the women in kimonos, with boudoir caps covering
their lumpy heads. They would have sent in strange children for things like yeast cakes and loaves of bread. And
why did not some of them come in at night when the new
helper was off duty?

As for accosting Gillis on suspicion, Tony was too wise
for that. Patronage had a queer way of shifting itself in
Harlem. You lost your temper and let slip a single 'nègre.'
A week later you sold your business.

Spread over his soap box, with his pudgy hands clasped
on his preposterous paunch, Tony sat and wondered. Two
men came up, conspicuous for no other reason than that
they were white. They displayed extreme nervousness, looking about as if afraid of being seen; and when one of them
spoke to Tony it was in a husky, toneless, blowing voice,
like the sound of a dirty phonograph record.

'Are you Antonio Gabrielli?'

'Yes, sure.' Strange behavior for such lusty-looking fellows. He who had spoken unsmilingly winked first one eye then the other, and indicated by a gesture of his head that they should enter the store. His companion looked cautiously up and down the Avenue, while Tony, wondering what ailed them, rolled to his feet and puffingly led the way.

Inside, the spokesman snuffled, gave his shoulders a queer little hunch, and asked, 'Can you fix us up, buddy?' The other glanced restlessly about the place as if he were constantly hearing unaccountable noises.

Tony thought he understood clearly now. 'Booze, 'ey?' he smiled. 'Sorry—I no got.'

'Booze? Hell, no!' The voice dwindled to a throaty whisper. 'Dope. Coke, milk, dice—anything. Name your price. Got to have it.'

'Dope?' Tony was entirely at a loss. 'What's a dis, dope?'

'Aw, lay off, brother. We're in on this. Here.' He handed Tony a piece of paper. 'Froggy gave us a coupon. Come on. You can't go wrong.'

'I no got,' insisted the perplexed Tony; nor could he be budged on that point.

Quite suddenly the manner of both men changed. 'All right,' said the first angrily, in a voice as robust as his body. 'All right, you're clever, You no got. Well, you will get. You'll get twenty years!'

'Twenty year? Whadda you talk?'

'Wait a minute, Mac,' said the second caller. 'Maybe the wop's on the level. Look here, Tony, we're officers, see? Policemen.' He produced a badge. 'A couple of weeks ago a guy was brought in dying for the want of a shot, see? Dope—he needed some dope—like this— in his arm. See? Well, we tried to make him tell us where he'd been getting it, but he was too weak. He croaked next day. Evidently he hadn't had money enough to buy any more.

'Well, this morning a little nigger that goes by the name of Froggy was brought into the precinct pretty well doped up. When he finally came to, he swore he got the stuff here at your store. Of course, we've just been trying to trick you into giving yourself away, but you don't bite. Now what's your game? Know anything about this?'

Tony understood. 'I dunno,' he said slowly; and then his own problem whose contemplation his callers had interrupted, occurred to him. 'Sure!' he exclaimed. 'Wait. Maybeso I know somet'ing.'

'All right. Spill it.'

'I got a new man, work-a for me.' And he told them what he had noted since King Solomon Gillis came.

'Sounds interesting. Where is this guy?'

'Here in da store—all day.'

'Be here tomorrow?'

'Sure. All day.'

'All right. We'll drop in tomorrow and give him the eye. Maybe he's our man.'

'Sure. Come ten o'clock. I show you,' promised Tony.

VI

Even the oldest and rattiest cabarets in Harlem have sense of shame enough to hide themselves under the ground —for instance, Edwards's. To get into Edwards's you casually enter a dimly lighted corner saloon, apparently— only apparently—a subdued memory of brighter days. What was once the family entrance is now a side entrance for ladies. Supporting yourself against close walls, you crouchingly descend a narrow, twisted staircase until, with a final turn, you find yourself in a glaring, long, low base- ment. In a moment your eyes become accustomed to the haze of tobacco smoke. You see men and women seated at wire-legged, white-topped tables, which are covered with half-empty bottles and glasses; you trace the slow-jazz accompaniment you heard as you came down the stairs to a pianist, a cornetist, and a drummer on a little platform at the far end of the room. There is a cleared space from the foot of the stairs, where you are standing, to the plat- form where this orchestra is mounted, and in it a tall brown girl is swaying from side to side and rhythmically proclaim-

ing that she has the world in a jug and the stopper in her
hand. Behind a counter at your left sits a fat, bald, tea-
colored Negro, and you wonder if this is Edwards—Edwards, who stands in with the police, with the political
bosses, with the importers of wines and worse. A white-
vested waiter hustles you to a seat and takes your order.
The song's tempo changes to a quicker; the drum and the
cornet rip out a fanfare, almost drowning the piano; the
girl catches up her dress and begins to dance. . . .

Gillis's wondering eyes had been roaming about. They
stopped.

'Look, Mouse!' he whispered. 'Look a-yonder!'

'Look at what?'

'Dog-gone if it ain' de self-same gal!'

'Wha' d' ye mean, self-same girl?'

'Over yonder, wi' de green stockin's. Dass de gal made
me knock over dem apples fust day I come to town. 'Member? Been wishin' I could see her ev'y sence.'

'What for?' Uggam wondered.

King Solomon grew confidential. 'Ain' but two things in
dis world, Mouse, I really wants. One is to be a policeman. Been wantin' dat ev'y sence I seen dat cullud traffic-
cop dat day. Other is to git myse'f a gal lak dat one over
yonder!'

'You'll do it,' laughed Uggam, 'if you live long enough.'

'Who dat wid her?'

'How 'n hell do I know?'

'He cullud?'

'Don't look like it. Why? What of it?'

'Hm—nuthin'—'

'How many coupons y' got tonight?'

'Ten.' King Solomon handed them over.

'Y' ought to've slipt 'em to me under the table, but it's
all right now, long as we got this table to ourselves. Here's
y' medicine for tomorrer.'

'Wha'?'

'Reach under the table.'

Gillis secured and pocketed the medicine.

'An' here's two-fifty for a good day's work.' Uggam
passed the money over. Perhaps he grew careless; cer-

tainly the passing this time was above the table, in plain
sight.

'Thanks, Mouse.'

Two white men had been watching Gillis and Uggam
from a table near by. In the tumult of merriment that re-
warded the entertainer's most recent and daring effort, one
of these men, with a word to the other, came over and took
the vacant chair beside Gillis.

'Is your name Gillis?'

' 'Tain' nuthin' else.'

Uggam's eyes narrowed.

The white man showed King Solomon a police officer's
badge.

'You're wanted for dope-peddling. Will you come along
without trouble?'

'Fo' what?'

'Violation of the narcotic law—dope-selling.'

'Who—me?'

'Come on, now, lay off that stuff. I saw what happened
just now myself.' He addressed Uggam. 'Do you know
this fellow?'

'Nope. Never saw him before tonight.'

'Didn't I just see him sell you something?'

'Guess you did. We happened to be sittin' here at the
same table and got to talkin'. After a while I says I can't
seem to sleep nights, so he offers me sump'n he says 'll make
me sleep, all right. I don't know what it is, but he says
he uses it himself an' I offers to pay him what it cost him.
That's how I come to take it. Guess he's got more in his
pocket there now.'

The detective reached deftly into the coat pocket of the
dumfounded King Solomon and withdrew a packet of
envelopes. He tore off a corner of one, emptied a half-
dozen tiny white tablets into his palm, and sneered triumphantly. 'You'll make a good witness,' he told Uggam.

The entertainer was issuing an ultimatum to all sweet
mammas who dared to monkey round her loving man. Her
audience was absorbed and delighted, with the exception
of one couple—the girl with the green stockings and her
escort. They sat directly in the line of vision of King

Solomon's wide eyes, which, in the calamity that had descended upon him, for the moment saw nothing.

'Are you coming without trouble?'

Mouse Uggam, his friend. Harlem. Land of plenty. City of refuge—city of refuge. If you live long enough——

Consciousness of what was happening between the pair across the room suddenly broke through Gillis's daze like flame through smoke. The man was trying to kiss the girl and she was resisting. Gillis jumped up. The detective, taking the act for an attempt at escape, jumped with him and was quick enough to intercept him. The second officer came at once to his fellow's aid, blowing his whistle several times as he came.

People overturned chairs getting out of the way, but nobody ran for the door. It was an old crowd. A fight was a treat; and the tall Negro could fight.

'Judas Priest!'

'Did you see that?'

'Damn!'

White—both white. Five of Mose Joplin's horses. Poisoning a well. A year's crops. Green stockings—white—white—

'That's the time, papa!'

'Do it, big boy!'

'Good night!'

Uggam watched tensely, with one eye on the door. The second cop had blown for help——

Downing one of the detectives a third time and turning to grapple again with the other, Gillis found himself face to face with a uniformed black policeman.

He stopped as if stunned. For a moment he simply stared. Into his mind swept his own words like a forgotten song, suddenly recalled:

'Cullud policemans!'

The officer stood ready, awaiting his rush.

'Even—got—cullud—policemans——'

Very slowly King Solomon's arms relaxed; very slowly he stood erect; and the grin that came over his features had something exultant about it.

AN ARMY WITH BANNERS[1]

By KATHARINE FULLERTON GEROULD

(From *Harper's Magazine*)

L EWIS HUNTING, like thousands of other young Americans, was a bond salesman. He had a kind of wayward handsomeness that endeared him to women, together with a deep voice and a gravely pleasant manner—both purely physical attributes—which prevented his good looks getting on the nerves of the men he dealt with. He was moderately successful in business, was always well dressed and provided with the comforts of life. A good many of those comforts, naturally, went into his expense account; but when he was not traveling, he lived with his widowed mother, whom he partly supported, in a commonplace but not uncomfortable suburban house. His mother, who adored him, accepted everything he would give her as the reward of her adoration. His father had hoped to send Lewis to a good technical school, but he died at an unlucky moment for Lewis—at the precise time, that is, when Lewis had finished his high school course and could be considered old enough to earn his living. College would have meant sacrifices on his mother's part which she would have thought unnatural when she had a son who was six feet tall. Lewis also would have thought them unnatural—for *his* mother; though he saw the mothers of other young men moving into apartments and doing their own work without thereby disfiguring the noble countenance of Nature.

Lewis Hunting was no moralist. He had to work, and he did work. He was much away from home, and he fell into a few casual adventures that would have shocked his mother hopelessly. These adventures were very few, however; not because Lewis minded doing things that would have shocked his mother, had she known about them, but because even

near-dissipation costs money; and he never forget that his
financial margin was hers, not his own. The adventures
were fairly sordid, as the limited contacts offered to a
young man in strange cities are apt to make them, and his
cynicism was deepened by them. In his later twenties
Lewis was living about as lonely an existence as a young
bond salesman can. When he was at the home office, he
spent most of his evenings with his mother (she complained
a great deal of loneliness)—reading, talking or listening to
her phonograph. When he was abroad in the land—which
was most of the year—he mitigated the solitude of hotel
rooms with visits to movie theaters or pool rooms. Mild
flirtations he could find anywhere, owing to his good looks
and engaging smile; but he was very wary of anything more
intimate or dramatic. He knew very little about women,
though he considered that he had plumbed female psychol-
ogy with an unerring lead line. Most women, he decided,
were on the make and no good. Girls he had known at
school, who had married his more prosperous comrades,
seemed—unless they were sunk invisibly into nurseries—
as shameless as the others. One or two of them, indeed,
made love to him; and that shocked Lewis almost as much
as it would have shocked Mrs. Hunting.

You see him, then—young, bewildered, faintly unhappy
and vaguely aspiring beneath the cynicism that kept its
visible smoothness in the face of the smuttiest story or the
most shameless of feminine advances. The fact was that
Lewis would have expanded most naturally in the society
of the nicest people, and he never met them. Mrs. Hunting made it a virtue to be too delicate and too sorrowful
for social contacts, and he had no relations that would have
knit him up, in this or that city, with the local aristocracy.
He was diffident with men who had been through college—
probably no one ever knew how he had grieved over the
frustration of his and his father's hopes—and his diffi-
dence took the form of refusing, with such, to mix business
and pleasure. So even old customers, once rebuffed, did
not ask him to their homes. Being, on the whole, irre-
ligious, he eschewed all sociabilities that had a sectarian
tinge.

Not a very strong person to stand up against circumstances or events or other people's desires. That cynicism of his, after all, was only skin-deep, and the boy beneath was soft. When Netta Jacobs decided to marry him, he was virtually helpless, for Netta was not only supple and alluring—she was clever. When I say clever, I do not mean to praise her understanding or her wit. She was clever like a very clever animal: she had the instinct of self-preservation so strongly developed that she selected without difficulty the tone, the gesture, the look that would serve her purpose. She was a finished egotist, if you like, though "egotist" seems too big a word for her. It implies cerebration, and Netta had no cerebration. She had the protective coloring of the white ermine, the adaptability of the giraffe that can lengthen its neck to crop the topmost leaves, of the creature that has developed a lung fit to breathe both air and water. Only, unluckily, she was neither giraffe nor fish; she was human and capable of passion—of that complicated emotion which does not afflict the lower mammals. The lion stalking his prey is far less terrible than the person who wants to possess another human being, not only physically and financially but socially, mentally, and morally. Netta never put it to herself in that way, but it was so. She fell in love with Lewis Hunting, and her whole organism set itself automatically to the task of acquiring him. It is not often that one person desires another with the totality of his being. Thus Netta desired Lewis. She had no moral sense; but if she had had one, that too would have clung to him. Lewis, of course, had not the faintest chance against her; and between the hour when he first saw her in Jere Wheaton's office, and the hour of the wedding among dusty palms and withering blossoms in the living room of her married sister's apartment, only four months elapsed.

They lived with Lewis's mother in the not uncomfortable suburban house. Netta intended to change all that; but the best equipped organism recognizes impossibilities—temporary ones. In order to get his mother to consent to the marriage at all, Lewis had had to make absurd and vast concessions. She made it clear to him that if he chucked

her and married without her consent, he would literally end
her life. Besides, there was the question of money. Either
Netta would have to live with Mrs. Hunting, or Mrs. Hunting would have to go to a cheap boarding-house. Netta,
who would not have cared in the least if Mrs. Hunting had
had to live in a Salvation Army Home or the State peni-
tentiary, realized that she would have to give in. For the
time being, Lewis was not yet completely her creature,
and you might as well ask him to break a blood vessel as
to turn his mother by force out of her house. Nothing
would be easier for her than to make—after marriage—the
situation impossible.

That, of course, she proceeded to do, though it took a
fairly long time on account of Lewis's protracted absences
from home. Given Mrs. Hunting, it was quite easy.
Lewis's mother, deprived of her dominance, was acutely
uncomfortable. She hated Netta, she thought Lewis deluded and doomed, and she kept herself within bounds only
because she knew she was playing a losing game. If Netta
had been a gentle soul, Mrs. Hunting would probably have
made her supremely unhappy. Netta was not a gentle
soul, and she made Mrs. Hunting unhappy instead. When
Lewis was at home, both women made him feel them
pathetic—suffering untold things for love of him. Netta
managed that, too, better than her mother-in-law.

A year, two years wore away, and Lewis began to know
despair. Netta was all his, and her kisses made it clear.
But she hated his mother, she hated their mode of existence; she was moving slowly but surely to the total elimina-
tion of Mrs. Hunting from their lives. So much, for a time,
was he Netta's that if she had asked anything less, she
might have had it. But what she asked of him, he felt,
was to kill his mother. Even for Netta he could not slay.
And there came, inevitably, a time when he criticized her
for asking him to.

They had it out at last, one evening in their own room,
when he was just back from a month's trip in the South.
Lewis, who had been listening to mocking-birds and smelling cape-jessamine—his sojourns were seldom in such romantic lands—came back with reawakened yearnings, the

old hope of beauty revivified in his foolish heart, to find his home uglier than ever. His mother was querulous and plain, and his wife—though as she caught him to her breast in greeting and let her bright eyes and hair shimmer above him, he was ravished again—seemed hard, for all the cheaply perfumed softness of her body. He felt that there was no kindness in her and wondered, for the first time, if Netta would ever develop that tenderness which is the loveliest by-product of passion.

Lewis bent over his suitcase, unpacking things and flinging them about; while Netta, standing between the twin beds, removed and folded counterpanes and pillow covers and wound the clock on the bed-table. Little, intimate, beloved gestures . . . but somehow tonight he did not love them. If he closed his tired eyes, he could smell the jessamine. Netta's rustlings forbade him to hear the mockingbird.

He straightened himself finally and snapped the suitcase shut. Netta came towards him in all the luxury of orchid négligée and cap.

"Tired, honey?" She stretched her arms and yawned a little.

The answer to that was "No." If he said "Yes," she would be close to him, enfolding him, comforting him, making him forget everything but the physical fact of her. That, he did not wish. "I've got a beastly headache," he said quietly.

The barrier was now built between them, and she walked away to her dressing-table. "Want some aspirin?" she asked over her shoulder.

"No, thanks." Lewis often made these little mistakes. By his refusal of aspirin he revealed to her that he had no headache.

"Oh—just cross."

"Isn't it enough to make anybody cross—the kind of thing I come back to?"

"I'm very sorry you have to come back to it, Lewis. But you would have it that way, you know."

"You certainly don't try to make it any better."

"You'd better drop that right now," she warned him.

"It doesn't seem to occur to you that, at least, when you come back to it, I'm here. I live with it, weeks on end, when you aren't here."

"If you mean, Net, that it's all mother's fault, you're wrong. She wasn't like this until you came and made her so. What makes the house so deadly is that you quarrel with her all the time. I'm always having to apologize to one of you for the other. I'm about fed up with it."

"Oh, you are, are you? And what about me? I've been pretty patient, I think, but if you're going to crab things, I think I'll have my say. I tell you I live with it all the time. It's a good deal worse when you're not there, because she's afraid of you. And I don't intend to live with it much longer."

He didn't want to quarrel, he reflected wearily. Why did he have to? But his exacerbated nerves spoke for him. "I honestly believe it's more your fault than hers, because you're young and strong and she's old and weak. She's a sick woman, half the time—has been for years. It won't be for long, Netta."

"You can bet it won't be for long," she murmured intensely. She, too, was irritated; irritated because, as always, his figure there before her set her heart to beating. She did not want to quarrel, either; she wanted him to make love to her. He wouldn't; and therefore they quarrelled. But Lewis surprised her. Standing there with folded arms, looking gravely across at her, he went on, "If you'd have a kid, Netta, I believe everything would come straight. Mother would forget all about both of us if she had a grandchild to fuss over. And you'd be too busy and happy to mind little things."

She did not recover at once from her astonishment. "You honestly mean that, Lewis? You'd like me to have a baby?"

"I'd like us to have a baby, of course," he answered quietly. "What did you suppose?"

"Well, if you want a child, Lewis"—she too spoke very quietly—"you'll have to marry somebody else. I'll never have one if I can help it—and I guess I *can* help it."

"I don't doubt it." He turned away.

Netta, however, was not through. She had waited long enough for this issue to define itself. As well now as any other time. He had given her the cue with his reproaches.

"And I've got something else to say," she proceeded. "I love you, Lewis, and you know it. I've tried out this idea of yours about living with your mother. You can't say I haven't given it a chance—for more than two years. Now, either it gets broken up and you and I take an apartment by ourselves, or I take a job and have a room of my own in town, and you stick with her if you want to. But you can't have us both any longer. And I wouldn't live in this house even if she went away. I don't want a house, any-way, unless I'm a millionaire. It's up to you."

His face crimsoned. "You know as well as anything that I can't run an apartment and this house both."

"I'm willing to take a job, anyhow," Netta returned triumphantly.

"It would take all you made in any job to dress you. The kind of thing you put on your back costs money."

"How about your own clothes?"

"I have to be decent to do business. But I don't buy myself fur coats and mesh begs—or the sort of thing you've got on at the present minute. I'm not blaming you for wanting clothes, Net—I guess every woman does—but unless we live right here I can't swing it. Even if you earned money yourself, I couldn't afford to keep mother in this house, with a maid, while we were somewhere else. I'll be making more money next year. We'll see. It would be pretty hard on mother to leave her; but maybe if I can afford to keep her here, the way she is . . ."

"All right," Netta's voice trembled. "I'll look for that job—*and* that room. It isn't of any importance to me that your mother should live in this house—or any house or whether she has anybody to work for her or not. I've lived with her for two years, and you can take it from me, she's the limit. You can live with her if you want to. I won't—not another week! This family stuff doesn't go down with me—any of it." She laughed unpleasantly. "If you come to your senses any time and want to treat your wife properly, you'll know where to find me. I've never looked at another man and don't expect to. There's nothing gay about me."

Curiously enough, it was just at the moment when Netta declared herself innocent of intent to wrong him that the idea of divorce first entered, explicitly, Lewis Hunting's mind. In that tired nervous hour he did not care whether she flirted—or more—with a dozen men. He had come to her that evening after a journey that had reawakened old desires—for peace, for sweetness, for calm domesticity, for affections normally diffused, for passion expressed in ways that were not wholly of the flesh. Netta knew as well as he what he could do and what he could not. She asked of him to forsake all duties and take her to some perfumed lair where they could lie as beasts at ease. He no longer cared much for his mother—Netta had finished off that job very neatly—but her hold on him was immemorial. He had no desire to live with her, but he would never fling her out of doors to die. If Netta would only wait another year— but she wouldn't wait, she said; and after all (he asked himself) what would they be waiting for? Netta would not have a child, she would not have a home, she would not have anything—except love-making, which must some day cease. In that hour he knew that he could not endure forever the life Netta offered him, and from that moment, really, began his wary plotting for freedom. Standing there delicately clad, flushed and tempting, she was desirable in his eyes . . . but, inevitably, after two years she had ceased to be a miracle. She, so prodigal of lures, had neglected every lure she might have spread for his incorporeal imagination. Even passion must be bolstered up, quickened, preserved by something besides itself. Netta, he thought coldly, had counted too much on passion. Oh, yes, he could kiss her and draw her bright head to his shoulder —and like it; but her perfume would destroy the memory of jessamine, her voice the echo of the mocking-bird. Tired, tired he was. . . .

"All right, Netta. Take your job and hire your room. Perhaps you'll come to feel differently about it." And already he was hoping that she wouldn't.

She breathed hard. "You mean it? You'd rather have your mother than me?"

"No, I wouldn't. I don't like the way we live. But I'm not willing to kill her to please you. So if you can't stand it any longer, you'll have to do as you like. As I say, you may change your mind."

She wept softly. "I love you so, Lewis. It isn't fair."

His lips tightened. "And I love you, Netta. But it doesn't seem to be enough, does it?" He kept the width of the room between them. He did not wish to be drawn into the quick charm of her proximity. "I shall have to be away a good deal the next months. They're thinking about a Western branch, and I may have to talk it up out there, more or less. It would be worse than ever for you here, I suppose."

"And when you come back, Lewis, are you coming to your mother or to me?"

He hadn't thought of that. But of course he couldn't plan anything yet. "We could both come here, at those times, couldn't we?" he temporized.

Her anger flared up. "No! When I'm once out of this house, I'll never set foot in it again—except for a funeral."

That was the end, he thought. Funny that she shouldn't know it was the end—which was not reasonable of Lewis, for cruel things had been said before and ignored if not truly forgotten.

"We'll talk tomorrow. I'm awfully tired now. Good-night." He slipped into his bed, leaving her to put out the lamp and raise the windows. His tone was utterly spent, and beyond "Good-night" she did not speak to him again.

That was the most explicit talk they had. Earlier there had been bickerings, but all the quarrels were intended to be—and were—smoothed out and composed. These particular statements and retorts were never cancelled.

Netta, who really wanted Lewis more than anything else, had made the mistake of permitting herself, temporarily, to want something else more: freedom, frank expression of her hatred and weariness, the luxury of a defiant gesture. Lewis, at the same moment, came to the belief that what he wanted was peace—and love only if it brought peace in its train. Alas! he wanted even more than peace: seemliness in the ordering of his life, beauty in its texture—intimations of immortality, perhaps. But peace was what he called it. "A man has a right to some peace"—thus he cloaked, or approximated, his yearning.

Destiny then made, in his direction, a few positively affectionate gestures. He wanted to get away, and it became his professional duty to get away. His firm decided to establish a connection on the Coast and kept Lewis for some months traveling between Far Western cities. Twice, in the interval, he came East for hasty visits to the home office. He worked hard on this job; put his very best into it; for he intended to demand, when arrangements were completed, a Western post. Out there, it seemed to him, he could create life anew. Time enough to make domestic plans when he got his business completed.

Netta had found her job—she made not at all a bad secretary—and had duly given Lewis the address of her office. On his first arrival in the East he telephoned to her. Over the telephone she spoke eagerly—caressed him, as it were; and Lewis exhilarated by Western air, soothed by long absence of domestic fret, found tenderness creeping back into his own voice—almost, indeed, into his heart. He could see her vivid figure across the channeled space between them. He told her he must go to his mother's for the night, asked her to join him. It was good tactics, though at the moment he was not thinking of tactics; he merely wanted every one to be happy. Perhaps, once out there in another atmosphere, all three of them. . . . But Netta's voice slid sharply into reproach, and he felt again all the menace that lay in her vividness.

"Indeed I will not, Lewis. You can go and see her, of course, but I'm not going to. I should think you'd want to see me first, but if you don't, you can go and have dinner with her and then come back and meet me. I can't spring you on my landlady very well, since she's never seen you, but we can live at a hotel while you're here."

His voice changed too. "We can talk about that later. There's no reason why you shouldn't be decent and go out with me, just for tonight."

She did not know that it was an ultimatum; she misread his annoyance, taking it for impatience, and laughed harshly. "Not much, Lewis! When you want me, you'll come to me. I'm a good wife, but I'm a darned poor daughter-in-law. . . . Where do I meet you tonight?"

"You don't meet me anywhere—tonight."

He hung up the receiver, and she heard its sharp click. Even then she did not suspect. She was still gloating over the first warmth of his voice and could not know that the warmth had meant very little—that her chance had been very small and that she had thrown that chance away. Lewis did not so much blame Netta for her attitude to his mother as accuse her, in his heart, of being a person who would make no sacrifices to any situation that might arise. Mrs. Hunting was not so much a special case as the sort of thing that, in a hundred forms, might happen to any one. Netta was hard and always would be. Even suppose his mother were dead: there would always be this or that thing to strike Netta as intolerable. It was the principle of the thing. No; they would never find that peace which, more than ever in an unfamiliar and beautiful landscape, had seemed every man's right. Netta waited in vain for a sign from him. She got none.

Netta, unaware that Hunting was expecting to be definitely settled in the West, thought a waiting game the wisest. If he once came back to living in his mother's house, he wouldn't be able to bear her absence. He'd come running, she believed. But he never did live there without her, and the place never had a chance to stir old memories. He was continuously away and, except in connection with divorce, Netta did not enter his mind. Her clutch was finally off him. He seemed to himself to know her wholly, to be completely aware of her character and to spurn it with reason. He did not know Netta wholly, as he was later to discover; but at this time he felt supremely capable of judging her.

Lewis, whom marriage and discontent had greatly matured, did good work for his firm. When he demanded his promotion and his transfer, he got them both. He had worked overtime for many months, giving to his business not only all his mind but all his secret stores of energy. He was not working for a woman this time, but to get rid of one. The spur was equally effective. When the "flu" hit him in San Francisco, it found him ready prey. Later, facing a limp and helpless convalescence, he asked for a long leave of absence, and it was granted. The length of the holiday he asked was the period needed for a divorce under Nevada laws.

In spite of increases and promotions, in spite of the absence of Netta's bills, Lewis had not a large store of money with which to buy his freedom. He would have, he realized, to send less money to his mother, and he wrote her frankly to that effect. He rather dreaded her answer, though he was grim enough about his own intentions. He need not have been afraid. Mrs. Hunting, who could not have lived in an apartment and fended for herself in order to give his youth more scope or his career more chance, could find both strength and money when it came to getting rid of the daughter-in-law she detested. She could even find the old adoration for Lewis, which had been much obscured by jealous resentment. She saw herself once more—with Netta out of the way—playing a winning game with her son; and her heart overflowed with kindness to him. When these troubles were over, she and her darling boy were going to be happy once more as they used to be. There is no doubt that she meant what she said. She really believed that they had been happy before his marriage; she thought of him as her darling boy. When she dismissed her expensive maid, got an ancient cousin in to keep her dismal company, bade Lewis send her no money until he was free and, in addition, sent him a handsome check, she felt these actions right and natural, a duty and a pleasure. Mrs. Hunting had despaired, and now she had hope. Lewis would now be bound forever to his self-sacrificing, generous, devoted mother.

Most people's emotions are even more muddled than their minds; and there can be no question that Mrs. Hunting, playing her unanswerable trumps, loved Lewis more than she had ever loved him. His emotional rejection of Netta she took for an emotional acceptance of herself. She

saw herself preferred: and it warmed her confused heart.
Lewis was misread by his mother as he had been by his
wife. He knew perfectly that they had not been happy
before Netta came, and he thought his mother's sacrifices
belated. Though he was grateful for her assistance, the
past could not be undone, and no new relation could be
built up. He was grateful that she helped instead of hin-
dering, as he was grateful for fine weather in place of
storm. His loyalty was perhaps increased by gratitude,
but the quantity of his affection for her had long since
been fixed. He wrote to her regularly and with the utmost
kindness; but it was too late for her to push any further
into his heart.

Perhaps he was the happier that no intimate relation
needed readjusting. For the first three months of Lewis
Hunting's sojourn in the little Nevada town were by all
odds the happiest of his life. He saw his future clear, and
for once he saw it bright. He had been afraid—though
reassured by his lawyer—that Netta would put up a fight;
but the fact was that Netta could not. She had no money
with which to fight the case; and she discovered very soon
that, though New York would have held her a virtuous
wife, from the point of view of the more sensitive state of
Nevada she had sinned. She had refused to live under
what was legally her husband's roof; she had explicitly refused to give him children or a home, even to speak to his
aged mother; she had indulged, indeed, in an absolute orgy
of mental cruelty. These things were easily proved. It
would have taken money to deprive Lewis of his decree,
and money she had not. Nor did Lewis have enough to
tempt any lawyer to take her case "on spec." Netta knew
that she was beaten. Yet—had she but known it—she had
allies dimly mustering on her side. Netta was all instinct,
and fate looks on instinct with a kindly eye.

Until strength flowed back into him Lewis was content
to lie on the tiny porch of his tiny apartment, staring at
the Sierras; and the exertion of going out to his meals and
seeing his lawyer, when necessary, was sufficient to his
weakened body. After some weeks, however, he tired of
watching, in solitude and silence, the dwindling snow

patches. Energy returned, subtly heightened by the hope that was his. As the months counted themselves off, he felt Netta a lesser and lesser burden—slipping, slipping from his back. His shoulders ached less with the weight of her. Cheerfulness returned, and he began to welcome the ordinary human contacts. He was not looking for excitement, of which he well knew there was plenty. Neither poker, roulette, bad whiskey, nor rash divorcées appealed to him. Though not over-fastidious, he did not care to seize the day. He hoped, instead to seize the whole of life. Certainly he intended sometime to marry again—some girl opposed at every point to Netta; intended to have a home, and kids, and a car, and a radio set, and (so far had he become infected with the West) a view. He didn't know just what she would be like, but he would not find her here.

The doctor whom he felt obliged to consult suggested a car and long drives in the open. He finally bought a small one out of his mother's check, knowing that he could sell it again. But to face the inhuman beauty of that landscape one needs a human companion; some one who is equally dwarfed and conquered by the uncaring peaks and the hostile desert. Rather diffidently—you must remember that Lewis was not vain; he undervalued his charm, indeed, since it had brought him only Netta—he asked Mona Jeffers to drive with him; once, and then again and again.

The girl—a poor relation—was companioning a cousin who soon found that she need not depend on Mona for excitement. Indeed, Mona was a mere hindrance to Mrs. Tilton on most occasions. She needed the girl there on general principles and would not send her home; but she wanted her out of the flat a large part of the time. Mona's insipidity, to Mrs. Tilton's mind, was complete. She used her as she needed her, but she used her less and less—especially after she discovered roulette and acquired a rather shady lover. So the colorless Mona was free to sit beside Lewis while they drove afar. Her quietness, her decency, her very lack of good looks soothed him who was tired alike of Venus and the Furies. Love never entered his head. He expected that shadowy future bride to be handsomer than Mona— for men demand everything and are not satisfied

until sex blinds them into thinking they have got it. They
were blithe days for Lewis: health recovered, hope enlarg-
ing itself on his horizon, the weeks passing swiftly by, the
little car for magic carpet, and Mona to exorcise the demons
of the hills. Every one was civil to him, and he rejected far
more advances than he accepted. All pointed to his being,
through a long life, a happy and useful citizen. Lewis, who
was an unimaginative creature, found sanctions all about
him for his content. He called them omens or "hunches."

Without being superstitious or sentimental one may suspect that Nature lays traps for mortals, and that the trap
is no less a trap for being seldom sprung. No doubt, for
that matter, a man often comes through unscathed. There
is a spot—a sharp turn of the precipitous road, where a man
is uplifted for an instant, defenseless and naked to his
stalkers above him on all sides—which goes (not without
reason) by the name of Dead Man's Point. The term in-
herits from the days when those who fetched gold from
Virginia City were apt to lose it—and necessarily their
lives—at this place. For a few moments as he toiled past
a man became, in the nature of things, a target; his best
friend would have taken imaginary sight and aim. When
you had finished him—in the old days—the disposal of the
body offered no difficulties. You rolled him over the preci-
pice into the trackless gorge, and sheriffs were thereby con-
founded. Booty on that road is now as rare as bandits.
Nature, however, pays little attention to the infinitesimal
changes of human history: her traps remain traps. Some
spots are forever sinister, and this is one of them. The gold
may have gone, but, for a softer generation, the view
remains; and a foolish youth with bad liquor inside him,
driving a car too fast, is as perilous as two guns and a total
lack of morals ever were.

There was nothing in Lewis Hunting's heart to cope with
that view, which is desolate and terrifying—and beautiful—
beyond most. He was not in its class; nor was Mona. But
the mere size and scale and arrangement of it impose themselves. You *must* turn back to look, at Dead Man's Point,
before you forsake that range for others. Lewis and Mona
turned to look—and Johnny Stevens, innocent of every-

thing but that foolish drink, crashed into them at a curious tangent. Mona was flung free, falling, with infinite bruising of her tender flesh, upon rock; but the tilt of the car was such that Lewis was half caught beneath it. It rocked horridly like a hanging stone—one of those natural wonders that attract tourists—and then, rolling over, slid down the path of the corpses. Lewis, whose hands had stretched out instinctively and caught themselves with desperation in a stiff clump of sage, was left—though precariously—behind buttressed for the moment by a few stones of which the car in its final plunge had made nothing. They could not deter the machine, but they sufficed to deter him until Johnny Stevens, sobered by the shock, had dragged him to what is known as safety. Mona came later—half fainting, half crying, but not badly injured. By the time a fresh car came over the pass and picked them up, Lewis was luckily unconscious. They wound slowly home, and Nature —a beast, first, last, and all the time except when she is broke to the service of God—resumed her wise, incomparable smile. A little thing like loose wreckage cannot mar a view like that.

Science, which loves the part more than the whole, took hold of Lewis Hunting and made him one of her choicest fragments. No one could have blamed those able surgeons for being proud of themselves; but, true to type, they were not that: they were proud of Lewis. Half a healthy man is better than a whole man with a trace of sepsis; and Lewis— both legs neatly shorn off between knee and hip—was Exhibit A, a victory, an exultation. His blood was pure, his heart strong, his constitution magnificent, his recovery just what the recovery of the normal man should be. He had not hampered either Nature or Science in any way. The doctors felt affection for him because of his strong heart and untainted blood, and assured him earnestly that there was no reason why he should not live for fifty years. Lewis heard the words but did not measure their full significance until later.

Numbers of people came to see him in the hospital; flowers and fruits stood about until his eyes wearied of them. He was setting his teeth harder than he had ever done in his life, and he could not unclasp his jaws to breathe the sweetness of roses or taste the pulp of figs. His lawyer had, at his request, written—not telegraphed—to his mother; and in the letter lay a plain request that the news should be kept, by hook or crook, from Netta. The lawyer humored him, writing precisely what Lewis wished; but as that miraculous convalescence progressed, he wondered. No one, of course, would be such a brute as to suggest to Lewis that he change his plans to match his prospects. But—well, *but*. . . . They moved him to the hotel when he left the hospital, and guests and employees vied with each other for the task of pushing his wheelchair in and out of the elevator and dining room. A visiting nurse did the necessary things for a time, but the wounds healed as by a miracle. Six weeks after the accident Lewis was tensely calm: adjusting himself; writing to his firm; trying to apprehend, little by little, what a man with no legs would be able to do for fifty years. His mental mood had not yet relaxed to despair, and his body inflicted no fevers, no relapses upon him. But as he had not reckoned with Nature, so he had not reckoned with Netta, who was Nature's protégée.

Mrs. Hunting—distraught, half maddened—had for a time kept Lewis's command not to let Netta know. But though Netta never read newspapers and had few intimate friends, the news eventually came to her. Some one had noticed the identity of names. The moment Netta heard of it, she asked permission to absent herself, and rushed to Mrs. Hunting's suburban home. She made no mistakes this time: her instincts served her well. Lewis's mother had become, by this stroke, her chief ally, and from the first moment Netta treated her as such. Within an hour she had got from Mrs. Hunting precisely what she wanted. Nor is Mrs. Hunting to be too much blamed for playing into Netta's hands. She had cried over the maiming of her boy, her heart had indeed been well-nigh broken. Yet, confusedly, she saw him as wreckage—beloved wreckage, no doubt; but there was no triumph in possessing him. She had wanted him all to herself, and now, inevitably, she had him thus; and her weak old shoulders trembled under the

burden. Being everything to him, as he had hitherto de-
fined it, was being the chief recipient of his favors. The
poor woman was discouraged to the marrow; she had no
gift for meeting new and shattering situations. Her griev-
ance against Netta had always been on her own behalf—not
really on her son's. She was, of course, leagues away from
understanding Lewis, who had indeed never done her the
honor of explaining himself to her.

Netta cooed over her, Netta wrapped her in pity and
compliments, Netta expressed remorse as inclusive as it
was vague. Only the last of their talk need be recorded;
and much had been decided between them earlier.

"But, Netta, how can I let you go when he told me not to
let you know?"

"You can't keep me from him. My boss will lend me the
money to go, if I ask him."

"No, no. I'll give you the money. But do you realize
what it means, Netta?"

"Do I realize? What do you take me for? I realize that
Lewis is down and out, forever."

The feeble tears stood in Mrs. Hunting's eyes. "Yes,
that's true. He is. What are you going to do when you
get there?"

"Take care of him, of course. He's still my husband."

"You forgive him for wanting to divorce you?"

Netta's mouth twisted. Forgiveness was something she
had never in the least understood. "It has all been a horrible mistake. And now Lewis will realize it. He'll find
that his wife is going to stand by him, no matter what has
happened. Bygones are bygones."

"Netta"—the older woman's voice shook—"I didn't
know you had it in you. I guess I never understood you
before." She had never been further from understanding
Netta than she was at that moment, but she spoke in the
utmost honesty. To stick to a broken man who could give
her nothing, who had cast her off with insult . . . why,
Netta was wonderful.

"You're going to take him back," she marveled humbly.

"Sure I am."

"He ought to worship you, Netta."

Even Netta was a little at loss to answer that. "Lewis doesn't worship people, I guess. But we'll be all right."

"I never did believe in divorce," sighed Mrs Hunting. It was quite true, and she felt reminiscently ashamed of having so welcomed her son's.

The two women kissed, and Netta, with Mrs. Hunting's check in her bag, departed to pack and make reservations. Lewis's mother watched her go, and pure admiration filled her heart. She wouldn't have expected it of Netta who could so easily, after the divorce, have married again. If only the dear Lord would help her to carry it through! A little toneless prayer went up that night from Mrs. Hunting's lips that Netta might find her strength and her reward. Netta, meanwhile, alert and flushed, was moving about her room, packing her trunk and humming. Never had she felt less need of pity. *She* was again for Cydnus, to meet Mark Antony.

Her train, she found, would arrive at a hideously inconvenient hour; so she stopped short of her goal, had a night's rest in another town, and motored over in the happy morning light. Her heart was beating hard as she faced the hotel clerk and registered. His quick, excited glance of sympathy and admiration encouraged her. She realized afresh the tremendous handicap in her favor. She was, after all, still a wife.

"I'll telephone up," stammered the clerk.

Netta bent across the counter and smiled at him gently. The result was to make him feel that some men had all the luck. For a hopeless cripple to get any woman back after trying to get rid of her—and such a good looking one. . . .

"No," she said. "I've got to see him. And I think it will be easier for both of us if I just walk in. I came as soon as I heard. Does he suffer?" She dropped her voice sympathetically.

"Not now. He's made a wonderful recovery, they say."

She nodded. "I'll just go up and knock at his door. What is the number?"

He told her. "Shall I give you a room?"

Netta flushed a little. "Suppose you wait until I come down. Here is my trunk check."

The elevator girl stared at Netta when she revealed her name and her errand. As soon as Netta was well down the corridor, the girl shot the car to the basement where her favorite bell boy would be haunting the pool-room entrance. She crooked a finger at him. "Say, Ted, who'd you s'pose I just took up to Mr. Hunting's room? His wife! Gosh, she's a wonder—and some looker. Goin' to take him back, I guess. Don't you ever talk to me about women again. There's some of 'em that's worth all the men in creation." The elevator rose, preventing retort.

Netta already had laid her finger on the pulse of Nevada. She had been a little afraid of this special atmosphere which, she thought, might be like nothing else in our great country. But apparently, even in the stronghold of divorce, fidelity was valued. The mere glances of the clerk and the elevator girl had made that clear. Nevada itself would back her, she now suspected, just as Mrs. Hunting had done. She knocked at Lewis's door and entered.

Lewis sat by the window, a rug spread over him from the waist down. He turned, expecting a bell boy. He saw Netta instead, and so profound was the shock that it seemed instantly inevitable. The fact was too monstrous for doubt. There was hopelessness beneath his hot flush, though his voice was cold and stern.

"Netta! Why are you here?"

Netta took off her gloves, went into the bathroom and washed her hands. She came back, drew up a chair near (but not too near) him and sat down. Only then did she speak.

"I'm here to talk to you, first of all, Lewis. And then to see what I can do for you."

"How did you hear about this?" He pointed at the rug.

"It must have been in the papers. Some one spoke to me about it, finally. So I went to see Mother Hunting, and she told me everything."

"Did she know you were coming out here?"

"Why, of course she knew, Lewis. She helped me to come and gave me her blessing."

More virtue went out of him as he heard these words.

"My mother doesn't understand anything about my position," he said harshly. "There's nothing you can do for me. Sorry you had the trip. And now you had better get out as soon as possible. How did they happen to let you up here?"

Netta made no show of temper—which was ominous, Lewis thought. A row, he considered, would be the very best thing that could happen.

"Well, you see, Lewis dear, I am still your wife. And I think" she spoke gently to veil the brutality of what was to come—"most people would feel that a man in your position couldn't refuse to see his wife, if she were willing to see him. It isn't as if you ever had any real grounds against me, you know. I suppose you thought you'd marry again. Well, I don't see how you ever can, do you?"

"Of course I shall never marry again," he said shortly. She had got beneath his skin—Netta always did—and he felt weak tears starting.

"Somebody's got to take care of you, Lewis, you know. And if your mother and I are willing to do it, between us, I guess you can only be thankful to us. I shall keep on working, of course."

"I'd rather starve," Lewis answered simply.

"That's foolish," his wife replied mildly "—dead silly. Where would you starve? And how? You can be very sure of one thing, Lewis. Your friends aren't going to look after you while your own family stand ready to do it."

"Why do you come and badger me like this?" It was weak, and he knew it; but he could not tell her in plain words that he hated her. The loss of his physical integrity somehow made it impossible to utter so complete and violent a truth.

Netta rose. "I suppose if I told you I loved you, Lewis, you wouldn't understand. But I've always loved you. You knew when you left me, when you tried to divorce me, that I loved you. Do you suppose a woman who didn't love you would come back to you, after the way I've been treated, and after what has happened to you? You can put it up to your precious lawyer if you want to. I guess you'll find that even in the state of Nevada people will

consider that a wife who's ready to forgive what I'm ready
to forgive, and to take care of you the rest of your life, is
worth paying some attention to."

"It's no use talking, Netta. I don't love you—not a
damn bit. What do you want me for?"

She bent over him, not touching him. "Darned if I
know, Lewis. But I do want you—and I intend to have
you. I don't see how you're going to stop it. No, you
needn't worry—I'm not going to kiss you. Some day"—she
looked at him strangely, scrutinizingly—"you'll be asking
for it. I'll wait for that, thanks."

A bell boy knocked and entered just then to take Lewis
down to the dining room. If he was half an hour earlier
than usual, he can hardly be blamed. The hotel was buz-
zing from lobby to kitchen. Word had already gone forth
upon the streets of the town concerning the beautiful for-
giving wife who had appeared like an angel in the desert.
It must be remembered that in Nevada the presumption
against the forsaken spouse is not very strong.

"You had better go down alone today, Lewis," Netta
said. "I'll go out and do an errand or two, and lunch later."

She left them in the lobby. There were two people she
wanted to see before she talked with Lewis again. Thanks
to Mrs. Hunting, she knew the names of both, and a telephone book did the rest.

The interview with Lewis's lawyer came first. Netta
did not attempt to commit him to anything. She merely
announced her presence and her intentions; and she did not
fail to refer obliquely to the fact that, however the situation broke, there could be no money in it for any one.

"Of course I know you'll have to talk with my husband,"
she said finally, as she rose. "But the fact is that he's down
and out, and I'm willing to forget everything and work for
the rest of my life to support him. I'm afraid I am his only
chance." She shook her tawny head a little pathetically
and departed.

Netta permitted herself a sandwich and a cup of coffee
before the second encounter. It was possible, she realized,
that Lewis had fallen in love; and in spite of Netta's brave
sarcasms she knew it also to be possible that another

woman had fallen in love with him. If she, Netta, could keep on loving him, another woman might. And if the other woman were rich, she might even allow herself the luxury of a crippled husband. Her hand trembled a little as she rang the bell of Mrs. Tilton's apartment.

She could have shouted for joy, once face to face with Mona Jeffers. If she couldn't cut out that pale creature, she wasn't much good, she opined. She prepared to do battle, rather contemptuously. But Mona surprised her at once.

"We heard that you had come on, Mrs. Hunting. My cousin just came in from shopping. Things get round pretty quickly in this place." The girl was panting slightly, and Netta watched her, catlike, to see what would come. "Oh, I do hope it's true, Mrs. Hunting, that you're ready to make it up and take him back!"

So, even if Lewis wanted this chit, she didn't want him. She had only Lewis to fight, after all.

"I certainly am, Miss Jeffers. I only want to stand by him and take care of him, if he'll let me."

"Oh, how glad I am, Mrs. Hunting. Why"—the girl spoke softly—"it is almost worth while it should have happened if it brings you together again."

Precisely what Netta had thought; but she had not expected any one else to say it. Suspicion attacked her again.

"I wouldn't say that, Miss Jeffers. It's a pretty awful thing that's happened. But he's my husband, and I feel we belong to each other. The real reason I came to see you"—she went on very gravely—"was that I knew you were together at the time of the accident. I didn't know but you and he had fallen in love with each other—meant to get married when he got his decree."

The pale girl flushed. "Oh, no, Mrs. Hunting. There wasn't a thing—ever!" She gave a little involuntary shiver.

Netta noted the shiver and could have laughed aloud. Whatever Lewis might have wanted, this girl didn't want him. Poor old Lewis! His day of charm was over—excepting always for her. Funny: somehow he had "got" her for all time, but it looked as if he would never "get" any one else.

She smiled as she rose to go. "You must remember, Miss Jeffers, that Mr. Hunting has been trying to divorce me. I don't know yet what he will do."

"Do?" the girl exclaimed. "Why, of course he'll worship you. Not many women would do what you are doing."

Wouldn't they? Netta wondered silently as she went out upon the street. Well, perhaps other people didn't know what they wanted. She had never been troubled that way. But it was clear to her that no one was going to interfere with her taking on the whole burden of Lewis Hunting. Relief was in all their voices. Netta took a room at the hotel, but she did not try to see Lewis again. She dined outside the hotel and filled in the evening at a movie. In the theater she was aware of being covertly pointed out. Before retiring she sent a note to Lewis, saying that she should not see him until he sent for her.

Lewis, however, did not take long to capitulate. After talking with a few people he saw that, in the eyes of public opinion, he had no case. It was cold fact that Netta was behaving with great magnanimity. He was helpless, done for, and she was willing to take him on. The fact that he didn't want to live with her seemed very small in comparison—everybody blew it away, and indeed the mere hint of it seemed to shock. Half a man has no right to the prejudices and preferences of the whole man. How could he fight against the heroine of the hour? He sent for his wife on the second day, and she came at once.

"Well, Lewis?"

"Well, Netta."

That seemed to be all. Then he said haltingly, "I am very grateful to you, Netta."

"You've got reason to be," she answered briskly. "I'll move next door tomorrow, and you won't have to hire other people to wait on you. Perhaps I had better begin by taking you down to dinner tonight." She moved about the room, tidying it. Her presence seemed to flow into the farthest crannies of the chamber, and his nerves began the old gestures of revolt. There was never to be peace.

"Let's go down early," he said roughly.

"All right." She wheeled him into the elevator and

wheeled him out and into the dining room. As they moved through the palm room, she heard an unattractive citizen remark aside, "I've got pretty cynical, living in this place; but by heck, a woman like that almost gives me back my faith in human nature." Evidently Lewis had heard it too, for he flushed.

At the table he ordered, but ate little. Instead, he stared ahead of him—still flushed and curiously, stonily handsome. They talked very little. Netta too was flushed and shaken—with victory. She had got Lewis back forever, and food was unimportant. Money was the thing that was going to trouble her next.

Lewis was dealing with the future, as well as she. He was beginning to realize—the overheard words had thrust it on him—that not only must he live with Netta, endure her unmodulated hardness, perhaps even her strong caresses, but must always be humble with gratitude. He would have died rather than kneel to her, three months ago, when he had knees to kneel with; but, symbolically, he must do just that—forever.

"Let's stick round the lobby awhile," he proposed.

"All right, if you want to."

But suddenly he clutched the chair-arm. "No—upstairs!" He had wanted to put off being alone with her, but he had been wrong. It was more terrible to sit there with her, hero and heroine, under those cynical eyes made soft again by the spectacle of them.

"All right," said Netta again. "Just wait until I go to the newsstand and get some magazines." She left him, and he closed his eyes.

A voice in his ear made him open them. "It's terrible for you—her coming like this. But be brave. Nothing lasts forever. Be brave." The speaker passed on—a woman he had never known but whom, like all the other hotel guests, he had noted for her distinction of bearing and garb. She was not in the least of Lewis's—or of the others'—world, and she would never have employed a young woman so aggressive and sharp as Netta.

"Who is your friend?" he heard his wife ask. Strolling back with her magazines, she had noted the clothes, the air, the aspect of the older woman who had paused—though barely—by her husband's chair.

"I never spoke to her before, and I haven't any idea," he replied. "There are all sorts of people round this place."

He spoke very quietly. It was suddenly easier to be patient. Somehow that woman, with her mere passing murmur of sympathy, had picked his dignity out of the dust and handed it back to him. They had to wait for the elevator, and a cold draft assailed them, blowing directly through the little lobby from the street. Netta took off her scarf and folded it round his shoulders with a solicitous, possessive smile. The world looked on, with moist eyes. . . . Lewis set his teeth, squared his fine shoulders, and looked straight ahead of him with pride.

COWARD'S CASTLE[1]

By WALTER GILKYSON

(From *The Atlantic Monthly*)

JUDGE AVERY held his pencil poised above the type-written page of testimony, then marked the margin with a long firm line. He had not remembered the plaintiff's evidence was so clear; that young man had brought it out very nicely with the neat indirectness of his questions. On page forty-eight—he turned back the rustling sheets. Yes, the witness had said about the same thing. With a faint smile of satisfaction he leaned over and began writing on the pad that lay upon the book-rest of his easy-chair.

For a moment he paused to read what he had written, the pencil trembling slightly in his thin blue-veined hand; there was a look of critical appraisal in his worn face, something vivid, keenly alive, beneath the bloodless texture of his skin. He struck out a word, replaced it with another; the wrinkle between his eyebrows deepened and he smoothed the white hair above his forehead absently, then laid down the pad. That was the last finding of fact. He would dictate the whole and his conclusions of law before Court tomorrow.

It must be nearly five, he thought. The sunlight had shrunk to a dusty orange bar across the red carpet at his feet; through the open window he could hear the cooing of the pigeons, the soft rustle of their wings as they moved upon the stone sill. Against the opposite wall the yellow bindings of the books ran in converging rows to a well of still gray light that seemed to gather at the end of the room; the surface of the table in the center shone like a ruddy disk above its dark carven legs; through the curtains that hung above the doorway to his right he could hear the voices of the tipstaves talking in the empty courtroom outside.

Rodenbaugh was late. Evidently he was going to finish
the Minturn case this afternoon. A driving young man,
Rodenbaugh—he swept uncommon clean for a new broom.
The judge smiled a little grimly, glanced down at his knees,
unpleasantly sharp and narrow beneath the neat fold of his
trousers. Old age did queer tricks to the body, things that
he didn't like. No doubt it did the same things to the
mind. He was seventy-three. That was a warning in itself.
He rose and walked to the window, sniffed the dusty May
air. He was sorry he didn't get on better with Rodenbaugh.
It was hard, at first, to like any one who had taken Langdon's place on the bench.

There was a difference now, a very great difference. He
shook his head, turned and walked stiffly to his chair. The
fact that he felt the difference so keenly was a sign of his
age. In his youth the old lawyers had always complained
about the decay of the bar. And he had laughed at them
just as Rodenbaugh would laugh at him now if he heard
him. Only Rodenbaugh didn't laugh, that was the trouble.
He only smiled—a slow spreading of unparted lips, a nar-
rowing of his eyes, which—the judge sighed—was intensely
distasteful. But—maybe it was just as well. If Rodenbaugh once began to laugh he might laugh at himself all
day.

A step sounded on the marble outside, and the curtain
was pushed tentatively back. Old Walrath appeared, his
watery blue eyes searching the chamber with vague apology.
'Judge Rodenbaugh been here, Judge?' he asked. He moved
forward, then hobbled down the steps. 'I looked in his
room and he wasn't there. He said he wanted to see Mr.
Mercer at half-past three. Mr. Mercer's in the courtroom now.'

'He's still trying the Minturn case, Enoch. He's coming
here, though, before he goes home. I don't know what he
wants with Mercer. If he's been waiting long I think you'd
better let him go. You can call him when the judge gets
back.'

'All right, sir.' The old man paused, and a look of doubt
crept into his mildly truculent face. 'You think he won't
mind? I shouldn't like to get him mad just after he's come

off the bench. You know, Judge, he's got a way, when he's mad, of smiling just like a Chessy cat, and passing that tongue of his over you fit to take off your skin!' He pulled at his long white walrus moustache and gazed at the judge. 'I've been thinking he acts pretty fiery for a young man that ain't seen too much of court before he become a judge. I reckon'—his eyes moved solemnly to and fro—'I reckon that's why.'

Judge Avery looked at his knees; it was difficult to conceal his smile. Of course, he oughtn't to let Walrath talk to him that way. He ought to reprove him sharply, and the fact that he couldn't was clearly just another sign of his age. He straightened his face, looked up. Walrath was smiling at him in a curious way. Yes, by George, he was actually smiling at him paternally underneath that white walrus moustache. The old beggar! Really, he'd have to say something! 'Enoch!' He stroked his chin, gazed through his spectacles at the bent figure standing in the doorway. 'You're becoming too philosophical, I'm afraid, in your later years. I have a suspicion you've taken to psycho-analysis.'

'No, sir!' Walrath grunted. 'I never yet heard of it. Them experts talks of electrolysis in the accident cases, but I never yet heard of the sister you speak of. No, Judge—it ain't science—you know that.' He shook his head and began climbing the steps. 'It's just putting a long time in the courtroom, the same as you and me's both done—that, and a little looking round, as Judge Langdon used to say.' He paused, the curtain clasped in his big bony hand. 'I'm going out now and tell Mr. Mercer he can leave, and then I'll come back and get what papers you want for your bag.'

Judge Avery watched the curtain settle behind him, heard the slow stump of his footsteps across the marble. Old Walrath had stumped up and down those steps and across that marble for nearly fifty years; he had been a tipstaff when the judge first came to the bar. A gay ribald young fellow, then, with a rough tongue and a surprising knowledge of human nature, but good company, sitting on a table in the clerk's office, swinging his legs and imitating Melchior Van Zandt blowing his nose at a jury. There was time to linger in the clerk's office, in those days; time to do many things that were forgotten now. Law was a profession then, not a business; the lawyer reached out toward art and letters rather than toward certified public accounting. Then Bricknell translated Demosthenes and Judge Haynes wrote Horatian Echoes. Very faint but quite scholarly. And every one, strangely enough, spoke and wrote English. It seemed to be the mother tongue. He sighed. Even the law had changed; it had lost its pattern, its design; the fine threads of continuity were gone. Nowadays you matched facts as you matched silk, and extracted legal principles like a dentist pulling teeth. He rose, straightened his coat across his slender shoulders. He was old, quite out of date. In the hurry and press of modern life there is no time, and so forth—— Any young man could finish the sentence.

He gathered the papers from the chair, slipped an elastic about them, and thrust them into a green-baize bag. There was no use in waiting any longer for Rodenbaugh; he might as well take his walk and go home. The evening dreariness was coming over him; it made him peevish and irritable; he was likely to bite, to say something he didn't mean, if Rodenbaugh provoked him. He glanced at the table to see whether he had left any papers, then at the desk. For an instant he paused, a bent delicate figure, very clear against the square of ruddy light. The evening dreariness was, after all, a little more than age. He gazed at the pictures standing in leather frames within a shadowy recess of the desk. The bright knife-like sorrow of the past was gone, but in its place was a numb loneliness, a darkening vision, a dim sense of drifting with blurred, loosened feeling toward some unfathomable end. It would have been different if they had lived. He would have understood these youngsters better then. Old age had always to look through others' eyes; the vistas of its own past were overwhelming.

A sharp footstep sounded outside and the curtain rings jangled angrily. Judge Rodenbaugh's body filled the doorway, descended with an abrupt heaviness into the room. 'I hope you haven't waited, Judge,' he said. His small eyes moved obscurely beneath his thin eyebrows, his tall clumsy

presence seemed to permeate the place, to pervade it like a
harsh dominating breath. 'I wanted counsel to finish their
speeches this afternoon, so I could charge the jury the first
thing in the morning.' He seated himself in the chair by
the table, his thick shoulders thrown forward, his legs
stretched out. 'That little Kardos is a pitiful apology,' he
said.

'Was he trying for the plaintiff?'

'Yes. He tries a case as if he were selling shoestrings on
State Street. He's all tongue and no head. I've had to
listen to him now for two days, fumbling and backing and
filling, encumbering the record with all sorts of useless questions. Moran is against him—you know what a good one
he is! I think he was saying things to Kardos under his
breath all through the trial. I wasn't sure. Every now and
then Kardos would stop and get sort of gray and ask his
questions again. Each time he repeated he got worse, and
then Moran would get up with that suave easy manner
of his, and suggest that his friend first make known to himself what he wanted to ask, and, after a moment's silent
communion, make it known to the witness, who, in spite of
his lawyer, seemed like quite an intelligent man. He's a
quick one, Moran.' The judge shook his head. 'I like
him. He gives a case something—color, I guess you'd call
it.'

'That, or atmosphere,' answered Judge Avery. 'It's sometimes fatal to litigants, although we lawyers survive it. Well
—what did Kardos do?'

'Oh, he'd just smile that sickly smile of his, and move his
hands to and fro and wipe his face, and begin again. He'd
have been funny if he hadn't taken up so much time. You
know—that fellow Moran is a great trial-lawyer! I never
realized it so completely until today. I'd never tried
against him—I didn't try cases, the way you did, before I
came on the bench. It doesn't bother me, though.' He
smiled and his dark heavy face seemed to widen slowly.
'It's easy to handle things from back here, isn't it, Judge?'

'Yes,' said Judge Avery. His thin mouth closed, he
leaned forward a little, his elbow upon the table, and surveyed his companion with still luminous eyes.

'Well!' Rodenbaugh stretched back his shoulders, ran his hand through the unparted hair that lay like a wig above his forehead. 'I put an oar in myself now and then. Yesterday, after Kardos had floundered about for a while, I told him he ought to get a lawyer to try his case. Up jumped Moran with that friendly manner of his and said he'd be delighted to furnish his learned friend with a list in case he were not acquainted with the bar. The jury laughed and Kardos stood there wiping his face and moving his lips like a fish and then sat down. I told him to go ahead and he pulled up his chair and began shooting questions at the witness as if he were crying a sale. It was awful!' He leaned back, took some cigars from his pocket and pushed one across the table. 'I don't know what we're going to do with these fellows, Judge.'

'Neither do I.' Judge Avery ignored the cigar. 'Was there something you wanted to discuss with me? If not, I think I'll go home.'

'Yes, there was. I wanted to see Mercer too.' He rose, thrust his head through the curtains. 'Walrath!' he called.

'Yes, sir!'

'Did you get Mr. Mercer?'

'Yes, sir. He was here. He waited till half-past four.' Judge Avery heard the clump of Walrath's feet on the marble. 'Then I let him go, Judge. I told him I'd call him tomorrow morning.'

'You did! What did you do that for?'

'Judge——'

'Well, get him now if you're able to handle the phone! And remember, when I send for a man I want him to wait! Exercise the authority of your age and position, Walrath, but don't exercise discretion. When the vessels of the law become old crockery, they shouldn't go to the well too often. Move along now—don't stand there, looking at me like a fool.' He turned and descended the steps. 'Doddering old ass, Walrath,' he said.

'I told him to let Mercer go,' said Judge Avery. 'I thought you wouldn't want him to wait.'

'Oh!' The judge paused, a sulky look on his face. 'I see. I don't believe Mercer's so busy that an hour's wait would injure his practice.' He sat down heavily in the chair. 'What I wanted to talk to you about was this—'

'Do you mind'—Judge Avery's voice had a curious lingering drawl—'if we wait a minute? There's something I want to tell you, first.'

'No,' said Rodenbaugh shortly, 'go on.' He drummed on the table impatiently. 'Old Walrath's an ass,' he muttered under his breath.

Judge Avery smiled, a still frosty look in his clear blue eyes. Yes. Rodenbaugh deserved something. With the exercise of a little imagination he could give it to him completely in a way that he would thoroughly understand. He paused, his mind penetrating—invading the man before him. Then he leaned back, put his finger tips together, and the little smile on his lips grew sharp. There was a certain pleasure in the exercise of the imagination. Quite justifiable in this case. He would tell Rodenbaugh exactly what he was.

'It's about myself,' he said slowly. 'Old men are given to telling stories about themselves. I suppose that's the reason they're bores. But I think this will interest you as a younger man. Do you mind?'

Judge Rodenbaugh turned and stared at him. 'Not at all,' he said.

'That's very kind!' The words dropped like acid from the sardonic lips. 'I've been in a reminiscent mood all afternoon. As you're my defenseless colleague—brother, as the Reports call us—I'm afraid I'll have to impose on you.'

II

'It's curious,' he continued, 'how the memories of childhood come to the surface in old age. It's rather the way an ebbing stream discloses the soft formless ooze that lies beneath it. I can remember now just how I felt as a youngster, remember all my desires and fears with a surprising vividness. And I had plenty of fears.' He paused, nodding his head. 'I think I must have been afraid of everything, when I was young. In that way'—he lifted his eyebrows—'I'm sure I was different from you. Of course,

I never let any one know I was afraid. I buried it all deep down, created an image over it—an image of myself as a valiant, aggressive, reckless youngster. But I knew it was there all the time, and the very thought of it seemed to give me a savage desire to show my strength. And yet I couldn't when it came to the test. I was afraid to fight. The other boys knew I was and so I never made friends with boys of my own age. I always went about with the younger boys; they couldn't destroy this image I had created; on the contrary, it seemed to grow larger the more I was with them. I used to bully them like a regular little cad.

'You know'—he shook his head—'what boys are, Judge. Queer little animals; just as eager to maintain their prestige as any full-grown man, and just as clever about it, too.' He leaned back, crossed his sharp narrow knees. 'Did that thought ever occur to you?'

'I can't say it has,' Judge Rodenbaugh answered. His eyes searched his companion's face with a veiled wavering glance, then fell away. Judge Avery lifted his hand to his mouth, smoothed his upper lip.

'I suppose old men, like dead men, should tell no tales.' His smile seemed to vanish into a lurking shadow. 'I must tell you a little story and then we'll take up the matters you want to discuss. At boarding-school—I presume you went to Saint Thomas?'

The judge moved his head.

'It might have been better if I'd gone there, too. They sent me to Milford. Well, I wasn't a great success. I was quick enough in class, but that didn't count; for some reason the boys didn't like me. I wasn't good at athletics, I couldn't play football, and the cold punishment of the track simply filled me with dread. There was nothing of that sort that I could do and, naturally, I didn't become a leader, and I didn't want friendship on any other terms. So I put up my image and looked around for some younger boy to keep it in place.

'It was little Immanuel Pleasants the last term. I seem to remember him better than any of the others. He was the son of Agamemnon Pleasants, the teacher of Latin—a

thin, frightened, large-eared man with a white face and
eyes like a Sealyham terrier. Immanuel's mother was
named Lucilla, and, of course, we always called her Clytemnestra. They lived in a little house near the main building and were constantly asking unwilling boys in to tea.
Even as youngsters we recognized their "inferiority complex," as I believe the psychologists nowadays call it. Old
Aggie—I suppose he was thirty-five—used to call us "young
barbarians" in a timid jocular voice, and give us little half-
hearted pats on the shoulder and look at us with his doubtful evasive eyes. We thought he wasn't much of a man,
and I daresay he wasn't; and as for Clytemnestra we liked
her still less; there was something depressing about her red
swollen eyelids and the soft pink of her nose—as if she were
always having a cold. I think even Immanuel, at times,
doubted the worldly value of his parents, and I know some
of us used to encourage him in his attitude of unbelief. It
was always easy to encourage Immanuel on any subject.
He was susceptible to every influence about him; a pathetic,
eager little fellow, filled with an unreasoning desire to
please; one of those boys that hang about the older boys
and do things for them and talk about them a little breathlessly. I thought him quite absurd, with his weasel face and
his silly hat and his big translucent ears. I've often wondered'—the judge stared at the bookcase as if he had forgotten his companion—'what became of Immanuel. He
was manifestly unfitted for this world. I suppose'—he
looked at Judge Rodenbaugh—'you knew boys like that at
school?'

'Yes,' said the judge. He frowned and pulled heavily at
his cigar; behind the dissolving smoke his face seemed to
darken with a slow menacing flush. 'But I can't see —he
paused, then straightened up, looked at his companion.
'I can't see——'

'There's no need to,' interrupted Judge Avery. He lifted
his long thin hand from the table. 'Don't try. I'll be
through now, in just a minute. You must let me finish
about Immanuel. I rather like Immanuel! I almost feel
as if I'd invented him for you!' His smile was hard and
bright with a little curl at the corners. 'Now what was I

going to say? Oh, yes—I wanted to tell you about our play.

'Somewhere I'd picked up the story of King Agamemnon and the wily Ægisthus who killed him and married the faithless Queen Clytemnestra and, one dull afternoon when Immanuel and Kinsey and little Pollock were loafing in my room, I conceived the idea of putting the story into a play. I thought it would be amusing to see Immanuel act the part of his father, and I explained to him carefully just what sort of a silly ass Agamemnon was and how Clytemnestra fooled him. I remember I took particular pleasure in rolling out the word "Agamemnon"; little Kinsey and Pollock were tremendously pleased and Immanuel stood there with that foolish, half-frightened, expectant look he always had when we made fun of his father. But, when it came to acting the part, he rebelled and, of course, that made me angry and all the more persistent. I told him he'd have to do it or he couldn't go about with me any longer, but even that threat didn't seem to make any difference; he only stood there shaking his head, his queer little weasel face very sharp and pinched, his eyes flickering with a dumb-animal refusal. I remember it made me quite angry. I felt in some way as if Immanuel were threatening my prestige, depriving me of a satisfaction to which I was entitled. And so, to punish him, I began to imitate his father myself. Little Pollock and Kinsey went into screams on the bed and I rather expected Immanuel to laugh before I was through: laughing had always been his final mode of defense. But he didn't: he only stood there looking down, his stubby fingers twisting at the absurd pearl buttons his mother had sewed on his coat. So I went on, getting more and more savage as I went, it seemed as if his very speechlessness, the fumbling inarticulate motion of his hands, filled me with rage. I must have gone on for five minutes or so, when suddenly he hunched up his shoulders and lifted his arm to his face, and then ran to the door with a queer little squeak like a bat that's been hit with a towel. I heard some one calling after him in the hall and the next minute Danforth came to the door.

' "What's the matter with Pleasants?" he said.

'I felt startled and rather uncomfortable at Danforth's sudden appearance: he was captain of the baseball team, and one of the leaders of the school. He'd never paid much attention to me. Well, I put my hands in my pockets and walked over toward him. "Nothing, Danforth," I said. "We were horsing Pleasants a little, that's all. He can't take a joke." I shook my head in a superior manner. "He needs hardening up, I should say."

' "You think so!" Danforth looked at me with perfectly frank disgust. "I should say you needed it a bit yourself! Lying around all afternoon with a lot of kids when you ought to be out in the field! Why don't you take some one your size?" He waited a minute and then walked away. "You let Pleasants alone," he said when he reached the door. "It's filthy the way you devil the younger boys. When I get through practice this afternoon I'll put on the gloves with you, if you still feel you have to harden some one up!" He gave me an ugly smile and then disappeared down the hall.

'Well, I felt pretty sick. I remember that very clearly, but, unfortunately, what I don't remember is that it did me any permanent good. It was not until long after I was grown that I learned my lesson; and then, strangely enough, it took old Melchior Van Zandt and a little lawyer like Kardos to teach me. I don't suppose you remember Melchior Van Zandt. He was the leader of the bar in my time; and the kind of man we're not likely to see again.' The judge shook his head. 'The day of outstanding personalities has gone, I'm afraid. A high level reduces the lofty peaks—I believe that's the explanation given. You can take it or not, as you like. To me, at times, the plateau doesn't seem so high. Of course, that may be only age: the old are apt to see the great men of their youth through the eyes of their youth—and they loom very large. However,'—he shrugged his shoulders—'I must tell you about Melchior Van Zandt and the lawyer like Kardos.' He leaned forward a little, a cold stealthy watchfulness in his eyes. 'I think I'd been on the bench just about as long as you have when it happened.'

Judge Rodenbaugh lowered his head, stared at the

carpet with an angry frown. Then he rose, thrust his hands
into his pockets, his face turned away, his chin sunk in a
heavy fold between the square points of his collar. 'I don't
propose, Judge,' he began. His grating voice had an ugly
snarl that sounded like the snapping of empty jaws. 'I
don't propose to listen to this kind of thing any longer!'
He shut his mouth and the muscles above his jaws trembled
slightly. 'It's insulting and I'm not going to stand it!
You have no business'—he stared at the judge with eyes
that seemed curiously futile and stricken—'you have no
business——'

'Oh, yes, I have!' said Judge Avery. 'Sit down, please.'
He paused. 'Sit down, I said!' His voice leaped like a
sharp blue flame through the room. 'When the vessels of
the law become old crockery, there's a certain courtesy
due them, and that I intend to have from you.' He
stretched out his hand. 'Take your seat, please, and listen
until I've finished.'

For an instant Judge Rodenbaugh's stare met his; then
it wavered, seemed to turn sullenly inward. 'You presume
on your age,' he said, in a husky voice. He sat down
awkwardly. 'Also, I think you're presuming on my intel-
ligence. If you have any more to say, will you kindly be
brief? I don't care to spend the afternoon listening to
stories of childhood.'

'*My* childhood,' corrected the judge. 'I wouldn't presume to intrude on yours.' He looked pleasantly across
the table. 'I only presume on my age, as you said—that,
and a certain feeling for what I believe is called the art
of narration. Quite a remarkable art; I admit I practise
it very badly. But that doesn't matter so long as I hold
your attention. And what old Melchior Van Zandt said
to me is worthy of your attention.

'I'd been on the bench just about a month when it
happened. I was older than you are, and I'd tried quite
a number of cases. But, nevertheless, I was developing that
splendid sense of power you spoke of so feelingly just a
moment ago. There was a little lawyer who came into
my court in those days—he's dead now—who was rather
like Kardos, and he irritated me the way Kardos irritates

you. I remember one morning when I had a full list, he
came bustling into the courtroom with a great cloud of
witnesses behind him and that air of his, of terrible absurd
importance, which, in view of his hopeless incompetence,
always annoyed me intensely. Well, his case was reached
that afternoon and when I called it, he came fussing up
to the bar with his greasy frock-coat buttoned about him
and began to splutter at me, the way he always did. He
had a high squeaky voice, and his words seemed to come
out in bunches, as if he blew them out from the back of
his mouth. "Mr. Stover," I said,—the very sight of him
made me angry,—"as far as I can gather from what you
say, you want to butcher another case for us this afternoon." Then I looked around and waited for the laugh.

'Of course it came. It always does when the judge makes
a joke. I grinned down at Stover and he wrinkled his
forehead, then gave me a sallow little smile. "As long as
your Honor's made a shambles out of the court, I suppose
I might as well begin," he said.' The judge shook his
head. 'Pretty good, wasn't it?' he laughed. 'He didn't
leave me much to say! After Court old Melchior came
stumping into my chambers swinging his big green bag at
his side like a Hercules-club. "Avery!" he grunted. "You
deserved what you got this afternoon." He put his bag
down on the table. "I didn't think little Stover had it
in him. Remember!" He shook his head at me—he had
hair like the mane of an old gray lion. "The bench is the
coward's castle, my boy. You're safe, and the other man
isn't." Then he picked up his bag and stumped out.'

The judge sighed, smoothed his hair thoughtfully, passed
his hand over his cheek. 'It all seems so very long ago,'
he said. 'I'm afraid in recalling the facts I may have been
just a little vague. I only hope that I haven't bored you.'
He paused, then settled back in his chair, touched the tips
of his fingers together. 'And, now, what did you want to
discuss with me?'

'Nothing,' Judge Rodenbaugh answered. He rose with a
hesitant awkwardness, his face turned away. 'I've heard
that story about the shambles before. Unfortunately for

the truth of your autobiography it's never been connected with you.'

'Indeed?' said Judge Avery brightly. 'I must have made it my own then. It's not a bad story, though, is it?'

'No,' said the judge. He walked to the doorway. 'Walrath!' he called. 'Ask Mr. Kardos to step over, will you?' He turned sharply about. 'I've listened to you; now I'll ask you to wait until Kardos comes and then listen to me!'

'Certainly,' said Judge Avery.

III

'Mr. Mercer's here,' said Walrath. 'Mr. Kardos is on his way over. Do you want Mr. Mercer to come in?'

'No, I'll talk to him in the courtroom.' The judge rose from his chair and plunged through the doorway, the curtains dropping with a swift flap behind him. His voice reached the chamber the next moment, subdued to a low murmur from beyond the bench.

Judge Avery put down the Report, smiled quietly, and smoothed his upper lip. On the whole, he had done a good job. Rodenbaugh had wriggled, to be sure, but he had held the knife firm, cut to the proper depth. Surprising how his imagination had gone on; he never remembered letting it wander so far before unaccompanied by facts. Reading the *Electra* last night must have been responsible for Agamemnon and Clytemnestra. He laughed, tapped the end of his tortoise-shell spectacles on the table, then drew a deep breath, his fingers slowly turning his thin gold watch-chain. After all, had his story done Rodenbaugh any good? Human nature was a strangely resilient substance, inevitably coming back to the same shape, no matter how hard you squeezed it. And what business had he—or any one else—to squeeze it? That was what these damned reformers were always doing; blowing their moral ideas under every one's skin like so many flies! He walked to the window, gazed down at the automobiles moving through the dust-gold street like platoons of black glittering beetles. Maybe he had been a little magisterial in his attitude toward Rodenbaugh, exercised the prerogative

of age in a high-handed manner. Still—he shook his head
—the boy deserved it!

The murmuring in the courtroom ceased and Rodenbaugh's step sounded on the marble. As the curtains
swung to behind him, Walrath appeared. 'Mr. Kardos is
here, Judge,' he said.

'Send him in.' Rodenbaugh turned away, thrust his
hands in his pockets, and sat down facing the table. He
did not look up; in the silence that followed, the situation
seemed to Judge Avery just a little absurd. Then some
one paused at the doorway, moved the curtains timidly
to one side. 'Come in!' said Judge Rodenbaugh, a note
of exasperation in his voice.

Kardos seemed to stumble into the room. As he bowed,
it occurred to the judge in a sudden whimsical flash that
his round staring eyes were exactly like the black buttons
on his yellow shoes. He suppressed a smile, and inclined
his head. 'Sit down,' said Judge Rodenbaugh, nodding at
the chair in front of the table.

Kardos seated himself, then reached over, placed his
green hat on the table. It looked curiously jaunty on the
dark polished surface, arching above the reflection at its
side with an air of draggled impudence: the judge wondered whether Rodenbaugh appreciated it, and what in
the devil he was going to do with Kardos anyway, now
he had him. He leaned back, gazed at the pair with
vague amusement. Where in God's name did the young
men get those coats! There was something skirted and
dashing about Mr. Kardos's apparel—for such a little
man!

'Kardos!' Judge Rodenbaugh looked in his direction with
a slow downward glance. 'I want to apologize to you.'
He lifted his eyes, stared at him with smoldering hostility.
'I had no business to say what I did in court this afternoon.'

'Yes, sir!' Kardos nodded his head with a violent eagerness. 'I'm sure I accept your Honor's apology. I'm sure
your Honor's very generous to make me any apology at all!'
He spread out his hands and smiled at the judge, a watchful
look on his dark flat face.

'No.' Rodenbaugh frowned. 'I owe it to you. I'll admit'—his lip quivered with contempt—'you gave me provocation. But'—he thrust his chin down on his collar —'I owe it to you.'

'That's very kind,' said Kardos glibly. He leaned forward with an air of confidence. 'You see, Judge, I was asking the questions all right. Yes I was.' His low forehead wrinkled in a thick triangular crease just above his nose. 'I think maybe your Honor don't understand the way I work.' He placed a stubby forefinger on his palm. 'You see, Judge, I sort of feel around and ease off the witness's mind until he can tell me what I want, you know, just letting him loose and giving him a chance to think, and then new things come up and you get something maybe you overlooked when you came to court. So I just suggest'—he lifted a hand—'an idea, maybe, here and there— something that comes to me, maybe, on the spot. Of course I know your Honor thinks it takes up time, but'—he cocked his head to one side—'I get splendid results!'

'You do, eh! I wish I saw some of them in my court!' Judge Rodenbaugh's little eyes gleamed balefully.

'Your Honor hasn't heard me try many cases,' Kardos said. His smile was almost benevolent in its assurance. 'Where I live I get most of the business now of that kind.'

'You do, eh?' The judge grunted. 'That doesn't speak well for your neighborhood! From the way you talk you sound to me very much like a fool! Why don't you prepare your cases instead of trying them by mental telepathy?'

Kardos laughed. To Judge Avery, watching his face, he didn't seem at all disconcerted. 'Your Honor has a forceful way of putting things,' he said. 'If your Honor will permit me to say so, I don't think your Honor quite understands what I mean.'

'No, and you don't yourself. How could you when you think round and round like a mule tied up in a field!' The judge grinned, shot a glance at Judge Avery. 'What you need, Kardos, is direction, straightness of mental line. I'm afraid your mind's built on a circular pattern.'

'Wheels?' said Kardos.

'Within wheels,' Rodenbaugh answered. 'In my opinion you're not fit to appear before any sensible jury. You ought to practise trying cases on a phonograph in the privacy of your home. You could encumber the record then all you liked.' He looked at Judge Avery again.

Kardos caught the glance and a little grin touched the corners of his lips. He gazed at Judge Rodenbaugh with sharp, motionless eyes. 'Your Honor says very smart things,' he observed, in a tone of impersonal appreciation. 'I suppose that's the reason we all like to try in your Honor's court.'

'What?'

'I suppose that's the reason we all like to bring our cases before your Honor.'

'You do, eh! Well, I don't know about that!' The viciousness faded from the judge's voice, and he stretched out his legs and looked tolerantly at Kardos. 'My tongue may be just a little bit quick, but you fellows need it sometimes.'

'That's true, Judge!' Kardos nodded his head. 'Your Honor always gives us what we deserve. And besides, Judge,'—the motionless lustre of his eyes seemed to break into tiny points,—'we like a little amusement in the court-room.'

'Yes?' The judge thrust out his lower lip. 'Well, you furnish it all right.'

'And so does your Honor.'

'I do, eh?'

'Yes, sir.' Kardos seemed cautiously to expand, to relax in a posture of intimate friendliness. He glanced over his shoulder at Judge Avery, then surveyed Roden-baugh with an unruffled face. 'I hear that everywhere, Judge.'

'Indeed!' The judge's mouth widened, and he smoothed his chin. 'Well, I do the best I can for you, Kardos. In your case it's never hard.' He crossed his knees, sank farther back in his chair. 'You fellows fumble so with your facts,' he observed contentedly. 'And I think you must get your law from the *Evening Telegram*.'

'Your Honor feels that way because of your Honor's

superior mind. That's another reason we all like to try in your Honor's court. Your Honor gets things done.' Kardos sighed wistfully. 'Your Honor's court is not like the other courts.'

'No?'

'No, sir!' Kardos repeated with emphasis. 'I remember I said, when your Honor was appointed, there's a young man, if your Honor will forgive the word, that's going to stir things up on the bench. It's the kind of thing we need, and I said so, Judge, right down in my ward in public, and in private conversations. He's a young man that know's the law, and knows how to handle a courtroom, I said. He's got a heavy hand and a sharp tongue, and that's what a judge needs more than anything else.'

'You think so, do you?' Rodenbaugh lifted his chin, arched his eyebrows amiably, and his lower lip relaxed.

For an instant Judge Avery surveyed him, then he turned away, gazed out at the pigeons, softly rustling their wings in the square of orange light. He was very tired; if they didn't stop in a minute he was going to get up and go home.

'Yes, I do, Judge Rodenbaugh! That's what I think.' Kardos's chair creaked and Judge Avery could hear the scratch of his sleeve on the table. 'And I says to them, Judge,'—he heard Kardos's voice rise with a lingering sinuous accent,—'I says to them, Judge, there's a man that ought to go higher!'

'Indeed!' The word echoed through the chamber, hopeful, faintly ironic, foolish.

'Yes, I did, Judge Rodenbaugh! That's exactly what I said. There's a man that ought to go higher. He's only just begun his career, Judge Rodenbaugh has. And I'm telling you, Judge,'—Kardos hitched his chair closer,— 'what I says goes, in my ward, with a lot of my own people!'

'Hm!' A look of doubt crossed Judge Rodenbaugh's face, and his fingers moved restlessly on the table.

'And I'm telling you, Judge,'—Kardos paused, then rose with an air of authority,—'I don't think you've realized what I could do for you. No, you haven't.' He shook his head with an impudent cunning. 'I speak for my own

people in my ward. I can do a lot, I can. And Judge,'—
his voice seemed to creep through the silence,—'I could
use an appointment now and then, when they come your
way.'

For an instant no one spoke. Judge Avery could feel
the silence about him expand, grow tense with unuttered
meaning. He waited, a little smile on his lips. Then
Rodenbaugh sprang from his chair, his fist beating against
the table. 'Get out!' he fairly bellowed. He stretched out
his arm. 'Get out, I say!'

Kardos turned, seemed to leap through the doorway.

'My God!' The judge stumbled against a chair, picked
it up with both of his hands. 'Avery! Did you ever hear
anything like that in your life?' 'Never before today,' said
Judge Avery.

HOW DOES IT FEEL TO BE FREE?[1]

By MANUEL KOMROFF

(From *The Atlantic Monthly*)

AFTER the usual breakfast he was taken downstairs, given a bath, a fresh suit of civil clothes, and brought to the office. Here he was presented with several documents and a five-dollar bill.

The warden got up from his desk, 'I see by your papers, Joe, that you have been here twelve years. Well, you have been a good prisoner; good-bye and good luck to you.' They shook hands.

He was led through the yard to the gate. The moment had come. He stepped through. Again they shook hands before the gate was closed behind him and locked—locking him free.

He carried his hat in his hand as he started along the road and down the hill. He was confronted by a fresh, bracing breeze and a most bewildering sense of vastness—a vastness bathed in light. His eyes blinked, and his steps were short and hesitating.

On top of the high gray wall a guard, rifle in hand, walked in the same direction. 'Good-bye, Joe,' he shouted. 'How does it feel to be free?'

How does it feel to be free? To be confined, bottled-up, held in check, restricted, controlled—and suddenly turned loose upon a dizzy world!

A gray mist has surrounded it all. Imagine yourself completely enveloped as though your life had been becalmed by a fog. A fog through which it is difficult to see. Only overhead can you see a tiny circular opening through which the bright sky shines like a sparkling jewel. Soon you discover that the mist has hardened about you. The fog has encased you completely, except for that far-away opening overhead. You examine the walls and find that they are composed of long narrow ribbons of gray celluloid hung from what appears to be a small hoop in the sky. No—you have more space than that. Your walls are round, but you have ten feet from side to side. And every side is alike. From the sky to the ground your life is encased in a celluloid tube made of cold gray ribbons, and you are unable to see what is outside of yourself.

But when you examine the walls closer you find that the strips are made entirely of little squares, and each square has a queer design. You had not noticed them at first, but everywhere you look and as far up as you can see you find the little squares. Then on examining them closer you discover that each square is a separate little picture in which you yourself appear! Each square a frozen moment of your life. Each picture a tiny recollection dimmed and made gray by that rapid piling-up—that multiplication called the Past.

Frozen memories in miniature. As though the ribbons were discarded cinematographic records—records of your discarded past—complete and shameless.

There are different scenes of long ago; some are comforting and some are horrid. At some you tarry, but others you are happy not to see at all. Those high up are hard to see, though some seem clear and fairly distinct. You make vague guesses at what they are, and some you are sure you recognize. It is like a game. The forgotten past hangs over you as high as you can see, and a circle of light comes through from the sky.

The whole thing is quite natural, and at first you see nothing very strange about the affair; a little odd, perhaps, or maybe like a dream; but it does not seem very startling until suddenly you discover that the sequence is wrong. Why should it be wrong? Why do the scenes not follow one another as they happened? Why is this thing all helter-skelter?

You try to select and arrange, but the task is enormous. Here and there and everywhere are pictures that you have not included and some that you would like to—if you could only cut them away with a penknife. Yes, cut little toy-windows so you could see clearly outside—the outside world —the real world that at present you can see only by looking through your own experiences, and see dimmed by the shadows of past images. But you have no knife that could sever. And it would not help.

Oh, how tired you are of it all! How dreary, how oppressing, how monotonous! Days are gray and nights are gray. You are tired of yourself—the constant repetition of yourself. If you could only run away. But the cylinder is light, airy, and nimble. It rotates as you run. You are imprisoned in this strange thing called life—life dreary and gray—surrounded by cameos and smudges of black.

The sequence is wrong. You try to escape. The walls are pliable, and with pressure could yield. You wedge a hand through, and another; you work a foot through, making still another opening, but at no time can you manage to get your body through. Then, too, where would you go? You give it up; and in time you are resigned and engage in that restful play of thinking back and of looking out at the real world through the lightly tinted squares.

You see the world—the real world that is made of kisses and snow. Of fire, milk, dreams, straw, water, tobacco, and children. You watch the real world that is built solidly of things that do not last—built firmly of vital sparks that cannot endure.

Every now and then you discover a new square or two added to your walls. Something that happened only yesterday; but what was in its place before you are unable to tell, try hard as you may.

In a year many different pictures have presented themselves. In three years a fair number are new; in six, three-quarters are added pictures; but in twelve hardly any of the old remain and these seem greatly dimmed. A comforting dimness. Time makes all things restful.

In the outside world you can see children playing. They are playing with matches, lighting old brooms and paper, and running across the fields with trailing flames and shooting sparks. They had never done this before.

You watch closely. They are putting fire to the whole business! Suddenly a flash, a puff of smoke, a blaze of light, and there you stand on a hill confronted by real colors and a free, bracing breeze. In the distance the frightened children are running and you hear one whimper, 'I did not know it could burn.'

Everything is sky and land. You are surrounded by a vastness bathed in light.

You blink at the glamour of it all, as with hesitating steps you wander down the road to—The station is a mile away. Here a train comes from somewhere and can take you to—exactly where you do not know, but it can take you there. You must go!

That is how it feels to be free.

At the station Joe changed his five-dollar bill to buy a ticket and a plug of chewing-tobacco. The train carried him home—to the city of his former life.

Here the streets are paved with stone. Square next to square, with hardly a crack between. Cruelly mortised by man for the benefit and convenience of his fellow men. Long lines cemented together so that mud and dirt are not tracked about—tracked into the little pigeonholes called homes.

Joe reached home all right. His wife had been dead a number of years and his children had all grown up and married. Old memories were quite dim. He hardly knew them, and they certainly did not recognize him; but it was all very pleasant.

In the evening they all had supper together—that is, after the babies had been put to bed in one room. The table was dressed as in a movie, the room was bright with lights, and everything was merry.

A steaming chicken was brought on and the oldest son stood up, removed his coat, and rolled up his cuffs before carving. 'Now, dad, I'm going to cut for you this-here leg, first and second joint,' and, pointing the knife at him, 'also a good big chunk of the white meat.   Mollie, dish the gravy.'

They spoke about the comic strips in the illustrated newspapers, about recent screen-dramas, about dance records for the phonograph, about everything that amused them. The checkered past was carefully avoided.   They were all quite intelligent and they said they understood.

Joe had a nice home.   He could stay about the house and just 'rest up.'   The children had seen all kinds of reunions in the movies, and would do their best to make him happy. They gave him a room to himself, a warm pair of carpet slippers, a pipe with a yellow stem and fancy gold band, a pair of cotton-flannel pajamas, razor blades, and everything that a male mortal needs for comfort.

But Joe spent a most uncomfortable night.   The large meal did not agree with him and kept him awake.   The rushing light of morn came blaring into the room.   He looked about.   Small photographs hung on the walls.   There were scenes of Niagara Falls, Yellowstone Park, and of big trees in California.   Little gray squares dotted the walls— views that Joe had never experienced.

It was all very natural that Joe should be a bit uncomfortable at first.   The children said that they understood, and that it would take a little while for him to feel really at home.

Joe proceeded to make himself comfortable.   He tried the carpet slippers, but found them loose, soft, and uncomfortable.   The pipe was a nice thing, too, though he did not really enjoy smoking.   The pictures he removed from the walls, and then he drove nails on which to hang his coat and pajamas.   He greatly distrusted the closet, where it was dark and where mice perhaps were free to wander.

He amused himself by collecting old bits of wire that he found on old picture-frames and in the basement of the apartment house.   It gave him great pleasure to send the wire down the neck of a bottle and watch the odd twists and coils it would make in the bottle—as though it were life itself going through its many painful convulsions.   He kept the bottle on the open fire-escape in front of his window.

Just as soon as Joe found that the friendliness of his children was quite genuine he proceeded to make himself really comfortable. He brought up some thin boards to slip under the mattress of the cot. This made it much firmer. He nailed up the closet door and painted the rods of the fire-escape black, under the pretext that its former color showed the dirt too much. At night he had several times been bothered by a notion that there might be rats about and that his cot was too low. This he soon fixed by bringing up some old wood from the basement and raising the cot so that it resembled an upper berth in a cabin. He was careful to eat very little meat and kept closely to a diet of soup and hot cereal. Day by day he was feeling more comfortable. Now only one thing more needed his attention. The room was too large! Too large for one person. This he remedied by rigging a pole across the room and hanging down a heavy curtain dividing the space in half. It also divided the window. Now all seemed cozy.

By this time the bottle on the window was packed tight with bits of wire. He carried it down to the basement and broke it over an ash can. The heavy wad of iron wire was freed from its container. It was nothing but a rusty solid mass, the same shape as the bottle that now was scattered in fragments.

He turned it in his hand and examined it closely. Was it an experiment that had failed? Did he imagine that the tough springy wires would jump back to their former state once freed? No. It was a rusty solid mass, brown as a cough mixture and shaped like a bottle. If he had a label he could paste it on and mark it—'Free!'

He brought it back to his room and carefully put it in its place on the window. Then he climbed up on his cot.

Outside it rains, and outside it snows, and then the sun sings forth and dries up the long lines of pavements made of stone cunningly mortised. From his cot he can see a tiny bit of sky—a small bright opening far away. Now and then a figure walks across a neighboring roof and reminds him of the man on the high wall who held a rifle in his hand and shouted, 'How does it feel to be free?' From his cot he can see glimpses of the outside world—the real

world that is made of kisses and snow.   But between him
and the great outside is the window-ledge upon which stands
that rusty, packed-together wad of wire, shaped like a
bottle.

HAIRCUT[1]

By RING LARDNER

(From *Liberty*)

I GOT another barber that comes over from Carterville
and helps me out Saturdays, but the rest of the time I
can get along all right alone. You can see for yourself
that this ain't no New York City and besides that, the
most of the boys works all day and don't have no leisure
to drop in here and get themselves prettied up.

You're a newcomer, ain't you? I thought I hadn't seen
you round before. I hope you like it good enough to stay.
As I say, we ain't no New York City or Chicago, but we
have pretty good times. Not as good, though, since Jim
Kendall got killed. When he was alive, him and Hod
Meyers used to keep this town in an uproar. I bet they
was more laughin' done here than any town its size in
America.

Jim was comical, and Hod was pretty near a match for
him. Since Jim's gone, Hod tries to hold his end up just
the same as ever, but it's tough goin' when you ain't got
nobody to kind of work with.

They used to be plenty fun in here Saturdays. This
place is jam-packed Saturdays, from four o'clock on. Jim
and Hod would show up right after their supper round six
o'clock. Jim would set himself down in that big chair,
nearest the blue spittoon. Whoever had been settin' in
that chair, why they'd get up when Jim come in and give
it to him.

You'd of thought it was a reserved seat like they have
sometimes in a theayter. Hod would generally always
stand or walk up and down or some Saturdays, of course,
he'd be settin' in this chair part of the time, gettin' a haircut.

[1] Copyright, 1925, by Liberty Weekly, Incorporated.
Copyright, 1926, by Ring W. Lardner.

Well, Jim would set there a w'ile without openin' his mouth only to spit, and then finally he'd say to me, "Whitey,"—my right name, that is, my right first name, is Dick, but everybody round here calls me Whitey—Jim would say, "Whitey, your nose looks like a rosebud to-night. You must of been drinkin' some of your aw de cologne."

So I'd say, "No, Jim, but you look like you'd been drinkin' somethin' of that kind or somethin' worse."

Jim would have to laugh at that, but then he'd speak up and say, "No, I ain't had nothin' to drink, but that ain't sayin' I wouldn't like somethin'. I wouldn't even mind if it was wood alcohol."

Then Hod Meyers would say, "Neither would your wife." That would set everybody to laughin' because Jim and his wife wasn't on very good terms. She'd of divorced him only they wasn't no chance to get alimony and she didn't have no way to take care of herself and the kids. She couldn't never understand Jim. He *was* kind of rough, but a good fella at heart.

Him and Hod had all kinds of sport with Milt Sheppard. I don't suppose you've seen Milt. Well, he got an Adam's apple that looks more like a mushmelon. So I'd be shavin' Milt and when I'd start to shave down here on his neck, Hod would holler, "Hey, Whitey, wait a minute! Before you cut into it, let's make up a pool and see who can guess closest to the number of seeds."

And Jim would say, "If Milt hadn't of been so hoggish, he'd of ordered a half a cantaloupe instead of a whole one and it might not of stuck in his throat."

All the boys would roar at this and Milt himself would force a smile, though the joke was on him. Jim certainly was a card!

There's his shavin' mug, settin' on the shelf, right next to Charley Vail's. "Charles M. Vail." That's the druggist. He comes in regular for his shave, three times a week. And Jim's is the cup next to Charley's. "James H. Kendall." Jim won't need no shavin' mug no more, but I'll leave it there just the same for old time's sake. Jim certainly was a character!

Years ago, Jim used to travel for a canned goods concern over in Carterville. They sold canned goods. Jim had the whole northern half of the State and was on the road five days out of every week. He'd drop in here Saturdays and tell his experiences for that week. It was rich.

I guess he paid more attention to playin' jokes than makin' sales. Finally the concern let him out and he come right home here and told everybody he'd been fired instead of sayin' he'd resigned like most fellas would of.

It was a Saturday and the shop was full and Jim got up out of that chair and says, "Gentlemen, I got an important announcement to make. I been fired from my job."

Well, they asked him if he was in earnest and he said he was and nobody could think of nothin' to say till Jim finally broke the ice himself. He says, "I been sellin' canned goods and now I'm canned goods myself."

You see, the concern he'd been workin' for was a factory that made canned goods. Over in Carterville. And now Jim said he was canned himself. He was certainly a card!

Jim had a great trick that he used to play w'ile he was travelin'. For instance, he'd be ridin' on a train and they'd come to some little town like, well, like, well, like, we'll say, like Benton. Jim would look out the train window and read the signs on the stores.

For instance, they'd be a sign, "Henry Smith, Dry Goods." Well, Jim would write down the name and the name of the town and when he got to wherever he was goin' he'd mail back a postal card to Henry Smith at Benton and not sign no name to it, but he'd write on the card, well, somethin' like "Ask your wife about that book agent that spent the afternoon last week," or "Ask your Missus who kept her from gettin' lonesome the last time you was in Carterville." And he'd sign the card, "A Friend."

Of course, he never knew what really come of none of these jokes, but he could picture what *probably* happened and that was enough.

Jim didn't work very steady after he lost his position with the Carterville people. What he did earn, doin' odd jobs round town, why he spent pretty near all of it on gin, and his family might of starved if the stores hadn't of carried them along. Jim's wife tried her hand at dressmakin', but they ain't nobody goin' to get rich makin' dresses in this town.

As I say, she'd of divorced Jim, only she seen that she couldn't support herself and the kids and she was always hopin' that some day Jim would cut out his habits and give her more than two or three dollars a week.

They was a time when she would go to whoever he was workin' for and ask them to give her his wages, but after she done this once or twice, he beat her to it by borrowin' most of his pay in advance. He told it all round town, how he had outfoxed his Missus. He certainly was a caution!

But he wasn't satisfied with just outwittin' her. He was sore the way she had acted, tryin' to grab off his pay. And he made up his mind he'd get even. Well, he waited till Evans's Circus was advertised to come to town. Then he told his wife and two kiddies that he was goin' to take them to the circus. The day of the circus, he told them he would get the tickets and meet them outside the entrance to the tent.

Well, he didn't have no intentions of bein' there or buyin' tickets or nothin'. He got full of gin and laid round Wright's poolroom all day. His wife and the kids waited and waited and of course he didn't show up. His wife didn't have a dime with her, or nowhere else, I guess. So she finally had to tell the kids it was all off and they cried like they wasn't never goin' to stop.

Well, it seems, w'ile they was cryin', Doc Stair come along and he asked what was the matter, but Mrs. Kendall was stubborn and wouldn't tell him, but the kids told him and he insisted on takin' them and their mother in the show. Jim found this out afterwards and it was one reason why he had it in for Doc Stair.

Doc Stair come here about a year and a half ago. He's a mighty handsome young fella and his clothes always look like he has them made to order. He goes to Detroit two or three times a year and w'ile he's there he must have a tailor take his measure and then make him a suit to order.

They cost pretty near twice as much, but they fit a whole lot better than if you just bought them in a store.

For a w'ile everybody was wonderin' why a young doctor like Doc Stair should come to a town like this where we already got old Doc Gamble and Doc Foote that's both been here for years and all the practice in town was always divided between the two of them.

Then they was a story got round that Doc Stair's gal had throwed him over, a gal up in the Northern Peninsula somewhere, and the reason he come here was to hide himself away and forget it. He said himself that he thought they wasn't nothin' like general practice in a place like ours to fit a man to be a good all round doctor. And that's why he'd came.

Anyways, it wasn't long before he was makin' enough to live on, though they tell me that he never dunned nobody for what they owed him, and the folks here certainly has got the owin' habit, even in my business. If I had all that was comin' to me for just shaves alone, I could go to Carterville and put up at the Mercer for a week and see a different picture every night. For instance, they's old George Purdy—but I guess I shouldn't ought to be gossipin'.

Well, last year, our coroner died, died of the flu. Ken Beatty, that was his name. He was the coroner. So they had to choose another man to be coroner in his place and they picked Doc Stair. He laughed at first and said he didn't want it, but they made him take it. It ain't no job that anybody would fight for and what a man makes out of it in a year would just about buy seeds for their garden. Doc's the kind, though, that can't say no to nothin' if you keep at him long enough.

But I was goin' to tell you about a poor boy we got here in town—Paul Dickson. He fell out of a tree when he was about ten years old. Lit on his head and it done somethin' to him and he ain't never been right. No harm in him, but just silly. Jim Kendall used to call him cuckoo; that's a name Jim had for anybody that was off their head, only he called people's head their bean. That was another of his gags, callin' head bean and callin' crazy people cuckoo. Only poor Paul ain't crazy, but just silly.

You can imagine that Jim used to have all kinds of fun with Paul. He'd send him to the White Front Garage for a left-handed monkey wrench. Of course they ain't no such thing as a left-handed monkey wrench.

And once we had a kind of a fair here and they was a baseball game between the fats and the leans and before the game started Jim called Paul over and sent him way down to Schrader's hardware store to get a key for the pitcher's box.

They wasn't nothin' in the way of gags that Jim couldn't think up, when he put his mind to it.

Poor Paul was always kind of suspicious of people, maybe on account of how Jim had kept foolin' him. Paul wouldn't have much to do with anybody only his own mother and Doc Stair and a girl here in town named Julie Gregg. That is, she ain't a girl no more, but pretty near thirty or over.

When Doc first come to town, Paul seemed to feel like here was a real friend and he hung round Doc's office most of the w'ile; the only time he wasn't there was when he'd go home to eat or sleep or when he seen Julie Gregg doin' her shoppin'.

When he looked out Doc's window and seen her, he'd run downstairs and join her and tag along with her to the different stores. The poor boy was crazy about Julie and she always treated him mighty nice and made him feel like he was welcome, though of course it wasn't nothin' but pity on her side.

Doc done all he could to improve Paul's mind and he told me once that he really thought the boy was getting better, that they was times when he was as bright and sensible as anybody else.

But I was goin' to tell you about Julie Gregg. Old man Gregg was in the lumber business, but got to drinkin' and lose the most of his money and when he died, he didn't leave nothin' but the house and just enough insurance for the girl to skimp along on.

Her mother was a kind of a half invalid and didn't hardly ever leave the house. Julie wanted to sell the place and move somewheres else after the old man died, but the mother said she was born here and would die here. It was tough on Julie as the young people round this town—well, she's too good for them.

She's been away to school and Chicago and New York and different places and they ain't no subject she can't talk on, where you take the rest of the young folks here and you mention anything to them outside of Gloria Swanson or Tommy Meighan and they think you're delirious. Did you see Gloria in Wages of Virtue? You missed somethin'!

Well, Doc Stair hadn't been here more than a week when he come in one day to get shaved and I recognized who he was, as he had been pointed out to me, so I told him about my old lady. She's been ailin' for a couple years and either Doc Gamble or Doc Foote, neither one, seemed to be helpin' her. So he said he would come out and see her, but if she was able to get out herself, it would be better to bring her to his office where he could make a completer examination.

So I took her to his office and w'ile I was waitin' for her in the reception room, in come Julie Gregg. When somebody comes in Doc Stair's office, they's a bell that rings in his inside office so as he can tell they's somebody to see him.

So he left my old lady inside and come out to the front office and that's the first time him and Julie met and I guess it was what they call love at first sight. But it wasn't fifty-fifty. This young fella was the slickest lookin' fella she'd ever seen in this town and she went wild over him. To him she was just a young lady that wanted to see the doctor.

She'd came on about the same business I had. Her mother had been doctorin' for years with Doc Gamble and Doc Foote and without no results. So she'd heard they was a new doc in town and decided to give him a try. He promised to call and see her mother that same day.

I said a minute ago that it was love at first sight on her part. I'm not only judgin' by how she acted afterwards but how she looked at him that first day in his office. I ain't no mind reader, but it was wrote all over her face that she was gone.

Now Jim Kendall, besides bein' a jokesmith and a pretty good drinker, well, Jim was quite a lady-killer. I guess he run pretty wild durin' the time he was on the road for them Carterville people, and besides that, he'd had a couple little affairs of the heart right here in town. As I say, his wife could have divorced him, only she couldn't.

But Jim was like the majority of men, and women, too, I guess. He wanted what he couldn't get. He wanted Julie Gregg and worked his head off tryin' to land her. Only he'd of said bean instead of head.

Well, Jim's habits and his jokes didn't appeal to Julie and of course he was a married man, so he didn't have no more chance than, well, than a rabbit. That's an expression of Jim's himself. When somebody didn't have no chance to get elected or somethin', Jim would always say they didn't have no more chance than a rabbit.

He didn't make no bones about how he felt. Right in here, more than once, in front of the whole crowd, he said he was stuck on Julie and anybody that could get her for him was welcome to his house and his wife and kids included. But she wouldn't have nothin' to do with him; wouldn't even speak to him on the street. He finally seen he wasn't gettin' nowheres with his usual line so he decided to try the rough stuff. He went right up to her house one evenin' and when she opened the door he forced his way in and grabbed her. But she broke loose and before he could stop her, she run in the next room and locked the door and phoned to Joe Barnes. Joe's the marshal. Jim could hear who she was phonin' to and he beat it before Joe got there.

Joe was an old friend of Julie's pa. Joe went to Jim the next day and told him what would happen if he ever done it again.

I don't know how the news of this little affair leaked out. Chances is that Joe Barnes told his wife and she told somebody else's wife and they told their husband. Anyways, it did leak out and Hod Meyers had the nerve to kid Jim about it, right here in this shop. Jim didn't deny nothin' and kind of laughed it off and said for us all to wait; that lots of people had tried to make a monkey out of him, but he always got even.

Meanw'ile everybody in town was wise to Julie's bein' wild mad over the Doc. I don't suppose she had any idear how her face changed when him and her was together; of course she couldn't of, or she'd of kept away from him. And she didn't know that we was all noticin' how many times she made excuses to go up to his office or pass it on the other side of the street and look up in his window to see if he was there. I felt sorry for her and so did most other people.

Hod Meyers kept rubbin' it into Jim about how the Doc had cut him out. Jim didn't pay no attention to the kiddin' and you could see he was plannin' one of his jokes.

One trick Jim had was the knack of changin' his voice. He could make you think he was a girl talkin' and he could mimic any man's voice. To show you how good he was along this line, I'll tell you the joke he played on me once.

You know, in most towns of any size, when a man is dead and needs a shave, why the barber that shaves him soaks him five dollars for the job; that is, he don't soak *him*, but whoever ordered the shave. I just charge three dollars because personally I don't mind much shavin' a dead person. They lay a whole lot stiller than live customers. The only thing is that you don't feel like talkin' to them and you get kind of lonesome.

Well, about the coldest day we ever had here, two years ago last winter, the phone rung at the house w'ile I was home to dinner and I answered the phone and it was a woman's voice and she said she was Mrs. John Scott and her husband was dead and would I come out and shave him.

Old John had always been a good customer of mine. But they live seven miles out in the country, on the Streeter road. Still I didn't see how I could say no.

So I said I would be there, but would have to come in a jitney and it might cost three or four dollars besides the price of the shave. So she, or the voice, it said that was all right, so I got Frank Abbott to drive me out to the place and when I got there, who should open the door but old John himself! He wasn't no more dead than, well than a rabbit.

It didn't take no private detective to figure out who had played me this little joke. Nobody could of thought it up but Jim Kendall. He certainly was a card!

I tell you this incident just to show you how he could disguise his voice and make you believe it was somebody else talkin'. I'd of swore it was Mrs. Scott had called me. Anyways, some woman.

Well, Jim waited till he had Doc Stair's voice down pat; then he went after revenge.

He called Julie up on a night when he knew Doc was over in Carterville. She never questioned but what it was Doc's voice. Jim said he must see her that night; he couldn't wait no longer to tell her somethin'. She was all excited and told him to come to the house. But he said he was expectin' an important long distance call and wouldn't she please forget her manners for once and come to his office. He said they couldn't nothin' hurt her and nobody would see her and he just *must* talk to her a little w'ile. Well, poor Julie fell for it.

Doc always keeps a night light in his office, so it looked to Julie like they was somebody there.

Meanw'ile Jim Kendall had went to Wright's poolroom, where they was a whole gang amusin' themselves. The most of them had drank plenty of gin, and they was a rough bunch even when sober. They was always strong for Jim's jokes and when he told them to come with him and see some fun they give up their card games and pool games and followed along.

Doc's office is on the second floor. Right outside his door they's a flight of stairs leadin' to the floor above. Jim and his gang hid in the dark behind these stairs.

Well, Julie come up to Doc's door and rung the bell and they was nothin' doin'. She rung it again and she rung it seven or eight times. Then she tried the door and found it locked. Then Jim made some kind of a noise and she heard it and waited a minute, and then she says, "Is that you, Ralph?" Ralph is Doc's first name.

They was no answer and it must of came to her all of a sudden that she'd been bunked. She pretty near fell downstairs and the whole gang after her. They chased her all the way home, hollerin', "Is that you Ralph?" and "Oh, Ralphie, dear, is that you?" Jim says he couldn't holler it himself, as he was laughin' too hard.

Poor Julie! She didn't show up here on Main Street for a long, long time afterward.

And of course Jim and his gang told everybody in town, everybody but Doc Stair. They was scared to tell him, and he might of never knowed only for Paul Dickson. The poor cuckoo, as Jim called him, he was here in the shop one night when Jim was still gloatin' yet over what he'd done to Julie. And Paul took in as much of it as he could understand and he run to Doc with the story.

It's a cinch Doc went up in the air and swore he'd make Jim suffer. But it was a kind of a delicate thing, because if it got out that he had beat Jim up, Julie was bound to hear of it and then she'd know that Doc knew and of course knowin' that he knew would make it worse for her than ever. He was goin' to do somethin', but it took a lot of figurin'.

Well, it was a couple days later when Jim was here in the shop again, and so was the cuckoo. Jim was goin' duck-shootin' the next day and had came in lookin' for Hod Meyers to go with him. I happened to know that Hod had went over to Carterville and wouldn't be home till the end of the week. So Jim said he hated to go alone and he guessed he would call it off. Then poor Paul spoke up and said if Jim would take him he would go along. Jim thought a w'ile and then he said, well, he guessed a half-wit was better than nothin'.

I suppose he was plottin' to get Paul out in the boat and play some joke on him, like pushin' him in the water. Anyways, he said Paul could go. He asked him had he ever shot a duck and Paul said no, he'd never even had a gun in his hands. So Jim said he could set in the boat and watch him and if he behaved himself, he might lend him his gun for a couple of shots. They made a date to meet in the mornin' and that's the last I seen of Jim alive.

Next mornin', I hadn't been open more than ten minutes when Doc Stair come in. He looked kind of nervous. He asked me had I seen Paul Dickson. I said no, but I knew where he was, out duck-shootin' with Jim Kendall. So Doc says that's what he had heard, and he couldn't understand it because Paul had told him he wouldn't never have no more to do with Jim as long as he lived.

He said Paul had told him about the joke Jim had played on Julie. He said Paul had asked him what he thought of the joke and the Doc had told him that anybody that would do a thing like that ought not to be let live.

I said it had been a kind of a raw thing, but Jim just couldn't resist no kind of a joke, no matter how raw. I said I thought he was all right at heart, but just bubblin' over with mischief. Doc turned and walked out.

At noon he got a phone call from old John Scott. The lake where Jim and Paul had went shootin' is on John's place. Paul had came runnin' up to the house a few minutes before and said they'd been an accident. Jim had shot a few ducks and then give the gun to Paul and told him to try his luck. Paul hadn't never handled a gun and he was nervous. He was shakin' so hard that he couldn't control the gun. He let fire and Jim sunk back in the boat, dead.

Doc Stair, bein' the coroner, jumped in Frank Abbott's flivver and rushed out to Scott's farm. Paul and old John was down on the shore of the lake. Paul had rowed the boat to shore, but they'd left the body in it, waiting for Doc to come.

Doc examined the body and said they might as well fetch it back to town. They was no use leavin' it there or callin' a jury, as it was a plain case of accidental shootin'.

Personally I wouldn't never leave a person shoot a gun in the same boat I was in unless I was sure they knew somethin' about guns. Jim was a sucker to leave a new beginner have his gun, let alone a halfwit. It probably served Jim right, what he got. But still we miss him round here. He certainly was a card!

Comb it wet or dry?

THE ILL WIND[1]

By ROBERT ROBINSON

(From *Collier's Weekly*)

A S best I can recollect, this is the way it happened:
I got up about the usual time that morning and went
out to get some kindling to make a fire with. Well, I
noticed that it was kinda still and sultry like, and I told
Martha when I got back in that I believed it was going to
come a storm. She said she hoped it rained, as the tomatoes
needed it bad. You see, we'd set out a five-acre patch of
them about a week before. I didn't tell her that I was
afraid that it was going to turn into a sandstorm. I knew
she'd have a fit. She always does.

Martha'd worked too hard. You see, we moved on this
place more'n fifteen years ago. We were young then, and
we figured we'd make no end of money. We came here from
Missouri 'cause we wanted to get a start so's we could give
the boy an education. We just had one kid then, Johnnie.
We got five now. But that ain't got nothing to do with the
story. As I was saying, Martha'd worked too hard. We
had to pay out the place, and it seemed like luck would
never break our way. The first year the sod didn't make
enough to pay expenses; then several years we were blown
out by sand; the drought got us a couple of times; and then
we had a good many other things to happen that kinda took
the wind out of our sails.

And then there was another thing that I hate to mention
that seemed to worry her no end. You see, Martha was
awful religious. She comes from that kind of stock. For
some reason or other I ain't never took to religion much. It
always seemed like foolishness to me. That kinda hurt
her. And when everything begin to go wrong she laid it to

me being so ungodly. I used to laugh and joke her about it, but she took it serious as ever'thing. She'd say:

"All right, you can joke about it all you want to, but some day you'll see. The Lord'll exact His toll; He'll make you pay."

Well, she got up, and as usual she cried a little. I didn't blame her. Poor old Martha! She'd had such dreams, and they'd all been blown away, as you might say. Then too she was a sick woman a lot of the time. She had the neuralgia and the catarrh, and between them, with all the work she did, they kept her feeling mighty poorly.

But, as I was saying, Martha got up, and after she'd had her little cry she was all right. She got Minnie up—that's our oldest girl—and they started getting breakfast. It weren't daylight yet, but the east was beginning to get sorta rosy like and you could kinda smell the sun a-coming. I rousted out Henry and Johnnie—they're our oldest boys—and we started to the barn to feed the stock.

Well, I saw that sure enough we were in for something. The red in the east had spread until it covered quite a bit of the sky, and it didn't look like it usually does. It was as if somebody had hung a thin yellow veil over it. And I noticed that there was a bank of dark-looking clouds hanging low against the northwest sky line. And so I yelled for Martha to leave breakfast alone and come milk before it started raining, or something. I was purty sure by that time that it weren't going to be no ordinary rain, but I didn't want Martha to know it till she had to.

I've seen a lot of west Texas storms, and I've seen them break records coming up, but I ain't never seen one that could keep in smelling distance of that one that morning. Why, do you know, by the time Martha and Minnie could get to the cow pen and get one cow apiece milked that bank of clouds was halfway up the sky and going so fast you could see it a-moving. The sun was just peeping over the horizon and looking so red and awful, and the air was so still, and you could hear for miles. I made out ever' word Old Man Holland said to one of his little boys, who it 'peared had done something he shouldn't, and it was more'n two miles over to their place. The air had a sort of press-ing-down effect. You kinda had to put out an effort to get enough breath to keep you from gasping. And sweat! It just poured down my face.

Well, I went on back in the barn and began shucking some corn to shell so as I could take it to town the next day, Saturday, and get it ground into meal. Directly I heard Martha let out a squeal and I knew something was up. I hurried out and saw her standing in the middle of the cow lot looking about her in a wild sort of way. She kinda looks wild, anyway, when she first gets up, with her hair a-stringing down and her dress askew.

"It's going to come a cyclone!" she yells to me. And then she tells Minnie to come on, and away they goes to the house lickity split. She hollers and tells me to come on and let's go down the cellar.

I looked about and, by heck, I felt like making a run for the hole myself. The cloud had spread away over the barn, and on both the east and west there was a rolling, working mass of sand a-tearing along the prairie at a terrific rate. Above I could hear the wind rumbling and growling, and about a mile and a half away I saw bearing down on me a black, awful-looking mass. And there weren't a breath of air a-stirring where I was. And hot! Gosh, but the sweat was just naturally pouring off me!

Well, you can tell the world that I made fast time getting to the house. By the time I was there Martha had all the kids out in the yard. We went down the cellar, and I managed to pull the door too just as the first whiff of wind hit.

Well, we stayed down there for I guess as long as thirty minutes. By that time the hardest part of the wind, it seemed, had passed. Now, that doesn't mean that it weren't blowing yet. Gosh, no! It was still moaning and whistling, making the craziest sound in the cellar flue. I stayed down there till I judged that it was safe to come out, and I started to open up. Martha she kicked some, but I told her I wanted to see what the wind had done to everything. I raised the door a little, and the wind got a whip at it. Danged if it didn't tear it right out of my hands and bust it into a dozen pieces against the ground. Then there weren't nothing else to do but come out.

Martha she grabbed the kids and said she weren't coming out, but when she saw me standing up she judged it was safe, so she took a chance and came about halfway up the steps. There came a moment's lull about that time. Now, I don't mean that the wind quit blowing. Land, no! I just mean that it didn't blow so hard for a minute or so. Martha saw that I knew what I was talking about, so she hustled the kids out, and they got ready to make a run for the house.

Well, about that time along came a hard gust and caught Molly—that's our second girl—right in the middle and blew her sky-winding. It didn't hurt her none, and I saw it, so I laughed. Now, maybe that didn't make Martha mad. Gosh! She started after Molly, who couldn't seem to get her feet, and danged if Martha didn't get turned over. Then I seen that it was time for me to take a hand, so I did. I got 'em both on their feet, but Martha, she couldn't seem to stand. She said it'd hurt her back; that she guessed that I was satisfied now that I had probably killed her; that that's what I'd been trying to do for a long time.

Now Martha she knew better than that, but when she gets all wrought up she jest has to say something like that. Of course her back weren't broke. It was just her imagination. She's got anything beat for imagining things that I ever seen. But you can tell the world that she gave me Hail Columbia just the same.

Well, I finally got 'em all safely in the house, and then I begin to try to see what damage had been done to the other buildings. I expected to see every one of 'em laying slap on the ground. I couldn't see very well from the window, but I could tell that at least a part of the barn was standing. Then I looked for the chicken house, but it weren't nowhere to be seen. Right then and there I said to myself that I had to go out and see about it.

Martha she didn't want me to.

"That's it. Go out and get yourself killed and then

what'll become of us?" she says with the tears a-running
down her cheeks.

Just for fun I put in, kinda innocent like:

"Why, Martha, I didn't think I amounted to much
around here anyway, to hear you tell it."

Well, sir, I hadn't no more'n got that out of my mouth
than I was sorry as heck that I'd said it. She begin to cry
and take on something terrible. Said that I was just making that up; that it was me that didn't care anything for
her; that I'd go out and get my neck broke and leave the
poor little children to be orphans. To quiet her I told her
I wouldn't go. And then I begin peering out of the windows of every room that gave me a view of the lots and
chicken house; and I begin to wonder out loud what had
become of them chickens. D'rectly Martha she says:

"Looks like you'd go out and see about them instead of
setting around in here and letting 'em blow away."

Now, that's just like Martha. It hadn't been five minutes before that she was crying because I was thinking of
going out. Anyway, I went.

Them chickens was a sight to behold. When the wind
took their house and sent it flying from over their heads
they was sent rolling and tumbling every which way. Least,
I guess they were from the way they were scattered. Some
of 'em had caught against the garden fence—it was made
out of hog wire—but most of 'em had been blown out
across the field where they'd been able to get protection
behind some new listed furrows that I had plowed only a
few days before.

The cow shed was gone and the fence was down. The cows
had drifted up against the wire fence that separated the pas-
ture from the fields. There they stood, their heads down, all
hunched up like they used to do on cold winter days. But
now, instead of snow caked on their backs, it was sand. Every
once and a while an extra hard puff would send 'em forward
like it was going to make 'em get in the fence. That kinda
skeered me, so I went back to the house and got Johnnie to
come and help me put 'em in the horse lot. Martha
objected to him going out, but he didn't listen, just came
a-tearing. He was tickled to death to get out. It was a

kind of picnic for him. Least, he 'peared to take it that way. All the kids seemed to be having a rip-roaring good time out of the storm. But you can tell the world that I weren't.

Well, we tried to drive them cows in the lot. Every time we'd turn them against the wind they'd blink their eyes, shake their heads, go a few paces, and then turn around and start tearing back to the fence. About the third time we tried it one of 'em went too far and got in the wire just as I was afraid she would. We tried to get her out, and she pulled and sawed about, which made it all the worse. She got all tangled up and tore down the wire.

We tried to get old Boss out of the fence, but she was helpless. Poor old thing! I seen that she was a goner, so to put her out of her misery I sent Johnnie in the house to get the gun. I told him not to let his ma see him, but it was wasted breath. She spied him on the road out and follered him just a-boiling. Of course she didn't know what he'd come after the gun for, and it skeered her. Then she saw what'd happened. Of course she laid it on to me. Land, how she did carry on!

We shot Boss. Then I went down and found out that the horses were faring purty well, considering ever'thing. They were all covered in sand, but that weren't nothing. I fed 'em and killed as much time as I could, 'cause I wanted to stay away from the house as long as possible. I knew good and well that Martha'd pour it onto me hot and heavy when I came in.

But, do you know, when I got in she didn't say a word for a long time. She was a-setting in the sitting room rocking back and forth in a chair that we'd got from Chicago a couple of years before. She just set there and rocked and looked at me so funny I felt downright creepy. I'd a whole lot druther she'd 'a' give it to me hot and heavy. Fact is, I tried to start her. I says, kinda funny like:

"Well, it looks like the good Lord don't like us none a-tall. Don't look like He'd 'a' treated you this way, Martha."

I thought sure that'd make her boil over, but it didn't. She just kept rocking back and forth and looking at me in that strange sort of way. I noticed a couple of tears that were running down her cheeks. They made little clear streaks through the dust. Maybe you think I wasn't getting skeered.

"What's the matter, Martha?" I asks in an anxious voice. She didn't answer a-tall.

"Do you feel bad?"

Still no answer. She just kept right on a-rocking and a-rocking, and she kept right on looking at me in that crazy sort of way. Then she says in a awful voice:

"The Lord's judgment has fell upon us."

Gosh, but I felt creepy! It was so gloomy there in the room in spite of it being broad open daylight. You see, the sun was hid behind dust clouds and the windows didn't let in much light, they were so dirty. The sand was a-drizzling down from the ceiling and a-coming in through the cracks around the windows and doors; the wind was howling about the roof of the house; and there she set and just rocked and rocked, and every now and then she'd say:

"The Lord's judgment has fell upon us."

I tried to get her to go to bed, but she wouldn't make a move; I got up and traipsed around trying to stir up some noise so's I could drive away that creepy feeling that she gave me with her rocking and saying in such a awful voice that the Lord's judgment was upon us. But somehow it didn't do no good. I began to be afraid that she was going crazy, and the more I watched her the more I believed it. I had often thought that she'd do it some time when she'd get on one of her tears.

Every now and then she'd raise her hands up toward the ceiling and make the craziest motions and mutter something under her breath. And all the time she just kept a-rocking and a-rocking.

I tried several things to arouse her. The kids were beginning to notice it and to get scared and to cry. Leastwise, the youngest ones was. Finally I happened to think of a bright idea. If I'd pretend I'd suddenly got religion, thinks I to myself, maybe she'd get cheered up and get over her spell. I kinda hated to do it because I hated to be a hypocrite, but, thinks I, circumstances alter cases, so I decided to take a shot.

I went around where she could see me and got down on my knees and begin to pray. I asked her to help me; said I felt the spirit of the Lord descending upon me. Then I knew at once that I'd hit the nail right on the head. She let out a shout and fell on her knees by my side, and such praying I never heard before. It actually skeered me, she was so wild about it. She'd throw up her arms and cry out at the top of her voice for the Lord to send down His blessed healing power and wipe out all my sins. The little kids, they got skeered and begin to squall with all their might, and Johnnie, Minnie and Mollie were struck dumb at first; then they fell on their knees and begin to pray. That only added fuel to Martha's praying.

"Lord," she screamed above the roar of the storm, "Thou seest this man's children on their knees to you pleading that you wash away their papa's sins; you see his wife that has lived with him in all his wickedness all these years, kneeling and asking you to send your healing grace."

About that time she got all choked up, and I decided it was time for me to give up, so I suddenly got up and told her that I saw the light; that I was saved.

Well, I've seen some wild ones in my time, but never one as crazy as she was for the next ten minutes or so. She begin to shout and jump around; then she threw her arms around my neck and praised the Lord so loud in my ear she nearly busted my eardrum; she sang and she shouted hurrah, hosannah, bless His precious name, and other such things, until the house fairly rung with her voice above the shriek of the storm. And Minnie, who is kinda like her ma in being religious and excitable like, begin to shout and sing too. Maybe you think that between them and the storm and the kids a-squalling there weren't some racket being made. I felt kinda foolish.

The rest of the day Martha was so cheerful it made me ashamed of myself.

Thinks I: why, if I'd 'a' known that it'd make so much difference to her I'd 'a' confessed a long time ago. I'd 'a' been a hypocrite to give Martha that much pleasure because she ain't had any too much joy in this life, anyway.

Well, I joined the church, and I ain't never had the nerve to tell Martha what a hypocrite I've been. She's been much happier. Of course she gets on a spell now and then, but not near as often as she used to. She's feeling much better too. I guess, all and all, it's a good thing, a mighty good thing. Anyway, that's how I come to be such a church-goer. They elected me deacon not long ago, said I was the regularest attending member they had. I don't feel near so bad about being a hypocrite, any more. The fact is, I don't know for sure that I am one.

THE OLD LADY[1]

By EVELYN SCOTT

(From *The Dial*)

THE old lady was often to be seen walking on the beaches
overlooked by the hotels. She had been tall, but was
now stooped, and always advanced slowly, and with the
help of a cane. In spite of the expensive soberness of her
dress, of fine stuffs not quite in the fashion, yet much dis-
cussed by the maids in her hotel who expected generous
remuneration for their services to her, the old lady had not
that aloof confidence in herself and her position which is
the usual endowment of wealth. She smiled too frequently
into the faces of those who looked at her, and her excessive
benevolence was like a subtle self-apology.

Her thoughts could not be read, and that was fortunate.
When she awakened in the morning in a stately bed, from
which, against an opposite wall of her large room, she saw
an *armoire* flanked with mirrors give back her image, she
always, when possible, avoided the contemplation of this
reflection; or, compelled to confront a revelation which
caused her pain, remarked inwardly, "Can it be I?" and
tried vainly to recall another almost-obliterated impression
of her own features. Queer that, remembering so distinctly
the most minute incidents of a past that had been filled
with dramatic interest, able to visualize with exactitude
the appearances of each of her friends, today dead or separated from her by years and oceans, she had so much difficulty in piecing together from fragments retained from the
lost years, even the vaguest representation of her own countenance as it had been caught in looking-glasses long ago.
People who had been dear to her, and even the people she
had once disliked, had not aged, nor had they died, in that

they existed continually in her thoughts in every moment of the time. Only her own personality, in its once-youthful aspect, had disappeared in the nothingness of a feeble present. She sighed, and said to herself, "Well, I never was pretty." Yet without being pretty she had commanded affection and even very strong feeling.

It frightened her a little that she had become some one whom she did not know, some one whom she could not look at with clear eyes.

For all the sadness which pervaded her meditations, she did not, with truth, call herself unhappy. She slept badly, dreaming often of her married daughter whom she had not seen for many months, and of a dead son; but always, after noting the thinning of the darkness by a dawn yet scarcely visible and feeling, upon her dry cheeks and in her scanty hair, the still wind which rushed in a tide of freshness from the suddenly audible sea, she would turn upon her side, and, as if some sentinel duty of the night had been accomplished, find that she could rest easily. Then, from this hour into the morning, she would sleep like a child and awaken when the sun was shining rosily upon the gilt-flowered bedroom walls, while the lace curtains between the window hangings of brown-and-cream brocade seemed to expand as with an ecstatic delicacy, and, in the gilded foliage of the dark plane tree beyond them, birds sang.

Her maid, entering the chamber, and bringing the morning coffee in an immaculate service, received a cheery *"Bon jour,"* but, offering to assist the old lady at her toilet, was invariably sent away with a refusal couched in the same terms. "Not yet, Françoise. The time for that has not yet come." And the old lady dressed herself. She waited for something miraculous to occur. Every morning approached her with an adventure which, finally, in the heat of noontime, had not revealed itself.

She felt that Françoise was a "good girl," who should be treated generously, and the maid, stout, handsome, and slyly officious, with the characteristics of a peasant initiate in the ways of the rich, adopted in her manner toward her prosperous mistress, the attitude of a mother. The old lady was not deceived as to the motives which prompted this consideration, yet, in the passiveness of temperament engendered by old age, did not condemn. "Well, poor girl. I must try and do something for her. I'll leave her something in my will." And the old lady felt drawn to the girl by the very exposure of self-interest which, it seemed, should have been repelling. To know that some one depended on you, if only for money, made you feel that your presence in the world was yet of importance. Generous pity relieved the heart of the old lady from the oppression of exhausted but persistent emotions which had no outlet. There was no one to whom the old lady could express herself.

Yes, she was lonely, though had she been asked if, in this loneliness, she wished to depart to an oblivion in which loneliness is not felt, she would have said, "No," sincerely and emphatically. Trifles which had once been of no account to her, objects and incidents which, in her youth, had failed to interest her, now compelled her whole attention and were infinitely precious. She loved her careful walks through the French town. She loved the hardy appearance of the cabbages planted in small gardens behind low fences covered with creepers. A neglected bush of marigolds, jutting ruddy-coloured blossoms beyond a wall, excited in her a tenderness for growing things. She watched the dark swallows in their bat-flights above a puddle in the road, and their shrill bleats, coming vaguely to her deaf ears, made her think of them innocently as lambs. Strong sunlight, stagnant upon the plaster façade of a dwelling, enchanted her. When, with a final exertion of her ever-waning strength, she climbed slowly, among heaps of refuse, to the summit of a crooked street which terminated on a hillside, and could gaze below her, between ancient roofs which interceded in the view, at the countryside—the still avalanches of the mountains, the small villages crushed under the red roofs that surmounted the houses, the acres of vines, tremblingly outspread in the soaring light of morning and resembling still lakes of green silk—the immense silence which lay beyond the town in which she was visiting seemed to her to enwrap her benevolently, and the whole world, dissension and struggle obliterated, was a friendly place.

It was only at noontime, in the heat of the day, when, after taking her luncheon in the table d'hôte downstairs and, with nodding head, listening for half an hour to some Spanish singers who, on a terrace ornamented with palms and young trees in pots and covered over by a pergola on which roses twined, were entertaining the guests of the hotel, she rested in her bedroom, that she felt depressed. The sunshine filled the street below her window, but the stillness it made, as the heat arrested the play of children and hushed their voices, and footsteps became so occasional that they echoed on the cobbles as footsteps echo in the night—this stillness was terrible and oppressive.

She lowered the Venetian blinds upon her balconies, and, in a semi-glow, in which the unchanging aspect of objects in her room became pronounced, she lay on her bed again, her eyes closed, and tried to sleep. Sleep was impossible. Her cheeks, pale and withered and covered by a scarcely-perceptible down of white, were hot and parched. With no relief from the violence of the light, that, even through drawn curtains could be discerned in the stolid brilliance of a stucco building opposite the hotel, she moistened her lips, several times adjusted the pillow beneath her head, and, without being conscious of the sounds she uttered, moaned slightly.

Her health was bad. At any moment she might have a recurrence of the heart trouble from which she suffered, a malady from which she would, at last, most certainly die. But it was not of death that she thought. Indeed she refused to think of death. It pleased her better to imagine that she would live a long time—a long, long, long time. And when, in her promenades, her steps turned inadvertently toward the cemetery, with its crumbling mausoleums making little intimate avenues for the dead below the black-green lines of conical cypress trees, she experienced, in her first glimpse of the tombs, decorated as for a perpetual holiday with wreaths of colored beads, black, violet, pale-blue, and white, and with bouquets of artificial flowers, a sudden shock of fright, of amazement—of some emotion which she did not attempt to describe—and turned back.

Why was she traveling like this, going all over Europe, from one hotel to another, rarely encountering an acquaintance and certainly not amusing herself in the ways habitual with tourists? In her young days she had been too much occupied with personal affairs to give much of her energy to travel. There was a great deal of the world that she had never seen. Now that her daughter was married, absorbed by interests in which the old lady had but slight part, and her son was dead, she, the old lady, had uninterrupted opportunity to see odd corners of the globe that had always intrigued her—even the names of the towns she visited were those that had, years ago, seemed to her remarkable. Besides she had a terror, continual if not dwelt upon, of being unwanted, and so, rather than remain as a tolerated outsider in her daughter's home, she had preferred the company of strangers who were not obliged to show her any attentions that were not quite spontaneous.

On the terrace of the hotel, under the pergola covered with roses and with foliage which had turned blue and artificial in the glow of the electric lamps, the old lady sat in the evenings, watching those who came and went from the dancing in the saloon, while she tried to make herself unobtrusive. If a young couple, approaching her, ignored her, and it could be seen that they were covertly making love to one another, the old lady moved further away into the shadows and out of hearing. There she was able, when lifting her gaze, to discern the stars which, at one instant, appeared to her quite brilliant, while the next minute she saw only darkness, and could hear, distant under the rotating melody of a waltz played by an orchestra, a rushing sound in her ears which might be the sea and might only be the beating of her own heart. She always preferred to think the sound was the sea, and then she would rise and walk about, still clinging to the shadows and, because she was forgotten, feeling her own person as the person of another whom she also desired to forget.

No, the day was happier than the night. She loved children. In her black dress and bonnet, she often walked, with her stick, along the beaches. There she encountered

children. She recalled the delights of her own childhood
and longed to be able, in some manner, to indicate to the
children, in some way which would convince them, that she
had been a child, and that childhood was not foreign to
her, as they supposed. And she was humiliated by something grotesque in this longing, as if she had convicted herself of a jealousy of youth.

The children paid no heed to her, and, screaming as they
ran, they brushed past her blowing skirts, brushed past
her and ran down to the sea. Feeling a pain which was so
ignoble that she refused to recognize it, she thought, "They
are so young. They don't understand." And she prayed
to be able always to love children as she did now, and to
wish for them, with her whole being, saturate with gratitude
for a happy past, a continuance of their light-heartedness.

After such an experience, returning to the hotel, she
wrote letters, to keep herself from growing "stale," as she
smilingly called it, letters to her daughter, letters to old
acquaintances—some of them had almost ceased to take
account of her existence— and the reward for this insistent
attention to those who were far away, perhaps forever, was
an interest in the coming of the postman, so keen that it
embarrassed her. Often the mails brought her nothing at
all, or there came a letter from some old friend who, bur-
dened with age, expressed herself entirely in the utterance
of complaints. "Poor Jane, poor Sally, poor Louisa," the
old lady would say, and try to evade the fact that she had
anticipated a letter of a different kind, a letter containing
something stimulating, something of especial interest, or
something complimentary to herself. It seemed to her that
her own troubles would have been quite bearable if only
her dear old friends could find, as she did, the philosophical
compensations of maturity. Occasionally, in her travels,
she encountered a woman like herself, old, isolate, seeking,
in new sights and scenes, a substitute for the personal
drama which was finished. "Poor woman," the old lady
would say of the other old woman, then, suddenly, realizing
that the one she pitied was like herself, and alarmed by the
sense of an intolerable identity, she would conjure up cheerful thoughts and, from that time forward, gently avoid the

new acquaintance, and this without any intention of being cruel, but simply to preserve something necessary to her.

"We must all live our own lives. We old people have no right to prey upon our children," she often said. And it was this conviction which made her, secretly, a little afraid of her grandchildren of whom her daughter sent her photographs—the daughter who, with the dead son, had been for many years the one absorption of the old lady's life. When she meditated upon the joys of maternity and the intimate relations of a family, the old lady became confused. In some manner, in spite of her devotion, her attitude toward her children had been an error, but an error which she would never be able to localize within her or describe to herself accurately. She only felt that such error, or its equivalent, must be common to all the world, and, in apologizing so constantly for herself, she apologized for others, too, and found that any emotion which was not pity had become incomprehensible to her. The most frightening thing of all was that pity itself required a defence, and her very desire to confess for herself and admit for others inadequacy, without condemning it, was the basis of her real apartness from her former life. She wanted to state all this intelligibly, but she had never been able to do so. Her thoughts became lost again in the past, when her eyes filled with tears and the grief she had felt at her husband's death came back to her—not the grief she had experienced at the time, to which her health had succumbed while her reason was threatened, but another despair which was without any quality of protest and which she vainly attempted to unify with the emotions of twenty years before. She even tried to grieve more, but without success.

It was her present incapacity for strong passion which drove her, in her phantomlike existence, to dependence on routine, and the concrete regularity of meal hours had become as important to her as any critical event. In the vast dining saloon with its glass front overlooking the water, she was punctual at one o'clock and at half-past seven, and, though her appetite was variable, she was always one of the last to leave the table. What nice young people those two in the corner were, the ones who were newly married, and what an excellent mamma was the stout woman of thirty with the little daughter. The old lady usually had some pleasant remark for the waiter who, good-humored and polite, was ready to serve her immediately upon her entrance into the room, though he was somewhat perfunctory and reserved his most refined solicitude for persons who, not poorer than she was, were more difficult to please. She liked hot coffee that burned her withered lips, and Michael was careful to bring coffee steaming and perfumed, and she drank it on the terrace. Yet she bored him. There was nothing beyond her guessed-at fortune to supply material for scandals or invite interest.

She did not resent living alone, but she was often conscious of her lonely appearance and of what it might suggest to others. She wished, on that account, to exhibit an occupation. When she went to the writing room or sat on the beach, she carried a book with her, turned over the pages carefully, and appreciated, perhaps, a paragraph of what she read, but many of the lines she perused might have been inscribed in some strange language as remote as a language of the Orient. Refusing to confront this incapacity to receive, mentally, the new impression, the secret of the universe was, to her, as if buried inscrutably in her own soul, and to be divulged—if ever—in a reconstructed understanding of what had happened to her, an understanding which included even the most trivial incidents of former days. To have lived, loved, borne children, and grown old was to have known everything. Why could she find no words to make this meaning of intimate things intelligible to her fellow men? Because she could not speak and make herself heard, it was often as though, in living so fully, she had never lived. Her heart beat in a troubled way. Her hands, on the leaves of her book, trembled, and she resisted being sorry for herself. She tried to take comfort in a religion in which her faith was no longer orthodox, and ended, finally, with this great pity for the world which did not ask to be pitied and despised pity—pity which was— she sometimes doubtfully conjectured it—the reflection of her own weakness. Then the only recourse from these vague and half-comprehended thoughts was to consider a

change to a new scene, a journey which would tax her
strength, in which, in speaking to Françoise, the old lady
would ridicule weakness and make light of it. Or she would
rise from her deck-chair and walk in the sunshine along
the beach.

The blue waters, angry and violent in the wind that
flapped her skirts, suggested to her a darkness of night in
which green fields are visible. The poetry of the comparison pleased her, as the image appeared unpremeditatedly
from her mind, and was like a memory of youth. As she
watched that steady onward movement of waters upon the
land, she experienced what was to her, in this day, a rare
moment, a moment of positive happiness.

Beyond the pier, where she walked, leaning on her stick,
the sea surrounded the dripping rocks of a headland. The
rocks were bronze-colored and porous, like gutted and petrified combs of honey, left there by bees of a giant size.
Above them, in jagged curtains of white foam, in the glow
of the sun, the surf towered. For an instant the suspended
curtain hung twinkling in the light, to descend, with the
transcience of dew and the indolence of a floating veil, upon
the agitation of waves which had conveyed it. The surface
of glass which was the ocean, voluminous and rocking, like
the sun-inflamed canopy of a glass tent, washed up and
down magnificently, somnolently, as a cradle gently rocked,
and the enormous tents of water, built up one after another,
were covered all over with globules of sunshine, round and
crystal, trembling like the drops that fall hesitatingly from
metal which, made over-warm, has begun to cool again.

Once more the foam concentrated in seething currents,
rushing together with subterranean hisses. The foam concentrated, lifted, and made a glittering edifice of snow,
harsh, exquisite, and momentary, like the Gothic traceries
of frost. The tower of marble, of a lacy substance, of the
purity of linen left long to bleach, but with the adamant
glitter of diamonds, sank easily, waned in prismatic reflections, and was no more than a pale breath, breathed on the
distance of the intense sky and evaporating like mist. Little water-spouts, such as pour from the gargoyle-mouths of
old fountains, ran steadily downward from crevices in the

stones. The tide rattled among the boulders. The sea
had subsided, only to come forward as before, but with a
more implacable ease. A glass tube, transparent on the
length of the shore, showed, in a bottle-blue wall, ribbon-
tangles of reddish seaweed, designed in the clear substance
with the design of objects caught in amber. The swell, with
its mounting undulations, resolved in long blades of crystal,
run high in the air in a concave symmetry in which sank
massive and transparent shadows that were the reflections
of the waves themselves, carving the beaches.

The old lady's bonnet-strings whipped out under her
chin, her wide black dress was full like a banner and beat
her legs, yet, though she steadied herself against the onslaught of winds, felt salt vapors upon her face, and was
obliged to squint and lower her wrinkled lids against the
glare, she saw everything vividly. The foam, curdling the
sands, sticky amber and smooth as mirrors, was a flat scal-
lop, like a ruffle of soapsuds, and the scallops ran down
corruscations and runnels that were the imprints of wavy
hair, faintly golden. A cold smell of rotted fish and kelp
came to the old lady on the same breeze that wafted to
her the screams of the children, of the little boys in their
striped bathing costumes who were wading in the shallows.
And little girls in white, little girls, barefoot, with sand-
buckets and shovels, their short skirts tilted behind their
flying legs, were heard shrieking happily as they swooped,
like a flock of small gulls, straight down to the water's
edge. More obscurely, as from a more vast distance, the
old lady heard the voices of the grown-up bathers, who,
swimming far out into the breakers, were carried, with
heads bobbing, to an immense height, lifted, by the indifferent sapphire waters, as upon the flashing shoulders of
armored giants.

Then she turned toward the sultry horizon, where the
brilliance of the day succumbed to the overshadowing of
clouds, and to something less visible—perhaps an emana-
tion from the light itself—which was like unseen smoke.
Beyond the cobalt welter of sun and waves, incessantly
flaked as with white flowers, a boat balanced quietly under

one sail, stood, upon the emptiness, like a swan upon a still lake, its head under its wing.

The old lady was fatigued by this unforeseen intensity of visual appreciation. She had come to the end of the pier, and, turning reluctantly, began to retrace her footsteps to the hotel. On the shore she noted the rosy and dusked loftiness of the retreating mountains, their peaks somber under the fogs of a summer rainstorm, while on the rusted slopes the deep green of the trees suggested a relief of velvet on an old brocade, the crushed foliage of the pines and cork oaks hinting at the tactile qualities of variegated mosses. The fashionable hotels along the waterfront, built in stucco and somewhat in the Spanish style, ancient houses in the town with walls of plaster or rubble, all showed in a violent radiance of sinking sun in which the pallor of white surfaces and the redness of far-off roofs received a remote emphasis on objects which seemed the minute dwellings of dolls.

And the old lady was suddenly overcome by an emotion which she afterwards preferred to forget. What she felt, as she turned from her promenade, the sea-wind stinging her flaccid cheeks, was an immanence of death, which came to her from nowhere out of nothing—from the cries of the children, from the boat, the breeze, from the vast water that flowed after her. Yes, most of all from the sea, the sea flashing in the sunshine, the great sea, monotonous, voracious, untouched, and merciless. "I shall die," she thought, "but *they* will die, too." In "they" she included the people in the village, the bathers in the surf, and the ladies in their organdie frocks and flowered hats, with the gentlemen in flannels, gentlemen dressed so precisely, if carelessly, in imitations of the English style—the old lady, as she approached the termination of her walk, could now see them all. And the quiet gale that swept past her from some space infinitely distant, beyond even the clouds of the coming rainstorm, was the breath of a holocaust. *"They"* were all dead, all the people who covered the security of the land, people the old lady loved and had loved, indeed people who were dead already. That the sea was, had been, and always would be—long, long after these, the young, the happy, the oblivious, had ceased to live—this sea, of which she herself was afraid, so that she had never undertaken an ocean voyage without a tremor, the sea comforted her with an immense and terrible comfort, so that, for an instant, her spirit flamed coldly and intensely. All was light, sunshine, happiness, and moving waters, and all was death, forever and ever death—though she scarcely called it so exactly, or by that name.

Then her eyes grew dim. The peculiar accuracy with which, the moment before, she had viewed and absorbed the details of her surroundings, faded in her habitual hesitance and vagueness. She began to think of saving her strength, of getting back to the hotel in time for her tea when she would eat some nice little *brioches*, of buying Françoise a new dress. Entering the hotel lobby at just quarter to five o'clock, weak and at peace as after some exhausting victory, she gave to her heart the shadowy acknowledgment of its new strength, and, in spite of her cheerful resolutions, was conscious of a faint, austere bitterness.

OLD MAN LEDGE[1]

By MAY STANLEY

(From *The Pictorial Review*)

BEYOND Bald Head a long white curve of beach held the old house in an encircling arm. There were no other buildings in sight. A thick growth of stunted spruces ran down to a meadow covered with coarse beach-grass, and the house stood on a small rise of ground at the edge of the meadow, commanding an unbroken view seaward. On one side the foundation had rotted away, so that the gray, weather-beaten dwelling leaned slightly as though striving to catch the faint murmur of the tides.

Out at sea the waters glowed vividly, reflecting the brilliant colors of sunset in wavering bars of rose and mauve and gold. The surface of the bay heaved gently, thrusting long rollers beneath the fishing boat as it swung in a wide curve around Bald Head.

"Thar she is!" Orin Pettishall twitched the tiller-ropes as he spoke. The boat swung obediently toward an old dock which made a gray blot against the background of white sand.

The girl nodded. "Bigger'n I thought 'twuz," she said happily. "I wuz over here onct cranberryin' when I wuz leetle, but it's bigger'n I thought 'twuz then."

"Yeah, it's a good house," he agreed, "even ef 'tis kind uv old. Still an' all, 'tain't old when ye think they's oak beams in it. Paw says Captain Beath got some uv the beams fer his house outer his vessel—arter she wuz wrecked on Old Man Ledge out thar."

"Wonder how long ago 'tis?" Emily Whidden glanced seaward. Half-tide revealed the jagged rocks of Old Man Ledge standing up sharply above the water.

"Dunno. 'Fore paw's time, fer 'twuz grampy told him."
He swung the boat deftly in beside the dock and made it
fast. "Looks like the house's kinder settlin' ter the one
side. Hev ter straighten her up fust uv all. Come on! I
got ter see how much fixin' the dock'll need."

With Emily beside him he went proudly across the dock,
keeping a sharp lookout for loose or rotting boards. Reaching shore, they paused involuntarily and stood, hand in
hand, looking up at the old house.

"Nicer'n I thought 'twuz goin' ter be," the girl murmured.

"Guess she's goin' ter be wuth what I'm payin' fer her."
He tried to speak calmly. "Seven hundred dollars ain't
sich a lot when ye think 'at they's twenty acres goes with
it—all this here shore-front an' back inter the woods a
piece. Paid the real estate fellers two hundred dollars
cash money, an' I got three years ter find the rest in."

Emily nodded. She had heard the story from Orin a
half-dozen times today, but it did not lose interest with
repetition.

"We kin do 'at easy," she said. "I kin hev chickens an'
put in a garden. 'Twon't cost us much ter live."

"An' they ain't no reason ter put off gittin' married," he
declared. "We kin git married soon ez I git the house fixed
up a mite an' a fish-house built."

"Guess we kin," she assented shyly.

They went quickly up the slope, along a path overgrown
with weeds and blackberry brambles. Emily cried out with
pleasure at sight of a great hedge of yellow lilies which
lifted their slender stalks defiantly above the encroaching
weeds. At the front of the house a bricked walk led up to
a hooded doorway. High-backed seats had once stood on
either side. One of them was still in good repair, but the
other sagged forlornly on its broken supports.

" 'Nough fixin' ter keep me busy fer a while, I guess,"
Orin commented as he unlocked the front door. It swung
open with painful creakings, showing a square hall with
doors on either side. "S'pose this must 'a' been the parlor."
He led the way into a fair-sized room with windows looking
directly toward sea. Now they were so dark with dust and

spider-webs that little light came through. Opposite the
door a stone fireplace yawned.

"It'll be nice here when we git it fixed up." Emily looked
about the room curiously. "Le's see the rest uv it."

They passed through the door at the back which led into
a small bedroom, returned to the hall, and inspected in turn
the dining room, kitchen, and woodshed on the opposite side
of the house.

"Le's go down in the yard an' see what the well's like,"
Emily proposed.

"I'd oughter go down cellar an' hev a look at the foundation," he objected. "Ef I wait any longer it'll be too
dark ter see anythin'. You go an' hev a look at the well
while I'm down cellar."

"A' right. I won't be long."

She ran down the steps, paused for a moment while her
eyes searched for a path, found it, and ran lightly along,
pushing aside weeds and brambles. Near a clump of
spruces she saw the well-sweep and was going toward it
when her glance was caught by something at the left of the
house—something which showed gray in the surrounding
greenness.

"Wonder what's thar?" Making her way through the
intervening growth, she cautiously lifted a matted bramble,
then dropped it with a startled exclamation and began to
run back toward the house.

"Orin!" she called. "Orin!"

Orin came out on the back porch, his face reflecting the
satisfaction he felt.

" 'Tain't goin' ter be much work ter fix up the foundation. Not near so much——" He paused at sight of her
white face. "What's come ter ye?"

"Thar's a grave out thar!" Her voice was trembling.
"Somebody's grave! I see it when I wuz goin' down ter the
well."

"Guess ye must be mistook," he said wonderingly.
"Never heared tell uv nobody bein' buried here."

"I see the gravestun ez I wuz goin' down ter the well,"
she explained breathlessly. "It's kind uv layin' down. Ye
kain't hardly see it 'ceptin' it ketches the light. Come an'

see fer yerself." She led him down the path, unmindful of the brambles which caught and tore at her skirt. "Thar 'tis!"

Orin Pettishall stared at it thoughtfully, then stooped and tried to read the words cut in the moldy stone.

"Too dark," he said at length. "Torch's down in the boa-at. I'll go git it."

"Let me go fer it—I'd ruther."

"What's the matter?" He glanced up, conscious of the fear in her voice. "Ain't scart uv an ol' gravestun, air ye?"

"N-o. Only I'd ruther go." She hurried off.

Left to himself, the boy sat down beside the grave and gazed proudly up at the house. His house! Pretty nice to be able to buy it and move into his own home this fall, when he and Emily were married. Pretty nice! If lobster prices stayed up he'd maybe be able to pay something more on it before Christmas. He was whistling jubilantly when Emily, hurrying back, thrust the torch into his hands.

"Read what it says!" she directed.

Holding the light close to the moldy stone, he read slowly: " 'Sacred—to the m—Nehemiah Hill—departed'— they's a big chip out uv the stone here—'May thirtieth, eighteen hundred an' fifty-two—Greater love hath no man than this'—I kain't read no more; it's chipped off some."

" 'That a man lay down his life for his friends.' " The girl finished the quotation in a hushed voice.

"Wonder who he wuz—Nehemiah Hill? I ain't never heared tell uv no Hills 'round here."

"Dunno." She rose, shivering. "Le's go back, Orin. It's gittin' late."

"I wanted ye ter see the cellar afore we go."

" 'At'll keep," she said hastily, and turned to the path which led down to the dock.

When he had started his engine and the fishing boat was chug-chugging its way back to West Harbor, Pettishall turned to the girl.

"What come ter ye, Em'ly?" he asked. "Ye ain't said a word sense we started. 'At grave didn't upset ye none, did it?"

"Yes—kind uv."

"It don't do no hurt, fur ez I kin see." Disappointment made his voice cold. "Thought ye liked the place."

"So I do, only——"

"Only what?"

She turned to face him. "Dunno ez I c'd live whar they's a grave," she said slowly. "It's a nice place an' all, only I dunno ez I c'd live whar they's a grave."

"Dunno what makes ye feel like 'at. An' anyways we got ter live thar. I bought the place, ain't I?"

"Yes."

"Wa-al, we got ter live thar, ain't we?"

She was silent.

"We got ter live thar, ain't we? Seein' I bought it, we got ter live thar." Frustration, injured pride, bewilderment, were in the words.

"Dunno ez we hev," she retorted. "Leastways, dunno ez *I* hev. They ain't nothin' ter *make* me!"

He did not reply, but stared straight in front of him, head up and lips set in a stubborn line. She could talk like that! That was all she thought of their home, the home he was planning to get ready for her! Well, if that was the way she felt about things——

"Orin!" Her voice was timid.

"Yes."

"I ain't meanin' ter be cross ner spiteful. It's only——"

"Only ye don't like the place I bought fer us. Wa-al, guess they ain't nothin' more ter be said."

"A' right," she replied coldly, "ef 'at's the way ye feel. I ain't goin' ter stay by myself, day in an' day out, 'ith a grave ter keep me comp'ny. I'd like the place fine ef the grave wa'n't thar. Even ef we knowed who 'twuz——"

"I kain't he'p it, way things air," he interrupted. "I didn't know 'bout the grave when I bought the place, but it wouldn't uv made no diff'rence ter me ef I hed knowed. Way I see it we got ter live thar, grave er no grave."

She shook her head sorrowfully. "No, I ain't goin' ter live thar. I knowed I wouldn't soon ez ever I see the grave. I jes' kain't an' they ain't no use in talkin' uv it!"

"Wa-al," Mrs. Whidden said cheerfully, "what ye think uv the place Orin bought?"

Her daughter, heavy-eyed from a sleepless night, looked up and said drearily, "A' right, I guess."

"Mercy me! Is 'at all ye think uv it?"

"Did ye know somebody wuz buried thar?" Emily demanded. "Right beside the house?"

"Mercy me!" Mrs. Widden exclaimed again. "I been cranberryin' in the medder a coupla times sense the ol' captain died, but I never seed no grave. Whose is it?"

"Dunno. Name on it's Nehemiah Hill. D'ye know who 'at is?"

"Never heard tell uv no Hills in these here parts," Mrs. Widden shook her head solemnly. "They's Hills over Lewiston way an' they's a fambily—say, Paw," as the door opened to admit Jeremy Widden's bulk, "did ye know somebody wuz buried over ter the ol' Beath place?"

"Never heard tell uv it." Widden clumped across to the sink and drank hugely from a tin dipper. "Here's Hannah Anne Pettishall comin'. Mebbe she'll know."

" 'Lo, ev'ybody!" Mrs. Pettishall panted genially. She was a huge woman whose bulk almost filled the doorway and quite overflowed the rocking-chair which Mrs. Whidden pushed forward. "I'm all outer crochet-cotton," she explained, "an' I thought I'd run over an' borrer a mite ter last till I kin git some f'om Po'tland."

"Yeah, I got some," Mrs. Widden replied, "same number ez what ye're usin'. D'ye know 'bout thar bein' a grave on the place Orin jes' bought?"

"Never heard tell uv one. Mebbe 'at's what made Orin so grumpy—wouldn't say a decent word breakfus'-time." She wiped her face meditatively with a corner of her apron. "My, it's hot fer this time uv year! Ef ye hurry up an' git married, Em'ly Widden, ye'll still hev summer fer yer weddin'."

"I ain't goin' ter git married," Emily said dully.

"Ye ain't *what?*" her elders demanded in chorus.

"Me an' Orin hed words las' night," Emily replied in a dull voice, " 'bout 'at grave. An'—an'—we hed words."

"D'ye mean ter say you an' Orin fit?" Mrs. Pettishall demanded. "Wisht ye'd hurry an' make up ef ye did, so's he won't be so grumpy."

"I tol' him I wouldn't live no place whar they's a grave 'longside uv the house."

"Fer any sakes!" Mrs. Pettishall stared at her prospective daughter-in-law in frank amazement. "Ye don't mean ter say 'at jes' 'cause they happens ter be a grave——"

"Wa'al, ef' 'at's the way Em'ly feels I guess she's got a right," Mrs. Widden broke in.

"Now, Maw!" Widden counseled. "Stay out uv it an' let the young folks fight things out fer tharselves."

But his wife was not to be so easily silenced. "Tell yer maw 'bout it, Em'ly," she commanded soothingly. "Tell yer maw what the trouble is. Ye didn't want ter live thar 'count uv the grave? Wuz 'at it?"

Emily nodded.

"Wa-al, I mus' say——" Mrs. Pettishall began heavily.

"Orin said we'd hev ter live thar," Emily explained. "An' I said I didn't hev ter. An' he said——" She dissolved into tears.

"Wa-al, he didn't hev no right ter say it!" Mrs. Widden stormed. "Guess my girl ain't goin' ter set up housekeepin' in no graveyard!"

"Orin didn't aim ter live in no graveyard," Mrs. Pettishall returned sharply. "I mus' say, Lucindy——"

"An' he kin jes' stay 'way f'om Em'ly!" Mrs. Widden threw down the wooden needle with which she had been knitting trap-heads, crossed the kitchen, and took her disconsolate daughter into her arms. "Thar! Ye don't need ter take on! Ye don't hev ter do nothin' ye don't want ter!"

Mrs. Pettishall got to her feet.

"Ef ye'd leave the young 'uns 'lone, Lucindy, an' mind yer own business," she said angrily, "they'd mebbe git things patched up! Stan's ter reason they won't so long ez ye keep interferin'!"

"Who's interferin'?" Mrs. Widden demanded belligerently.

"You, fer one! I mus' say I think Orin's patient to put up 'ith Em'ly actin' like she's doin'——"

"Thar now, Maw! Ca'm yerself!" Widden interposed.

"An' ef I wuz in his place I wouldn't stand fer it!" Mrs.

Pettishall continued bitterly. "They's other girls——"

"Now, now, Hannah Anne!"

"Ez fer you, Jeremy Widden," Mrs. Pettishall turned to him, the slowly kindling wrath of a fat woman in her voice, "ef ye wuzn't so petticoat-ruled an' put upon in yer own house ye'd do better——"

But here Mrs. Widden found voice. "Ef ye'll jes' go out uv my house, Hannah Anne," she said majestically, "an' stay out it's all I ask. I don't want you ner none uv your fambily ter darken my doors ag'in!"

"Now, Maw——" but the sound of the kitchen door slamming to behind Mrs. Pettishall drowned Widden's vain attempts to make peace.

Before nightfall every one in West Harbor knew that Lucinda Widden had put Hannah Anne Pettishall out of her house because Hannah Anne didn't want Orin to marry Emily Widden, that some one of whom no one had ever heard was buried over on the old Beath place, and that the real estate people had given Orin Pettishall a hundred dollars to take the place off their hands. Additional zest was given to these rumors when, in the store that afternoon, the elder Pettishall told Jeremy Widden that he'd just as soon have back the trawl which Widden had borrowed, and Widden had retorted that any time Pettishall wanted to pay for having the new engine put in his boat he'd better do it.

West Harbor gasped! Nothing so exciting had happened since the time Hepsibah Gutch and Lefey Williams quarreled one day at dinner and threw hot soup at each other. This was even worse than Hepsibah and Lefey!

Fred Hosmer said that in his opinion "growed-up folks hed oughter hev more sense'n ter fight like kids."

Will Ellery retorted that "it's all in the way a feller looks at things. Some folks ain't got 'nough spunk ter start a fight."

On which Fred Hosmer promptly invited Ellery out into the back yard if he had any doubts about there being enough spunk around to lick any Ellery that ever walked!

Some one intervened and a truce was patched up. Thereupon Mrs. Will Ellery, indignant at the insinuation directed against her husband, instituted a campaign against Mrs. Fred Hosmer, whose dearest wish it was to be elected president of the church sewing-circle. She was defeated by three votes and indignantly resigned, taking with her six devoted friends who were among the best workers and who had always cooked lavishly for box socials and baked-bean suppers.

Mrs. Uriah Goomes was heard to say that no one but a fool would think of marrying Orin Pettishall, anyway. He was too smart and always trying to get ahead of other folks. It was time he stubbed his toe. Which remark, duly repeated, immediately dissolved friendly relations between the Goomes and Pettishall families and led Mrs. Widden to remark caustically that maybe Emily wasn't such a fool as some people seemed to think and, anyway, she wouldn't ever be fool enough to marry any one as lazy as Uriah Goomes, who, with his family, would have starved last winter if every one in the Harbor hadn't turned to and fed them!

Alva Ryder, the storekeeper, told some one that in his opinion the whole trouble started with the Widdens and Pettishalls and ought to have stayed there. Folks were foolish, he said, to mix up in other folks' rows. Every one on hearing this said that it was no wonder Alva Ryder thought West Harbor folks foolish. The way they'd dealt with him, year in and year out, paying the awful prices he charged for everything, would make any one think they were weak in the head! Hereafter they would buy groceries in Bath or Portland or else do without.

Meetings at the schoolhouse had to be discontinued. No one but old Uncle Henry Breedon, who was too deaf to hear anything, would go to meeting after the Sunday when the Reverend Amos Putney preached from the text, "Blessed are the peacemakers," and referred pointedly to local difficulties. Every one felt that Brother Putney might say what he liked about people who danced or played cards or smoked—that was his business. But any disagreement we might have with the Goomeses or the Pettishalls or the Widdens was our own business and why did he want to interfere? Besides, hadn't the Widdens and the Pettishalls and the Goomeses been the first to start trouble? Well, then, what could you expect?

Time failed to heal the dissensions, which, indeed, grew in number and bitterness as the weeks went by. Two of West Harbor's most respected citizens charged two others, equally respected, with stealing lobsters from the former's traps. The fish warden was pressed into service and spent several long, chilly, and fruitless nights in watching for the supposed offenders. He did not catch any one, but the sight of a mysterious figure "pokin' 'round" on Jim Mears's dock so upset Mrs. Mears that she took to her bed and remained there until Jimmy, junior, was born. Thereafter she laid blame for the undeniable fact that Jimmy wasn't very bright to the scare which Warden Jim had given her, and talked darkly of suing the State and getting even with somebody.

With the Sunday meetings discontinued and the sewing-circle disrupted West Harbor women no longer convened save in groups of two or three. Friendly borrowing of a cup of sugar or the "lend uv 'nough flour ter make a mess uv biscuits" had ceased. Crochet- and dress-patterns were no longer exchanged.

When the Fred Hosmers drove to Bath in their car they did not, as in former days, stop to ask folks if they wanted anything from town, but drove straight ahead. Fishermen no longer gathered in Alva Ryder's store in the evenings to exchange news of the Portland market or to "swap yarns." The chair dedicated to the fisherman who could tell the best story was empty evening after evening. Down at the fish-houses or out in the boats solitary figures worked sullenly, refraining from looking up or giving a friendly hail when another boat passed.

Such was the state of things when Grammy Tagel— grandmother to the Ellerys and the Tagels and great-aunt of Hannah Anne Pettishall—came over from Augusta for a visit.

At first Emily Widden had refused to admit even to herself that her quarrel with Orin was serious. He would come over to see her, she was quite sure, and they would talk things over. Then Orin would sell the old Beath place and

buy somewhere else. She *couldn't* live beside a grave.
Nobody could! But Orin would see how things were, once
they had a good talk.

But Orin did not come. The days became weeks, and
still, to Emily's dismay and hurt surprise, he made no sign.
She couldn't believe he meant to stay away. Surely he
was just mad at the fuss every one was making and the
things she herself had said. But he would get over it soon.
Then he would come to see her and they would talk things
over. From her father Emily learned that Orin had begun
to "fix up" the old house in his spare time. Mereen Tagel
had gone over to help him repair the foundation and build
a fish-house.

The girl's spirits sank at the news. She was forced to
admit to herself that Orin had no intention of selling. And
that meant he didn't really care for her or how she felt about
things. He had never cared! Perhaps—the awful thought
smote her like a blow—Orin must be going to marry some
one else. He wouldn't be fixing up the house unless he
planned to live there soon. The girl ceased to watch for his
coming. At night she cried into her pillow quietly and
unobtrusively as she did everything else. She refused to
say anything when her mother railed angrily at the Petti-
shals, and only her pale, miserable face and red-rimmed
eyes told Mrs. Widden her daughter was not forgetting
Orin Pettishall—that she would never forget him.

And Orin was no happier. A hundred times he planned
to see Emily, to talk with her. Then he would remember
that Emily did not really care for him, that she had turned
her back on the home he had bought for her, refusing to
live there. What was the use of going to see her when she
didn't think enough of him to give up that silly feeling
about a grave? Some time she would be sorry for acting
like she did!

He would fix up the old place and live there alone, the
way Captain Beath had done. Perhaps he would die there,
alone. Emily would come to the funeral. Maybe she would
cry when she saw what she had done—sent him away to
die. Or, perhaps, she wouldn't care enough to come to the
funeral. She would marry some one else, and when she

heard the news she would say, "He was always queer. Went away to live alone with nothing to keep him company but a grave. No wonder he died!" Orin resolved bitterly to live. What was the use of dying when nobody would care what happened to you?

The only comfort he found was in hard work. He rose before dawn, hauled trawl, carried his fish to market, then came back to work on the old house until approaching twilight warned him it was time to bait trawl for the next day's set.

All through the quiet afternoons of late August he worked about the place, completing his fish-house, cutting away weeds and brambles from paths long unused, resetting bricks in the walk, repairing the broken settle. Sometimes he pictured Emily sitting here in the long summer evenings, busy with her sewing. He would be down at the fish-house baiting trawl. Emily would come out after the supper dishes were washed and wait here for him. When all the tubs of trawl were finished he would come up to sit in the other high-backed seat. They would talk or, perhaps, just sit listening to the tides along the beach.

He shook his head angrily, winking back unmanly tears. Emily would never sit there in the quiet evenings. One seat would always be empty. When his work was done he would come up to the house. There would be no one to welcome him. He would sit there, watching the empty place—an old, old man—alone.

West Harbor folks looked on Grammy Tagel as a "character." Perhaps, in days not so far gone, she would have been known as a soothsayer, and people would have consulted her when grave decisions were to be made and followed her shrewd advice. But now she was just an old woman with a philosophy wrought out of long, hard years, an old woman who didn't hesitate to tell folks what she thought of their words and actions, and who took an unbounded interest in the affairs of those about her.

Although more than ten years had passed since Grammy Tagel moved to Augusta to make her home with a married granddaughter she still kept in touch with all the principal events of the Harbor. She knew about all births, marriages, and deaths. She could tell you who had moved away in recent years and who had "built new"; had accurate information regarding those who had "perfessed" religion at the annual revival meetings and those who were still unsaved.

Today, with her chair drawn comfortably close to the stove, the old woman turned inquiring eyes on Hannah Anne Pettishall.

"What's wrong 'ith Orin?" she asked. "Looks kinder meachin' ter me."

"Yeah, he's meachin', a' right," Mrs. Pettishall agreed. She carried a pan of cookies to the oven, put them in, dusted the flour from her hands, and wiped her face thoughtfully with a corner of her blue-and-white-checked gingham apron.

Grammy Tagel waited patiently.

"I hate ter say it," Hannah Anne went back to the table and began to roll out another mound of cooky dough, "but it looks ter me like he's still takin' on 'count uv Em'ly Widden."

"Which Widden?"

"Em'ly—Lucindy Means's girl. Ye mind 'at Lucindy married Jeremy Widden, Uncle Uriah's first. The other boy, Lige, went ter Po'tland, an' folks say he's doin' well workin' in a garage. Makin' money hand over fist, Uncle Uriah says. I dunno."

"Don't seem like Orin's old 'nough ter be keepin' comp'ny." Grammy Tagel deftly brought the conversation back. "Wuzn't nothin' but a leetle squirt when I went off ter Augusty. Wuz they keepin' comp'ny, did ye say?"

Mrs. Pettishall nodded. "Yeah, fer more'n a year. Right up ter the time Orin bought the ol' Beath place——"

"Did he, now? Ye hedn't told me afore. He's a smart boy ter buy it. Reel sightly place."

" 'At's what I say—mercy! I fergot the cookies!" Snatching the pan from the oven, she tested its contents anxiously, found them unharmed, and transferred the cookies to a plate. "Hev one, Aunt 'Miry?"

"Don't mind ef I do. An' 'n what happened?"

"Wa-al, right arter he bought the place Em'ly found a grave thar—leastways she *says* she did—an' started actin' up. Lucindy, who'd oughter hed more sense, ups an' sides 'ith Em'ly. Says 'at no girl uv hern is goin' ter set up housekeepin' in a graveyard. The very idear! I'm a good-tempered woman, ez ev'ybody knows, but I don't stand fer bein' put upon, an' I give the hull Widden fambily a piece uv my mind."

"An' 'n what happened?"

"Folks 'at hed any sense tuck my side an' some tuck 'tother. Stirred up considerable to-do, ez ye might say."

"Sh'dn't wonder," Grammy Tagel commented dryly. "What'd Orin an' his girl do?"

"They ain't spoke sense—not 'at I know uv. An' ef Orin hez any right pride 'bout him——"

"Guess he's got pride 'nough. I've allus noticed 'at young folks hez too much pride 'bout things 'at matter." The old woman got stiffly to her feet. "Guess I'll go 'long over an' set 'ith Jerushy Spinney fer a spell. Still in bed, ain't she?"

"Yes, an' likely ter stay thar. Doctor said 'smornin' 'twuz the wust stroke he'd ever see anybody hev."

"Sh'dn't wonder. Allus hed considerable temper, Jerushy hed, an' temper brings its own reward. You comin' 'long?"

"No, don't guess I kin. Got a mess uv biscuits ter make when I git these here cookies done an' a couple uv pies."

"Wa-al, I won't be long."

Gathering an ample gray shawl about her shoulders and grasping her stick, Grammy Tagel went down the steps and along the path to the Spinney house. But she did not spend many minutes there. On learning that Mrs. Spinney was asleep she declined an invitation to come in and sit for a while, and turned to hobble along the road.

"Mercy me!" Mrs. Widden exclaimed, "ef 'at ain't Grammy Tagel comin' ter see us!" She hastened to the door. "Come right in, Grammy! I wuz kinder wonderin' ef ye'd drop in ter see us er ef ye wouldn't—things bein' like they air." She ushered her visitor into the kitchen.

"When ye git ter be my age, Lucindy," Grammy Tagel replied, "ye won't pay much 'tention ter folks' foolishness"; then, as Emily put down her crocheting and came forward to place a chair for the old woman, "Ye don't say this is Em'ly! My, ain't she growed up!"

"Sure is," Mrs. Widden rejoined. "Kain't make myself b'lieve it sometimes."

Grandmother Tagel regarded the girl searchingly, nodded as though some question in her mind had been answered satisfactorily, and said, "I stopped in ter see Jerushy Spinney on my way over. They been wonderin' ef they'd oughter move her downstairs, but I tol' 'em ter wait till they'd talked 'ith you. I said ef anybody'd know whether they'd oughter move her it'd be Lucindy Widden."

"S'pose I best go over some time today," Mrs. Widden mused.

"Yes, ef I wuz in yer place I'd go right now an' see how things air. I'll jes' set here an' talk whilst ye're gone."

"Wa-al, I won't be long."

When Mrs. Widden's apron-clad form had disappeared up the road Grandmother Tagel beckoned to Emily.

"Come here an' set down by me," she said. "I got somethin' ter tell ye 'at mebbe ye'll be glad ter hear."

The sunshine of early afternoon had disappeared, swallowed up in threatening, black clouds which trailed sooty vapors faster and faster across the sky. Fitful gusts of wind had begun to lash the tops of the long rollers into foam. Waves climbed higher and higher, vainly seeking to escape the fury of the wind. Like a toy in the hands of an angry child the fishing-boat was tossed and shaken violently to and fro. It slipped sideways in the trough of a wave, started sluggishly to climb, stopped half-way, and buried its nose in the water, which swept over the canvas covering the bow and flew backward in sheets of spray.

The girl, who had until now been working frantically over the engine, started up, grasped the tiller-ropes, and coaxed the bow up into the wind. With no power to keep it going the little craft dropped off again and swung about. The next wave caught it a violent blow and poured water over the canvas until the floor of the boat was awash.

"Ef I c'd only make this en-jine go!" Sweat stood out on the girl's face in spite of the bitter chill which had crept

into the air. Lifting an arm impatiently, she swept the
damp hair back from her forehead and once more bent over
the lifeless engine.

It had seemed such an easy thing to do a half-hour back.
She had left Grammy Tagel sitting by the fire and hurried
down to the dock, the old woman's words ringing in her
ears: "They's only one time ter put trouble straight an' 'at's
right away."

She hadn't even noticed that a storm was gathering. Her
father's boat was not at the mooring. That meant he had
gone to Portland. He wouldn't be back before five or six
o'clock, and she couldn't ask any one to take her—not with
the whole Harbor knowing about her quarrel with Orin.
It had seemed such a simple thing to just take Will Ellery's
boat for an hour. He wouldn't be using it again until
tomorrow morning and the engine was the same as her
father's. Who would think that it would stop when she
was out here opposite the Head?

A huge, wind-driven mountain of water towered suddenly
above the helpless boat, crashed down, just missing the bow
and blotting out the world in a welter of foam. A white
squall! She *must* make land somehow. The boat wouldn't
ride out a squall with the engine crippled.

She couldn't even hope for the chance of a tow. The
weather-wise fishermen had seen the storm coming and were
all safe in harbor. If only the engine would start she could
still make the shelter beyond Bald Head although wind
and tide were sweeping her each moment farther and
farther out to sea.

Against the frail shelter of canvas the wind was now
beating with long moans that ended in furious shrieks. All
around the drifting boat the waves rose, horrible monsters
with the foam of madness on their lips. They struck
against the boat with blows that made the frail thing
tremble like a creature in the last agony of fear. It plunged,
rose, and plunged again, vainly striving to shake off its
tormentors. Long, jagged streaks of lightning played across
the sky and were reflected fearfully in the black, tossing
water, but no rain fell. If it would only begin to rain!

The sea would grow calm with the rain lashing across it. But still the pent-up torrents remained in the black clouds. Wind and sea screamed across the world.

Suddenly a new sound, a sound as of giant drums beaten furiously, made the girl creep to the stern of the boat, heedless of the lashing spray, and stare westward.

Old Man Ledge! The helpless boat was being carried straight toward it, to the place where mighty waves lifted high in air before crashing down on the jagged teeth of the reef. No boat could live once it was caught in the grip of that swirling water! The girl sank to the floor of the boat, shivering convulsively, her fear-numbed hands still clutching the tiller-ropes.

At sight of the approaching storm Orin Pettishall ceased work on the dock and went up to the house to close windows and make everything secure. Kindling a heap of driftwood he had piled in the fireplace, he sat down before it to watch the leaping flames. The wind struck against the old house, rattling windows and screaming angrily around the gables. Through the windows, which looked westward, the boy could see inky clouds rolling above the water and watch the giant waves pounding across Old Man Ledge.

"Gosh, I hope ev'ybody's in!"

Even as he spoke Pettishall's eyes were caught by a black speck which showed for a moment on the crest of a wave, then sank from sight. When it appeared again the speck was farther out. It was some time before it rose again, and then the young fisherman's experienced eyes told him something was wrong. No one would dare go near Old Man Ledge in such a storm. He looked again, then hurried out of the room. A moment later he was running down toward the dock, struggling into a sweater as he ran. By the time he reached his boat, started the engine, and headed out toward sea, the storm had burst in full fury.

Yielding to the furious onset of wind and sea, his boat checked, then came up stanchly to its work, water and spray streaming from the canvas covering, rising and plunging while the engine coughed convulsively. Pettishall bent over the engine, nursing it with care against the onslaughts of flying spray while he guided, almost instinc-

tively, the desperate battle his boat was making. Twice
only did he catch sight of the helpless craft which was his
goal and each time his heart came up into his throat sick-
eningly, for it seemed that no power on earth could snatch it
away from the threatening reef. Still he urged his boat
on, confident in its strength, in the power of the engine
choking and coughing at its labor.

A third time the drifting boat rose. "Will Ellery!" the
boy gasped in astonishment, but the wind caught up the
words and seemed to drive them back into his mouth. Now
he was near it! He swung his own boat out in a wide
circle, rope coiled in his hand ready to throw. A figure in
oilskins scrambled to its feet and called something which he
could not hear. His spray-blinded eyes tried to measure
the distance between the boats. He threw the rope, only
to see it fall short in the boiling water.

No one but a fisherman, born and bred to the world-old
cruelty of the sea, could have coaxed his boat once more
near the disabled one, fighting inch by inch nearer to the
reef, the roar of its waters beating in his ears and the driven
spray striking against his face like flying needles. Only a
fisherman, fighting desperately for the life of another, would
have dared swing his boat in until for one ghastly moment
it stood poised on the crest of a giant wave, directly above
the one which wallowed helplessly in the trough beneath.
It slipped, clung to the wall of water for the eternity of a
second, then plunged, barely missing the other. In the
moment he shot past, Pettishall flung the rope outward.
As it was caught and made fast he saw the girl's white face
and knew who it was he had come out to rescue.

Blinding torrents of rain had begun to fall, drawing a
swirling white curtain across the water. Presently the rain
would cease and the sea grow calm, but there could be still
no question of rounding the Head. He would have to
take Emily ashore with him instead of bringing her home.

Towing the crippled boat as far back of him as the
length of his painter permitted, Pettishall at last gained
shelter. After making his own boat fast to its mooring
he drew in the other.

Emily looked up and made a brave attempt to smile.

Glancing sharply at her blue lips and haggard face, the boy swept her into his arms and put her down in the dory.

"Hev ye ashore in a minute." Swiftly he moored the second boat and then dropped into the dory with her. When they reached the dock he asked anxiously, "S'pose ye kin go up the ladder?"

"Sure I kin." She stood up, swayed, and would have fallen had he not caught her.

"I kin walk now," she told him when he had climbed with her to the dock, and went slowly beside him along the path to the house.

In the living room the fire still burned. Orin threw an armful of wood on it.

"Set up here close an' git yerself good an' warm," he said. "Maw left a dress here the day she come over ter clean fer me. I'll fetch it fer ye."

When he returned a second time, after leaving oilskins and seaboots in the kitchen, Emily looked up and smiled.

"I'm a' right now," she told him. "I wuz jes'—jes' kinder upset."

"Yes," he returned grimly, "sh'dn't wonder ef ye wuz. What wuz ye doin' out in 'at boa-at? Ye might 'a' been— ef I hedn't happened ter see ye—" The words stuck in his throat.

"I'd 'a' been drownded," she said soberly, "ef ye hedn't come out. I'd 'a' struck the ledge in no time. I wuz comin' here," she explained simply. "I hed ter see ye."

"Comin' ter see me?" he echoed incredulously. "Comin' here?"

She nodded. "I hed somethin' ter tell ye—somethin' 'at made me want ter git here fast ez ever I c'd. Set down here by me. I kin tell it plainer ef ye do." She nestled her cold fingers in his.

"It's what Grammy Tagel tol' me," she began, " 'bout this house an' the grave out yan an' how they happened ter be. She wuz only a young 'un when it happened, but she says 'at she minds the awful storm an' hearin' folks tell 'bout how Captain Beath's vessel wuz wrecked on Ol' Man Ledge an' nobody saved, only jes' him. Seven men in the crew an' only him saved, an' he wouldn't 'a' been ef it hedn't been fer one uv the men. Him an' Captain Beath hed gone ter school tergether an' they'd allus been friends, Grammy says.

"They wuz hangin' onto the dory, jes' the two uv 'em. The vessel was bustin' up an' they wa'n't no trace uv the other men. Twict Captain Beath wuz washed off, but the other feller got him both times an' fetched him up. The las' time he says, 'Ye got ter hang onto the plug-strap. It's yer turn,' he says, but Captain Beath allus said arterwards 'at it wuzn't his turn.

"Grammy says 'at when the captain come ter hisself he wuz layin' on the beach here. The storm wuz over an' the sea wuz all shinin' an' blue. He got up onto his feet an' called fer his friend an' then went 'round lookin' fer him, but they wa'n't nobody else thar—only the shinin' water an' the white beach an' the tide comin' in. They never found no sign uv the other feller, never——"

"The other feller," Orin asked in a hushed voice, "who wuz he?"

"Arter a while the captain built him a house here, so's he c'd allus see the place whar him an' his friend wuz tergether fer the las' time. Grammy says 'at when folks made him see 'at his friend hadn't been saved it wuz then he put up the gravestun—kinder so's they c'd be tergether like they'd allus been. He uster tend it an' put flowers on it an' got inter the habit uv settin' out thar an' talkin'.

"They wa'n't never nothin' in the grave, nothin'! Grammy says 'at's the way things often is—'at folks makes trouble an' sorrer fer tharselves an' fer others over things 'at wa'n't never thar in the fust place—like—like I done——" The words were lost in a passion of tears.

The boy swept her into his arms, murmuring broken words: "It's a' right! They wa'n't never nothin' wrong, Em'ly. It's a' right!"

Emily stood up at length, wiping the tears from her eyes. "Look," she said, "the storm's breakin'."

The rain, which had been pattering steadily on the old roof, had ceased. A broad band of sunlight streamed through the western window, flooding across the quiet old room like a benediction.

"Come on," the girl said in a low voice, "it'll be a good time arter the rain ter pull weeds. We got ter git all the weeds 'way f'om 'round the grave. I'm glad they's lots uv lilies still so's I kin trim it up nice. Arter a while they'll be bayberry an' maple leaves fer me ter put on it—an' in winter they'll be pine."

SIX DOLLARS[1]

By WILBUR DANIEL STEELE

(From *The Pictorial Review*)

WHEN Tansy Snow was a young man of eighteen or nineteen he went one night to the Stone Fold. The Stone Fold is an islet lying about two miles to the southeast of us. There is a house on it built of stones, and a sheep-shelter, and toward the southern end three thorn trees.

Tansy took his father's skiff and steered straight through the shoals that lie that way, guided by the lamp in the garret of the house. Donna, who had been in town with her father two days before, told him she would put it there when the old man was asleep and the dogs shut up.

Donna Salisbury wasn't pretty. And she would have been better for a mother's care; better to look at. As you'd expect, living with only a shepherd father, her clothes were heavy, stout things, fitted mostly by guess, and none too clean, and her hair was thick and untended, and the color of her father's sheep. But she was strong, stronger than a boy, and if her face had a dull look, there was something behind the dullness that would make a fellow stop to look again, especially when stars were bright enough to cast shadows among the rocks and the gray grass.

Tansy couldn't understand why he should want to have anything to do with her. He'd been to the Academy and now he had a position in the new bank; he had to wear decent clothes every day, clean collars, and polished boots; it went deeper than that: he had every day to be a decent *man* and wear a clean conscience; otherwise the pointing finger of the banking business would find him out—bound to—in the long run of a man's life.

He had been to the Stone Fold three times, steering by the light. This time he was coming simply to say he wasn't coming. It would be awkward telling the girl. For a day and a night he had been busy trying to think up something humane, but at the same time final. Finished. Chopped off.

He hadn't guessed how awkward it would be, after all. They couldn't talk there on the beach on account of the dogs; they had to go along a way. Occasional clouds, great fluffs of things, sailed over the sky, and in the dark when they covered the stars Donna led him, taking his fingers in her strong, dull, warm, eager hand.

He would have said it at the first turn of the shore, but the surf on the bar there was too loud; he didn't want to shout. He would have said it when they started inland toward the thorn-trees, but now they had got into the wind, the full weight of the wind that came in from the open sea and bore the great clouds among the stars and made a living sound among the grasses. He would have said it under the thorn tree, but under the thorn tree was Donna.

It was half-past two when he left the island, and he hadn't said it yet. What he *had* said he could hardly remember. Sometimes words, fragments of sentences, promises, will come from a man's mouth as if it were some one else speaking: things he doesn't mean at all.

He pushed the skiff off the sand, holding it by the painter. "When'll you be again?" she whispered.

Now was the time to tell her. She might have seen how pale he was; might have helped him by saying something. But she was a dumb young thing and she hadn't a word. Of a sudden he reached into his pocket and pulled out the money he had there and thrust it into her hands.

She was a dumb one, and she couldn't make it out. "What's this?"

"I want you should buy yourself some present or other." "Huh?"

The dogs in the sheepfold began to bark. Tansy jumped into the skiff and pushed off, leaving Donna to stand there, dumber than ever.

He had a fair wind back and put up the sail.

It was six dollars he had given her, a lot of money, the whole of his first week's wages. There were things he could have bought with that: a new tire for his bicycle, and a Young People's Union pin to give Elsie Baker on her birthday. But it was all right. Better to start off clear —not a debt outstanding—no matter what the cost might be.

Even yet, though, he didn't feel quite right. When he got home and up to his room he had three hours to sleep, but he couldn't sleep. He was disgusted with himself. His memory reviewed the night with shame and loathing. He saw the path down which he had started, and even if he had got out of it now, it was disgusting to remember.

All next day he felt drugged and haggard. He made mistakes with figures, so that Mr. Matheson had to speak to him. But what was it? He'd paid, hadn't he? Squared up? Given everything he had to the girl?

Yes, but how about the Lord God? Slowly, as the day went by, he saw this. You can't pay God with money.

There was a sociable at Center Church that night. He had asked to see Elsie Baker home. He looked so ill at supper time that his mother advised him to stay in. To her surprise he acquiesced without trouble. He went upstairs. When he was half undressed for bed, however, he couldn't do it. Getting dressed again, he stole out the back way and went and stood behind a tree near the church and watched the people going in.

The windows were bright and there were sounds of a good time, a hymn, then after a decent interval laughter and runnings about, games. Tansy walked across the street and stood at the steps.

He had given the girl everything he had. Can you give more than you have? And, anyway, any girl that would do that!

Yes, yes; but how about the Lord God?

He went around to the wagon-shed, and in the dark there he fell on his knees. "O, Heavenly Father, I've walked in evil; I've committed a grievous sin; I beg Thee to forgive me in Thy mercy. I repent. O God, I repent; I do, I do, honestly! Honestly, God, honestly——"

In the church they were singing "My Country, 'Tis of Thee."

Tansy got up and brushed off his knees. His weariness was gone, like a heavy coat he might have taken off and left there in the shed. In its place there was a sense of security and well-being, such as comes after a bath at the end of a sweaty day. He slipped back to his room and put on his blacks, and, coming down the front way, he said he thought he would go to the sociable. There was no turning him.

Actually he didn't go in, but waited on the steps. There was something about his feelings that would no more have mixed with the romping and the din than oil will mix with water. Yet it was marvelous just to sit apart and listen to it, especially when the organ struck into some familiar air, and all sang, soprano and alto, tenor and bass. It was marvelous to be whiter than snow, one with God, a little child.

He saw Elsie home, after all. It was only a couple of hundred yards, down the shore street and up London Lane, but he would never forget it. It was the first time he'd known that love and reverence could be one and the same thing. Earthly love and religious reverence.

Elsie was so pretty, so enchanting in ribbons and laces, so pure, as pure as a flower on which God's sun shines and God's rain falls unfailing, as if He were saying in the sun and rain: "Of such is the portion of them that think none but healthy thoughts and dream none but wholesome dreams; yea, even to the third and the fourth generation."

Elsie's great-grandfather it was who gave the land for the Atheneum. Her grandfather rescued the missionaries in Paul Straits, and founded the "Light in Darkness." Her father and mother were in the forefront of everything for decency and right living, and they were well-to-do.

The forefathers of that girl on the Stone Fold—what could they have been? By what steps of wrong thinking, of evil impulses given way to and higher impulses denied, must that strain have come down?

But now, because something had been changed in him, Tansy could think of her with nothing but pity.

In London Lane the lights, shining up under the willows, made it seem the nave of some dim cathedral, in which a boy and a girl walked together. And then Elsie was up on her stoop and he stood at the foot of the steps.

"W-e-l-l?" she said. The light from the two long panes flanking the door fell softly on either side of her figure.

"Elsie," he said, "excepting for my father and mother there's nobody in the world but you amounts to *that*, with me."

"What *are* you saying, you silly?"

She came back down the steps to read the silly's eyes. She was so good she didn't guess the risk. He could have grabbed her and kissed her.

But not he; not now! He kept his hands behind him.

"Elsie, you wait and see. Some day I shall be the biggest man in this town." It wasn't like boasting. "For your sake," he might have said.

He marveled as he walked homeward. On one side there were loveliness, niceness, world's goods; on the other unloveliness, a hard living, the scorn of friends. Yet did God ask him to choose the stony way? By a miracle, no. God asked him to choose the way it would have been the part of even the worldly-wise to choose.

Marveling so, as he crossed above the White Boys' place he spied a pin-prick of light away out beyond the Point. It was as though it rested on the low neck of sand, a fallen star.

"Tonight?" He felt angry. "She's got her cheek, I must say!"

On impulse he went down to his father's wharf, cast off the skiff's painter, and got in. He would finish *that* off. He would tell Donna what was what. Straight from the shoulder! Then, before he had got the oars out, he realized that it was only the devil tempting him, weaving any arguments at all, just to get him out there to the Stone Fold again.

He made the boat fast and went home. His parents were still up. He shook his father's hand and kissed his mother on the brow. She eyed him with a knowing little smile. "Been seeing Elsie Baker home?"

Tansy stood with his jaw out.

"I've made a decision to-night," he said. "Some day I shall be the biggest man in this town."

He married Elsie Baker on the day he was made assistant cashier at the bank. Within three months he was cashier.

People trusted him. "No need to count your money when it's Tansy passes it out of the till." His word was as good as a bond; better, for bonds can be lost or burned or stolen.

Old man Baker bought the Dow residence in the Brick Walk, had it renovated, and gave it to the couple as a wedding-present. Nothing could have been fitter. It was the smallest of the big houses built at the height of the California days, brick for walls, slate for roofing, and a wrought-iron grill around the turf-plot. Four-square with the street, a house of strength and dignity. It was not too large, and that was fit, too. In the great-grandfather's family there were eleven children; in the grandfather's, fourteen; in the father's, three. Elsie herself had none.

It was a town house, pure and simple; the Dows had always been shorefolks, lawyers and doctors and the like. From the windows of the guest-chamber upstairs, full of leafy boughs and neighboring gables, you might have been a thousand miles from the nearest salt; the sewing-room was the same, and so was the west-chamber, that had always been known as "the children's room." Yet it is a hard thing to find a house in Urkey without some peep of the water; even at Gramma Pilot's, about as thoroughly shut in as any in town, you've but to climb to the garret to get a sight of blue under the rod of the drug-store chimney. We may wear Brockton shoes, but we're a web-footed race for all that.

And so it was from the "used chamber" in the new Snow home.

The first time they slept there after their wedding-tour to Boston Elsie awoke in the middle of the night. For a moment she couldn't say why. It was too queer. She didn't stir; simply lay there trying to think what it was

could be wrong. It wasn't for instants that she recollected
where she was, that she was married, that her husband
was there beside her. She slid a hand over his pillow to
touch his head. There was no head to touch. She was so
startled she didn't know what to do or think. She went
cold. Then, of course, when she began to paw around,
her hand found Tansy's back. He was sitting up in bed;
that was all.

"What *is* the *matter?*" she demanded, she was so upset.

"Nothing. Why, nothing at all." And he lay back on
the pillow.

But by and by, when he thought her asleep, he was up
again, on an elbow, looking at the window over the foot of
the bed. Like burglars.

You know the feeling of that. Up went Elsie without a
word, staring at that window too. And there was nothing
there. Nothing but the rear corner of Center Church, one
side, and the corner of the Nickerson house, the other, and
their one outlook on the harbor in the slit between. By
day there would have been a bit of the harbor, a segment
of the Point, and out to sea. Now there was nothing but
the spark of a chance light; it might have been at the
masthead of some vessel at anchor; it was too low for a
star.

She was provoked. "What *are* you *gawping* at?"

"Nothing. Why, nothing in the world. What makes
you think I——"

"Is it that light?"

"Wha—what light?"

"Well, I'm all afidget now."

He lay back and comforted her. They were young.

Next morning, at the chamber-work, Elsie made a dis-
covery.

"You remember that light last night, Tansy?" she laughed
at supper-time. "Well, 'twas nothing but old Cabe Sal's-
bury's light in his house over to the Stone Fold; you can
see how it ranges in daylight. Must be some one sick."

"Or else Cabe's a great student," she modified it when,
at bedtime, she saw the lamp burning again in the window
on the Stone Fold.

"What you say to closing those blinds?" Tansy suggested. "I vow there's a tang in the air to-night."

No, Elsie wouldn't listen to that.

"The best doctors nowadays say all the air you can have in your bedroom is none too much, even in winter-time. I'd suffocate."

It was the following day that Tansy began to seem restless. To begin with, he didn't see where they were going to expect much company, overnight, all their friends being local people, with houses of their own. So why didn't they shift into the front chamber, which was roomier, with two closets; and as for air, certainly there was as much air coming up the Brick Walk as there was in the church back yard.

"My *spare* chamber?" was all Elsie could gasp.

"Or even the west chamber——"

"The *children's* room?"

Elsie went straight to her mother about it. Her mother smiled. Phidela Baker had been a young woman once, with a new young husband and a new house of her own. "They're all the same; Providence made 'em so. Ever notice a dog that's made up his mind to lie down in a certain spot? Made up or no, he's got to wander and fidget a dozen times around it first, before he settles down. Don't you take on."

"But over and above everything," was the parting advice, "don't you start out by humoring him too much. Be cheery, but put your foot down."

So when Elsie found Tansy at work one of those days, surreptitiously, trying to get the bureau switched for the bed, and the carpet in a tangle with it, she put her foot down. He looked foolish to be caught so. His face got redder and redder.

"Light shines in my eyes. That is—in the mornings."

"Can you *imagine* how this room would *look?*" She demolished him ruthlessly, but all the while with a smile.

That smile of Elsie Snow's grew famous. No matter if this went bad and that worse, Tansy Snow's wife always had a smile, always seemed to be saying, like her mother before her: "Don't you take on; God will provide."

Her energy was amazing and fruitful. Once she was married and settled down, and since she had no children to stop her, she was able to be a power for good. She was a treasure for Tansy; she saved his pennies; where another in her place might have got trained help from the mainland she did with young girls to come in, carried the bulk of the house herself, and never looked the worse for it.

As she matured she rounded out amazingly; folks wouldn't have believed it, from the slip of a girl she had been. But no matter how full her hands were, they were never too full to spare a finger where help was needed. In the church, in the Dorcases, in the "Light in Darkness," in the Town Farm Association, at Easter, Thanksgiving, Memorial Day, the word came to be: "See Elsie Snow; she'll manage."

There were plenty to say that her capacity for managing didn't go for nothing in Tansy's affairs. Certainly, once, when he wouldn't have foreclosed on Mrs. Hemans's store—which was going to be a valuable property as soon as the fish-freezer was built—certainly then it was his wife showed the common sense of the two, asking him plainly: "Which do you figure you owe the most to, Sarah Hemans or the men and women and children that've got their all in your bank?"

Yet too much may have been made of that. Tansy was honest, and honesty goes a long way. When he made a statement across his desk in the bank-block—it mattered not whether it was to the highest or the humblest—that statement held. And yet, again, in another way, where would he have been if it hadn't been for her? People would really have forgotten that he was alive.

Tansy had turned out a silent and unsociable man. He never went to the post-office; his mail came to the bank. From there home he took the back way; that was about the only place, except church, you'd ever see him, and then half the time he wouldn't see you, walking as he did with his eyes on the ground, studying.

A silent man is a wise one: that's common knowledge. Tansy ought to have been Selectman. Yet he never was. It hurt Elsie. Fall after fall, as town meeting came and passed, and somehow or other Tansy's name wasn't mentioned, it got deeper and deeper under her skin. Of course nobody ever knew. It wasn't anything you could say anything about. But it was bitter when she recollected the young Tansy standing at the bottom of the steps and vowing: "Some day I shall be the biggest man in this town."

She never mentioned it directly to her husband. The nearest she came was when she would plague him: "Why *don't* you see more of folks? I declare, I can't make you out. What good does it do going to church if you don't take a hand in any of the activities? Or in town affairs? See here now, So-and-so and So-and-so are coming in after supper about the cake-sale, and I want you to put on your blacks and stay down awhile—and talk. 'Twouldn't harm you to crack a joke, even. Be cheery!"

Tansy would change his collar and put on his blacks. He never crossed his wife; never put *his* foot down. Never but once. That was when Elsie, perceiving at last that there was to be no one for the "children's room," and moved by something too vague to say, suggested they might be more comfortable in the west chamber, after all, as he himself had said. It was the first time she had ever heard him speak as he did. "We'll stay where we are." And they had stayed.

But so he would freshen up after supper and come down as she bade him and sit, absent of eye and mind, in a corner of the cake-sale conference. Ten minutes. Half an hour. Then presently, as things warmed up, like dew under the heightening sun, he would be found to be not there. "Studying," his wife would have to tell them with a sigh. "What can a body do with a man whose work is never done? Up there in the dark, from now to bedtime, like as not, studying, studying. You'd never guess. But I declare if some folks were to work the amount Tansy Snow does, and take on so blessed little about it— Well, well. And now, who's it arranged shall get the paper for the streamers and festoons?"

So Tansy would sit there, studying. All alone in the

"used chamber," in the dark, in his shirt-sleeves, in the rocker. Studying, studying.

First, in the early days, he thought it was a sin. It seemed to him that it must be Satan himself who was putting that lamp in Donna's garret on the Stone Fold, night after night after night, to mock him, around the very corner of the church of God, and beckon him from the very pillow where he lay beside his wife.

At first he was angry. "The cheek of her!" She knew he was married, must know it; she had been in town with her father many times; he had seen their boat. Yes, he had seen *her*—at a distance. Angry and scared. Anything to escape that ray that poisoned his thoughts, his dreams! Any room, any window, but that! Angry, scared, and *fascinated!* That was the worst. Fascinated, so that it ate a hole in the fabric of his honesty, like a moth-hole, tiny enough to escape notice, but big enough to let a lie through.

"I've to step upstairs and get my slippers, wife dear."

"You're tired, Tansy; let me go."

"No, no, you stay by the fire and read; I'll be but a moment, dear."

For a while he was ashamed of himself. He ran to the stairs and started down if he heard Elsie coming. He felt he ought to make it up to her somehow, pet her, show himself ten times more fervent than it was in his nature to be. But that couldn't last. Nothing that's not in a man's nature can last. What *is* in his nature will out.

It's in the nature of islanders to be weather-vanes. As the weather goes, so do our spirits. There's none that hasn't, in some one of his generations, had a ship. So, even though her husband was a confirmed shore body, Elsie never thought it anything out of the way that he should be weather-tender, and show it by fidgeting and prowling on nights when the fog came and the wind was in the east.

Through the spring and summer of their first year there was prevailing fair weather, and only rarely a night like that—a blessed one (at first) when the star on the Stone Fold was blotted out—a torment (later on) when Tansy was upstairs as much as down, stealing peeps, dreading,

hoping. In September, though, there came a real spell,
five days of it as thick as a hat. In the night of the fourth
a lobsterman named Antony Coral claimed to have seen
Mr. Snow of the bank in a dory in Chalk Ground Slough,
toward the Stone Fold—was near to running into him—
fact!

If a tale like that had been let go far it might have
harmed a man in Snow's position. But it didn't go far.
Before his mates at the dock had got through guying the
credulous "Portugee," he began to wonder if he hadn't
been asleep at his oars, after all, and dreaming dreams, and
he never brought it up again.

One thing about that night is certain, however: Tansy
wasn't at home. Another thing is certain: it was he that
was rowing the dory in Chalk Ground Slough, toward the
Stone Fold. And it wasn't above five minutes after he
had avoided collision with Coral's lobster-boat that, close
aboard the island beach, he made out finally a disk of warm
light the size of a penny, up in that part of the vapors
where Donna's garret window ought to be.

That settled it. That made it another thing. Had it
been no more than spite, Donna wouldn't have wasted
oil and wick in weather that would smother the spark in
twenty rods, and never a chance in God's world for Tansy
to see and suffer. It was something in *her* made her do it,
then; like an act in some ritual of memory. Turning his
boat around, he rowed for home. What he had found out
filled him with a sense of pity. No, not pity. There was
solemnity, tragedy in it, but it wasn't pity, nor sorrow.

After that he began to lose his feeling of shame when he
made excuses to slip away upstairs, till he made them no
more. He no longer stole peeps from the window; he
sat there brazenly, "studying." As time went by, if the
good people gathered in Elsie's parlor—if they could have
seen him at the moment of his escape upstairs—they
would never have known him for Tansy Snow. His face
was contorted. He shook his fist. "———the lot of you,
you gabbling, gossiping little parcel of busybodies, you and
your holy little schemes, your little brains! The devil!
What claim have you on *me?*"

But when he had reached the bedroom and found the rocker and sat down with his back to the bedpost and his sock-feet on the window-sill, little by little the lines would vanish from his face. Little by little as he watched the fallen star, or thought of it shining in secret there, he forgot to hear the busy voices below; he heard the wind running in gray grasses and the living sound of breakers on far-strewn reefs and the dry rustle of leaves in a thorn tree. And what had happened was that he was no longer surrounded by walls and gables and hemmed in by the thoughts and needs and elbows of hundreds of industrious little two-legged vegetables; the walls had melted, his horizon was the horizon of dark ocean, and he walked in space.

And a girl walked with him—no, a woman—no (as time passed), more than a woman, a kind of goddess, sea-begot, earth-born, the soil of the mother still carelessly on her, and she the stronger for it, and slow, as the tides as slow, and generous, as the earth is generous with the seeds of life, and brooding calm as the sky is, which, knowing nothing, holds within itself all the generations of them that know all. Her hair was thick and tangled, because the grass grows so; eyes heavy, because they looked at things far off; hands large, because the blood that fed them was warm; and her words little words, because only little words can stay in the wind that blows from the caverns among the stars.

"The gray ewe dropped twins in that brush-patch. That's a good ewe."

And Tansy could imagine his own words as simple. "Yes, a good ewe."

"I like the feel of the wind, like tonight; there's rain to come. I like it to blow under my hair, the same as kisses. I love kisses."

"I love to kiss you. I love to be with you with nothing but water roundabout and nothing but stars above, and all on earth asleep, hushed up."

"They're awake in China, though, for the world's round like a ball."

"Most folks know the world's round, yet they think it's

flat. I love that in you, Donna; you can *feel* it, you can *see* it being round like a ball. And you can see the stars being round like balls as big as suns, to shine hot on other worlds where there were sheep and people living and having twins and dead under the grass a million centuries before Adam and Eve—and never a thought in all their races whether it should be a thousand or twelve hundred on the Dee Nickerson house, or something useful like aprons or something tasty like doilies at the Dorcas meeting next Tuesday week. You see it. You feel it."

"Yes, Tansy, I see it. I feel it."

"You and I. I love you. And here we are at the tree."

Nor could he any longer, caught in the net of fantasy, recognize the thing as sin. *There's* revenge for you. To have grown to be a man who didn't know right from wrong. Tansy, whose honesty was his strength!

After all, he wasn't a man; he was two men. It was the other that became president of the bank, director in both the new freezers, and owner of considerable property in the town. No one knew his duplicity. How was it possible? Certainly, after living with him ten years, his wife didn't know. Donna herself, who might have guessed, might have wished, even Donna couldn't *know*. He could assure himself there was no one. So he had forgotten what had happened that night in the wagon-shed behind the church (and almost under his window now). He had forgotten God, who never forgets.

But God moves in a mysterious way. It was a mystery to all "what it was bit Tansy" in his thirty-sixth year. There he was one week, a bit stoop-shouldered perhaps, but wiry for all that and going his way. Honest Tansy, who ought to have been Selectman—and why didn't *some-body* ever put him up? And there he was the next week, and talk of galloping consumption. Or Bright's disease. Or what?

They couldn't have got it out of him; he was too close of mouth. Nor dig and delve as they would they couldn't get it out of Mrs. Snow. She didn't know; that's why. He sleeps poorly; that's about all she could say. He would toss, his head as restless on the pillow as if it wore a crown of thorns. Once when he thought her asleep he got up and went into the spare chamber. From the hall where she had stolen she saw him with a candle staring at his own face in the bureau glass. The night-puffed face, the thinning hair, the stooped shoulders—in the mirrored eyes there was the look of a soul in hell, self-pity, self-hate, self-mockery.

Elsie was worried in earnest. When, without warning, a day or so later, he announced: "We'll try the west room a spell for a change," she was quick to humor him. Yet it came to nothing. Before she had so much as a bed-sheet shifted, there he was back, bareheaded: "Let it be as 'twas."

Here are the facts. Tansy oughtn't to have gone near the docks. For years he had kept clear of them, by instinct more than by reason. Now the mysterious way God took was to make him careless. It was a bright and innocent morning anyway; insurance was wanted on a big yawl; it's better to see a risk with your own eyes than to go by hearsay. (If you can see the risk.)

Alongside the yawl three single-handers were lying, the men in them sorting their last night's catch; lusty, brawny young fellows, a pleasure to the eye with their deep color and their flashing grins (more pleasure to the eye than a banker in a night-shirt before a looking-glass). And their voices, in the clear of the morning, were gay and strong.

Five years later Tansy could have repeated every syllable of every word:

"Looks o' that catch o' yourn there, Eddie, you didn't set no very likely place last night, did ye?"

"Aw, leave Eddie be, Sam. Didn't ye hear the terrible thing? Got a good fare o' haddock, Eddie did, only he had to heave the best part away. Turn out to be moth-millers when he come to look. Whatcha make o' that?"

"Laugh, you fellows; I like to hear ye. But if ye really want to know who 'twas fishin' the Stone Fold las' night, don't ask me; ask Codhead Collins; he's the boy'll know."

"All right, all right, don't jump so. All reminded me was, I was thinking I noted a new little face on the beach over there when I come by the old girl's last week. And a new batch o' wash on the line."

"Godfrey! How many's that she's got now?"

"Don't ask me; I ain't the only dory in the fleet."

It wasn't consumption; Tansy didn't cough. Nor Bright's disease; it didn't act that way. The doctor said it was just insomnia, and it came from too much work. Human flesh can't stand studying at a desk the livelong day and then in a bedroom rocker half the night. He advised, and Elsie insisted, that Tansy ease up, go off somewhere, and take a holiday.

"No, I'll just see it through," was all Tansy would say.

When he said that morning: "We'll try the west room a spell," it was a confession of rout. Once away from that window he might forget; that's how he figured it. He hadn't yet got it through his head that God never forgets. At the bank, who should be waiting to see him but two of those trawlmen, Eddie and Sam. It was something about a loan; Tansy hardly knew; the business was done mechanically; the whole sudden thing *he* saw was that he wasn't to be let escape; that God had sent those wind-browned lusty young fellows as a sign and reminder that by no hiding of his eyes was he to be let forget. He faced it.

When the emissaries were gone he got down on his elbows on his desk and looked at his conscience, and he saw that in all those years of letting his imagination run to that island, instead of keeping it home of nights where it belonged, he had been doing a sinful thing. Now for atonement he was given a cross to bear. In the long run, unless he bore it without flinching, the failure would find him out. It was then, forgetting his hat, he ran home to Elsie with his "Let it be as 'twas."

"As 'twas!" The irony! As though it could be any nearer to what it had been than heaven is to hell.

He tried never to flinch. Shirt-sleeves and sock-feet, "as 'twas," he sat there whole evenings through. No longer did he stride across the wind-blown grass with Donna by his side. He ran at a crouch under cover of the brush-patches, peeping, spying. Or he lay hidden as near as he dared to the thorn tree, holding his breath and listening—to youth.

Almost as bad as the jealousy was the shame. Beginning by boasting he would be the biggest man in town, he had

ended by being the least in a shady brotherhood, the scum-
miest of the scum of the waterfront.

Sometimes he had to flinch a little; sometimes, revoking
the image of the goddess he had created, he would rail at
them. And now his *"I was the first!"* was the whine of a
whip, and he had to grovel:

"Lord, when I have borne enough, in Thy mercy take it
away."

There came a time when it seemed it was to be taken
away. Mercy's instrument was Austin Dow, the proprietor
of the Seaside Lunch that came with the steamer, along
with other changes, when the old packet-schooner gave up.
More and more excursionists were coming for the day's
sail from Gillyport, with an hour ashore at noon, and Dow
got to thinking he'd have a sign put on his roof, a big fellow, one you could read from the harbor coming in, with
"SHORE DINNERS OUR SPECIALTY" in letters five feet high.
And he wanted a license from the town.

It came up in special meeting in January, and it made a
stir. There were forward-looking people who realized that
times had changed, and they spoke in favor. There were
just as many against it, though not quite so apt at saying
why; anyway, it would be an eyesore to the worshipers
coming out of Center Church, that monstrosity on a roof
across the street. And then a man got up in the back of the
hall and asked permission to speak.

The man was Tansy Snow. If it had been George True,
the town dummy, folks wouldn't have been struck so dead.
And that was only the beginning. From the first the thing
that had made it look as though Dow might get the vote
was that it was the business men that were with him; it
was the sentimental old ladies (male and female) that were
against.

And now to hear Banker Snow, the busiest business man
of them all, the dried-up human calculator, the man with no
sentiment, no romance, no imagination beyond set-down-
five-and-carry-two—to see him standing there like a born
revivalist—and to hear him carrying on—diving back into
history and coming up again—his face running sweat and
his eyes as big as quarters with earnestness—reciting the

beauty and dignity and grandeur of our island metropolis
—recalling the impressions of his boyhood, the simple no-
bility of that shore-street sky-line, as great epochs had
builded it slowly—and then taking the proposed sign-board
as a symbol of all the ills the mainland suffers from, making
bigness an idol, bustle a religion, the dollar a god to trample
them in the dust—it was too much for the town meeting.
When it came to a vote, there wasn't a voice for the lunchroom: Dow was too done up even to lift his own.

No one was more amazed than Elsie Snow, or more
thrilled. If Tansy didn't fathom what he had done, or
what was to follow, she did. As she took him out and home
through the streets where people lingered she held him by
the arm, "the biggest man in town"; you couldn't fool Elsie
Snow.

When they had undressed and she had blown out the
light and gone to lift the window, she stood for a moment
dreaming down at Dow's lunchroom on the shore, bright
in the moonlight in the bottom of the crevice between the
Nickerson house and the corner of the church, and, "By
gracious," she mused, "it never till this instant occurred to
me, but it would've cut off half our one and only sea-view,
that monstrosity of his."

No, there was one more amazed than Elsie.

Staring out through the moonlight, and through the darkness when the moon had set, Tansy Snow was wondering:

"Why in the name of the Eternal did I do that?"

Elsie was right about consequences. The town waked up
and rubbed its eyes. Tansy Snow had pulled the wool over
them for a couple of decades, but he couldn't do it any
more. From the minute he sat down after his speech in
meeting there wasn't a question in anybody's mind but
what he'd be chosen Selectman the coming autumn, in place
of John Matheson, who was "getting through." If he'd
take it, that is.

What a question! As we used to say: "Will a duck
swim?" And yet very presently here was Elsie Snow going
around with another kind of smile and another and mysterious light in her eye. She was a wonder, Elsie was.

How did she get wind of it? you'll ask. But you must

remember that, what with being chairman of this, manager
of that, and corresponding secretary of the other, the
banker's wife had in her hands the ends of more underground wires than any dozen in Urkey, and under-water
wires too, tapping the gossip of all the towns and pre-
cincts the length of the Cape. And wise in politics, she
knew that two and two, coming at the right time and at all
dramatic, are apt to make nearer forty than four. And she
knew that there is a tide in the affairs of men. And she
knew that it never rains but it pours.

She could hear them at Gillyport: "Well, they say
Honest Tansy Snow opened up his mouth at last, and the
man's a spellbinder; vow he is." And at Barnstable: "They
knew him, and they knew he meant it; he ain't the kind to
spout for spoutin' sake, Banker Snow ain't. And they do
say there was a good many noses blowed there toward the
end."

But Elsie knew more than that. Piecing it together in
her astute mind, from a hint here, an allusion there, a slip
of somebody's tongue or pen, she knew a thing that only
three men in the Congressional District happened yet to
know. And this was that "the party," what with the chill
of old blood and the heat of bad blood, was secretly in a
bad way indeed; that it wanted a doctor, and wanted one
quickly—with the autumn elections coming forward, and a
member of Congress to be sent to Washington. No vet-
eran; no silver-trumpeting old war-horse. No, a new name,
a fresh fame, a clean slate.

"And where, oh, where," thought Elsie, "where will the
lightning strike?"

Selectman? Selectman of a village? That was why
she smiled. Since Barlow Atkins left Congress in 1884
people in Urkey had almost forgotten that an islander could
sit under the dome in Washington. "The biggest man in
this town." She remembered the young Tansy standing up
straight in London Lane. Well, she'd see.

One afternoon in mid-July the Knights came over in the
steamer *Senator Bates* for their annual "time," a clambake
at Blue Goat Cove in the evening and the sail back home by
moonlight later on. When they had marched the length of

the shore street behind their band and got a start for the cove, they took half the population with them, but they left three of their own number behind.

The sail was all right for these three, but they weren't much on clambakes. They'd rather loaf around the old town, looking at the houses. Perhaps they were interested in architecture. Or perhaps it was lightning-rods. They were Mr. Claude Byram of Gillyport, Captain Charlie Slocum of Barnstable, and ex-Senator Bates himself, and they were the three men in the district who knew what Elsie knew. As they strolled they talked. They talked about Henry Poor, the young lawyer in Provincetown, who, unheard of a year ago, had just won the Province-land suit for the Commonwealth. They talked of the new man who was making such a name for himself as head of the Highmarket Academy—a scholar—no taint of politics there. And once or twice, lingering near the end of the Brick Walk, "Well, here's where *he* lives," they temporized. "What do we say?"

But they couldn't seem quite to say. They had to talk it all over again. Six o'clock passed. They had a snack at Dow's place, and then it was seven, and then it was eight. Elsie Snow wasn't the woman to wait forever. It was in the drug store, where they had stopped for cigars, that she brought them to earth.

"Captain Slocum, as I live! And *Mr.* Byram! And—*not* Senator *Bates!* Well, I declare, who'd have thought to find *you* drifting around our little town, and without a soul to manage for you? I give you my word——"

She gave them her word it was an outrage, and that even if there wasn't a committee of welcome, there was a home that would be honored by their presence, and a fresh lemon layer-cake, and a drop of rhubarb wine, put down the year she and Tansy were married. And Tansy *would* be tickled.

It seemed providential; seemed to help to clear their minds. When they had arrived, most easily, most pleasantly, at the foot of the Snow steps, they slackened pace and let their hostess go on in ahead.

She made it simple for them. "I'll run on and see Tansy's fit to be looked at; he's that much of a home body, he's probably in slippers now."

"I guess, Mrs. Snow," the Senator called after her, spokesman for the three, "I guess you can tell Snow *we'll* be tickled to see *him*."

All the woman could think, and that over and over, was, "This is the greatest day in Urkey's history."

Tansy, hearing voices, was half-way upstairs. She bustled him up the other half, the news on her tongue, but then it was too enormous to tell.

"Get into your blacks, and *hurry*," she bade him; "there's company."

As she turned and swept downstairs again to put the company at its ease with ash-trays and cake and rhubarb wine, the chosen of fortune felt along the wall for the chamber door with a sigh. Why wouldn't people let him be?

Once inside, he started toward the window, of habit a quarter-century old. Then he remembered he was to hurry. Company. Who? Why had there been that note in her voice? Perhaps at last it was somebody about the autumn meeting and the Selectmanship. Oh, Tansy knew. He never let on, but he wasn't a fool And he wanted it—as he'd never wanted anything. Why? For the name? Yes, in a way. More than anything in life, he wanted to be able to go to that window and throw back the taunt of that leering eye of light.

"Yah! Take a look at me—the man that's trusted above all others! Selectman! The biggest man in this island and this town! You, and your 'moth-millers,' your dirty, filthy nobodies, look at me! Yah!"

But he had been told to hurry. In that funny way— hurry! It was the Selectmanship! As good as done already. Because he had been an upright citizen and an honest man. Here he was at the window, after all.

It wasn't a "Yah!" It wasn't a sound, nothing formed, just a formless outlashing of a life that was tired in secret; secretly, prematurely old. Then, as he looked again, he lifted a hand and drew it across his eyes.

"Fog coming in. Won't have much of a moonlight sail, that crowd."

He removed his hand and stared. There was no fog. The sky was as clear as glass and full of stars. He put his other hand on the bedpost. The bedpost was solid, anyway.

"Good God! What's—wh-what's happened? What's wrong?"

Elsie couldn't keep them occupied forever, even with cake and rhubarb wine. Minutes are minutes to such men. When fifteen had passed, and Slocum had looked at his watch twice, she went to the stairs and called. Then, laughing, "What would you do with such a man?" she marched up to find him. The bedroom was dark, and he wasn't there. She went to the spare chamber, to the west chamber, down the back way to the kitchen. She returned to their bedroom; he *must* be there.

She felt on the bed, the chair; she stood staring out of the window.

She shut her eyes and opened them again. A curious uneasiness, having nothing to do with the company downstairs, seemed to lay hold of her.

"Fog," she said to herself.

She turned around. What was the matter with this room tonight? Why was everything so—so—so wrong—so lost—so funny? She touched the bedpost. It was solid enough. She glanced toward the window again.

She laughed. She saw what was wrong, and it was ridiculous. For two dozen years, without knowing it, she had depended on seeing a light there when the weather was clear. When it was thick, there was no light; no light, it must be thick. And here it was clear, and no light. Absurd, but it had given her the jumps.

That shows what habit is.

Rid of the spell, she remembered what she was about. Her lips whiter and whiter with anger, running on frantic tip-toe, she searched the house.

Coming through the parlor she was all cheer. "Tansy'll be down directly," she promised them, and, slipping out of the door, she was gone.

Time passed. Once or twice they heard a voice calling "Tansy! Tansy!" off in the distance, among the houses and lanes.

They got to talking. "You can't tell me this fellow Poor hasn't made a big impression, especially down-Cape." "Yes, but he's a lawyer, and that means politician to lots of people. Now this man McDowell over at the Academy——"

When Mrs. Snow reappeared it was awkward. They didn't want to seem to run, but there was a man Byram ought to see, and there was the boat.

They got out backward, Slocum saying: "We're right sorry not to have seen Snow," and the old Senator adding a word of kindness: "The talk's been up our way that your husband's slated for the next Selectman over here. I'm glad of that; he ought to make a good one, from all I hear."

Elsie stood staring at the closed door when they were gone.

"Selectman!" she whispered. *"Selectman!"*

All the poison of all the years came pouring out. "I'll *see* him Selectman! I'd kill myself first! He shall stay a stick till the day of his death, he shall. A dumb, stupid stick—stick-in-the-mud! *Ohhhh!"*

In the kitchen of the house on the Stone Fold they were playing pachisi down on the floor. The board was an old one, held together with court-plaster; most of the men were buttons, and there were only two dice left. Despite these defects, however; despite the two youngest, two babies, creeping in continually and grabbing and getting slapped; and despite the paralytic old shepherd in the chair behind the towel rack, who wanted attending to now and then— despite these handicaps they played with a quiet concentration, watching each the moves of all the others, alert for cheating, a gamin shrewdness in the eyes narrowed under the forelocks of tangled hair. It was an old game with them; yet tonight there was something new about it; as new as though it had been another game altogether, or the same game transported to heaven, where all is light.

"Better'n that old lantern!"

"Better'n two lanterns!"

"Better'n *ten* lanterns!"

So, from time to time, between moves, carried away afresh by realization, they joined and gloated.

"Better'n a *hundred* lanterns!"

The dogs were barking outside. An old one from under the stove sniffed toward the door, bristling. The players paid no attention, but the grandfather began to screech at the top of his lungs: "Shan't have it! Shan't! Ain't nobody no decency? With *her* there? Etta, you tell 'em go way. It's an unholy sin—comin' round a night like tonight —that's what it is! Etta!"

"Shut your face!" Etta threw at him as, without haste, she got up from the floor. She was a woman of twenty-odd, the mother of one of the infants underfoot. "Remember, you, it's my next move!" she threatened the others; then again to the old man: "Won't you shut up, f' gracious sake!" and finally to the door: "Well, well, 'tain't locked, is it? *Come in!*"

The door opened. Those on the floor sat up straight. Etta retreated a step, taken aback to see a stranger.

"What d'y' want?" she muttered.

The man kept standing there, staring at her; staring at her squat, strong-muscled figure, her lowering face, her hair, thick and matted about her head, the color of unwashed brown sheep. She didn't like it.

"Who are ye, and what d'y' want? Y' dumb?"

But the old shepherd began to screech now: "*I* know 'im! I seen 'im many's the time over to the village. I see ye, Mr. Snow. I know ye well, Banker Snow. Well, I vow! Draw out a chair for Mr. Snow, Etta. Florry! Frank! Scabby! What a parcel o' dummies! Git a chair for Banker Snow."

"What d'y' want?" Etta persisted, unmoved.

Snow lifted a hand and passed it down over his face, which looked drawn and moist. Like a man talking in his sleep, he asked: "What's wrong with Donna?"

That seemed to loosen all tongues at once. The kitchen was as full of voices, of a sudden, as it was of the yellow glare.

"Donna's dead."

"Donna's in there; wanta see 'er?"

"Ma went sick and she got worse and died off."

"Donna ain't boss no longer, she ain't."

"We got the lamp down."

"We gone and got the lamp on 'er now, for *all* 'er."

"At last we got the lamp."

Snow seemed to see the lamp for the first time. Like a man walking in his sleep he went to look at it. It was worth looking at. It stood on its own stand, a good four feet high; its finely swelled reservoir had variegated chasings of brass and nickel all over it; it had an extra-size chimney without a nick, and two wicks, one within the other. A lamp for any parlor in the world. All the parts that could be rubbed were as bright as a new one in the store. It had been looked after, like new; the price-tag, even, had never been taken off. It hung from the stem of the regulator, and the mark was still legible on it amongst the spotting of flies. Tansy read it.

"$6."

Some folks have a God of Mercy. And some have a terrible God.

THE HOME TOWN[1]

By MILTON WALDMAN

(From *The London Mercury*)

HIGH, high up in the spire of a New York office building (higher than the forty storeys which is the maxi-
mum that the foreigner's imagination, even when abetted by
observation, seems able to compass) sat a depressed and
lonely little man. He was lonely because he was alone,
and unaccustomed to so being; his present occupation was
to discover why he was depressed.

The little man was a very important person. On the door
by which one entered one might read in reverse, "Powell,
Prescot and Shipton, Publicity and Advertising Engineers.
Henry J. Powell, Pres." Though the letters appeared black
through the frosted pane, on the other side they were bright
gold. If, after entering one looked over Mr. Powell's head
through the window beyond, where the streets and roofs
of New York extended to the south, one saw a few of the
things for which he was celebrated. Not many hundred
yards out of that window is the famous *Lesson in Economy,*
the masterpiece commissioned by the Bungalow Savings
and Trust Company. It is an animated electric sign, which
at night shows the reception of depositors' money at a window of the bank, its passage to a huge transparent safe
wherein the piles of currency and checks undergo a met-
amorphosis into bricks, lumber, bathtubs, and shrubbery,
and fly away to a garden spot in the suburbs to arrange
themselves into neat little bungalows of an exact pattern
with rows of neighbours of similar origin. At the conclusion
of the performance, which requires about three minutes, all
lights go out save those in the most recent bungalow, on the
steps of which are seen a man, a woman, a small boy and a
dog, above the ruby caption "You can Do This Too!"

[1] Copyright, 1926, by Milton Waldman.

A quarter of a mile further on is visible the radiantly coloured *tableau vivant* of the Searchlight Stores, entitled *Nothing Too Good for Milady,* which, around the charming figure of a modish young woman, exhibits, in smaller pictures, the Searchlight's myrmidons stalking tigers, leopards and cobras' skins in the jungles of India, ostriches' feathers in the deserts of Africa, caterpillars' skeins in a sleepy garden in Japan; one beholds the pearl divers in the shimmering waters of the Orient, and chained gangs of Kaffirs plucking diamonds out of the obdurate rock in Rhodesia. But a few steps further, on the other side of the street, is the striking *Don't Be Miserable When Enjoying Yourself,* which presents an invalid and her nurse contentedly reading novels while being wafted over the worst of roads in a monotone motor, whilst on a parallel and greatly superior road a competing car and its occupants are being gradually disintegrated. The editor of a magazine for which Mr. Powell had once written an autobiographical article had presented his contributor as "The Monarch of the Upper Reaches of American Cities," a just, but inadequate tribute to his manifold activities.

For Mr. Powell was more than a mere creator of striking advertisement displays. He was, in his way, a philosopher, and in the modern sense a poet as well. In the article referred to he expounds the philosophy of publicity as it has never been done before. He demonstrates clearly and succintly that publicity, like all the best poetry, is a form of self-expression; only the advertiser, instead of informing the reader of the state of his private feelings, often an awkward affair to the latter, or proclaiming the beauty of Nature's handiwork, which the public is well able to observe and judge for itself, reveals the merit of the thing which his (the advertiser's) creative urge, and perhaps Fate, have set him to producing. Publicity thus redounds to the common weal in two ways: by holding the advertiser to a high standard and by elevating the taste of the public to a level which it could never attain without the explanatory counsels of the expert makers of the things the public required. For example, the manufacturer of rubber heels, by illustrating to the pedestrian reader the advantages of his conception, makes a promise, sets for himself an ideal which it is both his duty and pleasure to live up to; while the pedestrian, if not thus made aware of the maker's ideal, would either be sapping his vitality by continuing to bustle about on leather heels, or his purse, by ignorantly satisfying himself with inferior rubber ones. The article concludes:

> The world can't *guess* the work you've done,
>   'Tis *you* must let it know,
> 'Twill give you then the prize you've won,
>   And, giving it, will glow.

The photograph of the author, which accompanied the article was at first sight disappointing. One anticipated that a man who had done big things would keep his appearance in harmony with his achievements; but instead of the burly shoulders, broad face, square jaw, thin lips and acquiline nose which the reader expected to see, he was confronted with the portrait of a round, stoop-shouldered little man, whose black hair was brushed back from his forehead in Beethoven fashion, whose eyes were deep-set and speculative rather than keen, and whose chin violated all the canons by merely rounding off in a perfunctory way the boyish countours of his cheeks. He wore a black coat of ministerial cut and a flowing black tie. Yet, to those who knew him, Powell's appearance was the best possible index to his character. They were astounded by his miracles, but stood in awe of his dreams.

Now, for the first time in forty years of activity, he felt lonely and depressed. His success, achieved always in the company of men and by dint of untiring effort, had hitherto left no room for either emotion. There was always something to do, somebody to see, at best and worst some pleasant creative vision to think about. But a week since, business being dull, his associates had departed in a body and gone their separate ways to observe the ritual of Old Home Week. This latter, a ceremony springing jointly from native sentimentality and respect for humble beginnings, requires that the men in the cities who have made their way in the big world should retrace their steps to the towns and villages which have given them birth and join in

tribute to its virtues. All the absent are welcome, but the
occasion is dedicated rather to the successful than to the
prodigal sons.

So Prescot and Shipton and the younger partners, Wynn,
Jacobson, Bottinelli, Senkowsky, and the rest took leave,
and now, five days later, the head of the firm sat in his
studio of gleaming mahogany, leather and brass, perusing
their exuberant accounts of the various local festivities.
Prescot wrote from a little desert village in the Southwest
of a Chamber of Commerce dinner in his honour, of a political conference for the selection of a congressional candidate
in which his opinion was deferred to, of being asked to lead
the subscription towards a War Memorial in the public
square. Wynn, in his best "copy" manner, chronicled a
round of rustic frolics in Minnesota. Bottinelli sent him a
clipping from a newspaper in a Southern California town,
which related the installation of a stained glass window in
the church where the young Italian had been christened
and in which he now made the dedicatory address. And so
on, each in his turn contributing to his chief's forlorn sense
of being out of it all. He had few friends besides associates,
and they were absent on similar missions, as he knew from
a week of solitary luncheons and dinners. It was a dreadful thing, he reflected, for a man to have no interests outside his profession. These others had something to carry
them on, to look forward to. It made life more complete,
more harmonious, to have the roots of one's aspirations in
one's beginnings, to wish to honour one's past by means of
one's future.

He looked back and recalled the early years from which
his manhood had so completely divorced itself. Born in a
village in southeastern England, he had emigrated with his
father, long since dead, to New York. Many other images
now intervened between himself and the one he was trying
to reconstruct, the dormant blur of red roofs and green
fields which was Edginden as he had last seen it. Gradually
the focus became clearer and he saw a valley and two inter-
secting roads which wound their yellow lengths rapidly
away over the surrounding hills and disappeared. At their
intersection was a gray church steeple, a few shops clus-

tered in two rows on the north-and-south road, some grey, some yellow, some burnt red, a few timbered or brick houses more openly spaced, then the fields beyond, with the white wall or tiled gable of a farmhouse revealed through the trees—old, old trees, sycamores, tall oaks, chestnuts in full white bloom; he wondered what an Old Home Week would be like in Edginden.

He doubted that it would be a success. Very few of Edginden's sons went away. Those that did seldom came back, never for the purpose of paying a tribute of sentiment to their birthplace. Besides, there was little that Edginden wanted, very little indeed. It grumbled extensively, but semed only in need of those things which Providence alone could supply. He tried to picture himself returning to join with other absent ones in receiving welcome and admiration, in dispensing bounty of cheer and money. He found that he could not even recall the faces of any absent ones, or in fact of any one likely to be still alive. Of what good——

He went to the window. Over the roofs and spires of New York he could see the Atlantic glittering in the setting sun. A slim silvery object was moving rapidly out into the bay, its ribbon of smoke settling slowly down on the unruffled water behind it. He unconsciously put his hands behind his back, in Napoleon fashion, and narrowed his eyes. It was worth the trying, anyway, he decided; at least he knew that nothing else would ease the new-born ache in his heart.

London pleased and puzzled him. It gave him an impression, first, of vast size; through mile upon mile of small brick houses, one just like the other, the train raced to Waterloo Station—so many miles of repetition; he felt as one does in a semi-dream, when time loses all proportion; only his watch showed him that the row he was seeing at any instant was an actual extension in space, not in his imagination, of all the others he recalled seeing. The bustle of the station, huge and ugly, the ceaseless, punctuated buzz of queer vocal inflections that awoke old echoes, the enormous taxicab, more like a private car, save for its dirt

and decrepitude, and again rows of houses as like as peas.
It was endless—infinitely larger than New York, with its
variety and its immovable water boundaries. It was late
at night when he finished his dinner, and he was too tired to
leave the hotel for further investigation, but he fell asleep
with the curious reflection that all comparisons he had seen
or heard of between New York and London were the exact
reverse of the truth . . . the latter was infinitely the greater
in its mass of teeming life, but rough, inchoate, not nearly
so finished as the former.

Next day confirmed his impression. He sauntered about,
examining everything attentively, minutely, reconstruc-
tively, he might have said, the while unconscious of the
curious glances he attracted; the broad black hat which he
affected intensified the peculiar inward concentration of his
eyes and enhanced the contrast with the youthful, inde-
cisive curve of the lips and jaw above the negligé collar and
flowing black tie. What opportunities to remake this
enormous London, to shape this formless monster's endless
possibilities! The buildings seemed stunted, totally inadequate to house the world-famous businesses whose clumsy
signs he saw on them. He found his London correspondents,
a firm of indisputable skill, importance and solvency, in a
side street, occupying a narrow house four storeys high, and
entered by a former servants' doorway; its floors sagged, its
stairways creaked, and no amount of paint and electricity
could raise it to his conception of what was due to the
business it housed. After long search he stumbled by mere
chance on the offices of a periodical with which he annually
spent thousands, to find its affairs placidly going on in a
converted stable in an old courtyard. The narrow streets
offered, on a larger scale, the tangle of horse, vehicle and
pedestrian to be seen in any American farm town over-
crowded by market day. The electric signs of Piccadilly
Circus and Leicester Square which would have caused his
associates to guffaw, brought a frown to his forehead. So
many people, so much riches—and how carelessly employed.

Before long he began to wish that he could start at the
beginning and put some system into this amiable, haphaz-
ard metropolis. His desire was extremely practical. He

knew it would not do to take the whole thing down and build it up again on carefully planned lines. That would be too expensive, and he was aware that there might be prejudices against so drastic a proceeding. He merely desired earnestly to use in a proper manner the material now being so sinfully wasted. As an instance, one couldn't straighten the Thames, of course, useful as that might be; but one could put to better purpose the many open spaces of its bridge-heads to relieve their uninformative blackness at night—although in this respect he saw immature efforts at improvement. He wanted to knock out the dingy shop windows that prevailed everywhere, even in the West End, and replace them with something worthy of Fifth Avenue.

Even outside the question of rebuilding, on small scale or large, Powell was pained by the neglect of opportunities that fairly shrieked at him for recognition and adoption. To disregard them indicated either lack of vision in the English, or downright sloth. Perhaps it was due to the race's well-known self-satisfaction. But what just a little imagination could do. He recalled with what eagerness he had undertaken the publicity for a New York restaurant which boasted seventy-five years of active life. "The stock which conquered the West and fought the Civil War found sustenance at this historic hostelry. Lincoln ate here while on his arduous campaign for the Presidency; it was Grant's first stopping place after being banquetted in all the palaces of the world. Three-quarters of a century's experience in the polite art of entertaining ensures you those amenities which, to the epicure, are *sine qua non* when dining out." And here almost hourly he saw restaurants scattered from Richmond to the City whose weatherbeaten signs diffidently proclaimed three hundred years of uninterrupted cookery. What could they not boast of in the way of association, of rich material for justifiable *réclame*. Without doubt there were still extant tables in those places under which Cromwell and Wellington had put their boots, pegs on which plumed Cavalier and stiff Puritan hats had hung side by side. A complacent smile lingered for a moment as he recalled how neatly he had effected the sale of Schindler, the antique dealer's, two colonial chairs, in which Clay and Webster were supposed to have sat while visiting a famous Concord wit. *The Seats of the Mighty* was the neat caption by which the attention of newspaper readers was attracted to the photograph of the chairs convincingly occupied by the shades of the departed statesmen, and within twenty-four hours a millionaire had purchased them for ten thousand dollars.

He made profound calculations on the revenue Westminster Abbey would derive from the proper dissemination of facts regarding its peculiar relation to the nation's great dead; a quantity of judiciously prepared, wisely distributed newspaper paragraphs illustrating in word and picture the glory of *The Fane of Fame*, as he mentally entitled it, would probably, in the course of ten years or so, enable it to double its available space for coronations, etc. He wandered about the Tower with a guide and a compatriot, and received the latter's cordial agreement to a suggestion that a special 'bus line from Charing Cross would not only make the great monument more accessible, but would soon pay for itself if the vehicles were made in the form of tumbrils (he was not quite sure whether sixteenth-century England employed tumbrils, but that could be adjusted later), and the driver and the conductor attired, say, as Walter Raleigh and a headsman.

He left Victoria Station in the morning, having purchased half-a-dozen magazines to beguile the journey, but as the train issued into open country, which he had previously traversed in the dark, he forgot them in an unexpected interest in the countryside. In a very few minutes he had gained a more favourable impression of British advertising capacities than a week in London had given him. The signs were, indeed, fewer to the mile than in the best parts of the United States, but they were undeniably on the increase. From a professional point of view he found them sufficiently large and colourful, and on the whole well designed as regards employment of space. His only criticism was directed at their literary weakness. Here, for instance, was a blue background, a red and white tin, and the legend "Buy Tucker's Tinned Spinach—it saves Time." The alliteration was not bad, but the idea was primitive, an archaism in advertising. Here, a mile further along, was a merry Roundhead in a green coat offering the passer-by a glass of liquid with the words "I drank it in 1650—it's even better today." That was all right to begin with, he thought, his lips pursed like an infant's in doubt, but more could be made of it. He reflected a moment, and smiled happily to himself as the vision of the board repainted flashed on him:

We distilled our first whisky in 1650.
We have averaged 10,000 cases a year since.
No customer of ours ever voted for Prohibition.

It was only a rough sketch, but it pleased him, and he looked forward to his mission with content.

He arrived at Edginden before he was aware, and for a moment looked about him in bewilderment. What had been an adventurous descent forty years ago had passed unnoticed in the railway carriage, and the little grey railroad station failed to fit into the picture. He passed down the stone platform, noticing coloured posters inviting one to exotic south coast watering places he had never heard of, engaged a lonely Ford and in a quarter of an hour found himself at the Unicorn. As he stepped out of the car the smoke of the railroad train was just fading into the trees at the brow of the hill to the west. It vanished, and Edginden seemed to appear from behind it unchanged from half-a-century before. The Unicorn himself, imperceptibly faded, was pawing with his forelegs one side of the shield-shaped sign from the top of which his horn protruded. Through the low curtained bow-window was still faintly visible the portrait of a rubicund gentleman in wig and red coat; the only sounds might have been echoes from the past —chickens flapping their wings in a nearby yard, the rumble of a distant cart, the creak and drip of water being drawn from a well. Suddenly he heard a winnowing machine; he lifted his head, detected a faint odour of petrol, looked about inquiringly, and pushed the green door of the inn.

An ample, white-haired old lady gave him an unsmiling welcome, ignored his request for a room with a bath, in-

formed him that dinner would be cold and served at half-
past seven, and disappeared. A red-faced maid, in black
calico dress and white apron immediately issued from
another door and led the way up a flight of narrow, steep
and noisy stairs. Her long legs moved so rapidly that his
short ones were unable to keep up, and he only found his
room by searching around until he perceived his black
patent leather bag on a bed almost as high as himself. The
maid had gone, but reappeared several moments later with
a pitcher of hot water, following her own knock so closely
that he had no time to recover the substantial portion of
his garments he had already removed.

The window of his room gave on the hills; for a long
time he stood regarding their smooth rectangular patches
of emerald and bronze; his eye followed the road past
fence and house and barn to the purple of the crest; and a
feeling of forlornness came over him compared to which the
lonesomeness of the week in New York was vague and
feeble. It being due merely to the absence of people he
cared about, their return sooner or later would have made it
right. For this there was no cure; it came out of the essential isolation in which all human beings live, that terrible
isolation against which men devise the most fantastic activities, in order to avoid facing it. It was like his first illness
after his mother's death, when his pains and fears seemed
to mean nothing to any one. He decided to go downstairs
and have a drink with the landlady.

The latter had no objection to his drinking, but declined
to join him. The bar was empty, it being outside of hours.
He ordered a whisky and soda, and drank it slowly; he
detested the stuff and was a teetotaller on principle, but
lacked the courage to drink his favourite orange squash in
this environment. Besides he realised that the latter was
not an avenue to the sociability he craved.

"Nice place you have here," he began.

"There's worse," she replied.

Not being in a position to debate this he began afresh.

"Do you get many Americans here?"

"Some. Are you an American?"

He warmed at this first indication of personal interest

slight as it was. "Yes—that is, I live there. As a matter of fact, I was born in England."

"Couldn't tell it any more," she commented, wiping up the counter and significantly setting out a fresh glass. "Which part?"

He had braced himself for this moment. "Right here, in Edginden," he said, in the soft voice he reserved for the announcement of his most startling projects.

This time she was clearly interested. She scrutinised him carefully and said, "It's queer I don't remember you. I know everybody who has ever lived in these parts this sixty years."

"My father was George Powell."

She reflected an instant. "I remember," she finally declared. "He was from Portsmouth and married Jacob Gunn's girl; the old man set them up in a shop there, but it didn't go and they came here to live on the farm. I remember when you were born; you were only a little fellow when your mother died and your father took you off to America." She mused a moment. "Just fancy, you being Sarah Gunn's boy." In her abstraction she returned the glass to its place on the shelf behind her.

Thus was Powell welcomed home. In a general way his reception elsewhere resembled Mrs. Unicorn's (This being the name by which he thought of the landlady). Those that remembered him as a boy, like those that did not, viewed him with curiosity as a tripper rather than as a son come home. When he gave an impressive sum toward the restoration of the church roof, which had for years bided this event, relying meantime on the slender revenue derived from the solicitation of a torn sheet of paper in the vestibule, he received a formal letter of thanks from a committee and a shy, grateful handshake from the rector, but neither mentioned his sentimental reason for the act, nor treated it as other than the gift of a whimsically-minded rich man.

The end of a week found him as far removed from the end of his mission as if he had never come. By now he had company to drink with him in the bar and most of the natives greeted him in the street, pointing him out as the donor of the large sum toward the church's restoration; but any of this might have happened to any stranger. He wanted to be there as of right, to be at home while he remained, regretted as a departing son when he left. He realized that thus far he had moved little towards that happy goal. He had made no enduring impression; these people were as far from understanding the warm impulse he felt to pour out his energies in their behalf, to receive their cordial assurance of mutual bond and kinship, as he was from understanding how they found life permanently tolerable without electric light, gas or bathtubs. He wanted earnestly to plant some seed which would not only blossom into a thing of utility and beauty for Edginden, but would in its very nature prove to succeeding generations of its children that only one of themelves could have conceived the idea of it.

Numerous tentative projects floated through his brain, but the most favoured children of his imagination all seemed ill-suited to his purpose. The best, the only gift worthy of the name was the power of growth, and he could see no possibility of expansion in Edginden. He might set on foot tactfully a wide publicity campaign to set forth the unique advantages of the place, but he frankly doubted that it had any. There was no manufacturing, and no logical reason why any enterprising manufacturer should choose it for a site. He was reasonably certain that it would not, unlike the thriving small towns of America, buy up tracts of land and offer them gratis as an inducement. Nor could he conceive that the local squire, a stentorian fox-hunting giant who owned the land at both ends of the village, would sanction the placing of signboards, no matter how artistic, and for no matter what public purpose, in his domain. He was sure that these people wanted their town to grow, that was only human. But how to achieve it, how to overcome their dimly perceived prejudices and make them all pull together toward this end, for that he was beginning to despair of finding a solution.

Then, one day, he unexpectedly found it. He was passing Roger Martin's shop and decided to drop in. Martin was his most intimate acquaintance in Edginden. Each vaguely remembered the other as a boyhood playmate, and each had a dislike of whisky, which drew them together in a corner of the Unicorn's cosy pub. Martin had an unlimited curiosity about the New World, and Powell a tireless pleasure in gratifying it.

The shop, in a more pretentious locality, would have been called an antique shop. Here it served a more humble and daily need; though filled with quantities of old vases, pots, bowls, urns, cups and other household articles in copper, pewter and brass, with a fair sprinkling of old chairs, tables and chests in oak and walnut, its chief business was to supply Edginden homes, and particularly its kitchens, with the commonplace utensils necessary for containing and cooking. The sale of old things was subordinate to their mending, and to the making of new things.

Powell enjoyed watching almost any form of human activity, and found his place in Martin's old wing arm-chair soothing; it was where he always sat while exchanging sentences with the latter between the agreeable strokes of hammer on copper. The place was silent, however, as he entered, and its owner was standing by his work-table, which was pushed against the rear windows of the shop, overlooking a tiny walled garden now abloom with red tulips and purple iris. Martin was a little man, smaller even than Powell; his grey hair was thin at the top, but thick, crisp and curly over his neck and ears; his distinguishing features were red, wrinkled cheeks which dimpled when he smiled, merry twinkling eyes, a disorderly white and black moustache, and prominent upper teeth. At the moment he was attentively examining a bronze vase, in the form of a cylinder imposed on the flattened top of a sphere. He nodded over his shoulder to his visitor.

"This has just come over from your country," he said. "A lady who passed this way once and bought some of my things sent it to me from San Francisco to see if I could copy it. She wants to make them both into lamps. Isn't it a beauty?" He lovingly fingered the dull patine of the bronze, lifting it in both hands.

Powell was impressed by something else, however. So this little fellow had a clientele extending to San Francisco.

Strange. "Do you often sell things in America?" he asked.

"Oh, yes," responded the smith, still caressing the vase. "I've a number now to go to New York and Boston. There are some of my things in India and Australia, too," he added proudly. "Hardly a month passes without my getting an order from abroad."

Powell remained silent, thinking rapidly. So there was an activity of Edginden with a fame beyond its confines. These bits of brass and copper were known and desired by folk living at the ends of the earth.

"Why do you keep such a small shop?" he demanded suddenly.

Martin set the vase down; it gave the deep-toned ring of the G string of a violin gently brushed in passing. "It's bigger than I need now," he said, turning round in surprise.

"But you could extend the business, couldn't you? If you already have customers in San Francisco and Sydney, in New York and—" the alliteration failed him and he hurried on, "Why man, you could make a big thing of this."

Martin had before this failed to follow the American's mental flights; now he stood puzzled, his hands holding the shoulder-straps of his long blue apron, his head on one side like a sparrow's, looking down on the other.

"But all that doesn't keep me and Jim busy full time." Jim, the assistant, was at this moment occupied in wheeling a crying infant up and down the walk in front of the shop, the while its mother was at the chemist's two doors away. "I've had more work outside of Edginden this year than ever before, and I still have plenty of space and time to spare."

"Yes, but listen, man!" Powell was in the full ecstasy of sudden inspiration. He got up and walked over to the other; his eyes seemed to come out of their shadowy retreat and were flashing. "Don't you see that if there is a little demand for your stuff, you can make a big one? It isn't as if you were limited to this place. Put your wares out into the world. Advertise! I'll bet all I've got you can triple your business in a year and make it a hundred times as big in three. People are going in for the old-fashioned stuff. Why, I'll do the job for you for nothing. I'll make your shop and Edginden famous. This is the chance I've been looking for. Give me a free rein and Martin's Brass and Copper will be known wherever English is spoken, and then some!" He was aflame with his vision. He saw himself at last in his proper rôle, his ordained relation to his native place.

"But how?" persisted the bewildered little shopkeeper. "If you just doubled the business it would be too big for me; I couldn't do the work."

"You wouldn't have to," snapped the other; then, lowering his voice and putting his hand on the other's shoulder, continued, "Quantity production! That's the answer. It's my function in the world to show people how to sell large quantities of things. That's efficiency, economy. It makes more and better things, and everybody happier. We'll instal the proper equipment, and you will just watch and see that the thing's done right. We'll put up a model plant, get in outside labour—why man, can't you see what this will mean to you and your town?"

But Martin's troubled expression, instead of vanishing, became more anxious. "I don't think you can make these things with machinery," he explained plaintively, "I've made most of the metal utensils in the village myself, but sometimes they buy them outside, and very soon they are brought in for repair. Most often they are not worth the trouble. They are like that table in the garden—when Jim came to help me we were too busy to make one for him, so I had that one sent down from London. It's no good after two years. You can see how the top is warped and the legs have gone to pieces. This one I'm using my grandfather made."

The American cogitated a moment. "I don't see that," he affirmed presently. "Copper is copper, and brass is brass, and if you get the right material and see that it's made right, you will have done your part of the job. You can turn out the same designs a thousand times faster, and give employment to a thousand more men. Can't you see the difference it will make? We'll get the railroad to run

right into the town instead of three miles off—why we'll
put the place on the map!"

Martin became of a sudden very serious. "I—I'm not
sure we want that. We had a hard time keeeping the railroad out of here in the first place, and I'm afraid we
couldn't do with a lot of strangers. It would turn things
upside down. I've always done my best to please the
people here and I know what they like. And when I bought
a bed from Sam Greene or clothes from Bartlett or medicine from Rollo Hines I knew they were giving me their
best, just what *I* wanted. We are sort of used to each
other and understand each other. I don't think we should
get along so well if we had a lot of new people to deal
with." He was apologetic, diffident, eager to explain his
position, but underneath, Powell felt, stubborn in his prejudices; for the first time he began to be slightly exasperated.
Convinced not only of the worth of his intentions but of the
soundness of the plan that had taken hold of him, feeling
himself on the verge of bringing a great boon to Edginden,
he was annoyed at the other's failure to fall into step with
him. He was already visualizing the miraculous, mushroom
growth with which he was familiar, for which he had often
been largely responsible, and the unlooked for opposition
dumbfounded him. He had often had difficulty in selling an
idea, in convincing people that they would get their money's
worth; he had never as yet encountered, even remotely,
opposition to his underlying philosophy. It had never
occurred to him that men might look otherwise on expansion. Martin, sweet of temper, and shy in manner, began
to symbolise an obtuse, almost sullen unresponsiveness in
the people he was so eager to serve. If only he could come
to some common ground, if he could argue against objec-
tions he could understand. His hopes were being dashed to
pieces on a rock so unsubstantial that he could not even
see it.

"But what would the world be like if everybody—" he
began, when the door opened and the proprietress of the
Unicorn joined them, her parade to the back of the shop
punctuated by the clatter of furniture and the toppling of
metal ware. The aisle was narrow and irregular, Mrs. Uni-

corn very wide and quite direct in her progress. She carried in her hand a copper tea-kettle of unusual pattern, the spout coming from the top of the kettle and issuing through a large, graceful handle.

She ignored Powell and addressed Martin directly.

"Roger, that girl of mine has gone and smashed this kettle against the stove," she said, exhibiting a gash in the fair copper surface. "Can you mend it?"

He took it from her and examined it carefully. A pathetic look of distress settled on his face. "I'll try, Miriam," he observed finally, "I shall let you know if I can't."

"Well, do it as soon as you can, and don't let it cost too much," she said pointedly, and took her departure.

As soon as she was out of the door Powell laughed. "Serve her right if you made her scrap this and sold her another kettle," he remarked, "she's tight as a vice."

Martin did not reply for a moment. He continued to examine the kettle, real pain showing in his eyes. He put aside the vase from San Francisco, selecting some tools, lit his brazier. Finally he said to his companion, "I hope I can make this right. It's one of the best things I've ever turned out of this shop." He turned back to his work.

Powell's smile faded. The three-coloured, full-page advertisement he had been inwardly contemplating, which was to blazon to the world "Edginden for Excellence—Martin's Metalware is as durable and beautiful as the English village in which it was made" crumpled up and disappeared as if it had been dropped into a large fire. He pondered the other's words a moment, noting keenly at the same time how he fondled the injured utensil. An expression of understanding crept slowly over his face, and he stole out softly without disturbing the absorbed craftsman.

FIRE AND WATER[1]

By GLENWAY WESCOTT

(From *Collier's Weekly*)

I

THE sky rolled from side to side like an animal in pain,
outstretched on the soft, saturated trees. Now and
again there was a groan of thunder, and lightning flickered
with a glitter of enormous eyes, rolling in their sockets.

I was driving back to my father's farm from the village.
The downpour beat on the buggy-top, splashing to the
ground and spattering the rubber laprobe. I disliked the
smell of the wet harness leather and the sweating horse,
wishing to enjoy the sour fragrance of the vegetation half-
floating, half-rooted, in the fields. The lantern hanging
from the dashboard hollowed out a space in the darkness
into which the rain poured as bright as tin.

As I crossed a small bridge the lantern-light fell for a
moment on the dripping hat and red face of a man who was
leaning against the cement rampart. It was a neighbor
named George Stearns. Should I have stopped to give him
a lift? He was less than half a mile from home; he would
be drunk and troublesome, furthermore I should have had
to wake his wife and daughter, while he alone would roll
quietly into the hay-mow.

It was his custom to return from the village in this condition three or four nights in the week, always on foot,
since his daughter Amelia would not let him take the horse.
His drunkenness was proverbial, and every one who used
that road had seen him stumbling through the underbrush,
collapsing backwards into a ditch, or drawn up patiently
out of the way of hoofs and wheels. Weather meant nothing to him; he dug his way through the drifts, lay in the

[1] Copyright, 1925 (under title "This Way Out"), by P. F. Collier
& Son Company.
Copyright, 1926, by Glenway Wescott.

mud, lurched into cold creeks, but always got home. He
was well liked by his neighbors, who took a certain pleasure
in pardoning a manly weakness, and praised his good
nature whenever his bad habit was mentioned. One
autumn, having swigged too frequently from a bottle behind a beam in the wagon-shed, he dropped his pitch-fork
into the hopper of a threshing-machine, spoiling the blades
which cut the twine; but after the owner had cursed and
threatened, he was not even forced to pay for the damage.

As I passed the lamp rolled low, which Amelia always
left in a window to guide her father, I remembered a story
I had heard, how at the age of eight George had disappeared for a night and most of a day. His family had
lowered a lantern into the well, and shouted in the woods
around the sugar-bush, thinking of wild cats and wolves,
which still came out of the deep forests from time to time
to carry off lambs and ravish the chicken coops. His
hysterical mother peered into the bear's pen, half-expecting
to see strips of clothing on the ground and blood on the
animal's tusks. The whole countryside was aroused. At
last, after a mournful meal, his father had gone into the
basement with a candle and a pitcher to bring up cider, and
found the boy, drunk beside a barrel.

I thought then how one came to know people by the
accumulation of glimpses; the sight of George, wet and
drunk on the little bridge, a moment too fleeting even to
speak to him; and after that his solitude and my solitude,
in which my memory assembled other casual words and
brief encounters. In that country I met my neighbors
chiefly on the road. Thickets and piles of brushwood, the
gravel, the puddles, the barbed-wire fences, the hitching-
posts, and the piazzas, filled the corners of every picture of
their lives. A one-horse vehicle brought me near them, like
the field-glasses with which a naturalist detects a bird in a
tree, though its plumage is the color of the tree. All my
relations with George Stearns and his family, for example,
were of this kind: the talk of one of them and myself in a
buggy, or between one in a buggy and one standing beside
the wheel or on a porch; the look of one of them in a barnyard or a field. . . .

Thus about the nucleus of George's face in the rainstorm, previous impressions gathered, later images and later conversations were to gather, rounding out a pointless history. Recollections of similar men's lives served as intuition into his life, so that, as I turned in at my father's gate, I could see him behind me in the darkness, blustering and hiccoughing, slipping down in the flooded grass, I could hear his obstinate sighs in the wind as it pulled the clouds away.

His eighty-acre farm was a miserable piece of property. Gashed with gullies, the fields of red clay sloped acutely above the house and barn, which were almost hidden in the edge of a swamp. A lake lay like an immense ditch in the center of this swamp, and into it the rains carried the topsoil from increasingly arid fields. George's father had understood the weakness of his farm, and had kept the upper acres in sod-crops, filled the gullies with stone, planted clover to nourish the soil, rotted the grain-straw in the barnyard, and carted it with manure into the fields. But George preferred to forget these hard expedients, and the farm became, as it were, a portrait of himself. He planted only a little oats for the horse, a little corn for the cattle. The fences tottered and fell under loads of woodbine and wild grapes. In great pastures full of thistles two or three sharp-hipped cows gnawed the june-grass that grew between the stones.

George hired out by the day to his more ambitious neighbors. He was satisfied with this way of life; to move from farm to farm without responsibility, to work without haste or worry, to spend his earnings and his leisure in a saloon. The lot of his wife and daughter was not so agreeable. They lived like a pair of domestic animals in a pen: coarse trees on three sides, the tantalizing road on the other; no variety of duty or scene, no entertainment, no plans, nothing to expect. Inevitably their poverty would pinch closer and closer, and they were bound to a man who was happy and didn't care.

At first Amelia seemed to bear it better than her mother. As a tall, wry-faced girl Mrs. Stearns, having been assured by her brothers that she need not expect to be courted for her looks, had married George to avoid becoming an old maid. George's mother had suggested that he might settle down when he married, and she had to take the risk. The little house like a dry-goods box had seemed, in those days, a respectable home; but other people's prosperity had built all around it, to its shame, incomparable mansions with turrets, lightning-rods, and picketting around the chimneys, incomparable hip-roofed barns with the name of the owner stencilled under crossed flags; and George's house had deteriorated with his land and himself. Mrs. Stearns fretted less at her husband's shortcomings than at the looks of the place.

"Everything's goin' to pieces," I heard her complain one day. "It's the worst lookin' place in the county. Look at that broke rig with the weeds growin' through the wheels. The tools all out gettin' rusted. I'll be switched if the mare don't look mangy!"

"Oh stop it, Ma!" Amelia muttered. "I'm tired of that kind of talk!"

"Nobody goes by on the road," her mother went on, "nothin' to see, nothin' to do. And me sick. Your pa gets the best of it, he gets out among folks. We women don't get no further'n you could throw a stone."

Amelia marched across from the sink, her round shoulders raised, shaking her dish-towel angrily. "Who's to blame for this God-awful marsh? What's the good of whimperin'? Who's to blame, I ast you? Better go to bed, Ma, and rest."

When the girl went out to do her milking, the sick woman shuffled off to bed. If it rained she tossed back and forth on her bed, kept awake by the water which gushed in all the gullies, washing the best of their land down to the lake. The temporary rivers gurgled and grew thick, without foam, and ended as suddenly as they had begun. It seemed that soon there would be nothing but rocks between the fences.

Amelia was a short, flat-chested girl with muscular arms and extremely wide hips. Her chapped and freckled skin seemed to have been drawn tightly over the bones of her face—over the long nose, the cheek-bones exactly in the center of her cheeks, the receding but stubborn chin—a face in which were combined poor health and great strength. Her eyelids fluttered so much that one could not remember the eyes, and her thin lips pouted habitually.

She did all the work, had always done it. As a child she went to school only during the winter months, and ceased altogether at fourteen when the school inspector could not force her to go. She kept the house decently clean, baked, churned butter, made her own clothes, and nursed her increasingly bed-ridden mother. Then there were the chores: she gave the cattle frozen corn-fodder to supplement the straw which they ate from the stack, milked them, and took the can to the cheese factory, and pumped from the stinking vat her share of whey for the pigs. I had seen her staggering down ditches which she had shovelled in the snow drifts, her long arms almost pulled from their sockets by the slopping pails of swill, or stooping over the smoke from a kettle-shaped stove which melted the ice in the water-trough. At butchering time she worked elbow to elbow with the men, scraping the bristles from the carcass soused in boiling water, and she alone cut up the pigs, rubbed and smoked the bacon, and ground the sausage. She watched over the old sows when they farrowed, sometimes far into the night, lest they eat their young. Her last duty was to turn down the lamp in the kitchen window where her father could see it as he stumbled up the road.

In October I was driving to the village before dawn to meet a cousin at the station. An odor, iced and musky, came out of the woods. The dewy red leaves looked swollen, and the thickets very large with mist. My horse was willing, and I enjoyed the road, pointed like a rod into distant hollows and forests or lifted up to pierce the sky, feeling an absolute solitude. But when I came near the Stearns farm I saw some one waiting for me. It was Amelia, and she waved, and when I stopped, gripped the wheel with her red hands and stared at me, her face very sharp as if whittled away.

"Gerson, won't you stop and look at my pa. He's sick. I'm scared—scared to wake him up."

I followed her—not into the house, to my surprise—but

into the barn, where the light fell with a feeble quiver from
the two peepholes and innumerable cracks. Amelia pointed
into the nearly empty hay-mow, where I saw first a pair of
heavy boots, smeared with mud, the toes turned sharply
outward, and beyond them George's face, enormous, crimson, and disdainful, with hay in his hair and several stalks
in his moustache.

"I'm sorry, Amelia. He's dead."

"Oh Lord . . . I thought so."

"Is there anything I can do? Shall I tell anybody?"

"Well you can stop and tell Mrs. Bemis. You're goin' to
the village? Tell an undertaker to come, the cheapest
one."

"Is that all?" I repeated, shocked by her perfunctory
courage.

"Yeah, that's all." She sighed. "I got to wake up
mother and tell her."

Four months later she married a man named Nick
Richter. Her mother expressed a peevish gratification:
"Amelia couldn't stand it, bein' alone. I ain't much company no more." She grew weaker, and kept her newly
married daughter at her bedside all that winter, exercising
a tyranny with her eyes when she could not speak, and
they buried her in April.

There was a large funeral, for during the six months
by which she had survived her husband, the community
had decided that she was a martyr to his drunken shiftless-
ness. Amelia asked my father and me to bring two teams
to take people from the house to the cemetery, and she herself rode in my father's carriage with her only living uncle,
his wife, and another relative. But after the service she
separated herself from her family and climbed into the
front seat beside me, looking very tired, her face tight and
yellow, her mouth twitching as if with anger.

"I couldn't stand those sneaky women another minute.
My Aunt Cynthy and Mrs. Smart, the old hens. They
think I don't show a proper feeling. They'll start again's
soon as we get home, but I might's well have a rest, I guess."

"Good idea," I said.

"Of course I'll miss her and she was always good to me,"

she added timidly, as if to please me, and buried her pale nose in a handkerchief.

To change the subject I asked, "Are you and Nick going to stay at the farm?"

"I s'pose so."

"I thought you might try something else. The land isn't much good, is it?"

"No good at all. Worn out, sandy—stones and ditches. It's gettin' now so's it won't raise grass—never was manured any. And the fences are all down. God, I hate it!"

I asked why.

"Well, not just because it's poor farmin'. I don' know— the woods maybe, those rotten trees so close. It's no way to live; you see 'em all day and hear 'em all night. When I was a kid I used to be scared our house would slide into the lake. Was you ever down there? It just shows you what it's always been like. If you fell in, you'd have some chance—but if you was always in . . ."

Her voice weakened to a loud whisper. "You need some excitement. I never went nowhere, never saw nothin'—had to work. I guess you wouldn't have the nerve to get out of a dead hole like that if you knew you got to come back. That's why I never went to dances. I guess you'd jump into the lake for good—when you got home I mean."

I felt uncomfortable. "Why don't you sell the whole outfit and rent a house near town. Nick could make as much by the day as he does here."

She did not seem to listen. "And it's so awful still," she muttered. "My God. It's so still you can hear the slime dripping in the well."

I renewed my encouragement. "Sell it and go to town. Nick could make two or three dollars a day. Don't try to stick it out another year. Give yourself a chance. Have an auction," I said.

"Oh Lord," she cried. "Sell all that junk? It wouldn't bring thirty cents. Spread all that rubbish round the yard for a lot of old women to pick over? I should say not."

"Well, do something then," I said impatiently. We were in sight of the house.

"Oh, I couldn't," Amelia moaned. "I couldn't go off

and leave that house—everything the way it's always been. It'd be like leaving one of them, Ma or Pa, like not burying them," she said.

II

Nick Richter had married to improve his position. His father, a blacksmith, having speculated in Texas oil, had been forced, just before he died, to sell his house, his shop, and every hammer and horseshoe. Nick disliked his father's trade, and drifted in a radius of ten miles around the village, working by the day, week, or month, at odd jobs. He bought a horse and buggy when he could afford to, selling them if he lost his job, and looked for a wife at every Saturday and Sunday night dance for several years. But he danced with his jaw, his neck, and his elbows, and the boisterous girls merely laughed at him, so these entertainments left him lonely and discouraged.

The lake in the swamp below the Stearns house contained pickerel and black bass, which George had been too law-abiding as well as too lazy to exterminate with nets. Since the owner was a bed-ridden widow in Milwaukee, he was its virtual proprietor, and rented his flat-bottomed rowboat two or three times a week. Nick drove up before the barn one Sunday morning, two bamboo poles wagging behind his buggy, and Amelia showed him where to tie his horse and brought the heavy oars from the shed.

He was soon recognized as her beau. George had always puttered about the sheds on Sunday, and Amelia, leaving her chores to him, claimed her first regular holiday. They went to picnics, and drove from village to village, stopping at the saloons for soda and beer, and sat very late on the back porch. Sometimes they went to the lake to fish or pretend to fish.

I saw them there one morning just before George died, as I walked through the swamp on an old corduroy road. From the tall maples leaves floated to the ground like a harvest of ghostly oranges. Through a clearing I could see the murky hills, and when I approached the lake, the water glimmered between the boughs in mother-of-pearl strips. From the tottering boat-house a muddy channel

led out through the reeds to a cup-shaped harbor, separated
from the deep water by a sand bar. In this quiet place a
few lilies grew, the yellow thrusting their closed, hard
heads above the surface, the white spreading tufts of
petals like miniature swans.

Here the boat was at rest, the oars hanging from the
oarlocks. I stood on the shore for several minutes, unobserved, and then turned back into the woods. Nick crouched
in the bottom of the boat, half-hidden, and Amelia, sitting
on the broad back seat, held his head in her lap. Upon her
face there was a vague, pale look of ecstasy, an ecstasy of
possession without confidence and without hope.

There followed George's death, their hasty marriage, the
mother's illness and death. By spring Nick must have recognized the sterility of the farm, for he put in only the
patch of oats and the patch of corn, ploughed up the garden
for Amelia, and began to hire out to his neighbors as George
had done. He was a good worker in his sour, muttering
way, his shoulders bent forward like the wings of a large
hawk, his gaunt wrists extended stiffly. Perhaps his marriage was a disappointment; certainly he failed to feel the
security of a man of property, the serenity of a married man,
of which he may have dreamed. Perhaps he had been con-
taminated by Amelia's discontent. Perhaps he was afraid
of her: a weak swimmer who had ventured into what looked
like a stagnant pool, to find himself in the embrace of a
profound, indomitable current.

Early in the next harvest I stopped one afternoon to ask
Amelia if Nick could help my father any day that week.
The horizon was wrinkled with heat waves, the zenith as
dark as a sea, and one never ceased to hear the growling of
binders. In all the reaped fields the stubble was spotted
with bindweed like drops of blood. As I turned down
toward the swamp I observed the poverty of the fields
there, the exhausted soil gaping through the grass, the thin
stand of grain, the great parched gullies, the bogs where
the birds shouted over the ripe weeds. The trees slept in
the sunshine: not a leaf swayed, but sometimes one feathered prematurely to the ground.

My mare trotted in at Amelia's gate under the poplars

full of blackbirds. In the semicircle of forest the little house squatted, staring blindly from its windows. The sheds leaned against the barn. A sick dove staggered over the rocks by the water-trough. A little way from the kitchen door, some shirts and stockings and cotten sheets hung on a line stretched between two posts.

"Hello!" I shouted. No answer. "Amelia!" An echo, small and soft, came back from the woods: "Amee-lia!" I jumped out of the buggy and went up the steps, certain that if she had gone to town she would have taken in the washing. The kitchen smelled of boot-leather, manure, soft soap, and cooking, and there was another odor which I identified as that of moth-balls.

Could she be asleep? The pendulum of the clock creaked monotonously. I stepped inside and called again. The breakfast dishes lay in and around a dishpan of cold water, and the fire in the range was only a handful of pink coals. I felt the embarrassment of an empty house. Deciding that she had gone to the woods for blackberries, I drove away.

As I passed one of the farms owned by a man named Beacon, I saw him sitting on the lawn, a pitcher of water beside him, fanning his brick-red face with a newspaper. In hot weather he left the heavy work to his sons, since he weighed more than two hundred and fifty pounds. He beckoned to me and came down, wheezing and ponderous, to the road. "As you went by Stearns'," he asked, with the worried frown of a man who has a larger harvest than he can handle, "did you see anything of Nick?"

I shouted because he was deaf. "No, Mr. Beacon. I stopped at the house, but there wasn't anybody there."

"Whew," he sighed. "Nobody there. Queer. Nick's been helpin' us out, and he hain't showed up today. He al'ays sends word. I thought he must'a been sick."

"It is funny," I admitted. "Amelia wasn't there either."

"Well, it's a new wrinkle for Nick," he concluded mournfully.

I intended to stop at Amelia's again, but as I came back from the village I detected in the air a faint bitterness of smoke—so faint at first that I thought it had drifted down from a forest fire in the north. When I came to the top of a hill I saw it, hanging in a black mushroom over the swamp. I touched the mare with my whip and rattled into the alley, where the smoke was thick and steady and the color of wheat-chaff, blowing slowly overhead.

It was the Stearns house. Through a hole in the roof a great draught lifted the flame as if in a chimney. The yard was full of men, whose faces in the ruddy light were strange and glistening. Sweat dripped on their blue shirts. They were fighting the fire eagerly and with some skill; already they had chopped away the flaming porch. Three men in turn worked the handle of the coughing, spurting pump, and bucket after bucket of water was passed from hand to hand and emptied.

I saw immediately that Amelia and Nick were not there. Some buggies and an auto had stopped along the road, and several women looked on with interest, their summer dresses and parasols lending to the catastrophe an air of picnic. Among the spectators, but near enough to make his orders heard above the crackle and roar of the fire, the shouts, the axes, the creak of the pump handle, old Beacon was enthroned on a dry-goods box.

"Well my boy," he demanded, "what d'you think of this? Did they have any insurance?" He smiled wickedly.

Indignant at his suspicion, I tried to offer some explanation, to remember some clue. Then I shouted into his ear, "They hadn't any insurance. I remember. Amelia asked father about it, and he told her not to bother, but to sell out when she had a chance."

A look of perplexity, even of disappointment, passed across old Beacon's face, that resembled a great, sagacious beet. He swelled his cheeks and blew wearily. "Well, I'll be damned, anyway," he said.

The roof fell, splitting like paper, and after that the fire diminished. The floor sent up smoke and steam, but no more flame. The kitchen stove crashed through the charred boards into the cellar.

"But I don' know what these men are burstin' themselves for at this job," the old man said. "Looks to me like nobody's goin' to thank 'em for it. The mare and the cart're gone." He settled his damp cheeks in the folds of his neck.

"Oh," I shouted half-heartedly, "I guess they've gone to town. They'll be back, poor devils."

"But I knew better. My eyes had rested on the clothes-line; the washing which had hung there was gone, and on the ground beneath in an uneven row the clothespins lay. I remembered the harmless dying coals in the range. I remembered the unwashed dishes and the odor of moth-balls. I remembered what Amelia had said the day her mother was buried: "I couldn't go off and leave that house —everything the way it's always been."

Had they been in the house? Had they heard me call? Had they been hiding there, in the other rooms or behind a door?

The fire left a ruin shaped like a charred pot. The men drew off—wet, black, tired, and puzzled—washed their faces at the pump and rolled down their sleeves. The horses were untied, every one piled into one vehicle or another, and they drove away shouting; but those who spoke of the cause of the fire did so in pairs, very quietly.

From the charred and broken house the smoke went up straight to the sky. Now it was as soft as wool, now like a tower or shell. It widened over the swamp, casting a shadow upon the lake, and persisted until dusk with an even, melancholy trembling.

III

Years afterward, while I was stopping for a few days in a town in the western part of the State, a carnival set up its tents in a dance-hall park between the river and the tracks. I saw a van or two come down the main street, the horses' fetlocks stirring up dust in clouds which settled on their sweaty backs and on the faces of the man with his cheeks full of tobacco and the hatchet-faced woman who sat on the packing cases and rolls of canvas. That night two of the vagrants appeared at the boarding-house table where I took my meals. The shuttered dining room smelled like a po-tato cellar where the sprouts have nosed their way upward

and the scabby tubers have rotted for months, and when
the landlady trotted out of the kitchen and set down plat-
ters of meat in slabs as large as her hand, the regular
boarders looked with sick faces at their plates and at one
another.

But the theatrical ladies ate with the silent heartiness of
women paid to eat in a shop window as an advertisement
of whatever they ate. Chemises of shadow lace showed
through georgette shirtwaists, making their bodies look em-
bossed with garlands and butterflies. Under mats of blon-
dined hair fastened with rhinestone pins, their faces had an
identical appearance of porcelain, the hard eyes surrounded
by pencilled lashes and eyebrows, spots of orange rouge
exactly between the nose and the ear. Their nails cut in
triangles shone like celluloid. Grasping the knives and
forks vigorously, their eyes unfocussed, their red mouths in
motion, they ate the fat meat to the last drop of gravy, the
soggy pie to the last crumb.

The next afternoon I crossed the iron footbridge with an
aimless curiosity, into the Grove. The river was only a
trickle from puddle to puddle and gave off an odor similar
to that of cucumbers, and the reflections of narrow, green
and yellow leaves upon its surface were like the footprints
of innumerable birds on a flat of mud.

Five great wagons and a mud-caked Ford were drawn up
along the river. The horses grazed in an adjoining meadow,
the sweat dried in flakes on their backs, switching at the
flies and never lifting their heads to look at the noisy camp,
unfolded from the loads which they had drawn.

In the center, like a fat woman pirouetting, the merry-
go-round revolved laboriously. The mincing legs of its
horses kicked out behind, their foamless lips were parted,
and a pair of crimson tigers drew a chariot for those too
timid or too large to go astride. The power which set the
minute stallions and sky-blue bears gradually rocking and
circling came from a steam engine like a short-necked bottle,
whose whistle preceded the slapping and squeaking of the
leather belts and the outburst of shrill tunes from the calliope, when all the passengers, mostly children, had been
hoisted and set upright in the saddles.

A crowd of untidy women and shouting boys filled the alley between the tents. The refreshment booth, a great umbrella of canvas enclosed by planks laid from barrel to barrel, did a brisk business in ice-cream cones, in tepid drinks, in hot dogs and patties of ground meat stewing on a black griddle. A young man whose hair hung down in shoestrings and a plump woman with brown pouches beneath her eyes ran from side to side shouting, "What's yours?" and "Don't push plee-ase," storing the nickels and dimes in a cash-register drawer which opened and shut with a grating noise.

Next to it stood a "hit-the-nigger-baby" establishment— a hierarchy of dolls, and a pile of baseballs with which to knock them down, and a display of bad cigars and felt pillow-covers for prizes. Though it was Saturday afternoon few men were there to patronize it, for those who had worked all morning in the heat naturally preferred to lie on couches indoors, with newspapers over their faces.

The showmen's cheeks drooped with disillusionment and fatigue. Business was not good; business was never good, or never good enough. It was a hard life: shouting, luring, browbeating, laughing, and singing—eating the poorest food, counting the smallest coins, packing the tents, frayed finery, nigger-dolls, fangless rattlesnakes, and petrified Belgian babies; the boss and his wife going ahead in the Ford to rent the next park, the rest following slowly after the strong-smelling horses. They must have learned, the youngest Carnival Queen and the newest freak, that romance is for those who see, never for those who do, and underpaid as a profession.

I stopped to look at a picture of the dope-fiend, a moon-colored young man with scaly, presumably allegorical beasts nestling against his ribs. Hanging beside it were posters of Jocko, the Baboon-Man, who spoke the monkey language and ate raw meat, a snake charmer among her serpents which stood up in spirals as thick as trees, and the Fat Woman, a belted, brooched, and corsetted feather-bed, with oval fingers scarcely meeting across her tremendous chest. A nervous little man, who looked as if he might at any moment burst into tears, was lecturing a dozen people.

I was not tempted by his promises, for I could hear the tremolo of the young man who would say, "Cigarette smoking has made me what I am today," and the charmer crooning perfunctorily to her sick snakes; I could smell his ether and her toilet-water. I had seen a Wild Man from Java or Borneo or somewhere else who tore off the heads of live, squawking hens with his teeth and sucked their blood, and felt sure that this poor tent had nothing so sensational to offer.

The leaves of the maples, pockmarked and bleached by a common blight, loosened and glided through the windless air, the calliope played, the barkers grew hoarse, several babies cried. I went on to the next tent, labelled in great letters GAY PAREE, joining the crowd which gathered to see a free show before the performance.

Three women and a negro stood on a platform like a large bench. The women wore diaphanous slips, all beads and fringe, which did not cover a row of pink and green legs, two of which were crooked and four very fat. I recognized the ladies of the boarding house. They stared at the crowd with the solemnity of caged animals, apparently trying to look voluptuous on the couchless, cushionless boards. One of them pulled her blouse away from her body and stared avidly inside it. The negro who stood sleepily beside them crouched now and began to pipe, drearily and loud, on a sort of flute. The women stiffened, their lips parted, the pupils of their eyes grew large and cold. Three arms were lifted, and all their bodies throbbed, paused, and throbbed again. Then each one curved her waist extremely, first to the right side, then to the left, and each seemed to spring upward and relax like a bow from which an arrow has been shot. Three shrill cries and a tapping of the negro's foot marked the beat.

During the dance a woman came out of the tent behind the performers and sat down in the ticket-box. It was Amelia.

I was shocked and amazed. Seven years had passed. And the pair had vanished like a rock, not thrown, but laid in a pond. No one had suspected their intention, and after they went, their neighbors wondered why rather than where they had gone. The police could have traced them, but why should they have been traced? The farm, which was heavily mortgaged, went to a real estate agent who came out from time to time to stare at the ruin and to stamp over the miserable fields, not knowing what to do with them. Seven years ago. . . . Doubtless some one found out what had become of them, but I had been away from home for years and had never heard.

Amelia had changed more than I, and at first I was afraid she would give me a wild welcome—to what? The tent was all she had. But in a few moments I began to doubt if she would have recognized her own father. She sat there above me like a figure in a jack-in-the-box, took out a roll of tickets like a pulley-wheel, and counted the change in a box. Her small eyes drifted heedlessly from dull face to dull face: so many strangers, so many fools, so many tickets to be sold! She had forgotten me, forgotten above all what I remembered.

She was grotesquely fat. Her narrow lips had been pressed together by rectangular cheeks, there were deep crevices at her wrists, and the sharp chin was lost in a succession of double chins gathered into a tight necklace of amber beads as large as cherries. Her hair was drawn up in a pompadour over a visible brown rat, her purple velvet dress had worn leathery at the elbows. But it was evident, by the way she sat in that booth like a pulpit, that all this meant progress and prosperity. Every distortion of her face, every aggrandizement of her body proclaimed her contentment. Soothed by movement and noise, gorged by excitement, the girl who had resembled years ago a wistful rat, was satisfied.

I looked about for Nick, and his appearance between the flaps, coat-tails first, as he argued with some one inside the tent, silenced the music and arrested the dancing. He came forward and began to harangue the onlookers and to shake his large fists, straining the frock-coat which was buttoned too tightly over his chest. He had not changed, unless exaggeration be a change: his glance was still hurt and ominous, and there was the suggestion of a curse in the tone of his voice. It was plain that the carnival had not been his salvation. Amelia did not look at him but nevertheless she seemed, in her fulfillment, to mock his angry hands, the furtive hope of his eyes, his mastiff-jaw that would never dare to snap.

"You have here, ladies and gentlemen," he continued, smiling wanly, "the flower of Oriental art. It is no singing and dancing for children. There are things about it they would not appreciate. All these famous performers have appeared in Paris. The French do not relish tame entertainments. They like it hot, they like it strong. You have seen their free preliminary dance. It is only a sample of what they can do. The admission is ten cents. I advise you strongly to come in. The show starts in five minutes."

The women and the negro sauntered down the steps behind the flap. Nick disappeared. Amelia began to tear off tickets and make change, and presently she followed, never glancing at the stragglers or at me.

I did not see them again. I did not need to hear their story. For in the dusty grove were tents, the brass throats of the calliope opened again, and the whole town throbbed with music. Those silences in which she had heard "slime dripping in the well" were vanquished.

THE DEVIL–DRUM[1]

By BARRETT WILLOUGHBY

(From *The Century Magazine*)

O-O-M, oom-oom. O-o-m, oom-oom. O-o-m, oom-oom.
Up from the *kashim* the underground council-house,
came the beat of the devil-drum, pulsing hollow and strange
amid the scream of the gale and the rumble of icebergs
grinding below the snow-buried Eskimo village.

O-o-m, oom-oom. O-o-m, oom-oom. O-o-m, oom-oom.
Ah-king-ah, the medicine-man, was trying to change the
wind. Day and night for two moons the polar blizzard had
split its force on the bleak island pyramid thrusting up
through the ice of Bering Strait. It was a wind of death, a
devil's wind, piling floe on floe until the ice grounded, yet
keeping it ever a-stir. No life could exist beneath the pack
or on top of it, and in the igloos clinging to the white
slope of the shore the people, unable to hunt, were facing
starvation.

O-o-m, oom-oom. O-o-m, oom-oom. O-o-m, oom-oom.
In the temporary lull the hollow rhythm grew louder,
penetrating the walls of the missionary's igloo, where he,
the only white man on the island, sat alone before a table
clutching an open book with both mittened hands. The
twilight of the arctic noon made no impression on the thick
frost-crust of the window, but the wan rays of a kerosene-
lamp fell on the volume, and on the missionary's gray hair
showing above the dropped hood of his reindeer parka.
With every breath a shaft of vapor clouded the chill air,
for his supply of driftwood had vanished while the blizzard
was in its first month, and after he had shared his oil
with the village families there was little left for use in his
Eskimo heating-lamp.

The reverberation of the devil-drum was suddenly pierced by the wail of a wolf-dog dying under the teeth of its hunger-maddened mates. The man raised sunken eyes, blue and fervid with a terrible anxiety, and listened. The sounds of cannibalistic ravening sent a tremor through his body.

"God— God—" he flattened his palms on the open Bible and strained his thin face upward in desperate supplication —"God, Father, change the wind!" During a moment's silence his gaze remained fixed on something beyond the blackened ceiling of the igloo, beyond the driven ice-dust of the blizzard. Then in a voice that gathered confidence as he proceeded he filled the room with ringing phrases from the Book:

"He caused an east wind to blow in the heaven: and by his power he brought in the south wind.

"He rained flesh also upon them as dust, and feathered fowls like as the sands of the sea.

"And He let it fall in the midst of their camp, round about their habitations.

"So they did eat and were well filled."

O-o-m, oom-oom. O-o-m, oom-oom. O-o-m, oom-oom, the devil-drum beat a barbarous amen.

"They did eat and were well filled!" The missionary closed the Bible and firmly, as one who has found new courage, repeated the words in the Eskimo tongue. He rose from the table, a lean, little man even in his heavy furs, and crossed over to a corner where a canned-milk box did duty as a cupboard. From the curled bacon rind that hung there he cut a thin slice and slipped it hungrily into his mouth. Chewing a bit of it eased the gnawing in his stomach, which had not yet grown accustomed to one meal a day, a ration made necessary since he had divided the last of his provisions with the village.

Opening a door at the back of the igloo he made his stooping way into another larger room—the schoolhouse and church his own hands had built so hopefully six months before. Under his stiff fingers the light flared up from a bracket lamp, revealing a small wall-blackboard which had never known a chalk mark and the yellow lumber of benches that had yet to feel the contact of Eskimo garments.

In the beginning the Eskimos had treated him with the good-natured tolerance of their race. They accepted his presents, ate his food, and begged or borrowed from him in accordance with their code: The white man who outwits us is a better man than we, and we admire him; the white man we outwit is a fool. The unsuspecting little missionary, confident that he was making great strides into their friendship, was unusually generous; but the moment he tried to preach the word of his God, the moment he attempted to interfere with their customs, he found himself up against a glacial wall of resentment.

"Leave us alone! Leave us alone!" Milli-ru-ak, the hunter, had said to him in the squirrel-hunting season when the missionary went to remonstrate with him for biting off the nose of his wife's lover. "Leave us alone! Does the Eskimo force his way on the white man who invades his country? Why does the white man force his way on the Eskimo? Leave us alone!"

"But Milli-ru-ak, to bite off the nose of thy neighbor——"

"Listen, white man, to the law of my fathers!" The hunter's dark eyes narrowed. "Had my neighbor come to me and said: 'Milli-ru-ak, thy woman hath found favor in my eyes. Let us change wives during the squirrel-hunting, that our families may be allied when the children are born'; then would I have been proud that my neighbor should have taken his pleasure with my wife and I with his. But my neighbor was without honor. He waited until I was gone to the hunt, then like a thief he goes to my woman. I found him there. I bit off his nose. Such," said Milli-ru-ak, turning on his heel, "was the just law of my fathers."

Aghast at this disclosure, the little missionary persistently attempted to convince the hunter of his sins, and after a week Milli-ru-ak shot at him—by accident. The bullet passed harmlessly between the white man's arm and his body, embedding itself in the shaky pulpit he was building at the time. He could see the splintered hole now as he placed his open Bible upon it and reached for the dangling bell-rope behind the pulpit.

The *ding-dong* that marked the Sabbath day was caught up by the blizzard and carried with the boom of the devil-drum out over the polar wastes. Every Sunday and Wednesday since the completion of the meeting-house the missionary had doggedly rung the first and second bell summoning an indifferent people to listen to the word of his God. Not a soul had ever responded.

He rang the first bell longer than usual. Now that the magic of Ah-king-ah had failed to change the wind, now that the dogs were starving, and the people were eating the last of the moldy seal-meat originally intended for the animals, surely, he thought, they were ready to abandon their ways of darkness for the light of Christianity.

He allowed the bell-rope to fall, and poured a bit of oil from a deflated seal-skin container into the stone lamp in the middle of the floor. When the flame flared up from the moss wick he held his hands over it. Not for himself would he have used any of the precious oil, but he hoped that some curious Eskimo might come and, seeing the fire, spread the news of it in the village. The people might come to him then, since there was no oil in the native igloos—no oil for heating, no oil for melting ice for water, no oil for cooking the moldy seal-meat. Only the medicine-man had oil now.

The dogs outside had quieted, and the voice of Ah-king-ah's drum alone rode the gale. The little missionary, squatting over the lamp, kept turning his thin, expectant face toward the outside door. He was always looking for it to open, but it never did. Fifteen minutes dragged by before he rose and rang the second bell. In the silence that followed its last clang the *oom-oom* of Ah-king-ah's drum mocked him with his failure in the service of his Master.

Across the vapor of his breath the rows of clean new benches reproached him with their emptiness, and from the bare wooden walls frost-pegs on every nail-head pointed at him like accusing white fingers. He turned slowly and, mounting the pulpit, stood, his hands on the open Bible, his blue eyes looking down wistfully on the cheerless room. The smoky bracket lamp behind him threw his shadow, long and grotesque, across the bare benches, as if in pity trying to cover them. The sound of the devil-drum filtered in faint, taunting, but the missionary cleared his throat and, as was his wont, began his lonely Sunday service. His voice, forlorn and strange at first, grew firmer as he proceeded.

At the end he closed his Bible and turned out the light. There was a dispirited sag to his narrow shoulders as he went back to his living room. Today, because death was so near to them all, the Eskimos' animal-like indifference to him and his message made him feel small and forsaken; made him ache with the terrible longing of the lonely white man for his kind. For a moment he stood uncertain, his breath clouding the cold, stale atmosphere of the igloo; then with the air of one banishing personal weaknesses he shoved his parka hood over his head, drew the long fur about his face, and made his way out through the snow tunnel leading from his door to the open.

The force of the gale struck him flat against a trampled snow-bank where red stains still defied the covering of the wind-blown snow. Not a bone or a piece of fur remained of the dog who had died there an hour before.

The pallor of the arctic noon was filled with frost-dust borne on wind of such velocity that its passing was like the whiz of speeding bullets. Through the fur about his face the man peered at the ice-pack lying like a gray monster below him. Stationary it appeared at first, but as his eyes grew accustomed to the murky light, it became a thing of horrid life, heaving, quivering, forming itself into grotesque shapes with a slowness that was as sinister and relentless as death. Through the blizzard as far as he could see berg was creeping up over berg, grinding, crunching, to heights of twenty, thirty feet, until the masses tottered and crashed down on the other side, sending powdered ice streaming on the gale like ocean spray. The awful, insensate force loosed thus in a strange, unearthly land struck to the missionary's soul with primeval terror. He felt puny, insignificant, cruelly at the mercy of that tremendous wind which was blowing the ice-pack down from the pole and maliciously grounding it in the shallow

waters of the strait. For an instant something primitive
in him was near to endowing it with the malevolent personality the Eskimos were even then trying to placate
through Ah-king-ah's drum.

"God, Father," he prayed with sudden, panicky earnestness, "change the wind!"

O-o-m, oom-oom. O-o-m, oom-oom. O-o-m, oom-oom,
reverberated the devil-drum.

Far out on the pack, where death was certain, a dark
thing moved. It drew nearer the village, a great bull
walrus scouting vainly for leads of open water that meant
life to the small herd wallowing along in its wake. The scout
rolled its three thousand pounds from side to side over the
moving ice, dexterously fastening its tusks into the base of
each berg and pulling itself to the top. On the pinnacle
it reared still higher on its flippers, sniffing the air, tusked
head swaying, short-sighted eyes trying to pierce the thick
atmosphere. A moment of decision, and through the stridor
of the elements a bellowing grunt rumbled deep and lone,
signaling the advance of the herd. The valiant creature
wallowed on from point to point of vantage, progressing
through the zone of constant and terrible danger with a
courageous dignity that won admiration even from the
hungry missionary, who saw it as food, heat, life itself.

Opposite the village the walrus escaped the buckling of
the ice by a hair's-breadth, and drawing itself up to the peak
of a moving berg, paused longer than usual to toss its
mighty tusks in nervous apprehension of a new danger.
Just as the berg began to topple it sensed the presence of
human beings, and sent its wild trumpetings to warn the
herd. The gallant animal, too late to take any thought
for itself, plunged recklessly. A patch of black in the gaping angle between two floes, a slow closing of the frigid
trap, and a long-drawn despairing roar wove itself through
the hissing of the wind and the booming of the devil-
drum. As it died away, the ice was marked by a seeping
red stain.

The herd, panic-stricken at the loss of their leader, flung
themselves forward to destruction, leaving crushed bodies
to mark a spotted trail of death across the ice-field.

The last terror-driven creature was disappearing in the haze of the blizzard when a bent Eskimo battled his way down from the *kashim* to the edge of the heaving ice. He sheltered himself in the lee of a floe, looking long at the evidences of tragedy before him. Three wolf-dogs, scenting the blood, came out from under the snow and sat on their haunches to send their hunger-cry keening through the glimmering twilight. Starving though they were, neither man nor beasts dared venture over the few feet that lay between them and the meat tantalizing them on the creeping ice.

"O God, Father, change the wind!" prayed the missionary.

O-o-m, oom-oom. O-o-m, oom-oom. O-o-m, oom-oom, propitiated the devil-drum of Ah-king-ah.

II

When the white man saw the Eskimo, he started. Then tightening the hood of his parka against the stinging ice-dust, he began creeping cautiously away toward the sound of the drum. With every backward glance he quickened his progress. At last he would be able to enter the tunnel of the *kashim* while the guard was absent from his post; for though the missionary's presence had been tolerated in the igloos, he had never yet succeeded in forcing his way into the council-house. He had convinced himself that once in the *kashim*, where he could address the assembled village, he could persuade them to abandon their heathen incantations and fling themselves on the mercy of God.

He pressed forward eagerly toward the open jaws of a whale which formed the entrance to the tunnel. Despite his haste, he came to an abrupt halt inside the passage. A queer cross of driftwood lay there, warning strangers against entering the *kashim* while the medicine-man was performing the weird mysteries of his calling.

The missionary's hesitation was banished by his zeal, and a moment later he caught up a club from the stack of hunting implements near the opening and began to feel his uneven way along the icy stones of the tunnel. Half a dozen

steps plunged him into darkness where every movement of
his feet roused wolf-dogs driven to shelter by the storm.
They leaped, savagely snarling their hatred of the disturbing
white, and the missionary, knowing that one misstep would
send him sprawling under their slavering jaws, laid about
him with a club, beating a way through the starving
animals.

He advanced blindly until a glimmer of light at the end
of the tunnel guided him to the opening in the floor of the
kashim above. With a gasp of relief, he clutched the ladder
that led upward, and mounted. He was not observed as he
thrust his head into the dim room, hot and rank with
ammoniacal smells and the reek of close-packed bodies.
Miak, the witch-woman, huddled in one corner, tending
the wick of the medicine-man's stone lamp. It's smoky
light barely revealed the skin-covered shelf about the walls
where hunters, stripped to the waist, sat cross-legged and
cross-armed, their Mongolian faces set in earnest concentration. On the floor below them squatted the women, the old
men, and the quiet children, naked as fishes.

All eyes were on Ah-king-ah, the medicine-man—Ah-
king-ah who had successfully defied the Christianizing
efforts of two former missionaries. Many were the tales
told of the man's cunning and strength not only among the
Eskimo tribes, but among the whalers and the white traders
of the arctic. In the Season of the Sun, when the tribes
assembled on In-ga-lee-nay for the yearly Festival of the
Whale, it took Miak, the witch-woman, three days to sing
all the runes of his magic. Mightiest and richest shaman
of the high North was Ah-king-ah, and great in the eyes
of the Innuits, was the singing of Miak. So strong were his
words of enchantment, he could plunge a hunting-knife
through his vitals and dance with his necklace of bird-claws
dangling from the point behind. So marvelous were his
chants of wizardry that the sound of them formed kayaks,
which took him far to the moonless land, where spirits of
departed ivory-hunters yielded up their secrets to him.
Ah-king-ah had the spirit of a crow. Ah-king-ah was a son
of the wind. Ah-king-ah flew to the moon on the rays of
the ice-blink. Once he flew to Siberia and challenged Nan-

kum, the one-eyed shaman of the Chuckchees, to battle for
the supremacy of the North. Had not all the village seen
them fighting over the strait one morning—two great black
crows whose raucous screams sent chills to the hearts of
the bravest hunters? Mightiest shaman of the North was
Ah-king-ah. With his beak he had wrenched off the leg of
Nan-kum and flung it to the ice, cawing triumphantly,
while the cripple flapped away defeated to Asiatic shores.
Had not Milli-ru-ak found the leg where it fell, and was it
not the leg of a man? And did not hunters returning from
Siberian tundras report Nan-kum hobbling about on one leg
ever after? Great indeed was Ah-king-ah, the medicine-
man, and greater still would he be when he had changed
the wind that was bringing famine to In-ga-lee-nay; greater
and richer, for his price would be half the fruits of the village hunt for the space of six hunting moons.

The missionary's eyes fell upon Ah-king-ah, half crouch-
ing in the middle of the floor. He was six feet tall, and nude
except for a short, transparent garment made of the intes-
tines of seals and trimmed with the crimson beaks of sea-
parrots. He was beating upon the sacred devil-drum and
chanting runes treating of the secret things of spirits, while
his slim, naked feet made weird passes and performed
strange, halting steps. With every movement his superb
brown body rippled beneath the transparent shirt, setting
all the beaks clattering in measured cadence. Behind him
sat his three apprentices, swaying their naked bodies as
they thumped the floor with sticks adorned with wolf-tails
and gull-wings.

A sudden, sinuous motion, and Ah-king-ah was facing
the west. The drum began a soft, rolling accompaniment
to his rising, long-drawn croon. The tawny torsos of the
hunters, moving to and fro from the hips, caught the
light in zigzag waves.

Ah-king-ah's tones grew louder, the tempo of the drum
quickened, and its sound swelled until it became the voice
of the wind, the thunder of crashing seas, the expression
of nature in all her moods of fury. Swaying bodies responded. The people began to shout, to vent queer cries in
unison, urging the shaman to greater efforts, deeper magic.

Excitement grew until it was a very frenzy of earnestness
that increased the heat of the *kashim* and started the sweat
on the sixty bodies packed there. The reek of them was
sickening, the deluge of sounds deafening.

Suddenly everything stopped. Ah-king-ah grew rigid.
While the jade and amber beads dangling from the plugs
in his lower lip quivered into life, his dark face took on the
look of a demon. He flung out his arms, raised his chin,
and sent an intonation soaring through the din of the gale.

"Thou, Almighty Devil——"

"Stop!" The small figure of the missionary catapulted
to the middle of the room, one arm outstretched, one thin
finger extended. "Stop, blasphemer!" he shouted, lost to
all sense of danger in the fervor of his religious indignation.
"Servant of Satan! son of Belial! wouldst thou anger God
by thy sacrilege?" His pale eyes flashed in his twitching
face, his accusing fingers trembled. "God alone is mighty!
God alone is good! Oh, poor deluded ones,"——he turned
pleadingly to the stunned and wondering people——"shut
your ears to the evils of this sorcerer! Turn to the true
God, and the blizzard will die, and you shall have meat!"

In the smoky light the astonished expressions on the
dark faces changed. They grew sullen, grew threatening,
in a silence that was pregnant with hostility. One wolf-
step brought Ah-king-ah close to the white man, who became dwarfed and insignificant beside the powerful Eskimo.
Ah-king-ah's voice rang deep and mellow and supremely
exalted after the thin, excited tones of the missionary.

"The white man has spoken, my brothers. But——did we
of In-ga-lee-nay ask him for this God whom he says we
insult? The white man has broken in upon us. He has
crossed the sign that warns all strangers from our council-
house. He has spoken. Listen now to Ah-king-ah and
compare the wisdom of our tongues." He paused until the
murmur of approval went around the hunters' shelf. "Well
ye know that our people have lived on In-ga-lee-nay for ten
times a thousand moons, happy in the customs of the
ancient ones. Well ye know that our island and the
waters about our island have ever been the abode of plenty,
the breeding-place of birds, the dwelling-place of land-

creatures, the home of sea-creatures. In all the land of the Innuits no village has been so favored by the spirits. In no village but thine could a man sit in his doorway and shoot enough seals to give a feast."

The hunters grunted assent and gravely nodded their heads above their folded arms.

"Yea, my brothers, in the old time ye were happy. Your bellies were rounded and well filled. Skins of oil hung from your ceilings, and oil in plenty burned in the lamps of your igloos. This was the happy way of life under the wise laws of your fathers." Ah-king-ah shifted his drum from one hip to the other and resumed with quickened utterance:

"Then comes this white man from the South. Uninvited, he pushes his way into your igloos with the words of his God. He comes with the ringing of the bell that is bad medicine in the ears of the almighty devil, tossing in his hands the ivory ball of the world. Then, my brothers, from the Place of Winds strange evils have come upon you. Why? Why, my brothers?"

He allowed a moment's silence before he leaned forward and whispered slowly in a way that left the room ringing:

"The—almighty—devil—is—angry—with—you!"

In the hush that followed, the sound of the blizzard seeped in through the thick walls. Ah-king-ah suddenly flung himself upright, and continued in a voice that gathered volume as he proceeded:

"The almighty devil is angry with you for harkening to new words. Behold, your bellies grow flat against your backs. Your igloos grow cold. Your dogs consume each other. Oh, hear the words of Ah-king-ah, my brothers, whom the spirits have taught concerning these things of mystery." The shaman wheeled, and with a quick, accusing finger transfixed the missionary. "It is because of this white man and his ringing bell that the devil is angry!" he shouted. "Wherefore, I say, let this white man take his God back to his own kind—back to the land of his fathers!" The words rose to a shriek. "Let him take his God back to the land of his fathers!"

The muttering of the crowd broke loose in a yelling frenzy as men, women, and children took up the cry. In

the seething, sweating mass of humanity the missionary's
protests were lost; but the dauntless little man wrested
himself from the hands of the medicine-man's apprentices,
snatched the drum from the great Ah-king-ah himself, and
leaped to the now empty shelf of the *kashim*.

"Wait! Wait!" he commanded. His fist banged the
devil-drum, which none but a shaman might touch on penalty of death. The very magnitude of the sacrilege blud-
geoned the people into an aghast silence. "For the sake of
your starving women and children, listen to the words of
the white man's God. In the Book of which I have told
you it is written: 'Whatsoever ye shall ask in my name, that
will I do!' Oh, poor benighted ones, pray to God for help,
and He will answer. For two months ye have watched
Ah-king-ah with his devil tricks trying to change the wind.
His words are a lie within his mouth! His sorceries are an
abomination to the Lord. His——"

A lightning movement, and Ah-king-ah had snatched the
drum to him.

"We do not know this man's God, and we do not want to
know Him!" The shaman's mighty voice extinguished the
missionary's. "Let the white man take his God back to
the land of his fathers!" The rumble of the drum began,
and the shaman's feet resumed their weird passes. Again
and again he repeated the words. His rhythmic chanting
and the booming of the drum woke the mob spirit in the
people. The yelling crowd that surged threateningly
toward the missionary was led by Milli-ru-ak, who leaped
to the shelf and crooked his avid fingers about the white
man's throat.

"Stop, my brothers!" The medicine-man's authoritative
voice rang out. He had ceased his capering, and there was
a light of apprehension in his wary eyes. "Milli-ru-ak, lay
thy hands off! It is not well that the people of In-ga-lee-
nay do violence to such as he, for well ye know how the
long arm of the white man's law reaches even from the
South, where the sun sinks under the world, to the North,
where the water ends. Have ye forgotten the fate of the
three medicine-men, Sautock, Beelack, and O-tock-tock in
the year of the Red Death? They did but bind the man

O'Ryan until his spirit fled—the strange man O'Ryan, who swung the little cup of smoke before his God, and wore the long garment of a woman, with a cross about his neck. Remember my brothers, how in the Season of the Sun there came high chiefs from the South, mighty in anger, and with stars on their breasts glittering like the fishes' scales? Remember how they hanged Sautock, Beelack, and O-tock-tock high on the slope back of the village? Have ye the minds of children that ye can forget the long moons their bones rattled in the chains as the east wind lipped them? I, Ah-king-ah, to whom spirits whisper, tell ye it is not well that we do violence to a white man,"—he woke again the rumbling rhythm of the drum—"but let him leave us in peace to practice the ways of our fathers. Let him take his God back to his own land!"

"Yea! Yea!" The people took up the words in a clamoring chorus, while the shaman's three apprentices seized the protesting missionary and carried him to the opening in the floor. One of them placed his feet on the ladder. The other two pressed him down rung by rung until he found himself on the floor of the tunnel, where the eyes of starving dogs menaced him.

He stood uncertain for a moment while the *oom-oom* of the devil-drum rolled in his ears. Then blindly he groped and beat his way along the slippery passage.

"Oh, Thou, Almighty Devil—" The propitiatory chant of Ah-king-ah followed him out into the blizzard.

Darkness had already fallen. The malicious wind flung ice-dust like splintered glass through the fur about his face. He shut his eyes against the sting of it, and stumbled forward, a small, forlorn figure in the polar night. A gust flung him into a drift, and he crawled on his hands and knees until he encountered a dog asleep under the snow. He rose hastily, shivering as the roused animal's howls set all its mates wailing their hunger in the blackness.

Back in the chill emptiness of his igloo he swayed toward his bunk and, dropping on tense knees beside it, began to pray.

III

Day after day the blizzard continued unabated. The supply of moldy seal-meat dwindled, vanished. The people began eating the walrus-skin coverings of the oomiaks. They chewed the hide dry because there was no oil for cooking except in the house of the medicine-man. The thin-faced children and babies suffered mutely, sucking on seal-skin ropes, on thongs of snow-shoes, on anything that contained a bit of nourishment. The dogs, with uncanny prescience, left the habitations of their masters for the heights back of the village. There in the graveyard, where the iron chains still clanked a warning against the hanging-posts of Sautock, Beelack, and O-tock-tock, the gaunt beasts riddled the sepulchers and fought like werwolves over what they found. Not even Milli-ru-ak, the greatest hunter on In-ga-lee-nay, could battle his way up through the blizzard to shoot at them for food.

Hunger gnawed at the stomachs of the people and marked their faces with hollows, yet there were no lamentations, no visible evidences of despair. After the fatalistic manner of their race they waited patiently, stoically, for a change of weather—or for death.

One night the old mother of Miak, the witch-woman, froze to death. The next day every family moved to the *kashim*, where, by shutting out the air and huddling close together, the people could keep warm without oil. Once a day Ah-king-ah brought them hope and comfort by lighting the stone lamp and chanting magical words to the almighty devil.

The missionary in his igloo spent desperate hours on his knees pleading with his God to change the wind. In the darkness he paced his room, warming his thin body by the exercise and striving for courage by repeating over and over the promises of the Bible. Sternly he reduced the rations for his scant daily meal until hunger brought upon him that strange fanatical exultation which is akin to the ecstasy that causes the fasting prophet to prophesy, or the medicine-man to perform his greatest feats of magic. With the passage of each dreary day the conviction grew upon him that this unprecedented blizzard had been sent to test his zeal as a worker in the vineyard of the Lord. This blizzard was his opportunity to win an entire village from the heathen sway of the medicine-man. With every atom of his being the little missionary grew to believe that if once he could persuade the people to enter the meeting-house, if once he could induce them to pray to his God, the wind would die, and the hunters be able to get food.

This conviction forced him every afternoon through the gale to the *kashim*. He ignored every rebuff, ignored utterly the danger to himself, although he knew that Ah-king-ah, should he forget the fate of the priest-murdering medicine-men, might have him killed as a witch who had brought misfortune on the village. Sometimes, by dint of superhuman self-denial, he brought bits of hardtack for the strangely quiet little ones clinging to their mothers in the *kashim*. Always he pleaded with the elders to turn from shamanism to the true God. The Eskimos, apathetic from prolonged hunger, suffered his presence. While he was with them, there was at least the light of his kerosene lantern. Otherwise, the *kashim* was always in darkness now, for Ah-king-ah's oil was gone.

Construing this tolerance as an encouraging sign, the earnest little man brought his Bible, and standing under the swinging light of the lantern, he translated page after page of Exodus—the promises of the Lord to the Children of Israel, the feeding of the wanderers in the desert. But the Eskimos sat stolid, unmoved, apathetic. Even his ardent rendering of the miracle of the loaves and fishes fell flat. Ah-king-ah, as if in weary scorn of his rival, stretched himself on the skins of his shelf and slept, or appeared to sleep.

One day, by accident, the missionary read of the magicians and sorcerers who competed with Moses and Aaron at the court of the Egyptian Pharaoh. Milli-ru-ak raised his eyes from a sad contemplation of his ailing infant son asleep in its mother's arms. Miak, the witch-woman, leaned forward over her empty lamp to listen. A stir of interest went among the people. Here at last was something they could understand.

The white man had heretofore preached only a kind and

beneficent God, but seeing in this an opening in the wall of
their indifference, he plunged into detailed descriptions of
the misfortunes that had visited the Egyptians. His gaunt
face and sunken eyes glowed with fervor. Hunger lent a
delirious and terrible vividness to his speech. Vicariously,
the starving Eskimos were drowned in his Biblical rivers
of blood. They were tormented by plagues of frogs and
boils, locusts and lice. They were terrified by hails and
thunders. Aware of the Eskimos' almost idolatrous love for
their offspring, he loosed his tongue of all restraint when
he pictured the smiting of the first-born. To the sound of
the howling blizzard he dwelt long on the pathos of the dead
childish faces in those desolate homes along the Nile. Ah-
king-ah bestirred himself and sat up. There was a murmuring among the hunters. The mothers caught their children to their breasts and swayed back and forth, moaning.
The missionary, light-headed from hunger and emotion,
reeled under the swinging shadows of the lantern.

"Would ye, like the Egyptians, harden your hearts
against the word of God and bring death to your children?"
he shouted. "Oh, come, my friends! Come with me before
your little ones lie dead in your arms. Pray to Almighty
God and be delivered! Follow me before it is too late!"
Carried away by the effect of his eloquence on the hitherto
indifferent Eskimos, he caught at the lantern and lurched
forward toward the exit of the *kashim*. "Follow me to the
house of God!"

The mothers rose with hysterical cries. The hunters
began to get down from their shelf. But before the missionary had reached the ladder, Ah-king-ah was standing in
the middle of the floor. Calm and dignified, he made a
single motion with one hand. Not a soul moved farther to
follow the white man.

The next day, when the missionary climbed to the opening of the *kashim,* he found the hole covered. His knocks
and pleas for entrance met with no response, because
Ah-king-ah was sitting on the door to hold it down.

Night brought a drop in temperature and an increase in
the force of the gale. The grinding and crash of the ice-
pack seemed to threaten the very foundations of the island.

With the exception of the missionary, every soul on In-ga-lee-nay was packed in the *kashim*. Men, women, and children chewed desperately on dry walrus-hide and clung together to keep from freezing. The little ones wedged between their parents whimpered in misery. At last the company, weary from many wakeful nights, jerked and flung their arms about in troubled sleep.

When morning broke Milli-ru-ak's child was dead.

The wailing of the mothers mingled with the roar of the blizzard and the increased fervor of the medicine-man's incantations. Before the day was done, two more little ones died.

It was then that Milli-ru-ak, with three of the council men, appeared in the igloo of the white man.

"We will pray to your God," said the hunter, wearily.

The peals of the bell that summoned the people to the prayer-meeting were freighted with the little missionary's joy in the fulfilment of his mission. He had wrested a whole village from the dominance of the medicine-man!

The sunken eyes in his gaunt, unshaven face glowed with fanatic happiness as he looked down on the crowded room. Eskimos filled the benches, stood about the walls, and squatted on the floor about the last of his oil burning in the stone lamp below the pulpit. Of all the village only Ah-king-ah was absent. The people sat silent, grave, attentive, their eyes fixed on the Bible lying open on the pulpit.

The missionary began his exhortation, raising his voice above the raging of the blizzard and the rending of the ice-pack. Thrilled by a sense of achievement and inspired by faith, he spoke with a confidence and an eloquence he had never known before. Within him woke the spirit of the evangelist. During the hour he worked upon his congregation he felt himself rising to the sublime heights from which Jesus himself had dominated all physical conditions. So exalted was he that his preaching aroused a measure of faith in the starving Eskimos, even as the incantations of Ah-king-ah had done.

"Such is the might and goodness of our God," he shouted after he had combed the Bible for incidents showing the

stilling of storms, the feeding of the hungry, the raising of
the dead. "And He is the same yesterday, today, and forever! Oh, down on your knees, my friends!" he cried
with sudden vehemence. "Down on your knees and prove
him now—now!"

His impassioned utterance swept his listeners to their
knees, shouting, praying, pleading in long, fragmentary
prayers for food, for life, for a change of wind. The fervid
little white man leading them felt the whole room to be
charged with power—an invincible power that flowed from
him and from each one and definitely made its connection
with the Infinite Mind that rules creation.

When he sprang to his feet at the end of the supplication,
his thin face was alight.

"Go home, my people!" his voice rang out with confi-
dence. "Go home and wait on the salvation of our Lord.
Sharpen your spears; put an edge on your skinning-knives.
Make ready your gears, for the day of hunting is near!"

"If the white man's God answers, we will all become
Christians!" cried Milli-ru-ak, rising and bringing the
others with him.

"Yea! Yea!" came the chorus of assent. Miak, the
witch-woman, sidled close to the pulpit, putting out a
curious, but cautious, finger to feel the Bible.

"If the white man's God changes the wind," she croaked,
slanting a wise, bleary eye up at the missionary, "the
people of In-ga-lee-nay will come when the bell calls and
listen again to the words in the black medicine-book."

From the supreme heights of his faith the missionary
watched his fur-clad congregation depart, seeing in them
brands he had plucked from the burning, souls he had saved
from destruction. Finally, in his cold living-room, he
staggered toward his bunk and in sudden exhaustion sank
upon it. He had scarcely drawn the fur robes about him
when he was plunged into a heavy, dreamless sleep.

IV

He awoke to a hush so intense that his soul ached with
it. It was as if the world had died, leaving him the only

living thing upon it. After a moment's bewilderment he realized that the wind was still, and there was no sound of grinding ice! His nerves, for ten weeks made taut by the continuous shriek of the blizzard, relaxed with a suddenness that was like a fall from a great height. Like a man swimming in a sea of silence, he raised his hands, groping for the luminous-faced watch by his bunk. He saw, with a gasp of incredulity, that he had slept eighteen hours!

Still dazed with sleep and hunger, he crawled from his robes and hurried out into the glimmering twilight of the arctic day. Great as was his faith in the power of prayer, he was astonished at the sight that met his eyes.

Under dark, moving clouds strangely shot with silver the ice-pack lay quiet and gray. A quarter of a mile away an inky, jagged line marked a lead of open water among the bergs. Every hunter in the village was squatted along the lead, and, as he looked, a sudden fusillade of rifle-shots registered the death of seals coming up to breathe.

Along the shores women and children and old men swarmed laughing, shouting, as some one threw a seal-hook into a dead animal and drew it to the ice. They crowded about it, their excited yells increasing. Five minutes later they were devouring the steaming flesh, stopping often to toss bits to the dogs, which gulped it ravenously.

The missionary bowed his head, a great gratitude, a great wonder in his heart. God had listened. God had heard. The famine was over.

Like the blizzard, that day's hunting was unprecedented in In-ga-lee-nay. Thirty seals and a sixty-foot whale fell to the lot of the hunters. There was food in abundance, and oil for the lamps and for the torches that fluttered yellow lights over the ice-bound shores where the people worked joyously over the kill. All day the missionary moved among them. He was happy, elated. They were his flock, his children. In the flush of his joy he had to exercise considerable self-control to keep from calling attention to the glory of God's mercy. The following day, Saturday, was also filled with unusual activities, but he permitted himself to speak of the meeting of thanksgiving which he would hold

for them on Sunday. The Eskimos nodded, and laughed in
answer to his enthusiasm. Light-hearted, variable, they
had already forgotten the misery of the famine in the plenti-
tude of feasting.

But the children with whom he had divided his last hardtack came shyly to his side and took hold of his hands.
They had not forgotten. The little missionary had not
realized his utter loneliness, his craving for friendship, for
love, until he felt the clinging of their small, warm fingers.
His vision was blurred as, one by one, he gathered them up
in his arms and talked to them. Here indeed was his
work among these benighted little ones and their parents.
Here would he stay as long as he lived, teaching them the
ways of truth and civilization. His last thought that night
was of the meeting-house on the morrow filled with grateful Eskimos sending up their praises to God. Perhaps even
Ah-king-ah, the defeated, might come to listen to the Holy
Word and become converted.

Sunday morning found him up early preparing his ser-
mon. He melted ice, and for the first time in many
weeks was able to shave. As he lighted the blubber-lamps
to heat the meeting-house, he noted a small pair of fur
mittens left by some child who had accompanied its mother
to the first gathering. He picked them up and placed
them on the pulpit, intending to return them later. The
thought of the youngster sent him to the bottom of his
trunk for the flag he always carried with him. He could
not begin too soon to familiarize the little ones with their
country's flag, he thought, as he pinned the Stars and
Stripes above the blackboard in anticipation of the near
day when the people should send their children to school.

He rang the first bell, and then busied himself with a
rearrangement of the benches. Engrossed in happy
thoughts, he did not realize how swiftly time was passing
until he glanced at his watch. Half an hour had gone by
since his call to meeting! Apprehension stirred in him as
he reached for the cord to ring the second bell, but before
his outstretched fingers touched it, he stiffened in the attitude of arrested action.

O-o-m, oom-oom. O-o-m, oom-oom. O-o-m, oom-oom.

The air suddenly began vibrating to the deep boom of the devil-drum. His hand fell to his side. Incredulity, comprehension, anger, succeeded each other in his face. Without pausing to tighten his parka hood he rushed out into the calm arctic noon, and ran toward the *kashim* tunnel. One leap carried him over the medicine-man's crossed sticks at the entrance, the next plunged him into the darkness of the passage.

Beat of drum and pagan chanting grew louder as he thrust his head up through the opening in the floor which was once more the stage for Ah-king-ah. Behind the shaman stood Milli-ru-ak, with the three whale hunters who had helped him kill the whale. Bird-beaks and crab-claws on their scanty garments were clattering to every motion of their dancing bodies. Their feathered heads swayed above whale-charms of jade that dangled on cords about their necks. Four Eskimo maidens in primitive finery stood together, holding by its ivory chains the Ceremonial Cup of the Whale filled with blubber cubes. At intervals, when the medicine-man signaled, they held the cup aloft and uttered long, weird cries like gulls.

The people who had so recently prostrated themselves in supplication before the white man's God were now as fervently assisting Ah-king-ah in the ancient rites of thanksgiving to the Spirit of the Whale. Their faces glowed with happiness and well-being; their voices rose in joyous unison with the voice of the shaman.

At sight of the missionary the dancing and chanting ceased abruptly. Ah-king-ah took a confident step forward.

"Why does the white man bring his long face here to anger the spirits of the hunt?" he asked.

The missionary's sunken eyes passed slowly over the faces of the hunters squatted on the shelf, over the faces of the mothers and of the old men and the children below. His anger ebbed to a great hopelessness that showed in the weary sag of his shoulders. He was defeated, yet he climbed to the floor of the *kashim* and stood beside the half-nude figure of the giant shaman.

"Were your words then a lie within your mouths, ye people of In-ga-lee-nay?" he asked quietly. "Ye did prom-

ise this day to send up thanks to Almighty God for his
mercies. If these promises were lies, why did ye come to
pray with me?"

Milli-ru-ak started forward, his eyes narrowed with anger,
but the medicine-man gestured for silence.

"Listen to the words of Ah-king-ah!" He spoke with
primitive dignity, his authoritative voice instantly quelling
the murmur of the hunters. "It was I, Ah-king-ah, who
sent my people to the *kashim* of the white man."

The missionary turned incredulously.

"Long had I chanted the runes that please the almighty
devil tossing in his hands the ivory ball of the world," went
on the medicine-man. "And I knew the time was ripe for
fulfilment. Yet the wisdom of my fathers tells me that all
things change form, even as the ice-pack changes its face
in the arms of the wind. New spirits come. Old spirits die.
There is sorcery in all things. Perhaps there is sorcery in
the black Book the white man keeps. Perhaps there is
not. But I, Ah-king-ah, maker of medicine, am not a man
of wisdom if I protect not my people against it. Therefore I sent them to thee, white man, who knoweth the ways
of thy God in the black Book, but before I sent them I
promised that I, Ah-king-ah, who knoweth the ways of the
almighty devil, would stay alone, working for them my
strongest magic while they pray. They know my medicine is great, for, behold! the storm dies like the last grunt
of the stricken walrus and"—he drew himself up proudly,
resting his drum on his thigh—"it is I, Ah-king-ah, mightiest shaman of the North, who changed the wind!"

In the approving chorus that filled the room the missionary tried to make himself heard, but Ah-king-ah's voice
continued, vanquishing every other sound:

"And why should thy God be thanked?" he asked in the
earnest manner of one seeking to understand another's point
of view. "Thou hast told my people He is a good God
wanting to do only good to man. Why pray to Him when
he can do us no harm? But the almighty devil—he is evil,
evil. All his pleasure comes from doing evil to man. Therefore we must sing the magic runes that please him, so he
leaves us alone. Therefore we must dance before the Spirit

of the Whale to show our joy at the good fortune the devil has permitted. White man"—Ah-king-ah's shrewd dark eyes were not unkind as he looked down on the little missionary —"our ways are still the ways of our fathers. Thy ways are the ways of thy fathers. Leave us, then, and give thy thanks to whom it please thee." He raised the drum from his thigh and made a quick motion with it. As the booming sounded, the three apprentices sprang forward. Not un- gently they laid hold of the missionary and led him to the opening in the floor. Then rung by rung he was forced down the ladder until his feet touched the icy cobblestones at the bottom. The trap-door dropped above him, leaving him in darkness.

As he stumbled over wolf-dogs gorged with food and in- different with sleep, his ears rang to the thump of the devil- drum and the pagan chanting of well fed, joyous people. The sounds followed him from the passage into the awful pervading silence of the polar day. He dragged his forlorn figure back along the snowy trail to the meeting-house. His knees trembled. A sudden awareness of his isolation from his kind struck through his heart like a sickness.

Past the mocking bareness of the benches, past the black- board where the flag, loosed from three of its tacks, hung limp and dispirited, he made his way to the shaky little pulpit. He rubbed a fumbling hand across his eyes then, as a hurt child seeks the comfort of its mother's breast, his gray head sank on his folded arms, and he pressed his face against the open Bible.

Numbed by his disappointment, crushed by his failure, he lay, a small, defeated white man in the primitive fur garments of an alien race. Gradually into his memory began to crowd the long months of loneliness, sacrifice, and privation he had borne to bring the comforts of religion and the uplift of civilization to an ungrateful heathen people. For them he had given up everything a white man holds dear. For them he had been willing to give even his life. His work had been futile. Futility! The word stood out in letters of ice against the blackness of his misery. But he was at the end. He was through. In the spring, when the first boat came from the mainland, he would

leave In-ga-lee-nay. He *would* take his God back to his
own land, where there was at least the companionship of
his kind.

Sagging wearily against the pulpit, he was oblivious to the
passage of time, deaf to the increasing happy shouts from
the *kashim*. The oil in the lamps burned away, the sputtering wicks grew black. Unconsciously, one hand, opening
and shutting in anguish, had taken hold of something soft
and warm. When at last he raised his face from his
cramped arms, his eyes, dull with brooding, fell on the tiny
pair of mittens he had placed on the pulpit that morning.

For the space of a dozen breaths he stared at them,
then slowly, meditatively he began stroking them. Into his
tired mind crept thoughts of yesterday. Children had come
to him then—children with upraised, trusting eyes and
warm, clinging fingers. They had come because they believed in him. They liked him. They were potential
hunters and mothers of hunters. With their small clinging
hands they were already molding the future of their race.

Little by little the look of hopelessness faded from his
eyes, and a new determination crept into his thin face.
When he stepped from the pulpit he turned and pinned the
flag back into place, then hung the mittens on a nail beside
it.

It was very late for the second bell, but the missionary
crossed over to the bell-rope. His step was firm again, his
dogged chin upraised. He laid hold of the rope and began
pulling it vigorously, hopefully.

Out over the still, white bergs of Bering Strait two
sounds strove once more for dominance in the arctic air:

*O-o-m, oom-oom. O-o-m, oom-oom. O-o-m, oom-oom.
D-i-n-g-d-o-n-g, d-i-n-g-d-o-n-g. D-i-n-g-d-o-n-g.*

GIDEON'S REVENGE[1]

By ELINOR WYLIE

(From *The Century Magazine*)

GIDEON extinguished the flame wherewith he had lit his pipe; he dropped the match tidily behind the wall-flowers, and looked about him with quiet, but incredulous, joy. Standing at the door of the cottage, his head was stooped a little beneath the lintel, partly from actual necessity and partly in a courteous gesture of apology to this exquisite scene in which only children or delicately formed and tinted women might appear appropriate and untarnished. Above him the freshness of the honey-colored thatch contrasted pleasantly with the rose-purple of ancient brick; the watery sheen of the upper windows reflected a few hanging strands of straw, like gilded seaweed observed in the profundity of a wave. Inclosed by its clipped hedge, the garden lay like a small square pool of flowers drawn together in concentrated brightness, as if many larger and grosser gardens had been melted into one and poured into this narrow space. Across the green a dew pond reversed the sky to another pool, and permitted Gideon's vision to plumb without fatigue the utmost depth of the empyrean.

Gideon was a tall old man; his age was perhaps seventy. His face had more of the falcon than the eagle in its lines; the beaked nose, the bony setting of the large bright eyes, the hollowed cheek and temple, were all carved and polished to a pattern sufficiently bold, but light and restless and uneasy. His eyes were gray; his hair, which had once been reddish, had now the faintly yellowed whiteness of flax; it rose steeply to a crest above his brow. The garments which he wore hung somewhat awkwardly upon his emaciation—an emaciation suggesting austerity rather than weakness. The correct and shabby tweeds were excellent in themselves, molded to fit with easy perfection the scene and circumstance, but although they clothed with tolerable grace the mortal form of Gideon, they did not fit his soul. You saw him preferably in rusty black, with a hat remotely Spanish, and a cloak; decidedly the soul of Gideon wore a black cloak. And indeed at this very moment, within the cottage, Caroline was brushing just such a cloak preparatory to putting it away forever with beautiful cakes of gum camphor crumbling like soft and fragrant ice among its mysterious folds.

Gideon turned and entered the cottage; the rooms appeared deliciously chilled and shadowed by the green orchard to the east. Avoiding the larger chamber, where Caroline whisked fantastic garments into the bland, golden obscurity of a tulip-wood chest of drawers, he turned into the kitchen and surveyed its cool and ordered colors with minute approval. It was a room decorous and subtly bright, a place for the concoction of junkets and cherry pies. Gideon sighed with pleasure; it was a miracle that he, a lawless, bitter man, should have imagined this room and made it. Of course there had been the skeleton ready to his hand—the stone floor, the beams, the fireplace—but he had breathed upon cold ashes, and they had flowered like a domestic rose.

Caroline had climbed the steep little stairs to the attic; he could hear portmanteaus bumping about overhead like huge frolicsome beasts; he had a sudden picture of the trim, pink-faced servant surrounded by portmanteaus and kit-bags, labeled in dusty, barbaric scarlet, enormous in the gloom. He reflected with satisfaction that all his papers were already neatly pigeon-holed in his grandfather's desk and his mother's boule cabinet; Caroline was merely rummaging among ponchos and sombreros.

Slowly, with a fastidious, yet sensual, savoring of his delights, Gideon entered the other room and strolled down its entire length, stopping here and there to touch the lovely surface of wood perversely satin-skinned, or velvet worn and rosy as immemorial lichen. Here again was something more than human in the happy confluence of various times and manners; he had seen these objects scattered in obscure exile among the Victorian ineptitudes of his mother's vast drawing rooms, or lately huddled ignominiously in storage warehouses; he had purchased some of them carelessly at the ragged ends of the earth, and now they were gathered together under the green and glazing twilight of the apple trees to make a miraculous whole. He had bought a cottage, knocked down a partition or two, and engaged a certain number of pantechnicon vans; he had expected the place to be comfortable and rather absurd, and by some curious necromancy of chance it was grave and exquisite. It was as if it had always been so, and his. Between open windows, his desk was flooded by calm radiance.

As he fingered the firmly packed bundles of letters, bound with pink legal tape, or more sentimentally confined by blue ribbons, he considered the future with approval. It was eminently fitting; it was, indeed, inevitable. How, save under conditions of the most shining peace, could he hope to relax into that judicial clarity of mind so necessary to his great project? The hardships, the astringent horrors of his past career, had precisely steeled his hand to execution; it now remained for a poor, but honest, gentleman to judge the culprits before killing them, and Gideon was acutely aware of the propriety of being equitable to begin with, if only to augment the pleasure of being savage in the final sentence, the final act of revenge.

He stared retrospectively down the lurid vista of the last twenty-five years, his mind's eye blinking, for all its falcon look, in the full chemical glare of recollection. There had been, quite literally, singularly little sunlight in the vista, and that little had quivered to a tropical intensity removed by several continents from this subaqueous glimmer stained by apple trees. But mostly, he remembered, things had happened at night; that was, perhaps, the reason he had achieved so flattering and profitable a reputation as special correspondent.

Special! Oh, very special indeed! For who but Gideon would have been clever enough to be forever on the spot, the often bloody and unhealthy spot, where things were happening at night? What other nocturnal vigilance had so well observed, what vitriolic pen recorded, alike the curious minutiæ and the vast apocalypse of life? From the beginning to the end of that bewildering vista he had contrived to see the event strangely, and to make the strangeness vivid by his words. Also, he had advanced in wisdom and cunning; he recalled with contempt how crudely he had daubed hell-fire and sanguine upon his earlier efforts. In ninety-eight, when he had seen the *Maine* intemperately uncurl a million fronds of brilliance against the plushy dark, he could not, telling the dreadful thing beheld, curdle the reader's veins as now his lightest, coolest whisper curdled them. The latest of all his writings, the wry, amused account of Lenine stretched upon his crimson upholstery under the great glass bell like some horrible wax flower, blooming through unnatural, and electric, days, that was excellent, that was art.

II

And now, the quarter-century past, he was quit of restraints, of delicacies and decencies; now he was free of galling secret vows and public scruples. The very last of the Pennimans had died twenty years ago in the person of old Joseph; Gideon had kept his promise to Millicent, and Millicent herself had been dead for twenty-five years.

He was free to turn that intricate and fiery engine, his mind, upon the people he had hated and had, for a measured space of time, striven to forget. At first, after his wife's death, he had acidly regretted his promise to her— the promise given to the expiring appeal of her large blue eyes, but never ratified by their wedded spirits in this world or the vaguer one into whose ambiguities she had at once departed. He had kept the promise because it was a promise; he had been totally untrammeled by sympathy for its purpose or its beneficiaries. He had spared the Pennimans for a score of years; he had not written a book, no, not so much as an epitaph upon any of them until two decades had yellowed the latest of their tombs. It had been a hellish bore, but now he was glad he had refrained. The long and lenten abstinence from revenge had but given edge to his appetite and sharpened his powers to austere perfection.

Gideon drew a dozen slim and pointed pencils from a drawer of the desk; upon its dark-amber surface he placed a formidable pile of copy paper. The book loomed before his happy contemplation, tremendous, Protean, monstrous, yet alluring. A book, but not alone a book; a mighty chase, a dexterous unmasking, a trial, and an execution. And Gideon, at once Justice incarnate and the instrument of Justice, Gideon must be both judge and executioner. The book was to be a headsman's ax, savage, medieval, elegant, and efficient. Then, picturing a row of Penniman faces upon the spikes of Temple Bar, Gideon smiled a slight abstemious smile.

Apart from fancies, however charming, the facts were these; he reviewed them swiftly, leaning back luxuriously in a chair whose polished curves were as velvet to his neuralgic bones. The book was a debt to his own soul, long overdue, heavy with accretion of interest. He had waited, for Millicent's darling and ridiculous sake, until all kith and kin of hers were moldered into complete indifference. She had desired to shield them from anger and annoyance, for surely their fatted, gelded souls were incapable of pain; she had interposed her threadbare little body between their torpor and his vengeance. Very well; it had been so, but now he would remember it all, and set it down, and verily the page should shrivel beneath the fire of his revelation. Though they skulked in their sepulchers, shrouded in this their last cowardice, he would burn them out of oblivion; the flame of their destruction should ascend forever, purified and fervent, sweet in the nostrils of the brave. He would tell the tale; he would release that holy indignation which for so long had made his heart a fever.

Milly—that foolish nickname wherein her family, with characteristic impertinence, had clothed the golden pallor of her girlhood! If Gideon pronounced her name, he enriched the vowels with a foreign inflection which made it more Mélisande than Millicent. That was her proper appellation, that long soft veil of sound, fitting her sallow-flaxen beauty with an enduring garment.

She, who had lain so long asleep in his heart, should be brought forth once more into the wide, bright chamber of his mind; he would look at her in the unpitying glare of that illumination. She would stand, willowy and disarming, lovely and ineffectual, beside the solid, stolid forms of her murderers, the Pennimans. Gideon would look at them all; the Pennimans would tremble and grow pale, they would even grow thin perhaps; Millicent would smile. It would not be the smile of her later days, painted narrow and colorless by despair; it would be the smile of the beginning, of hope and casual courage and unconsidered joy. Gideon ground his teeth, thinking how the Pennimans had destroyed her gaiety and trust. She had loved her father and mother; she had even loved the unspeakable Ambrose, with his long nose and liquid, languid eyes; by love she had been broken and undone.

Of course they had opposed the match; they were obstructive by instinct and conviction, and Gideon, who had refused to be a barrister in order to write for the lesser journals, was sufficiently above them in family and below them in fortune to irritate their every prejudice. His wit inflamed their mental tissues like cayenne pepper; his tongue was gall and vinegar. They resented his height and were half afraid of his hair, which was never properly brushed; he seemed an enigma designed to insult them; his doing could not be other than wrong, but his mere being was the radical error. Gideon knew that, and the reflection soothed him; it meant that he had always, even without trying, done his best to please them: his best must always fail with the Pennimans, and he was glad he had not tried too hard. Millicent had tried too hard, and, in foredoomed endeavor, been destroyed.

He had been a strange son-in-law for the Pennimans; he had fluttered that dove-cote with a vengeance. Fat pigeons they were, and Ambrose with the melting gaze of a turtle above his little waistcoat's curve. And Millicent among them, white and fluttering, with her perpetual olive branch: she was truly a dove!

Without the Pennimans, pecking and obese, how far might they not have flown together, Gideon and Millicent, the falcon and the dove! God knew she had always wanted to be free; God had known it all along, in fact, and that was Gideon's quarrel with God, second only to his quarrel with the Pennimans. For the Deity, frequently invoked by that pious family, had apparently been moved by their flatteries rather than by Gideon's dignified silence; God had not saved Millicent even at the last minute: he had, by allowing her to die, given her back to the Pennimans. Gideon, who had never believed in God, found this impossible to forgive; in his indignation he realized that he was a Christian.

The Pennimans, outrageous to the last, had always blamed him for his wife's death; they had pecked her into shreds while he was cynically examining the Spanish-American War. They had not even taken the trouble to cable news of her illness; he had returned to find her *in extremis*. Gideon was frantic; the Pennimans were sorrowful and mildly complacent. They expressed surprise at his reappearance, and disgust at what they were pleased to term his neglect. Millicent had, apparently, been killed by the absence of a husband whose presence had always, according to the Pennimans, constituted a criminal menace to her health and sanity. The bronze door of the Penniman vault shut firmly upon her mortal remains; the family, in solemn conclave, decided that Gideon was sailing for South Africa with Milly's blood upon his hands. Gideon knew that their own hands were dabbled in her innocence.

Gideon found the South African War a personal convenience, but against the Pennimans he was very bitter, and his amazing despatches, colored and brilliant with hate, were only a partial relief to his feelings. He found it impossible to dislike the Boers with the authentic fervor so desirable in a special correspondent; quite deliberately he dipped his pen into his private gall before writing, and his passionate loathing for a respectable family at Wimbledon fired half England to a pure flame of patriotism. But it was all very unsatisfactory and rather troublesome, this inner pretense that Cronje and Wessels were in reality Mrs. Penniman and Ambrose. His despatches were devoured raw by the popular appetite, but he himself went hungry;

he starved for his revenge. Gideon, remembering those days, laughed heartily. How fierce he had been, and how frustrate!

The sunlight fell across his dusky golden desk, and still he remembered, and did not write. That was twenty-five years ago, and this was England, and he was old, but neither frustrate nor starving. The Gideon of the Transvaal had been a widowed Gideon of forty-odd, bereaved and raging— a Gideon who had but just observed the wife of his romantic youth go down to the grave shrunken to premature decay, quenched in body and soul, the clear flame withered, the bright stem trodden underfoot. For a long and parching term of years he had beheld her obliquely in the flawed mirror of her dying face; later he had shut his eyes while she slept in his heart. Now he looked at her again, in the cool and blessed light of these windows, in the peace of this quiet room; she was a girl again, and beautiful. But Millicent had always been beautiful.

It was the other Pennimans who had been ugly; how ugly he shuddered to recall. He drew a packet of papers toward him. These were photographs of the criminals, letters from Milly, letters from Ambrose, his own wild scrawls. Gideon adjusted his spectacles.

III

At seven o'clock Caroline lit the lamp; it was a pale unluminous yellow against the western window-panes, where rose color was fading. Half an hour later she placed a small tray at Gideon's elbow; the noiseless hand was also skilful, for the cutlet was done to a turn, the coffee superlative. Gideon ate and drank, thanking the stars now set in chrysoprase above the apple trees. At nine he put down the last of the letters and, lifting one of the photographs, examined it intently. A curious trembling seized him; he appeared a prey to obscure emotions, and his face was visibly convulsed.

The picture, a highly glazed *carte-de-visite* of the eighties, showed a family group augmented by one stranger: it showed, clearly enough, the four Pennimans and Gideon.

And the book? Gone, like a gorgeous thundercloud, tiger-streaked, into profound oblivion. Dead, like the Pennimans, who, in its death, were prodigally revenged.

Gideon stooped, and set a match to the fire. It flew upward like a sanguine flower, and the room was roseate instead of amber-yellow in the lamplight. Its colors glowed from new planes and facets; its shapes were subtly altered and enhanced. Caroline came in quietly with the whisky and soda.

Presently Gideon rose, and lit his pipe. A tall and solitary figure, he stood gazing into the lambent mystery of the fire; he sighed gently.

"I suppose I shall have to learn to dislike my neighbors," he told himself in a low voice. "One might write a grim realistic novel about those squat dark people at Skatt's Farm."

But at the back of his mind was a sick conviction that they were probably quite pleasant, harmless people, and after a little while he took his candlestick from the hall table and went upstairs to bed.

He jumped very quickly between the cool sheets, and fell asleep trying hard to hate the squat dark people at Skatt's Farm. But the dreadful part of it was that Gideon could not hate them.

THE YEARBOOK OF THE AMERICAN
SHORT STORY
OCTOBER, 1924, TO SEPTEMBER, 1925

ABBREVIATIONS

I. PERIODICALS

A. D. ....Arts and Decoration.
A. Merc. ....American Mercury.
A. W. ....All's Well.
Adv. ....Adventure.
Ain. ....Ainslee's Magazine.
Am. ....American Magazine.
Am. B. ....American Boy.
Am. H. ....American Hebrew.
Asia ....Asia.
Atl. ....Atlantic Monthly.
B. E. T. ....Boston Evening Transcript.
Blue Bk. ....Blue Book Magazine.
B'nai ....B'nai B'rith Magazine.
Book. (N. Y.) ...Bookman. (New York.)
Books ....Books. (New York Herald-Tribune.)
C. D. N. ....Chicago Daily News.
C. E. P. ....Chicago Evening Post Review of Books.
C. G. ....Country Gentleman.
C. R. Rep. ......Cedar Rapids Republican.
Cath. W. ....Catholic World.
Cen. ....Century Magazine.
Charm ....Charm.
Chic. Trib. ......Chicago Tribune Syndicate Service.
Col. ....Collier's Weekly.
Com. ....Commonweal.
Cos. ....Cosmopolitan.
D. D. ....Double Dealer.
Day ....The Day.
Dear. Ind. ......Dearborn Independent.
Del. ....Delineator.
Des. ....Designer.
Dial ....Dial.
Echo ....Echo.
Elks ....Elks Magazine.
Ev. ....Everybody's Magazine.
F. F. ....Farm and Fireside.
For. ....Forum.
Fron. ....Frontier.
Gal. ....Golden Galleon.
G. H. ....Good Housekeeping. (New York.)
Gol. ....Golden Book.
Guar. (Am.) ....Guardian. (Philadelphia.)

H. C. ....Hue and Cry.
Harp. B. ....Harper's Bazar.
Harp. M. ....Harper's Magazine.
Hear ....Hearst's International.
Hol. ....Holland's Magazine.
I. A. ....Inter-America.
I. L. M. ....Iowa Literary Magazine.
Ind. ....Independent.
Int. ....International Book Review.
Int. Arts ....International Arts.
J. F. ....Jewish Forum.
J. T. ....Jewish Tribune.
L. H. J. ....Ladies' Home Journal.
L. Rev. ....Literary Review of the New York Evening Post.
Leonardo ....Leonardo.
Lit. R. ....Little Review.
Liv. A. ....Living Age.
Ly. ....Liberty.
McC. ....McClure's Magazine.
McCall ....McCall's Magazine.
MacF. ....MacFadden Fiction-Lover's Magazine.
MacL. ....MacLean's Magazine.
Men. J. ....Menorah Journal.
Mid. ....Midland.
Mod. Q. ....Modern Quarterly.
Mod. R. ....Modern Review.
Mun. ....Munsey's Magazine.
N. A. Rev. ......North American Review.
N. Rep. ....New Republic.
N. Y. Sun ....New York Sun.
N. Y. Times ....New York Times Book Review.
N. Y. Trib. ......New York Herald-Tribune.
Nat. (N. Y.) ...Nation. (New York.)
O. R. ....Open Road.
Opp. ....Opportunity.
Outl. (N. Y.) ....Outlook. (New York.)
Pear. (Am.) ...Pearson's Magazine. (Chicago.)
Pict. R. ....Pictorial Review.
Pop. ....Popular Magazine.
Red. Bk. ....Red Book Magazine.
Rev. ....Reviewer.
S. E. P. ....Saturday Evening Post.
S. S. ....Smart Set. (New York.)
S. W. ....Southwest Review.
Sat. R. ....Saturday Review of Literature. (New York.)
Scan ....American-Scandinavian Review.
Scr. ....Scribner's Magazine.
Sea. ....Sea Stories Magazine.
Sh. St. ....Short Stories.
Strat. ....Stratford Monthly.

Sun. ....Sunset Magazine.
Tr. ....Transatlantic Review.
Tri. ....Trident.
V.F. ....Vanity Fair.
Va. ....Virginia Quarterly Review.
W.H.C. ....Woman's Home Companion.
W.M. ....Worker's Monthly.
W.T. ....Weird Tales.
W.W. ....Woman's World.
W.Tom. ....World Tomorrow.
Wave ....Wave.
World ....New York World.
Y.I. ....Young Israel.
Yale ....Yale Review.
(161) ....Page 161.
(2:161) ....Volume 2, Page 161.

II. BOOKS

Aces ....Aces.
Aces B. ....More Aces.
Aiken ....Aiken. Bring! Bring!
Arlen C. ....Arlen. Mayfair.
Aumonier C. ....Aumonier. Overheard.
Austin B. ....Austin. "13."
Austin C. ....Austin. William Austin, the Creator of Peter
                  Rugg.
Barbey ....Barbey d'Aurevilly. The Diaboliques.
Becke C. ....Becke. Yorke the Adventurer.
Bennett ....Bennett. Elsie and the Child.
Bierce C. ....Bierce. The Monk and the Hangman's Daughter.
Boyd B. ....Boyd. Points of Honor.
Bramah B. ......Bramah. The Specimen Case. (English edition.)
Buck ....Buck. Afterglow.
Busch ....Busch. Selected Czech Tales.
Cabell E. ....Cabell. Straws and Prayer-Books.
Child B. ....Child. Fresh Waters.
Cobb F. ....Cobb. Alias Ben Alibi.
Colette ....Colette. Cats, Dogs and I.
Connell C. ......Connell. Variety.
Conrad B. ....Conrad. Tales of Hearsay.
Contact ....Contact Collection of Contemporary Writers.
Coppard C. ......Coppard. Fishmonger's Fiddle.
Copy B. ....Copy, 1925.
Corvo ....Corvo. In His Own Image.
Cotton ....Cotton. Wall-Eyed Cæsar's Ghost.
Dargan ....Dargan. Highland Annals.
Eaton A. ....Eaton. The Best Continental Short Stories of
                  1923–24.
Eaton B. ....Eaton. The Best French Short Stories of 1923–24.

ADDRESSES OF MAGAZINES
PUBLISHING SHORT STORIES

I. AMERICAN MAGAZINES

Adventure, Spring and Macdougal Streets, New York City.
Ainslee's Magazine, 79 Seventh Avenue, New York City.
All's Well, Gayeta Lodge, Fayetteville, Ark.
American Boy, 142 Lafayette Boulevard, Detroit, Mich.
American Hebrew, 19 West 44th Street, New York City.
American Magazine, 250 Park Avenue, New York City.
American Mercury, 730 Fifth Avenue, New York City.
American-Scandinavian Review, 25 West 45th Street, New York City.
Argosy All-Story Weekly, 280 Broadway, New York City.
Asia, 627 Lexington Avenue, New York City.
Atlantic Monthly, 8 Arlington Street, Boston, Mass.
Blue Book Magazine, 36 South State Street, Chicago, Ill.
Bookman, 244 Madison Avenue, New York City.
Catholic World, 120 West 60th Street, New York City.
Century Magazine, 353 Fourth Avenue, New York City.
Charm, 50 Bank Street, Newark, N. J.
Chicago Tribune, Chicago, Ill.
Collier's Weekly, 250 Park Avenue, New York City.
Cosmopolitan, 119 West 40th Street, New York City.
Country Gentleman, Independence Square, Philadelphia, Pa.
Delineator, Spring and Macdougal Streets, New York City.
Designer, 12 Vandam Street, New York City.
Dial, 152 West 13th Street, New York City.
Double Dealer, 810 Baronne Street, New Orleans, La.
Echo, 1837 Champa Street, Denver, Colorado.
Elks' Magazine, 50 East 42d Street, New York City.
Everybody's Magazine, Spring and Macdougal Streets, New York City.
Farm and Freside, 250 Park Avenue, New York City.
Forum, 247 Park Avenue, New York City.
Frontier, Garden City, Long Island, N. Y.
Good Housekeeping, 119 West 40th Street, New York City.
Guardian, 720 Locust Street, Philadelphia, Pa.
Harper's Bazar, 119 West 40th Street, New York City.
Harper's Magazine, 49 East 33d Street, New York City.
Holland's Magazine, Dallas, Texas.
Hue and Cry, Woodstock, N. Y. (In summer months only.)
Independent, 9 Arlington Street, Boston, Mass.
International Arts, 3 Christopher Street, New York City.
Jewish Tribune, Marbridge Building, New York City.

Ladies' Home Journal, Independence Square, Philadelphia, Pa.
Liberty, 247 Park Avenue, New York City.
Little Review, 27 West 8th Street, New York City.
McCall's Magazine, 236 West 37th Street, New York City.
McClure's Magazine, 80 Lafayette Street, New York City.
MacLean's Magazine, 143 University Avenue, Toronto, Ont., Canada.
Menorah Journal, 167 West 13th Street, New York City.
Midland, Care of Mr. John T. Frederick, Iowa City, Iowa.
Modern Quarterly, 318 North Exeter Street, Baltimore, Md.
Munsey's Magazine, 280 Broadway, New York City.
New Republic, 421 West 21st Street, New York City.
Open Road, 284 Boylston Street, Boston, Mass.
Opportunity, 127 East 23d Street, New York City.
Outlook, 381 Fourth Avenue, New York City.
Pearson's Magazine, 157 East Ohio Street, Chicago, Ill.
Pictorial Review, 216 West 39th Street, New York City.
Popular Magazine, 79 Seventh Avenue, New York City.
Red Book Magazine, North American Building, Chicago, Ill.
Reviewer, Chapel Hill, N. C.
Saturday Evening Post, Independence Square, Philadelphia, Pa.
Scribner's Magazine, 597 Fifth Avenue, New York City.
Sea Stories Magazine, 79 Seventh Avenue, New York City.
Short Stories, Garden City, Long Island, N. Y.
Southwest Review, Dallas, Texas.
Sunset, 460 Fourth Street, San Francisco, Cal.
Woman's Home Companion, 250 Park Avenue, New York City.
Woman's World, 107 South Clinton Street, Chicago, Ill.
World Tomorrow, 104 East 9th Street, New York City.

II. British and Irish Magazines

Adelphi, 18 York Buildings, Adelphi, London, W. C. 2.
Blackwood's Magazine, 37 Paternoster Row, London, E. C. 4.
Blue Magazine, 115 Fleet Street, London, E. C. 4.
Bystander, Graphic Buildings, Whitefriars, London, E. C. 4.
Calendar, 1 Featherstone Buildings, High Holborn, London, W. C. 1.
Cassell's Magazine, La Belle Sauvage, Ludgate Hill, London, E. C. 4.
Chamber's Journal, 38 Soho Square, London, W. C. 1.
Colour Magazine, 53 Victoria Street, London, S. W. 1.
Corner Magazine, La Belle Sauvage, Ludgate Hill, London, E. C. 4.
Cornhill Magazine, 50a Albemarle Street, London, W. 1.
Coterie, 68 Red Lion Street, London, W. C. 1.
Criterion, 24 Russell Square, London, W. C. 1.
Dublin Magazine, 2–5 Wellington Quay, Dublin, Irish Free State.
Empire Review, Macmillan and Co., Ltd., St. Martin's Street,
    London, W. C. 2.
English Life, 9 East Harding Street, London, E. C. 4.
English Review, 4 Dean's Yard, Westminster, London, S. W. 1.
Eve, Great New Street, London, E. C. 4.

Fortnightly Review, 11 Henrietta Street, London, W. C. 2.
G. K.'s Weekly, 20–21 Essex Street, Strand, London, W. C. 2.
Gaiety, 10 Adam Street, Adelphi, London, W. C. 2.
Grand Magazine, 8–11 Southampton Street, Strand, London, W. C. 2.
Graphic, Graphic Buildings, Whitefriars, London, E. C. 4.
Green Magazine, Fleetway House, Farringdon Street, London, E. C. 4.
Happy Magazine, 8 Southampton Street, Strand, London, W. C. 2.
Home Magazine, 8 Southampton Street, Strand, London, W. C. 2.
Hutchinson's Adventure Story Magazine, 34–36 Paternoster Row, London, E. C. 4.
Hutchinson's Magazine, 34–36 Paternoster Row, London, E. C. 4.
Hutchinson's Mystery Story Magazine, 34–36 Paternoster Row, London, E. C. 4.
Illustrated London News, 172 Strand, London, W. C. 2.
Irish Statesman, 84 Merrion Square, Dublin, Irish Free State.
John o' London's Weekly, 8 Southampton Street, Strand, London, W. C. 2.
London Magazine, Fleetway House, Farringdon Street, London, E. C. 4.
London Mercury, 229 Strand, London, W. C. 2.
Manchester Guardian, 3 Cross Street, Manchester, England.
Nash's and Pall Mall Magazine, 1 Amen Corner, Paternoster Row, London, E. C. 4.
Nation and Athenæum, 10 Adelphi Terrace, London, W. C. 2.
New Age, 38 Cursitor Street, Chancery Lane, London, E. C. 4.
New Leader, Napier House, 24–27 High Holborn, W. C. 1.
New Magazine, La Belle Sauvage, Ludgate Hill, London, E. C. 4.
New Statesman, 10 Great Queen Street, Kingsway, London, W. C. 2.
Novel Magazine, 18 Henrietta Street, London, W. C. 2.
Outlook, 167 Strand, London, W. C. 2.
Outward Bound, Edinburgh House, 2 Eaton Gate, London, S. W. 1.
Pearson's Magazine, 17 Henrietta Street, Covent Garden, London, W. C. 2.
Premier, Fleetway House, Farringdon Street, London, E. C. 4.
Queen, Bream's Buildings, London, E. C. 4.
Quiver, La Belle Sauvage, Ludgate Hill, London, E. C. 4.
Red Magazine, Fleetway House, Farringdon Street, London, E. C. 4.
Romance, Long Acre, London, W. C. 2.
Royal Magazine, 17 Henrietta Street, Covent Garden, London, W. C. 2.
Saturday Review, 10 King Street, Covent Garden, London, W. C. 2.
Sketch, 172 Strand, London, W. C. 2.
Sovereign Magazine, 34–36 Paternoster Row, London, E. C. 4.
Spectator, 13 York Street, Covent Garden, London, W. C. 2.
Sphere, Great New Street, London, E. C. 4.
Story-Teller, La Belle Sauvage, Ludgate Hill, London, E. C. 4.
Strand Magazine, 8–11 Southampton Street, Strand, London, W. C. 2.
T. P.'s and Cassell's Weekly, La Belle Sauvage, Ludgate Hill, London, E. C. 4.
Tatler, 6 Great New Street, London, E. C. 4.

Time and Tide, 88 Fleet Street, London, E. C. 4.
Truth, 10 Bolt Court, Fleet Street, London, E. C. 4.
20-Story Magazine, Long Acre, London, W. C. 2.
Weekly Westminister, 12 Cursitor Street, Chancery Lane, London, E. C. 4.
Windsor Magazine, Warwick House, Salisbury Square, London, E. C. 4.
Woman, 34–36 Paternoster Row, London, E. C. 4.
Yellow Magazine, Fleetway House, Farringdon Street, London, E. C. 4.

THE BIOGRAPHICAL ROLL OF HONOR
OF AMERICAN SHORT STORIES

OCTOBER, 1924, TO SEPTEMBER, 1925

NOTE. *Only stories by American authors are listed. The index figures 1 to 11 prefixed to the name of the author indicate the last Roll of Honor in which his work has been included. The figure 1 refers to 1914, the figure 2 to 1915, etc. The Roll of Honor for 1914 appeared in the volume for 1915. The list excludes reprints*

ADAMS, DAVID ERNEST. Born in Wilton, New Hampshire, 1891. Educated at Phillips-Andover Academy and Dartmouth College. Graduate of Union Theological Seminary. Married. Congregational Minister. Lives in Ware, Massachusetts.
"Truth is Stranger——."

(10) AIKEN, CONRAD (*for biography, see* 1922).
Disciple.
Last Visit.
Strange Moonlight.

(10) "ALEXANDER, SANDRA." (MILDRED ALEXANDER LEWIS.) (*For biography, see* 1923.)
Gift.

(11) ANDERSON, SHERWOOD (*for biography, see* 1917).
Meeting South.
Return.

(6) ANDREWS, MARY RAYMOND SHIPMAN (*for biography, see* 1917).
Passing the Torch.

ANTHONY, JOSEPH. Born New York, 1897. B. A., Columbia, 1917. Author: "Rekindled Fires," 1918; "The Gang," 1921; "The Golden Village," 1924. Began as reporter for the *Newark Evening News*, then went into publishing work with Harper and Brothers, the National Association of Book Publishers and the Century Company. Spent two years in London, 1921–23, as manager of Century Company's foreign office. All writing done in intervals between various jobs. Lives in New York City.
Kill or Cure.

(11) ASCH, NATHAN (*for biography, see* 1924).
Gertrude Donovan.

(11) BEEDE, IVAN (*for biography, see* 1924).
Haywired.
Storm.

(3) BENEFIELD, BARRY. "Was born in a little, old mellow town in northeast Texas—oh, yes, there are old towns in Texas—by name Jefferson, in the piney woods, against the Louisiana border. There was some studying at school, much hunting and fishing down the bayou, a little teaching in the country districts, and then an ambitious leap to the State University at Austin. Followed newspaper work on *The Dallas* (Texas) *News* and on *The New York Times.* Thus prepared, he began writing advertisements and magazine fiction—mixed diet of what is called, foolishly, romance and realism. The record to date is some forty or fifty short stories, thousands of columns of advertisements and one novel, 'The Chicken-Wagon Family.' Works in New York City (advertisements), lives in Peekskill, New York (fiction)."
Blocker Locke.
Fiery Sweetness in the Air.
Guard of Honor.

(11) BENÉT, STEPHEN VINCENT (*for biography, see* 1920).
Harrigan's Head.

(11) BERCOVICI, KONRAD (*for biography, see* 1920).
Beggar of Alcazar.
Flood.
Law of the River.
Millstones.
Steel Against Steel.
Storm.
Tinsel.
Vineyard.

BIDDLE, FRANCIS B. Born in Paris, 1886. Educated at Groton School, Harvard College, and the Harvard Law School. Formerly private secretary to Mr. Justice Holmes of the United States Supreme Court. Now Assistant United States Attorney in Philadelphia, where he is also engaged in private law practice.
Aunt Jane's Sofa.

BROWN, KENNETH IRVING. Born in Brooklyn, New York, 1896. Educated at Rochester public schools and the University of Rochester. In naval service during the war. Ph.D. Harvard University, 1924. Has had travelling fellowship from Harvard University. Now professor of Biblical literature at Stephens College, Columbia, Missouri. "'The Christmas Guest' relates an actual occurrence, but the background has been changed from Greece to Colombia. During the war I was for a time on a merchant vessel carrying Government cargoes. On one trip we brought home a load of

lumber from the forests of Colombia, and during the course of that loading I visited the lumber camp described in the story."
Christmas Guest.

(10) BURT, MAXWELL STRUTHERS (*for biography, see* 1917).
Beauty and the Blantons.

BURTIS, THOMSON.
Man-Made Mutiny.

(5) BUTLER, ELLIS PARKER (*for biography, see* 1918).
Idealist.

(3) "BYRNE, DONN." (BRYAN OSWALD DONN-BYRNE.) Born in New York City, 1889. Educated at University College, Dublin, and in Paris and Leipzig. Married. Author: "Stories Without Women," 1915; "Stranger's Banquet," 1919; "The Foolish Matron," 1920; "The Woman God Changed," 1921; "Messer Marco Polo," 1921; "The Wind Bloweth," 1922; "The Changeling," 1923; "Blind Raftery," 1924; "An Untitled Story," 1925. Lives at Riverside, Connecticut.
Blue Waves of Tory.

(10) CABELL, JAMES BRANCH (*for biography, see* 1918).
Above Paradise.
Mathematics of Gonfal.

CARVER, ADA JACK. Born in Natchitoches, Louisiana. Educated at the Louisiana Normal College, Judson College, and Columbia University. Married. Won first prize in the third short story contest held by Harper's Magazine in 1924. Lives in Louisiana.
Redbone.

(11) CLARK, VALMA.
"Service."

(11) COBB, IRVIN S. (*for biography, see* 1917).
Nobody Sees the Waiter's Face.
Principle of the Thing.
Standing Room Only.

(11) COHEN, BELLA (*for biography, see* 1924).
Laugh.
Yetta's Fella.

(10) CORLEY, DONALD (*for biography, see* 1923).
Manacles of Youth.

(11) CROWELL, CHESTER T. (*for biography, see* 1924).
Devil Born in Them.

Giovanni and the Goddess.
Mary Fisher's Philosophy.
Pariah.

(11) DELL, FLOYD (*for biography, see* 1924).
"Hallelujah, I'm a Bum."

DICKENSON, MAY FREUD. Born in San Francisco. Educated in New
York public schools and at Hunter College. Went on the stage
and later married a mining engineer. Has lived in Alaska, On-
tario, and India. Now lives in New York City.
Mouse.

DINGLE, AYLWARD E. Born in Oxford, England, 1874. Went to sea
in 1899 as apprentice in a sailing ship. Served at sea twenty-
two years, during that time rising to command of square-riggers
and steamers. Served in Boxer Rebellion and Boer War. Began
writing in 1915. Is author of two novels and several hundred
short stories. Lives in Bermuda, but spends all possible time
cruising in a seventeen-ton schooner, "Gauntlet," wherever fancy
beckons.
Blow the Man Down.
Bound for Rio Grande.

(11) DOBIE, CHARLES CALDWELL (*for biography, see* 1917).
Arrested Moment.
Elder Brother.
Hands of the Enemy.

(11) DREISER, THEODORE (*for biography, see* 1919).
Glory Be! McGlathery.

DUDLEY, WALBRIDGE.
Harvest.

FAGIN, N. BRYLLION. "I am thirty-three years old. Married. I
have been errand boy, drug clerk, factory worker, government
clerk at Washington, lecturer and college professor. I have
received my education in the public and private evening schools
of New York, at Michigan State College, at Chicago, Columbia,
George Washington and Johns Hopkins universities. My first
paid contribution appeared in the *Atlantic Monthly* in 1918.
My name did not appear. Since then I have contributed prose
and verse to many magazines, popular and unpopular. 'Short
Story Writing: An Art or a Trade?' (Seltzer), 1923. A volume
of youthful storiettes, 'Of Love and Other Trifles' (Rossi-Bryn),
1925. I live in Baltimore.
Buttoned Up.

FISHER, RUDOLPH. Born in Washington, D. C., 1897. Educated in
Providence public schools and at Brown University. Graduate of

the Medical School of Harvard University, 1924. Married. Now engaged in medical research at Columbia University, as Fellow of the National Research Council.
City of Refuge.

(9) FITZGERALD, F. SCOTT (*for biography, see* 1922).
Absolution.

(11) GALE, ZONA (*for biography, see* 1923).
Dime.

(9) GEROULD, KATHARINE FULLERTON (*for biography, see* 1917).
Army with Banners.

(9) GILKYSON, WALTER (*for biography, see* 1922).
Coward's Castle.

(9) GRAEVE, OSCAR (*for biography, see* 1922).
Ferry Boat.

GREEN, PAUL. Born on a farm near Lillington, North Carolina. Has written stories, sketches, and plays of a section of the Cape Fear River country which he calls Little Bethel. At present, he is editor of The Reviewer and a member of the faculty of the University of North Carolina. Lives at Chapel Hill, North Carolina.
Man Who Died at Twelve O'Clock.

(2) GREGG, FRANCES.
Hunch-Back.

HACKETT, FRANCIS. Born in Kilkenny, Ireland, 1883. Educated at Clongowes Wood College, Kildare. Married. Came to America in 1900. Newspaper work in Chicago, 1906–09. Editor, Chicago Evening Post Literary Review, 1909–11. Associate Editor, New Republic, 1914–22. Author: "Ireland, a Study in Nationalism," 1918; "Horizons," 1918; "The Invisible Censor," 1920; "The Story of the Irish Nation," 1922; "Candor," 1924. Lives in Paris.
Unshapely Things.

HALL, JAMES NORMAN.
Forgotten One.

(9) HECHT, BEN (*for biography, see* 1918).
Lindro the Great.

(11) HEMINGWAY, ERNEST. Born Oak Park, Illinois. Married. Reporter on Kansas City Star before the War. Served on Italian Front during the War. Wounded, Croce di Guerra. Medaglia D'Argento, Valore Militare. Newspaper man in Europe since

1921. Written short stories since 1916. Amateur boxer and bull fighter. Author: "In Our Time," 1925. Long story, "The Bull Ring," translated and published serially in Der Querschnitt, 1925. Lives in Paris.
> Cross-Country Snow.
> Doctor and the Doctor's Wife.
> Mr. and Mrs. Elliot.

HIBBEN, PAXTON. Born in Indianapolis, 1880. Educated at Princeton and Harvard. F. R. G. S., F. A. G. S. Admitted to bar, but has not practiced law. United States Diplomatic Service, 1905–1912. Secretary International Tribunal of Arbitration at The Hague, 1910. Candidate for Congress, 1914. War correspondent, Collier's Weekly and Associated Press, 1914–1917; Leslie's Weekly, 1920–1921. Special correspondent in Russia and Near East of Chicago Tribune, London Daily Chronicle, L'Humanité and United Press. Enlisted as private in United States Army in 1917; captain, 1919; served at G. H. Q., A. E. F. Decorated: Orders of St. Stanislas of Russia, Redeemer of Greece, Sacred Treasure of Japan. Author: "Constantine I and the Greek People"; "The Famine in Russia." Lives in Indianapolis.
> Young Man with Great Possessions.

HOUSTON, MARGARET BELLE.
> Gold Picayune.

HOWARD, SIDNEY. Born in Oakland, California, 1891. Educated at the University of California. Studied play-writing at Harvard. With the American Ambulance in France and later aviator with the rank of captain. Since the War he has been on the staff of Life, The New Republic, Collier's Weekly, International, and other magazines. Married. Author: "Swords" (play), 1921; "Three Flights Up," 1924; "Bewitched" (play in collaboration with Edward Sheldon), 1924; "They Knew What They Wanted" (play), 1924; "Lucky Sam McCarver" (play), 1925. Has translated and adapted various European plays. Winner of Pulitzer Prize. Lives in New York City.
> Such Women as Ellen Steele.

(7)   HUSSEY, L. M. (*for biography, see* 1920).
> Conclusion.
> Reunion.

(10)   JITRO, WILLIAM C. G. (*for biography, see* 1922).
> Holiday.

(11)   KNOWLTON, CLARKE (*for biography, see* 1924).
> Bridegroom.

(10)   KOMROFF, MANUEL. "Born in New York City in 1890 under protest but in good humor. Tampered with schools and tried

a college or two under the impression that education was the mark of a gentleman. Discovered his mistake. Travelled far across Siberia and parts of China, and edited an English newspaper in Russia during the Revolution. Married an Englishwoman in 1918 and tried to support her by doing editorial work on newspapers.

He began writing stories through sheer obstinacy and still has the same wife he started with. His first stories appeared in Reedy's Mirror and The Dial after they had been rejected in other places, and in the face of everything he still keeps on writing when he finds time. He now works for a book publisher, but has an agreeable nature though a sharp and quick tongue.

In spite of his practical jokes his friends like him. He lives like a fool and by so doing hopes to die a wise man."

Beating of the Reed.
Grace of Lambs.
How Does it Feel to be Free?

(9) LARDNER, RING W. (*for biography, see* 1922).
Haircut.
Zone of Quiet.

(10) LEECH, MARGARET KERNOCHAN (*for biography, see* 1923).
Little White Village.

LEHMAN, B. H. Born 1889. Graduate, Harvard, A.B., Ph.D. Associate Professor of English in the University of California. Married. Lecturer and writer. Novel: "Wild Marriage," 1925. Residence, Berkeley, California.
Sons.

(11) LOWELL, AMY (*for biography, see* 1924). Died 1925.
Conversion of a Saint.

(10) MARQUAND, JOHN PHILLIPS (*for biography, see* 1923).
Old Man.

MARSH, HOWARD R. Born at Milwaukee, Wisconsin, 1893. Educated at University of Michigan. Publicity and article work, 1915–1920. Travels considerably. Lives at Jackson, Michigan, and Redlands, California.
Rebellion.

(7) MASON, GRACE SARTWELL (*for biography, see* 1920).
Gray Spell.

MATHEUS, JOHN F. Born in Keyser, West Virginia, 1887. Childhood passed in Steubenville, Ohio. Educated at Western Reserve University and Columbia University. Professor of Romance languages in the West Virginia Collegiate Institute since 1923. Married. Has travelled widely. Lives at Institute, West Virginia.
Fog.

MATHEY, FABYAN. Born in New Jersey, 1903. Educated at Princeton and Columbia Universities. At various times in his life has been lumberjack, longshoreman, and forest ranger. Is particularly interested in music, painting, and French and Scandinavian literature. Has been writing for two years—plays, poetry, and stories. Lives at Cranford, New Jersey.
Sunday.

(11) MONTAGUE, MARGARET PRESCOTT (*for biography, see* 1919).
Great Theme.

MOON, LORNA.
Wantin' a Hand.

(11) MORRIS, LAWRENCE S. (*for biography, see* 1924).
Apples of Gold or Pictures of Silver.

MOSLEY, JEFFERSON. Born in Texas. Educated at South Western University, Texas, and Oxford University. Former Rhodes scholar. Taught physics at South Western University, 1912–15. Has been in the Civil Service. Is now editor of research publication at the United States Forest Products Laboratory, Madison, Wisconsin. Won first prize in Forum short story contest, 1924.
Secret at the Crossroads.

MULLEN, KATE.
Interval.

(10) NICHOLL, LOUISE TOWNSEND (*for biography, see* 1919).
Green Ice.

(3) NORRIS, KATHLEEN. Born in San Francisco, 1880. Educated privately and at University of California. Married Charles G. Norris, the novelist, 1909. Author: "Mother," 1911; "The Rich Mrs. Burgoyne," 1912; "Poor Dear Margaret Kirby," 1913; "Saturday's Child," 1914; "The Story of Julia Page," 1915; "The Heart of Rachael," 1916; "Martie, the Unconquered," 1917; "Undertow," 1917; "Josslyn's Wife," 1918; "Sisters," 1919; "Harriet and the Piper," 1920; "The Beloved Woman," 1921; "Certain People of Importance," 1922; "Butterfly," 1923; "The Callahans and the Murphys," 1924. Lives on Long Island.
Masterpiece.

(8) O'HIGGINS, HARVEY J. (*for biography, see* 1919).
Love Story of a Silent Man.

(9) OPPENHEIM, JAMES (*for biography, see* 1918).
Last Man.

PARSONS, ALICE BEALE.
Love at 42 Altgeld Avenue.

(11) PETERKIN, JULIA (*for biography, see* 1924).
    Maum Lou.
    Sorcerer.

(6) PRATT, LUCY (*for biography, see* 1918).
    Dark Gate.

PRUETTE, LORINE. "I was born in Tennessee, November 3, 1896.
    At an early age I acquired the habit of going to school, and I
    seem to have kept it up nearly ever since, finishing—I trust—with
    a doctorate from Columbia University. My book, 'Women and
    Leisure, A Study of Social Waste,' was published last year. I
    have just completed a psychological biography of G. Stanley Hall,
    and my next job is to write a book on Industrial Sociology. I
    am one of the editors of 'Industrial Psychology' and have con-
    tributed to various scientific journals. Writing stories and going
    to the theatre are the chief joys of life. 'Smile of Victory' is my
    third story to be published. My home is in New York City."
    Smile of Victory.

(9) ROBBINS, TOD (*for biography, see* 1921).
    Bit of a Banshee.

(11) ROBIN, MAX (*for biography, see* 1923).
    Itzikil.

ROBINSON, ELSIE.
    Misunderstood Husband.

ROBINSON, ROBERT. Born near Taylor, Texas, 1899. Educated in
    Texas Public Schools and graduated at the University of Arkansas.
    Has worked at a variety of occupations ranging from harvesting
    to school teaching. At present engaged in recreation work as
    boys' supervisor at Mount Vernon, N. Y.
    Ill Wind.

(11) SHIFFRIN, A. B. (*for biography, see* 1924).
    Other Cheek.
    Trickle of Red.

(9) SPRINGER, FLETA CAMPBELL (*for biography, see* 1917).
    Legend.

STANLEY, MAY. (MRS. ELMER BROWN MASON.) Born in a pioneer
    cabin on Puget Sound, Washington. "Never attended school, but
    studied for a few months with an Oxford man when I was twelve
    years old. He taught me more important things than mathematics
    and history—to love trees and the sea and the books written
    about them." Newspaper worker since 1912, Washington and

Minnesota. Came to New York City in 1916, magazine work and musical criticism. Author: "Fair Weather Cometh," 1923. Lives in New York City, but spends most of the time on the Maine coast.
Old Man Ledge.

(11) STEELE, WILBUR DANIEL (*for biography, see* 1917).
Man Who Saw Through Heaven.
Sauce for the Goose.
Six Dollars.
Thinker.
When Hell Froze.

(11) SUCKOW, RUTH (*for biography, see* 1923).
Golden Wedding.
Start in Life.

(10) TARKINGTON, BOOTH (*for biography, see* 1918).
Shanty.
'Thea Zell.

TAYLOR, ELLEN DU POIS. Born in Huron, South Dakota. Educated at Huron College, South Dakota, and Northwestern University. Has been a publisher's proof reader, manager of the Chicago Little Theatre, director of the Speakers' Bureau of the Illinois Council of Defense, and has worked with women in politics. Lives at Chesterton, Indiana.
Calico.

(10) TOOMER, JEAN (*for biography, see* 1923).
Easter.

(11) VENABLE, EDWARD CARRINGTON (*for biography, see* 1921).
Lines on the Portrait of a Lady.

(11) VORSE, MARY HEATON (*for biography, see* 1917).
Sand.

WALDMAN, MILTON. Born in Cleveland, Ohio, U. S. A., 1895. Educated at Yale College, 1917. Journalist, New York and Cleveland. Assistant editor London Mercury since February, 1924. Author: "Americana," 1925.
Home Town.

(11) WESCOTT, GLENWAY (*for biography, see* 1924).
This Way Out.

(11) WHARTON, EDITH (*for biography, see* 1924).
Bewitched.
Miss Mary Pask.
Velvet Ear-Muffs.

(11) WHITMAN, STEPHEN FRENCH (*for biography, see* 1924).
      That Famous Love Affair.

(11) WILLIAMS, BEN AMES (*for biography, see* 1918).
      Finished Story.

WILLOUGHBY, BARRETT. "I am an Alaskan, white, Irish, and a Miss
      instead of a Mister. My first home was my father's trading
      schooner that cruised up and down the shores of Alaska. My
      people now have a trading post in Alaska. I received my educa-
      tion in a convent in the States, and from the traders, trappers,
      Indians, explorers, scientists and sea-faring men who make of my
      father's store a sort of wilderness club in the winter. I wanted
      to tell the world about my country and its people, so I borrowed
      some money and came down to San Francisco to begin in 1920.
      Went broke before my book was done. Became, for a year and
      a half, secretary to Frederick O'Brien, the South Sea writer.
      Then finished my book—'Where the Sun Swings North,' and I've
      been writing for myself ever since."
      Devil-Drum.

(9)   WOOD, CLEMENT (*for biography, see* 1922).
      Blue Circle.
      Mother.
      Tzagan.

WYLIE, ELINOR. (MRS. WILLIAM ROSE BENÉT.) Author: "Black
      Armor" (poems), 1923; "Jennifer Lorn," 1924; and "The Venetian
      Glass Nephew," 1925. Lives near New York City.
      Gideon's Revenge.

THE ROLL OF HONOR OF FOREIGN
SHORT STORIES IN AMERICAN
MAGAZINES

OCTOBER, 1924, TO SEPTEMBER, 1925

NOTE. *The index figures from 1 to 11 prefixed to the name of the author indicate the last Roll of Honor between 1914 and 1924 in which his work has been included. Thus the figure 1 indicates 1914, the figure 5 indicates 1918, etc. The Roll of Honor for 1914 appeared in the volume for 1915.*

I. BRITISH AND IRISH AUTHORS

(11) ARLEN MICHAEL (DIKRAN KUYUMJIAN).
   Ace of Thirteens.
   One Gold Coin.

(11) AUMONIER, STACY.
   Dark Red Roses.

(11) AUSTIN, F. BRITTEN.
   Battle Piece: New Style.
   On the Flagship.

BENNETT, ROLF.
   Cask.

(11) BIBESCO, PRINCESS ELIZABETH.
   "Peronnière Letters."

(4) BOTTOME, PHYLLIS.
   Wonder-Child.

(11) CHESTERTON, GILBERT KEITH.
   Arrow of Heaven.
   Asylum of Adventure.
   Curse of the Golden Cross.
   Man with Two Beards.
   Mirror of Death.
   Song of the Flying Fish.

(2) COLUM, PADRAIC.
   John Greggins—A Day in His Life.

(11) COPPARD, A. E.
   Field of Mustard.

COULDREY, OSWALD.
   Nandi in Pound.

COULTER, GEOFFREY.
   Decoy.

(9) DE LA MARE, WALTER.
   Connoisseur.

(7) ERVINE, ST. JOHN G.
   Mr. Peden Keeps His Cook.

(10) GALSWORTHY, JOHN.
   Last Card.
   Mummy.
   Water.

GERHARDI, WILLIAM.
   Big Drum.

HUGHES, RICHARD.
   Locomotive.
   Poor Man's Inn.

(11) HUXLEY, ALDOUS.
   Half Holiday.

JACOBS, W. W.
   Fickle Woman.
   Something for Nothing.

(11) KAYE-SMITH, SHEILA.
   Working Man's Wife.

(11) KIPLING, RUDYARD.
   Bull that Thought.
   Prophet and the Country.
   Wish House.

(9) LAWRENCE, D. H.
   Woman Who Rode Away.

(11) MAUGHAM, W. SOMERSET.
   Man Who Wouldn't Hurt a Fly.
   Mr. Know-All.

METCALFE, JOHN.
   Mole.

MEYNELL, VIOLA.
    Letter.
    Ten Minutes.

O'FLAHERTY, LIAM.
    Conger Eel.
    Wild Goat's Kid.

(11) POWYS, T. F.
    Painted Wagon.

RICHARDSON, ANTHONY.
    Old Mossy Face.

(11) WALPOLE, HUGH.
    Old Elizabeth.

WILLIAMSON, HENRY.
    No Eel for Nog.

(10) WOOLF, VIRGINIA.
    Miss Ormerod.

WRYNN, ANTHONY.
    Equinox.

II. TRANSLATIONS

(10) ANDREYEV, LEONID (*Russian*).
    Giant.

(6) D'ANNUNZIO, GABRIELLE (*Italian*).
    Bells.

DOSTOEVSKY, FYODOR (*Russian*).
    Christmas Story.

GOGOL, N. V. (*Russian*).
    Diary of a Madman.

(11) "GORKY, MAXIM" (*Russian*).
    Hermit.
    Story of a Novel.
    Strange Murderer.

GOURMONT, REMY DE (*French*).
    Evening Chat.
    Faun.

(6) JACOBSEN, J. P. (*Danish*).
    Two Worlds.

MARTORELLO, NOÉ S. (*Argentinian*).
  Pedro.

(11) SCHNITZLER, ARTHUR (*Austrian*).
  Lieutenant Gustl.

SILLEN, MARTA AF (*Swedish*).
  Two Sibyls.

VON HEIDENSTAMM, VERNER (*Swedish*).
  Sigrid the Haughty and Her Wooers.

THE BEST BOOKS OF SHORT STORIES OF 1925

I. American Authors

1. AIKEN. Bring! Bring! Boni and Liveright.
2. AUSTIN. William Austin. Marshall Jones.
3. COBB. Alias Ben Alibi. Doran.
4. FITZGERALD. All the Sad Young Men. Scribner.
5. Harper Prize Short Stories. 1924. Harper.
6. HEMINGWAY. In Our Time. Boni and Liveright.
7. KOMROFF. The Grace of Lambs. Boni and Liveright.
8. O'BRIEN, FITZJAMES. Collected Stories. A. and C. Boni.

II. British and Irish Authors

9. ARLEN. Mayfair. Doran.
10. AUMONIER. Overheard. Doubleday, Page.
11. BECKE. Yorke the Adventurer. Lippincott.
12. BLACKWOOD. Tongues of Fire. Dutton.
13. BRAMAH. The Specimen Case. Doran.
14. CONRAD. Tales of Hearsay. Doubleday, Page.
15. COPPARD. Fishmonger's Fiddle. Knopf.
16. CORVO. In His Own Image. Knopf.
17. DE LA MARE. Broomsticks. Knopf.
18. KENNARD. Level Crossings. A. and C. Boni.
19. LAWRENCE. St. Mawr. Knopf.
20. LYND. The Mulberry Bush. Minton, Balch.
21. MACARDLE. Earth-Bound. Harrigan Press.
22. MACHEN. The Shining Pyramid. Knopf.
23. MAYNE. Inner Circle. Harcourt, Brace.
24. MEYNELL. Young Mrs. Cruse. Harcourt, Brace.
25. SACKVILLE-WEST. Seducers in Ecuador. Doran.
26. SITWELL. Triple Fugue. Doran.
27. SMITH. The Little Karoo. Doran.
28. WATSON. Innocent Desires. Boni and Liveright.

III. Translations

29. BARBEY D'AUREVILLY. The Diaboliques. Knopf.
30. BLASCO IBÁÑEZ. The Old Woman of the Movies. Dutton.
31. EATON, *editor*. The Best Continental Short Stories of 1924–25. Small, Maynard.

32. EATON, *editor*. The Best French Short Stories of 1924–25. Small, Maynard.
33. Flying Osip. International Publishers.
34. GOBINEAU. Five Oriental Tales. Viking Press.
35. GORKY. The Story of a Novel. Dial Press.
36. MANN. Death in Venice. Knopf.
37. MAUPASSANT. Collected Stories (Volumes 10–15). Knopf.
38. PILNIAK. Tales of the Wilderness. Knopf.
39. REMIZOV. The Clock. Knopf.
40. ZWEIG.. Passion and Pain. Bernard G. Richards.

VOLUMES OF SHORT STORIES
PUBLISHED IN THE UNITED STATES

OCTOBER, 1924, TO SEPTEMBER, 1925

NOTE. *An asterisk before a title indicates distinction. This list includes single short stories and collections of short stories. Volumes announced for publication in the autumn of 1925 are listed here, although in some cases they had not yet appeared at the time this book went to press.*

I. AMERICAN AUTHORS

ABDULLAH, ACHMED. The Swinging Caravan. Brentano's.

AIKEN, CONRAD. *Bring! Bring! Boni and Liveright.

ALLEN, JAMES LANE. *The Landmark. Macmillan.

ANDERSON, ISABEL. The Kiss and Queue. Four Seas Co.

ANDREWS, MARY RAYMOND SHIPMAN. Pontifex Maximus. Scribner.

AUSTIN, WALTER, editor. *William Austin, the Creator of Peter Rugg. Marshall Jones.

BAILEY, PAUL. The Man Who Turned Mex. Dorrance.

BAILEY, TEMPLE. The Holly Hedge. Penn.

BANNAN, THERESA. Waifs of War. Syracuse, N. Y.: Syracuse Printing and Publishing Co.

BEACH, REX ELLINGWOOD. The Goose Woman and Other Stories. Harper.

BOYD, THOMAS. *Points of Honor. Scribner.

BUCK, MITCHELL S. *Afterglow. Frank-Maurice.

CLARK, BADGER. Spike. Badger.

COBB, IRVIN S. *Alias Ben Alibi. Doran.

COHEN, OCTAVUS ROY. Bigger and Blacker. Little, Brown.

COLLINS, CHARLES. The Sins of Saint Anthony. Covici.

CONNELL, RICHARD. *Variety. Minton, Balch.

Copy—1925. Appleton.

COTTON, JANE BALDWIN. *Wall-eyed Cæsar's Ghost. Marshall Jones.

DARGAN, OLIVE TILFORD. *Highland Annals. Scribner.

DE BRA, LEMUEL. Ways that are Wary. Clode.

FITZGERALD, F. SCOTT. *All the Sad Young Men. Scribner.

FOX, CHARLES DONALD, editor. Il Conte. Charles Renard Co.

FRENCH, JOSEPH LEWIS, editor. Great Pirate Stories—Second Series. Brentano's. Great Sea Stories—Second Series. Brentano's.

GLASS, MONTAGUE MARSDEN. Y'Understand. Doubleday, Page.

GONZALES, AMBROSE E. *Laguerre. Columbia, S. C.: The State Co. *The Captain. Columbia, S. C.: The State Co.

GRAY, CHARLES WRIGHT, editor. "Dawgs." Holt.

GREENE, L. PATRICK. The Major-Diamond Buyer. Doubleday, Page.

*Harper Prize Short Stories. Harper.

HASTINGS, WILLIAM THOMPSON; CLOUGH, BENJAMIN CROCKER, and MASON, KENNETH OLIVER, editors. *Short Stories. Houghton Mifflin.

HEMINGWAY, ERNEST. *In Our Time. Boni and Liveright.

HERRICK, ROBERT. *Wanderings. Harcourt, Brace.

HUMPHREY, MURIEL MILLER, editor. *The Best Love Stories of 1924. Small, Maynard.

JEWETT, SARAH ORNE. *The Best Stories of. 2 vols. Houghton Mifflin.

JOHNSTON, WILLIAM, editor. The World's Best Short Stories of 1925. Doran.

KENDRICK, ELSIE. The Rip Tide. Stratford.

KOMROFF, MANUEL. *The Grace of Lambs. Boni and Liveright.

LA MOTTE, ELLEN N. Snuffs and Butters. Century.

LARSEN, CAROLINE D. The Goosegirl's Love Story. Rutland, Vt.: Tuttle Co.

LYTLE, JOHN HORACE. The Story of Jack. Appleton.

MACMECHAN, ARCHIBALD. Old Province Tales. Doran.

MOORE, JOHN TROTWOOD. Uncle Wash, his Stories. Cokesbury Press.

*More Aces. Putnam.

NOBLE, EDWARD. The Mandarin's Bell. Houghton Mifflin.

O'BRIEN, EDWARD J., editor. The Best Short Stories of 1924. Small, Maynard.

O'BRIEN, FITZJAMES. *Collected Stories. A. and C. Boni.

O'SHAUGHNESSY, EDITH. *Married Life. Harcourt, Brace.

OVERS, W. H. Stories of African Life. E. S. Gorham.

POE, EDGAR ALLAN. The Best Tales of. Modern Library.

POOLE, ERNEST. *The Little Dark Man. Macmillan.

REEVE, ARTHUR B. The Boy Scouts' Craig Kennedy. Harper. Craig Kennedy on the Farm. Fourteen Points. Harper.

RICE, ALICE CALDWELL HEGAN, and RICE, CALE YOUNG. Winners and Losers. Century.

ROBINSON, KENNETH ALLEN, editor. *Contemporary Short Stories. Houghton Mifflin.

ROYSTER, JAMES FINCH, editor. American Short Stories. Scott, Foresman.

RUTLEDGE, ARCHIBALD. Heart of the South. Columbia, S. C.: The State Co.

SALTUS, EDGAR. Purple and Fine Women. Covici.

SASS, HERBERT RAVENEL. Way of the Wild. Minton, Balch.

SCHWEIKERT, H. C., editor. Short Stories. Harcourt, Brace.

SOCIETY OF ARTS AND SCIENCES, editors. O. Henry Memorial Award. Prize Stories of 1924. Doubleday, Page.

SPARLING, E. EARL. Under the Levee. Scribner.

STREET, JULIAN. Mr. Bisbee's Princess. Doubleday, Page.

URNER, MABEL HERBERT. The Married Life of Helen and Warren. Small, Maynard.

WITWER, H. C. Love and Learn. Putnam.

II. British and Irish Authors

ARLEN, MICHAEL. *Mayfair. Doran.
AUMONIER, STACY. *Overheard. Doubleday, Page.
AUSTIN, F. BRITTEN. *Thirteen. Doubleday, Page.
BECKE, LOUIS. *Yorke the Adventurer. Lippincott.
BLACKWOOD, ALGERNON. *Tongues of Fire. Dutton.
BRAMAH, ERNEST. *The Specimen Case. Doran.
CONRAD, JOSEPH. *Shorter Tales. Doubleday, Page. *Tales of Hearsay. Doubleday, Page.
COPPARD, A. E. *Fishmonger's Fiddle. Knopf.
CORVO, FREDERICK, BARON. *In His Own Image. Knopf.
DE LA MARE, WALTER. *Broomsticks. Knopf.
DELL, ETHEL M. The Passer-By. Putnam.
FLETCHER, J. S. The Secret of the Barbican. Putnam.
GILES, HERBERT A. *Strange Tales from a Chinese Studio. Boni and Liveright.
KENNARD, SIR COLERIDGE. *Level Crossings. A. and C. Boni.
LAWRENCE, D. H. *St. Mawr. Knopf.
LYND, SYLVIA. *The Mulberry Bush. Minton, Balch.
MACARDLE, DOROTHY. *Earthbound. Worcester: Harrigan Press.
MACHEN, ARTHUR. *The Shining Pyramid. Knopf.
MCKENNA, STEPHEN. Tales of Intrigue and Revenge. Little, Brown.
MAYNE, ETHEL COLBURN. *Inner Circle. Harcourt, Brace.
MEYNELL, VIOLA. *Young Mrs. Cruse. Harcourt, Brace.
MILFORD, H. S., editor. *Selected English Stories. Oxford University Press.
*New Decameron. Volume 4. Brentano's.
O'BRIEN, EDWARD J., and COURNOS, JOHN, editors. The Best British Short Stories of 1925. Small, Maynard.
OLLIVANT, ALFRED. Boxer and Beauty. Doubleday, Page.
REDMOND, I. P. The Master's Vineyard. Herder.
SACKVILLE-WEST, V. *Seducers in Ecuador. Doran.
"SAPPER." The Dinner Club. Doran. Out of the Blue. Doran.
SITWELL, OSBERT. *Triple Fugue. Doran.
SMITH, PAULINE. *The Little Karoo. Doran.
SQUIRE, J. C. The Grub Street Nights' Entertainments. Doran.
SUTTON, GRAHAM. Fish and Actors. Brentano's.
WATSON, E. L. GRANT. *Innocent Desires. Boni and Liveright.
WILLIAMSON, HENRY. *Sun Brothers. Dutton.

III. Translations

BANDELLO (Italian). *Tragical Tales. Dutton.
BARBEY D'AUREVILLY, JULES (French). *The Diaboliques. Knopf.
BERLIC-MAZURANIO, I. V. (Croatian). Croatian Tales of Long Ago. Stokes.
BLASCO IBÁÑEZ, VICENTE (Spanish). *The Old Woman of the Movies. Dutton.

CHIVAS-BARON, CL. (*French*). *Three Women of Annam. Frank-Maurice.

"COLETTE" (*French*). Cats, Dogs, and I. Holt.

DUVERNOIS, HENRI, *and others* (*French*). Jacqueline. Minton, Balch.

EATON, RICHARD, *editor*. *The Best Continental Short Stories of 1924–25. Small, Maynard. *The Best French Short Stories of 1924–25. Small, Maynard.

*Flying Osip (Russian). International Publishers.

GOBINEAU, JOSEPH ARTHUR, COMTE DE (*French*). *Five Oriental Tales. Viking Press.

GORKY, MAXIM (*Russian*). *The Story of a Novel. Dial Press.

IBÁÑEZ, VICENTE BLASCO (*Spanish*). *See* BLASCO IBÁÑEZ, VICENTE.

KELLER, GOTTFRIED (*German*). *The Fat of the Cat. Harcourt, Brace.

KUPRIN, ALEXANDRE IVANOVITCH (*Russian*). *Gambrinus and other Stories. Adelphi.

MANN, THOMAS (*German*). *Death in Venice. Knopf.

MAUPASSANT, GUY DE (*French*). *The Horla. Knopf. *The Little Rogue. Knopf.

OGAWA, MIMEI (*Japanese*). Rose and Witch. Overland Publishing Company.

PILNIAK, BORIS (*Russian*). Tales of the Wilderness. Knopf.

REMIZOV, ALEKSEI (*Russian*). The Clock. Knopf.

RUNG, OTTO (*Danish*). *Shadows that Pass. Appleton.

SEITZ, DON C., *editor* (*Japanese*). Monogatari. Putnam.

TOWNSEND, R. S., *editor*. *Short Stories by Russian Authors. Dutton.

VICTORIN, M. (*French*). The Chopping Bee. Toronto: Musson.

ZWEIG, STEFAN (*German*). Passion and Pain. Bernard G. Richards.

ARTICLES ON THE SHORT STORY IN AMERICAN MAGAZINES

OCTOBER, 1924, TO SEPTEMBER, 1925

Authors of articles are printed in capital letters. For articles in British and Irish periodicals, see "The Best British Short Stories of 1925." Unsigned reviews of minor importance are not indexed.

A

Aakjaer, Jeppe.
> By Waldemar Westergaard. Scan. Nov., '24. (12:665.)

AIDLINE-TROMMER, ELBERT.
> Yiddish Short Story. Men. J. Nov.–Dec., '24. (10:515.)

AIKEN, CHARLES E.
> James Stephens. Cath. W. Apr. (121:132.)

Aiken, Conrad.
> By Malcolm Cowley. Sat. R. (N. Y.) Jun. 27. (1:851.)
> By Robert Morss Lovett. N. Rep. Jul. 22. (43:242.)

ALDEN, STANLEY.
> George Gissing. Books. Feb. 22. (11.)

ALDERMAN, EDWIN A.
> Edgar Allan Poe. Va. Apr. (1:78.)

ALDINGTON, RICHARD.
> Katharine Mansfield. L. Rev. Jan. 10. (8.) N. Rep. Oct. 22, '24. (40:207.)

Aldrich, Thomas Bailey.
> By C. Hartley Grattan. A. Merc. May. (5:41.)

ALLEN, FLETCHER.
> Sheila Kaye-Smith. Int. Sept., '24. (2:726.)

ALLEN, HERVEY.
> A. E. Gonzales. Sat. R. (N. Y.) Mar. 14. (1:595.)

Allen, James Lane.
> By John H. Finley. N. Y. Times. Mar. 1. (2.)

ALLEN, LOUIS.
> Jack London. Dear. Ind. May 16. (2.)

American Short Story.
> By John Davis Anderson. Int. Mar. (3:251.)
> Anonymous. Book. (N. Y.) Nov., '24. (60:370.)
> By Herschel Brickell. L. Rev. Jan. 31. (7.)
> By Louis Bromfield. Books. Feb. 15. (3.)
> By Gerald Hewes Carson. Book. (N. Y.) Mar. (61:58.) May. (61:348.) June. (61:438.)
> By N. Bryllion Fagin. Int. Mar. (3:249.)
> By Charles J. Finger. A. W. Dec., '24. (7.)

By Henry B. Fuller. N. Y. Times. Jun. 28. (16.)
By Herbert S. Gorman. N. Y. Sun. Mar. 6. (16.) Int. Aug.
25. (3:616.)
By M. M. World. Jul. 5. (9S.)
By Lloyd Morris. N. Y. Times. Jan. 18. (6.)
By Edward J. O'Brien. L. Rev. Apr. 11. (2.)
By John Pentifer. A. Merc. Jan. (4:90.)
By Janet Ramsay. Books. Aug. 16. (10.)
By R. L. Ramsay. L. Rev. May 9. (14.)
By Paul F. Sifton. N. Y. World. Feb. 22. (7.)
By John F. Smertenko. Nat. (N. Y.) Apr. 22. (120:469.)
By Blanche Colton Williams. N. Y. Sun. Jan. 31. (7.)
By R. Heylbut Wollstein. Int. Mar. (3:249.)

ANDERSON, ISAAC.
Irvin S. Cobb. Int. Nov., '24. (2:906.)
Selma Lägerlof. Int. Nov., '24. (2:890.)

ANDERSON, JOHN DAVIS.
American Short Story. Int. Mar. (3:251.)

Anderson, Sherwood.
By D. A. Ind. Nov. 22, '24. (113:429.)
By William Rose Benét. Sat. R. (N. Y.) Oct. 18, '24. (1:200.)
By Louis Bromfield. Book. (N. Y.) Dec., '24. (7:71.)
By V. F. Calverton. Mod. R. Fall, '24. (2:82.)
By Joseph Collins. Book. (N. Y.) Mar. (61:22.)
By N. Bryllion Fagin. D.D. Jan. Feb. (7:91.) Guar. (Am.)
(1:246.)
By Charles J. Finger. A. W. Dec., '24. (7.)
By Waldo Frank. Guar. (Am.) Feb. (1:97.)
By Julius Weis Freind. D. D. Nov.–Dec., 24. (7:71.)
By Isaac Goldberg. Strat. Jan. (4:83.)
By Herbert S. Gorman. Int. Dec., '24. (3:15.)
By Harry Hansen. Nat. (N. Y.) Dec. 10, '24. (119:641.)
By John L. Hervey. A. W. Mar. (9.)
By Sinclair Lewis. Books. Nov. 9, '24. (1.)
By Robert Morss Lovett. N. Rep. Nov. 5, '24. (40:255.)
By Flora Merrill. N. Y. World. Mar. 22. (1 M.)
By Christopher Morley. Sat. R. (N. Y.) Aug. 15. (2:43.)
By Lloyd Morris. N. Y. Times. Oct. 12, '24. (6.)
By Frank Luther Mott. Mid. Jan. 15. (11:54.)
By Llewellyn Powys. Dial. Apr. (78:330.)
By Carl Van Doren. Cen. July. (110:362.)
By Virginia Woolf. Sat. R. (N. Y.) Aug 1. (2:1.)

Andreyev, Leonid.
By Julian Leveridge. L. Rev. Jan. 10. (2.)
By Princess Radzwill. Sat. R. (N. Y.) Oct. 4, '24. (1:164.)
By Joseph T. Shipley. Guar. (Am.) Apr. (1:261.)

Arlen, Michael.
By William Rose Benét. Sat. R. (N.Y.) Jun. 6. (1:802.)
By Herschel Brickell. L. Rev. (N. Y.) Jun. 13. (3.)
By Bruce Gould. Int. May. (3:399.)

By Joseph Wood Krutch. World. May 24. (4 M.)
By Shane Leslie. Int. Oct., '24. (2:769.)
By Robert Morss Lovett. N. Rep. Dec. 10, '24. (41:8.)
By Herman L. Mankiewicz. N. Y. Times. Mar. 22. (2.) May 31. (5.)
By David Martin. Book. (N. Y.) Nov., '24. (60:293.)
By Edmund Lester Pearson. Outl. (N. Y.) Jun. 10. (140:221.)

ARNESSEN, ELIAS.
Knut Hamsun. For. Jun. (73:852.)

Aumonier, Stacy.
By Stella Heilbrunn. Int. May. (3:426.)
By William McFee. N. Y. Sun. Feb. 14. (7.)

Austin, William.
Anon. N. Y. Times. May 31. (21.)

B

Balzac, Honoré de.
By Albert S. Guérard. S. W. Apr. (10:110.)
By Hugo von Hofmannsthal. Dial. May. (78:35.)

Barbey d'Aurevilly, Jules-Amédeé.
By Ernest Boyd. N. Y. Sun. Mar. 11. (16.)
By William A. Drake. Books. Apr. 19. (9.)
By John Eversharp. N. Rep. Aug. 19, '25. (43:351.)
By Paul Souday. N. Y. Times. Jul. 19. (12.)

"Barrington, E."
By Gerald Hewes Carson. Books. Oct. 5, '24. (8.)
By William Arthur Deacon. Int. July, '25. (3:535.)

BAUGH, HANSELL.
Short Story. Rev. Jul. (5:105.)

Beach, Rex.
By Carey Jeffreys. L. Rev. Aug. 8. (2.)
By Morris Markey. Int. Sept. (3:681.)

BEAZELL, W. P.
Washington Irving. World. May 3. (6 M.)

BEER, THOMAS.
Richard Harding Davis. Ly. Oct. 11, '24. (15.)
Henry James. Sat. R. (N. Y.) Apr. 25. (1:701.)

BELL, CLIVE.
Virginia Woolf. Dial. Dec., '24. (77:451.)

BELL, LISLE.
J. C. Squire. Books. Mar. 8. (11.)

BELLOC-LOWNDES, MRS.
Henry James. Sat. R. (N. Y.) Sept. 19. (2:139.)

BENÉT, WILLIAM ROSE.
Sherwood Anderson. Sat. R. (N. Y.) Oct. 18, '24. (1:200.)
Michael Arlen. Sat. R. (N. Y.) Jun. 6. (1:803.)
Richard Connell. Sat. R. (N. Y.) Aug. 8. (2:23.)
Joseph Conrad. Sat. R. (N. Y.) Mar. 14. (1:594.)
Charles J. Finger. Sat. R. (N. Y.) Dec. 13, '24. (1:380.)
John Galsworthy. Book. (N. Y.) Aug. (61:698.)

Bennett, Arnold.
  By George B. Dutton. Ind. Dec. 27, '24. (113:577.)
  By Kenneth Fuessle. Int. Jan. (3:98.)
  By Henry B. Fuller. Sat. R. (N. Y.) Nov. 29, '24. (1:319.)
  By Henry Hazlitt. N. Y. Sun. Sept. 26. (8.)
  By Joseph Wood Krutch. Books. Nov. 9, '24. (4.)
  By Frederic Lefévre. Liv. A. Mar. 28. (324:691.)
  By H. L. Mencken. World. Sept. 13. (4 M.)
  By Charles Wharton Stork. L. Rev. Jan. 3. (3.)
Bercovici, Konrad.
  By Ring W. Lardner. L. Rev. Oct. 18, '24. (3.)
BESTON, HENRY.
  Charles J. Finger. Books. Dec. 28, '24. (4.)
Bierce, Ambrose.
  By Ruth Guthrie Harding. Book. (N. Y.) Aug. (61:636.)
  By Edna Kenton. Book. (N. Y.) Sept. (62:77.)
  By Robert Littell. N. Rep. Oct. 15, '24. (40:177.)
  By Henry L. Mencken. World. Mar. 1. (3 E.)
  By George Sterling. A. Merc. Sept. (6:10.)
BISHOP, JOHN PEALE.
  Kenneth Burke. Sat. R. (N. Y.) Jan. 3. (1:427.)
BJÖRKMAN, EDWIN.
  Ernest Bramah. L. Rev. Apr. 4. (3.)
  Aldous Huxley. L. Rev. Oct. 4, '24. (4.)
  Thomas Mann. L. Rev. Feb. 28. (3.)
Blackmore, Richard Doddridge.
  By John Walker Harrington. Int. Sept. (3:666.)
Blackwood, Algernon.
  Anonymous. N. Y. Times. Feb. 22. (14.)
  By Louise Maunsell Field. Int. Jun. (3:482.)
  By Zona Gale. Books. Apr. 26. (1.)
  By Robert Hillyer. N. Y. Sun. Mar. 7. (7.)
  By Wallace Irwin. L. Rev. Mar. 7. (3.)
Bland, J. O. P.
  By Herschel Brickell. L. Rev. Dec. 27, '24. (3.)
Blasco Ibáñez, Vicente.
  By Arthur Livingston. Int. Jul. (3:543.)
  By Allan Nevins. Sat. R. (N. Y.) Jul. 4. (1:871.)
  By Henry Longan Stuart. N. Y. Times. May 31. (9.)
BOAS, GEORGE.
  Comte Arthur de Gobineau. Rev. Apr. (5:101.)
BOGAN, LOUISE.
  Viola Meynell. Sat. R. (N. Y.) Apr. 25. (1:703.)
BOIS, JULES.
  Anatole France. Cath. W. Jan. (120:567.)
BOLITHO, WILLIAM.
  G. A. Borgese. World. Mar. 29. (7 M.)
  Franz Kafka. World. Feb. 8. (6.)
  Carlo Linati. World. Jul. 26. (3 M.)
  Mario Puccini. World. Feb. 15. (6.)

By Carl Van Doren. Int. Dec., '24. (3:12.) Cen. Nov., '24. (109:129.)

By James Southall Wilson. Va. Apr. (1:150.)

Cable, George W.

Anonymous. Outl. (N. Y.) Feb. 11. (139:213.)

By Arthur H. Quinn. Sat. R. (N. Y.) Mar. 21. (1:609.)

CALVERTON, V. F.

Sherwood Anderson. Mod. Q. Fall, '24. (2:82.)

CARSON, GERALD HEWES.

American Short Story. Book. (N. Y.) Mar. (61:58) May. (61:348.) Jun. (61:438.) Sept. (62:40.)

"E. Barrington." Books. Oct. 5, '24. (8.)

Sarah Orne Jewett. Book. (N. Y.) Jul. (61:594.)

Short Story. Book. (N. Y.) Feb. (60:769.)

CARTER, JOHN.

Theodore Dreiser. N. Y. Times. Aug. 9. (5.)

Sidney Howard. Sat. R. (N. Y.) Feb. 14. (1:523.)

Mimei Ogawa. N. Y. Times. Jul. 26. (1.)

P'u Sing-Ling. N. Y. Times. Mar. 29. (6.)

Cather, Willa Sibert.

By Elizabeth Shepley Sergeant. N. Rep. Jun. 17. (43:91.)

By Walter Tittle. Cen. Jul. (110:305.)

Chekhov, Anton.

Anonymous. N. Y. Times. Nov. 2, '24. (2.)

By Louis S. Friedland. Sat. R. (N. Y.) Apr. 4. (1:654.)

By Maxim Gorky. Dial. Feb. (78:96.)

By Robert Littell. N. Rep. Mar. 25. (42:131.)

By Johan J. Smertenko. Nat. (N. Y.) Dec. 10, '24. (119:652.)

By Eliss L. Tartak. J. T. Jan. 2. (16.)

By Leo Wiener. Sat. R. (N. Y.) Apr. 4. (1:646.)

By Abraham Yarmolinsky. Guar. (Am.) May–Jun. (1:341.)

CHAPMAN, ELISABETH COBB.

Irvin S. Cobb. Ly. May 30, '25. (11.)

CHAPMAN, JOHN JAY.

Edgar Allan Poe. N. Y. Times. Nov. 2, '24. (2.)

Chesterton, G. K.

By W. Teignmouth Shore. Dear. Ind. May 2. (2.)

By Kathleen Woodward. N. Y. Times. Jul. 12. (2.)

CHEW, SAMUEL C.

Anatole France. N. A. Rev. Dec., '24. (220:296.)

Thomas Hardy. Guar. (Am.) Mar. (1:213.)

Arthur Machen. N. Y. Sun. Apr. 18. (6.)

Child, Richard Washburn.

By Vivian Radcliffe Bowker. Int. Feb. (3:211.)

By Blanche Colton Williams. N. Y. Sun. Apr. 18. (7.)

CLINE, LEONARD LANSON.

Stephen McKenna. Books. Sept. 27. (12 V.)

CLOSSER, MYLA JO.

Harry Leon Wilson. Book. (N. Y.) Jun. (61:458.)

Cobb, Irvin S.
> By Isaac Anderson. Int. Nov., '24. (2:906.)
> By Elisabeth Cobb Chapman. Ly. May 30, '25. (11.)
> By Wallace Irwin. L. Rev. Mar. 14. (3.)
> By Clement Wood. L. Rev. Oct. 18, '24. (15.)

COBLENTZ, STANTON A.
> Lafcadio Hearn. Int. Mar. (3:239.)

Colcord, Lincoln.
> By Samuel Eliot Morison. Yale. Oct., '24. (14:195.)

Collins, Charles.
> By Lawrence Lipton. Pear. (Am.) Apr. (53.)

COLLINS, JOSEPH.
> Sherwood Anderson. Book. (N. Y.) Mar. (61:22.)
> Joseph Conrad. Book. (N. Y.) Apr. (61:173.)
> Anatole France. L. Rev. Oct. 18, '24. (1.) Va. Apr. (1:94.)
> Lafcadio Hearn. Book. (N. Y.) Mar. (61:22.)
> Henry James. Book. (N. Y.) Jun. (61:477.)
> V. Sackville-West. L. Rev. Aug. 1. (2.)

COLLINS, J. P.
> Bret Harte. Liv. A. Dec. 6, '24. (323:515.)

COLTON, ARTHUR W.
> James Branch Cabell. Sat. R. (N. Y.) Aug. 22. (2:62.)
> A Conan Doyle. Sat. R. (N. Y.) Oct. 18, '24. (1:199.)

Connell, Richard.
> By William Rose Benét. Sat. R. (N. Y.) Aug. 8. (2:23.)

Conrad, Joseph.
> Anonymous. N. Y. Times. Dec. 7, '24. (3.) Aug. 9. (13.)
> By William Rose Benét. Sat. R. (N. Y.) Mar. 14. (1:594.)
> By Joseph Collins. Book. (N. Y.) Apr. (61:173.)
> By R. B. Cunninghame Graham. N. Y. Times. Jan. 4. (2.)
> By Ford Madox Ford. Tr. Oct., '24. (2:454.) Nov., '24. (2:570.) Dec., '24. (2:689.)
> By Julius Weis Freind. D. D. Oct., '24. (7:3.)
> By Kenneth Fuessle. Int. Jan. (3:98.)
> By John Galsworthy. Scr. Jan. (77:3.)
> By Edward Garnett. N. Rep. Apr. 8. (42:190.)
> By C. Lewis Hind. Outl. (N. Y.) Jan. 28. (139:138.)
> By L. D. Howland. Com. Apr. 22. (1:666.)
> By Percy A. Hutchison. Int. Sept., '24. (2:713.) May. (3:429.)
> By Charlton Laird. I. L. M. May. (42.)
> By Robert Littell. N. Rep. Feb. 4. (41: 287.)
> By William McFee. N. Y. Sun. Jan. 31. (7.) Book. (N. Y.) Jun. (61:500.)
> By H. L. Mencken. A. Merc. Apr. (4:505.)
> By Christopher Morley. Sat. R. (N. Y.) Dec. 27, '24. (1: 415.) Apr. 25. (1:707.)
> By Thomas Moult. Yale. Jan. (14:295.)
> By John Hyde Preston. Int. Jan. (3:137.)
> By Cecil Roberts. Book. (N. Y.) Jul. (61:536.)

By Ellen Burns Sherman. Books. Nov. 23, '24. (11.)
By Stuart P. Sherman. Books. Dec. 28, '24. (1.)
By Walter Tittle. N. Y. Times. May 17. (2.) Outl. (N. Y.)
    Jul. 1. (140:333.) Jul. 8. (140:361.)
By Mark Van Doren. Nat. (N. Y.) Jan. 14. (120:45.)
By G. W. L. Rev. Mar. 21. (2.)
By Charles R. Walker. Ind. Feb. 7. (114:161.)
Continental Short Story.
By Louis Bromfield. Books. Feb. 15. (3.)
By Matthew Josephson. Sat. R. (N. Y.) Jan. 10. (1:443.)
Coppard, A. E.
By Margery Latimer. Books. Sept. 6. (5 V.)
COURNOS, JOHN.
Fyodor Dostoevsky. L. Rev. Sept. 19. (2.)
Maxim Gorky. L. R. Jan. 24. (4.)
Short Story. L. Rev. Oct. 11, '24. (1.)
L. A. G. Strong. L. Rev. Sept. 5. (2.)
Lyof Tolstoy. L. Rev. Sept. 19. (2.)
COWLEY, MALCOLM.
Kenneth Burke. Dial. Dec., '24. (77:520.)
Conrad Aiken. Sat. R. (N. Y.) Jun. 27. (1:851.)
Crane, Stephen.
By Floyd Dell. Nat. (N. Y.) Dec. 10, '24. (119:637.)
By James L. Ford. Int. Oct., '24. (2:785.)
By Shane Leslie. L. Rev. Jan. 3. (7.)
By Stanley T. Williams. Yale. Oct., '24. (14:172.)
CRAWFORD, JOHN W.
D. H. Lawrence. World. Jul. 15. (95.)
V. Sackville-West. N. Y. Times. Jul. 5. (13.)
CROCKETT, MARY.
Gertrude Stein. Mod. Q. Feb. 2:233.)
CUNNINGHAME GRAHAM, R. B.
Joseph Conrad. N. Y. Times. Jan. 4. (2.)

D

DARGAN, E. PRESTON.
Anatole France. Sat. R. (N. Y.) Oct. 25, '24. (1:221.)
Davis, Richard Harding.
By Thomas Beer. Ly. Oct. 11, '24. (15.)
By Arthur Bartlett Maurice. Int. Jun. (3:458.)
By William C. Shepherd. Col. Nov. 29, '24. (39.)
By Vincent Starrett. Rev. Oct., '24. (4:352.)
DEACON, WILLIAM ARTHUR.
"E. Barrington." Int. Jul. (3:535.)
De Bra, Lemuel.
By Vivien Radcliffe Bowker. Int. Sept. (3:681.)
De La Mare, Walter.
By Herbert S. Gorman. N. A. Rev. Dec., '24. (220:372.)
DE MILLE, GEORGE E.
Edgar Allan Poe. A. Merc. Apr. (4:433.)

De Wit, Augusta.
    By E. H. Brewster. Yale. Apr. (14:596.)
DELL, FLOYD.
    Stephen Crane. Nat. (N. Y.) Dec. 10, '24. (119:637.)
DEUTSCH, BABETTE.
    Maxim Gorky. Books. Nov. 30, '24. (1.)
    Thomas Hardy. Books. Jan. 18. (10.)
DEVREE, HOWARD.
    Thomas Burke. N. Y. Times. Dec. 28, '24. (15.)
DIBBLE, R. F.
    Marcel Schwob. Nat. (N. Y.) Nov. 5, '24. (119:500.)
DOS PASSOS, JOHN.
    Thomas Boyd. N. Y. Sun. Mar. 28. (6.)
DOSTOEVSKY, FYODOR.
    A Page of Manuscript. Liv. A. Sept. 5. (326:551.)
Dostoevsky, Fyodor.
    By John Cournos. L. Rev. Sept. 19. (2.)
    By A. Donald Douglas. Int. Oct., '24. (2:787.)
    By Arthur Ruhl. L. Rev. Oct. 11, '24. (2.)
    By Alexander I. Nazaroff. Sat. R. (N. Y.) Aug. 8. (2:30.)
        N. Y. Times. July 19. (8.)
    By Dorothy Thompson. L. Rev. Jan. 3. (7.)
    By Abraham Yarmolinsky. N. Y. Times. Jul. 19. (9.)
DOUGLAS, A. DONALD.
    Fyodor Dostoevsky. Int. Oct., '24. (2:787.)
    Ring W. Lardner. Int. May. (3:409.)
Doyle, A. Conan.
    By Arthur W. Colton. Sat. R. (N. Y.) Oct. 18, '24. (1:199.)
    By Arthur Bartlett Maurice. Int. Nov., '24. (2:877.)
    By Melville E. Stone. L. Rev. Oct. 18, '24. (1.)
DRAKE, WILLIAM A.
    Jules-Amédée Barbey d'Aurevilly. Books. Apr. 19. (19.)
    Anatole France. Books. Jan. 25. (7.)
    Thomas Mann. Books. Feb. 1. (7.)
    Boris Pilniak. Books. Mar. 8. (7.)
    Aleksei Remizov. Books. Mar. 8. (7.)
    Carl Sternheim. Books. Aug. 23. (7.)
Dreiser, Theodore.
    By John Carter. N. Y. Times. Aug. 9. (5.)
    By Henry B. Fuller. N. Rep. Sept. 16. (44:104.)
    By Stuart P. Sherman. Books. Aug. 23. (4.)
    By Walter Tittle. Cen. Aug. (110:441.)
Duhamel, Georges.
    By André Thérive. Liv. A. Sept. 12, '25. (326:58.)
DUTTON, GEORGE B.
    Arnold Bennett. Ind. Dec. 27, '24. (113:577.)

E

EATON, G. D.
    Louis Hémon. Int. Aug., '25. (3:581.)

Ellingston, John R.
    Wilhelm Hauff. N. Y. Times. Aug. 2. (5.)
    Alfred de Musset. N. Y. Times. Aug. 2. (5.)
Eversharp, John.
    Jules-Amédée Barbey d'Aurevilly. N. Rep. Aug. 19, '25. (43:
        351.)

F

Fagin, N. Bryllion.
    American Short Story. Int. Mar. (3:249.)
    Sherwood Anderson. D. D. Jan.–Feb. (7:91.) Guar. (Am.)
        Apr. (1:246.)
    Short Story. D. D. Jan.–Feb. (7:116.) Int. Apr. (3:301.)
Ferber, Edna.
    By Flora Merrill. World. May 3. (1 M.)
    By Arnold Patrick. Book. (N. Y.) Apr. (61:164.)
Field, Louise Maunsell.
    Algernon Blackwood. Int. Jun. (3:482.)
    D. H. Lawrence. Int. Aug., '25. (3:613.)
    Viola Meynell. L. Rev. May 29. (3.)
Finger, Charles J.
    American Short Story. A. W. Dec., '24. (7.)
    Sherwood Anderson. A. W. Dec., '24. (7.)
Finger, Charles J.
    By William Rose Benét. Sat. R. (N. Y.) Dec. 13, '24.
        (1:380.)
    By Henry Beston. Books. Dec. 28, '24. (4.)
    By Herschel Brickell. L. Rev. Oct. 11, '24. (14.)
    By Eva Goldbeck. L. Rev. Jan. 10. (3.)
    By Harry Hansen. Books. Oct. 26, '24. (6.)
    By Joseph M. March. N. Y. Times. Dec. 28, '24. (15.)
    By C. A. Newman. Dear. Ind. May 21. (14.)
Finley, John H.
    James Lane Allen. N. Y. Times. Mar. 1. (2.)
Follett, Wilson.
    Thomas Hardy. N. Y. Sun. Apr. 18. (6.)
Ford, Ford Madox.
    Joseph Conrad. Tr. Oct., '24. (2:454.) Nov., '24. (2:
        570.) Dec., '24. (2:689.)
    Ernest Hemingway. L. Rev. Jan. 3. (1.)
    Robert McAlmon. L. Rev. Jan. 3. (1.)
Ford, James L.
    Stephen Crane. Int. Oct., '24. (2:785.)
    Edith Wharton. Int. Oct., '24. (2:785.)
Forman, Henry James.
    George Gissing. N. Y. Times. Jan. 18. (9.)
    Thomas Hardy. N. Y. Times. Apr. 12. (7.)
France, Anatole.
    Anonymous. Nat. (N. Y.) Oct. 22, '24. (119:434.) Nov. 12,
        '24. (119:512.) N. Y. Times, Oct. 19, '24. (7.) Guar.
        (Am.) Nov., '24. (1:2.) Tr. Nov., '24. (2:547.) Liv.
        A. Dec. 6, '24. (323:535.)

By Edwin Björkman. L. Rev. Jul. 3. (4.)
By Jules Bois. Cath. W. Jan. (120:567.)
By Ernest Boyd. Ind. Jan. 31. (114:133.) V. F. (N. Y.) Aug. (42.) Sat. R. (N. Y.) Jun. 27. (1:853.) Nat. (N. Y.) Nov. 5, '24. (119:488.)
By Gamaliel Bradford. Book. (N. Y.) Aug. (61:705.)
By Joseph Brainin. J. T. Oct. 24, '24. (11.)
By H. I. Brock. N. Y. Times. Jun. 14. (6.)
By Jean-Jacques Brousson. A. Merc. Sept., '24. (3:9.)
By Samuel C. Chew. N. A. Rev. Dec., '24. (220:296.)
By Joseph Collins. L. Rev. Oct. 18, '24. (1.) Va. Apr. (1:94.)
By E. Preston Dargan. Sat. R. (N. Y.) Oct. 25, '24. (1:221.)
By William A. Drake. Books. Jan. 25. (7.)
By W. L. George. N. Y. Times. Oct. 19, '24. (7.)
By James Graham. L. Rev. Jan. 17. (1.)
By Albert Guérard. Books. Sept. 27. (1.)
By Percy A. Hutchison. Int. Nov., '24. (2:851.)
By Emil Lengyel. N. Y. Times. Aug. 23. (5.)
By Robert Littell. N. Rep. Nov. 5, '24. (40:250.)
By Pierre Loving. Guar. (Am.) Apr. (1:276.)
By Marvin Löwenthal. Men. J. Feb. (11:14.)
By John Macy. Nat. (N. Y.) Nov. 5, '24. (119:489.)
By René Maran. Opp. Dec., '24. (2:370.)
By Arthur Bartlett Maurice. Outl. (N. Y.) Oct. 22, '24. (138:296.)
By Thomas Moult. Book. (N. Y.) Dec., '24. (60:465.)
By William Lyon Phelps. Scr. Feb. (77:210.)
By Princess Radziwill. For. Dec., '24. (72:827.)
By Burton Rascoe. Book. (N. Y.) Nov., '24. (60:337.)
By Harry Saltpeter. N. Y. World. Feb. 8. (6:1.)
By Pitts Sanborn. Nat. (N. Y.) Nov. 5, '24. (119:489.)
By Stuart P. Sherman. Books. Oct. 26, '24. (1.)
By Joseph Shipley. Guar. (Am.) Dec., '24. (1:1.)
By Paul Souday. N. Y. Times. Dec. 14, '24. (8.)
By Paul Vaillant-Couturier. Nat. (N. Y.) Apr. 15. (120: 406.)
By Carl Van Doren. Cen. Dec., '24. (109:286.) Jan. (109: 418.) Aug. (110:510.)
By Mark Van Doren. Nat. (N. Y.) Nov. 5, '24. (119:497.)
By Edward Wassermann. Book. (N. Y.) Apr. (61:197.)
By Louis Weitzenhorn. World. Jun. 21. (4 M.)
By Edmund Wilson. N. Rep. Feb. 11. (41:308.)
FRANK WALDO
    Sherwood Anderson. Guar. (Am.) Feb. (1:97.)
Frank, Waldo.
    By Burton Rascoe. A. D. Oct., '24. (41.)
FREDERICK, JOHN T.
    Charles T. Finger. Mid. May 1. (11:176.)

FREIND, JULIUS WEIS.
    Sherwood Anderson. D. D. Nov.–Dec., '24. (7:71.)
    Joseph Conrad. D. D. Oct., '24. (7:3.)
French Short Story.
    By Louis Bromfield. Books. Feb. 15. (3.)
French, Joseph Lewis.
    Anonymous. N. Y. Times. May 3. (13.)
FRIEDLAND, LOUIS S.
    Anton Chekhov. Sat. R. (N. Y.) Apr. 4. (1:654.)
FRIEDMAN, FRIEDA.
    Fannie Hurst. J. T. Jul. 10. (4.)
FUESSLE, KENNETH.
    Arnold Bennett. Int. Jan. (3:98.)
    Joseph Conrad. Int. Jan. (3:98.)
    Sir Philip Gibbs. Int. Jan. (3:98.)
FULLER, HENRY BLAKE.
    American Short Story. N. Y. Times. Jun. 28. (16.)
    Arnold Bennett. Sat. R. (N. Y.) Nov. 29, '24. (1:319.)
    British Short Story. N. Y. Times. Jun. 28. (16.)
    James Branch Cabell. N. Rep. Dec. 31, '24. (41:151.) Sept.
        16. (44:104.)
    Theodore Dreiser. N. Rep. Sept. 16. (44:104.)
    Henry James. N. Y. Times. Apr. 19. (4.)

G

GAINES, CLARENCE H.
    Robert Louis Stevenson. N. A. Rev. Mar. (221:567.)
GALE, ZONA.
    Algernon Blackwood. Books. Apr. 26. (1.)
GALSWORTHY, JOHN.
    Joseph Conrad. Scr. Jan. (77:3.)
Galsworthy, John.
    By William Rose Benét. Book. (N. Y.) Aug. (61:698.)
    By Herschel Brickell. L. Rev. Aug. 8. (2.)
    By Percy A. Hutchison. N. Y. Times. Aug. 2. (1.)
    By Mary Kolars. Books. Sept. 6. (4 V.)
    By Dorothy Martin. Yale. Oct., '24. (14:126.)
    By Harry Saltpeter. Int. Sept. (3:678.)
    By R. D. Townsend. Outl. (N. Y.) Sept. 16. (114:98.)
    By Mark Van Doren. Nat. (N. Y.) Sept. 2. (121:258.)
GARNETT, EDWARD.
    Joseph Conrad. N. Rep. Apr. 8. (42:190.)
Garnier, Clarence H.
    Viola Meynell. N. A. Rev. Sept.–Nov. (222:163.)
GEORGE, W. L.
    Anatole France. N. Y. Times. Oct. 19, '24. (7.)
    Edgar Saltus. Pear. (Am.) Apr. (17.)
Gibbs, Sir Philip.
    By Kenneth Fuessle. Int. Jan. (3:98.)

GILBERT, BERNARD.
    James Joyce. D. D. Jun. (7:174.)
GILBERT, KATHARINE.
    Thomas Hardy. Rev. Jul. (5:9.)
Gissing, George.
    By Stanley Alden. Books. Feb. 22. (11.)
    By Henry James Forman. N. Y. Times. Jan. 18. (9.)
    By Marette Quick. Guar. (Am.) Apr. (1:274.)
GLASGOW, ELLEN.
    James Branch Cabell. Books. Nov. 2, '24. (1.) Apr. 5. (3.)
GLASGOW, ELLEN.
    By Grant Overton. Book. (N. Y.) May. (61:291.)
Gobineau, Comte Arthur de.
    By George Boas. Rev. Apr. (5:101.)
GOLDBECK, EVA.
    Charles J. Finger. L. Rev. Jan. 10. (3.)
    Russian Short Stories. L. Rev. Apr. 11. (3.)
GOLDBERG, ISAAC.
    Sherwood Anderson. Strat. Jan. (4:83.)
Golding, Louis.
    By Elias Lieberman. Am. H. Jul. 31. (117:355.)
Gonzales, A. E.
    By Hervey Allen. Sat. R. (N. Y.) Mar. 14. (1:595.)
    By Herschel Brickell. L. Rev. Jan. 10. (2.)
GORKY, MAXIM.
    Anton Chekhov. Dial. Feb. (78:96.)
    Count Lyof Tolstoi. Dial. Feb. (78:96.)
Gorky, Maxim.
    By John Cournos. L. Rev. Jan. 24. (4.)
    By Babette Deutsch. Books. Nov. 30, '24. (1.)
    By Louis Kronenberger. N. Y. Times. Jun. 14. (9.)
    By Alexander I. Nazaroff. N. Y. Times. Jan. 4. (11.)
    By Vinton Liddell Pickens. Rev. Jul. (5:109.)
    By Nathan P. Stedman. Int. Feb. (3:203.)
    By Elizabeth Vincent. N. Rep. Feb. 25. (42:22.)
GORMAN, HERBERT S.
    American Short Story. N. Y. Sun. Mar. 6. (16.) Int. Aug.
      (3:616.)
    Sherwood Anderson. Int. Dec., '24. (3:15.)
    James Branch Cabell. N. Y. Times, Mar. 29. (11.)
    Walter de la Mare. N. A. Rev. Dec., '24. (220:372.)
GOULD, BRUCE.
    Michael Arlen. Int. May. (3:399.)
GOULD, LAURA STEDMAN.
    Lafcadio Hearn. N. Y. Times. Dec. 28, '24. (26.)
GRAHAM, JAMES.
    Anatole France. L. Rev. Jan. 17. (1.)
Grant Watson, E. L.
    By Llewellyn Powys. Books. Feb. 15. (4.)
    By Elizabeth Heywood Wyman. Int. Mar. (3:285.)

GRATTAN, C. HARTLEY.
 Thomas Bailey Aldrich. A. Merc. May. (5:41.)
 Kenneth Burke. Int. Dec., '24. (3:60.)
 Lafcadio Hearn. C. D. N. Dec. 17, '24.
GREENBAUM, BETSY.
 Russian Short Stories. N. Rep. May 27. (43:25.)
GREGORY, ALYSE.
 Henry James. Dial. Sept. (79:235.)
GUÉRARD, ALBERT L.
 Honoré de Balzac. S. W. Apr. (10:110.)
 Anatole France. Books. Sept. 27. (1.)
GUNTHER, JOHN.
 Arthur Machen. Book. (N. Y.) Jul. (61:571.)
 Rafael Sabatini. Int. Mar. (3:252.)
GWYNN, STEPHEN.
 C. E. Montague. Yale. July. (14:811.)

H

HAMILTON, CLAYTON.
 Robert Louis Stevenson. Int. Jan. (3:110.)
Hamsun, Knut.
 By Elias Arnessen. For. Jun. (73:852.)
HANSEN, HARRY.
 Sherwood Anderson. Nat. (N. Y.) Dec. 10, '24. (119:641.)
 Charles J. Finger. Books. Oct. 26, '24. (6.)
HARDING, RUTH GUTHRIE.
 Ambrose Bierce. Book. (N. Y.) Aug. (61:636.)
Hardy, Thomas.
 Anonymous. N. Y. Times. Dec. 14, '24. (7.) Mar. 1. (6.)
 By Ernest Boyd. Harp. M. Jul. (151:234.)
 By Angus Burrell. N. Y. World. Apr. 26. (6 M.)
 By Samuel C. Chew. Guar. (Am.) Mar. (1:213.)
 By Babette Deutsch. Books. Jan. 18. (10.)
 By Wilson Follett. N. Y. Sun. Apr. 18. (6.)
 By Henry James Forman. N. Y. Times. Apr. 12. (7.)
 By Katherine Gilbert. Rev. Jul. (5:9.)
 By George McLean Harper. Scr. Aug. (78:151.)
 By F. J. Harvey Darton. Liv. A. Feb. 7. (324:303.)
 By C. Lewis Hind. Outl. (N. Y.) Feb. 25. (139:297.)
 By Frederic Lefévre. Liv. A. Apr. 11. (325:98.)
 By William Lyon Phelps. Sat. R. (N. Y.) Jun. 6. (1:808.)
 By Henry Longan Stuart. N. Y. Sun. Jan. 19. (14.)
 By Carl Van Doren. Cen. Jan. (109:418.)
 By Louis Weitzenhorn. N. Y. World. Apr. 12. (6 M.)
HARMAN, HENRY E.
 Joel Chandler Harris. Book. (N. Y.) June. (61:433.)
HARPER, GEORGE MCLEAN.
 Thomas Hardy. Scr. Aug. (78:151.)
HARRINGTON, JOHN WALKER.
 Richard Doddridge Blackmore. Int. Sept. (3:666.)

Harris, Frank.
 By J. G. Jacobson. Pear. (Am.) Apr. (22.)
Harris, Joel Chandler.
 By Henry G. Harman. Book. (N. Y.) Jun. (61:433.)
 By Julia Collier Harris. Rev. Apr. (5:64.)
HARRIS, JULIA COLLIER.
 Joel Chandler Harris. Rev. Apr. (5:64.)
Harte, Francis Bret.
 By J. P. Collins. Liv. A. Dec. 6, '24. (323:515.)
Hauff, Wilhelm.
 By John R. Ellingston. N. Y. Times. Aug. 2. (5.)
HAWTHORNE, JULIAN.
 Nathaniel Hawthorne. Book. (N. Y.) Jul. (61:567.)
Hawthorne, Nathaniel.
 By Julian Hawthorne. Book. (N. Y.) Jul. (61:567.)
HARVEY DARTON, F. J.
 Thomas Hardy. Liv. A. Feb. 7. (324:303.)
HAZLITT, HENRY.
 Arnold Bennett. N. Y. Sun. Sept. 26. (8.)
Hearn, Lafcadio.
 By Ernest Boyd. Ind. Dec. 20, '24. (113:548.)
 By Stanton A. Coblentz. Int. Mar. (3:239.)
 By Joseph Collins. Book. (N. Y.) Mar. (61:22.)
 By Laura Stedman Gould. N. Y. Times. Dec. 28, '24. (26.)
 By C. Hartley Grattan. C. D. N. Dec. 17, '24.
 By Harry Salpeter. World. Jan. 25. (9.)
HEILBRUNN, STELLA.
 Stacy Aumonier. Int. May. (3:426.)
 Alfred Noyes. Int. March. (3:287.)
HELLMAN, GEORGE S.
 Washington Irving. Book. (N. Y.) Apr. (61:144.)
 Robert Louis Stevenson. Book. (N. Y.) Jan. (60:575.)
Hemingway, Ernest.
 By Ford Madox Ford. L. Rev. Jan. 3. (1.)
 By Edmund Wilson. Dial. Oct., '24. (77:340.)
Hémon, Louis.
 By G. D. Eaton. Int. Aug., '25. (3:581.)
 By Katherine Keith. N. Rep. Oct. 15, '24. (40:183.)
"Henry, O."
 By Edward Larocque. Tinker. Book. (N. Y.) Jun. (61:436.)
Herrick, Robert.
 By H. W. Boynton. Sat. R. (N. Y.) Sept. 19. (2:135.)
 By Herschel Brickell. L. Rev. Aug. 22. (2.)
HERRMANN, JOHN.
 Emile Verhaeren. Books. Feb. 22. (3.)
HERVEY, JOHN L.
 Sherwood Anderson. A. W. Mar. (9.)
HILLYER, ROBERT.
 Algernon Blackwood. N. Y. Sun. Mar. 7. (7.)

Hind, C. Lewis.
   Joseph Conrad. Outl. (N. Y.) Jan. 28. (139:138.)
   Thomas Hardy. Outl. (N. Y.) Feb. 25. (139:297.)
Hofmannsthal, Hugo Von.
   Honoré de Balzac. Dial. May. (78:357.)
Hopkins, R. Thurston.
   Rudyard Kipling. Liv. A. Nov. 8, '24. (323:342.)
Howard, Sidney.
   By John Carter. Sat. R. (N. Y.) Feb. 14. (1:523.)
Howard, Velma Swanston.
   Selma Lägerlof. Int. Nov., '24. (2:890.)
Howland, L. D.
   Joseph Conrad. Com. Apr. 22. (1:666.)
Hughes, Rupert.
   Wladislas Rejmont. Int. Feb. (3:170.)
Hummel, George F.
   By Johan J. Smertenko. Nat. (N. Y.) Apr. 22. (120:469.)
Hurst, Fannie.
   By Frieda Friedman. J. T. Jul. 10. (4.)
Hussey, L. M.
   James Branch Cabell. Guar. (Am.) Apr. (1:269.)
Hutchison, Percy Adams.
   Joseph Conrad. Int. May. (3:429.) Sept., '24. (2:713.)
   Anatole France. Int. Nov., '24. (2:851.)
   John Galsworthy. N. Y. Times. Aug. 2. (1.)
Huxley, Aldous.
   By Edwin Björkman. L. Rev. Oct. 4, '24. (4.)
   By Joseph Wood Krutch. Nat. (N. Y.) Nov. 5, '24. (119:499.)
   By E. A. Niles. Ind. Oct. 25, '24. (113:318.)
   By Shaemas O'Sheel. Sat. R. (N. Y.) Oct. 18, '24. (1:197.)
   By Raymond Weaver. Book. (N. Y.) Nov., '24. (60:262.)

I

Ibáñez, Vicente Blasco. *See* Blasco, Ibáñez Vicente.
Irving, Washington.
   By W. P. Beazell. World. May 3. (6 M.)
   By George S. Hellman. Book. (N. Y.) Apr. (61:144.)
   By William R. Langfield. Int. Jun. (3:443.)
   By Arthur Bartlett Maurice. Out. (N. Y.) May 27. (140:156.)
   By Lloyd Morris. N. Y. Times. Apr. 26. (3.)
Irwin, Wallace.
   Algernon Blackwood. L. Rev. Mar. 7. (3.)
   Irvin S. Cobb. L. Rev. Mar. 14. (3.)

J

Jacobson, J. G.
   Frank Harris. Pear. (Am.) Apr. (22.)

JACOBY, JOHN E.
  Henry James. Cath. W. Sept. (121:854.)
JAMES, HENRY.
  A Letter. Yale. Oct., '24. (14:205.)
James, Henry.
  By Thomas Beer. Sat. R. (N. Y.) Apr. 25.
  By Mrs. Belloc-Lowndes. Sat. R. (N. Y.) Sept. 19. (2:139.)
  By Ernest Boyd. Ind. Apr. 18. (114:448.)
  By Clarence Clough Bull. L. Rev. May 9. (6.)
  By Joseph Collins. Book. (N. Y.) Jun. (61:477.)
  By Henry Blake Fuller. N. Y. Times. Apr. 19. (4.)
  By Alyse Gregory. Dial. Sept. (79:235.)
  By John E. Jacoby. Cath. W. Sept. (121:854.)
  By James McLane. Yale. Oct., '24. (14:205.)
  By William Lyon Phelps. Int. Jul., '25. (3:521.)
  By Elfrida H. Pope. Sat. R. (N. Y.) July 11. (1:902.)
  By Ben Ray Redman. N. Y. World. Apr. 19. (6 M.)
  By E. S. Roscoe. Book. (N. Y.) Jan. (60:584.)
  By Carl Van Doren. Cen. Sept. (110:637.)
Japanese Short Stories.
  By Herschel Brickell. L. Rev. Jan. 3. (3.)
  By Rinsaku Tsunoda. W. Tom. Jun. (8:189.)
JEFFREYS, CAREY.
  Rex Beach. L. Rev. Aug. 8. (2.)
Jewett, Sarah Orne.
  By Gerald Hewes Carson. Book. (N. Y.) Jul. (61:594.)
  By Richard Le Gallienne. N. Y. Times. Apr. 19. (2.)
  By Fred Lewis Pattee. N. Y. Sun. Apr. 18. (6.)
JONES, LLEWELLYN.
  H. G. Wells. C. E. P. Oct. 24, '24. (1.)
JOSEPHSON, MATTHEW.
  Kenneth Burke. Books. Nov. 16, '24. (4.)
  Continental Short Story. Sat. R. (N. Y.) Jan. 10. (1:443.)
Joyce, James.
  By Ernest Boyd. World. Jan. 25. (9.)
  By Bernard Gilbert. D. D. Jun. (7:174.)
  By Lloyd Morris. Int. Apr. (3:321.)
  By Edith Rickert. N. Rep. Jan. 7. (41:181.)
  By Edmund Wilson. Dial. Nov. '24. (77:430.)

K

Kafka, Franz.
  By William Bolitho. World. Feb. 8. (6.)
Kallas, Aino.
  By Vivien Radcliffe Bowker. Int. Sept. (3:603.)
KATZIN, WINIFRED.
  Katherine Mansfield. Int. Feb. (3:212.)
Kaye-Smith, Sheila.
  By Fletcher Allen. Int. Sept., '24. (2:726.)

KEITH, KATHERINE.
    Louis Hémon. N. Rep. Oct. 15, '24. (40:183.)
Kennard, Sir Coleridge.
    By Russell Wright. Books. Sept. 20. (11.)
Kennedy, R. Emmett.
    By Margery Latimer. Books. Dec. 14, '24. (8.)
    By Jean West Maury. For. Jun. (73:927.)
    By C. McD. Puckette. Sat. R. (N. Y.) Jan. 3. (1:427.)
    By Edwin D. Sheers. Opp. Jun. (3:182.)
KENTON, EDNA.
    Ambrose Bierce. Book. (N. Y.) Sept. (62:77.)
King, Grace.
    Earl Sparling. L. Rev. Mar. 14. (2.)
Kipling, Rudyard.
    By R. Thurston Hopkins. Liv. A. Nov. 8, '24. (323:342.)
    By Grant Overton. Book. (N. Y.) Mar. (61:65.)
    By Alexander G. Stewart. Int. Jan. (3:100.)
KIRCHWEY, FREDA.
    British Short Story. Books. Jan. 4. (4.)
KOLARS, MARY.
    John Galsworthy. Books. Sept. 6. (4 V.)
KRONENBERGER, LOUIS.
    Maxim Gorky. N. Y. Times. Jun. 14. (9.)
    D. H. Lawrence. Sat. R. (N. Y.) Aug. 1. (2:4.)
    Thomas Mann. Sat. R. (N. Y.) Jun. 27. (1:851.)
KRUTCH, JOSEPH WOOD.
    Michael Arlen. World. May 24. (4 M.)
    Arnold Bennett. Books. Nov. 9, '24. (4.)
    British Short Story. Sat. R. (N. Y.) Jan. 24. (1:475.)
    Aldous Huxley. Nat. (N. Y.) Feb. 5, '24. (119:499.)
    Thomas Mann. Nat. (N. Y.) Mar. 25. (120:330.)
    Boris Pilniak. Nat. (N. Y.) Feb. 11. (120:163.)
    Aleksei Remizov. Nat. (N. Y.) Apr. 29. (120:496.)
    Osbert Sitwell. Nat. (N. Y.) Apr. 29. (120:496.)

L

Lagerlöf, Selma.
    By Isaac Anderson. Int. Nov., '24. (2:890.)
    By Velma Swanston Howard. Int. Nov., '24. (2:890.)
LAIRD, CHARLTON.
    Joseph Conrad. I. L. M. May. (42.)
LANGFELD,, WILLIAM R.
    Washington Irving. Int. Jun. (3:443.)
LARDNER, RING W.
    Konrad Bercovici. L. Rev. Oct. 18, '24. (3.)
Lardner, Ring W.
    By Donald Douglas. Int. May. (3:409.)
    By Robert Littell. N. Rep. Apr. 15. (Suppl., 1.)
    By H. L. Mencken. A. Merc. Jul., '24. (2:376.)

By Flora Merrill. World. May 10. (1 M.)
By Grant Overton. Book. (N. Y.) Sept. (62:44.)
By D. R. Ind. May 23. (114:590.)
By Gilbert Seldes. V. F. (N. Y.) Jul. (45.)
By Lawrence Stallings. N. Y. World. Apr. 13. (11.)
By Henry Longan Stuart. N. Y. Times. Apr. 19. (1.)
By Walter Tittle. Cen. Jul. (110:305.)
By Virginia Woolf. Sat. R. (N. Y.) Aug. 1. (2:1.)

LATIMER, MARGERY.
A. E. Coppard. Books. Sept. 6. (5 V.)
R. Emmet Kennedy. Books. Dec. 14, '24. (8.)
Charles Merz. Books. Nov. 2, '24. (2.)
Julia Peterkin. Books. Dec. 14, '24. (8.)

Lawrence, D. H.
By John W. Crawford. World. Jul. 5. (95.)
By Louise Maunsell Field. Int. Aug. (3:613.)
By Louis Kronenberger. Sat. R. (N. Y.) Aug. 1. (2:4.)
By Robert Littell. N. Rep. Jul. 8. (43:184.)
By Edwin Muir. Nat. (N. Y.) Feb. 11. (120:148.)
By Vance Palmer. Ind. Apr. 11. (114:414.)
By Edith Rickert. N. Rep. Jan. 7. (41:181.)
By Carl Van Doren. Cen. Sept. (110:639.)
By Eliseo Vivas. Guar. (Am.) Apr. (1:267.)

LEE, LAWRENCE.
E. Earl Sparling. Int. May. (3:427.)

LEE, MUNA.
Manuel Gonzales Zeledon. (Mayon.) N. Y. Times. Jul. 5. (9.)

LEFÉVRE, FREDERIC.
Arnold Bennett. Liv. A. Mar. 28. (324:691.)
Thomas Hardy. Liv. A. Apr. 11. (325:98.)

LE GALLIENNE, RICHARD.
Sarah Orne Jewett. N. Y. Times. Apr. 19. (2.)

LENGYEL, EMIL.
France, Anatole. N. Y. Times. Aug. 23. (5.)

LESLIE, SHANE.
Michael Arlen. Int. Oct., '24. (2:769.)
Stephen Crane. L. Rev. Jan. 3. (7.)

LEVERIDGE, JULIAN.
Lenoid Andreyev. L. Rev. Jan. 10. (2.)

LEWIS, SINCLAIR.
Sherwood Anderson. Books. Nov. 9, '24. (1.)

LIEBERMAN, ELIAS.
Louis Golding. Am. H. Jul. 31. (117:355.)

Linati, Cario.
By William Bolitho. World. Jul. 26. (3 M.)

Lincoln, Joseph C.
By Arnold Patrick. Book. (N. Y.) Jan. (60:593.)

LIPTON, LAWRENCE.
Charles Collins. Pear. (Am.) Apr. (53.)

LITTELL, ROBERT.
    Ambrose Bierce. N. Rep. Oct. 15, '24. (40:177.)
    Anton Chekhov. N. Rep. Mar. 25. (42:131.)
    Joseph Conrad. N. Rep. Feb. 4. (41:287.)
    Anatole France. N. Rep. Nov. 5, '24. (40:250.)
    Ring W. Lardner. N. Rep. Apr. 15. (Suppl. 1.)
    D. H. Lawrence. N. Rep. Jul. 8. (43:184.)
LIVINGSTON, ARTHUR.
    Vicente Blasco Ibáñez. Int. Jul. (3:543.)
LONDON, CHARMIAN.
    Jack London. Cos. Oct., '24. (78.)
London, Jack.
    By Louis Allen. Dear. Ind. May 16. (2.)
    By Charmian London. Cos. Oct., '24. (78.)
    By William McFee. N. Y. Sun. Mar. 28. (6.)
Longstreet, Augustus B.
    By Edgar Legare Pennington. Int. Oct., '24. (2:788.)
Louys, Pierre.
    By Paul Souday. N. Y. Times. May 17. (16.)
    By Ruth Willis Thompson. L. Rev. Sept. 12. (5.)
LOVETT, ROBERT MORSS.
    Conrad Aiken. N. Rep. Jul. 22. (43:242.)
    Sherwood Anderson. N. Rep. Nov. 5, '24. (40:255.)
    Michael Arlen. N. Rep. Dec. 10, '24. (41:8.)
    Ethel Colburn Mayne. N. Rep. Jul. 2. (43:242.)
LOVING, PIERRE.
    Anatole France. Guar. (Am.) Apr. (1:276.)
LOWENTHAL, MARVIN.
    Anatole France. Men. J. Feb. (11:14.)
Lynd, Sylvia.
    By Ernest Boyd. Ind. May 9. (114:533.)
    By Lewis Mumford. N. Rep. Jun. 24. (43:132.)
M., M.
    American Short Story. World. Jul. 5. (95.)
McAlmon, Robert.
    By Ford Madox Ford. L. Rev. Jan. 3. (1.)
McFEE, WILLIAM.
    Stacy Aumonier. N. Y. Sun. Feb. 14. (7.)
    British Short Story. N. Y. Trib. Dec. 14.
    Joseph Conrad. N. Y. Sun. Jan. 31. (7.) Book. (N. Y.)
        Jun. (61:500.)
    Jack London. N. Y. Sun. Mar. 28. (61.)
McKenna, Stephen.
    By Leonard Cline. Books. Sept. 27. (12 V.)
    By Dawn Powell. L. Rev. Sept. 20. (3.)
McLANE, JAMES.
    Henry James. Yale. Oct., '24. (14:205.)
Machen, Arthur.
    By Samuel C. Chew. N. Y. Sun. Apr. 18. (6.)
    By John Gunther. Book. (N. Y.) Jul. (61:571.)

MacMechan, Archibald.
    By Fraser Bond. N. Y. Times. Jun. 14. (19.)
MACY, JOHN.
    Anatole France. Nat. (N. Y.) Nov. 5, '24. (119:487.)
MANKIEWICZ, HERMAN J.
    Michael Arlen. N. Y. Times. Mar. 22. (2.) May 31. (5.)
Mann, Thomas.
    Anonymous. N. Y. Times. Feb. 22. (9.)
    By Edwin Björkman. L. Rev. Feb. 28. (3.)
    By H. W. Boynton. N. Y. Sun. Feb. 28. (7.)
    By William A. Drake. Books. Feb. 1. (7.)
    By Louis Kronenberger. Sat. R. (N. Y.) Jun. 27. (1:851.)
    By Joseph Wood Krutch. Nat. (N. Y.) Mar. 25. (120:330.)
    By Aldo Sorani. Sat. R. (N. Y.) Aug. 1. (2:13.)
    By Cuthbert Wright. Dial. May. (78:420.)
Mansfield, Katherine.
    By Richard Aldington. L. Rev. Jan. 10. (8.) N. Rep.
        Oct. 22, '24. (40:207.)
    By Grace Z. Brown. Book. (N. Y.) Aug. (61:687.)
    By Winifred Katzin. Int. Feb. (3:212.)
    By John Montgomery. D. D. Nov.–Dec., '24. (7:73.)
    By A. R. Orage. Cen. Nov., '24. (109:36.)
    By Mary Ross. Books. Oct. 19, '24. (3.)
    By T. K. Whipple. Sat. R. (N. Y.) Dec. 6. '24. (1:342.)
MARAN, RENÉ.
    Anatole France. Opp. Dec., '24. (2:370.)
MARCH, JOSEPH M.
    Charles J. Finger. N. Y. Times. Dec. 28, '24. (15.)
MARKY, MORRIS.
    Rex Beach. Int. Sept. (3:681.)
    Julian Street. Int. Aug. (3:618.)
Marquis, Don.
    By Stuart P. Sherman. Books. Feb. 8. (1.)
MARTIN, DAVID.
    Michael Arlen. Book. (N. Y.) Nov., '24. (60:293.)
MARTIN, DOROTHY.
    John Galsworthy. Yale. Oct., '24. (14:126.)
Maupassant, Guy de.
    By Paul Souday. N. Y. Times. Sept. 13. (7.)
    By Henry Longan Stuart. N. Y. Sun. Jan. 17. (6.)
MAURICE, ARTHUR BARTLETT.
    Richard Harding Davis. Int. Jun. (3:438.)
    A. Conan Doyle. Int. Nov., '24. (2:877.)
    Anatole France. Outl. (N. Y.) Oct. 22, '24. (138:296.)
    Washington Irving. Outl. (N. Y.) May 27. (140:156.)
MAURY, JEAN WEST.
    R. Emmet Kennedy. For. Jun. (73:927.)
Maxwell, W. B.
    By Grant Overton. Book. (N. Y.) Jan. (60:611.)

Mayne, Ethel Colburn.
    By Robert Morss Lovett. N. Rep. Jul. 22. (43:242.)
MEADOWS, GEORGE D.
    James Branch Cabell. Cath. W. Aug. (121:705.)
MENCKEN, H. L.
    Arnold Bennett. World. Sept. 13. (4 M.)
    Ambrose Bierce. N. Y. World. Mar. 1. (3 E.)
    Joseph Conrad. A. Merc. Apr. (4:505.)
    Ring W. Lardner. A. Merc. Jul., '24. (2:376.)
    Edgar Allan Poe. World. Aug. 16. (3 M.)
    Short Story. World. Feb. 22. (3 E.)
    Robert Louis Stevenson. A. Merc. Nov., 24. (3:278.) Jan.
        (4:125.)
MERRILL, FLORA.
    Sherwood Anderson. World. Mar. 22. (1 M.)
    Edna Ferber. World. May 3. (1 M.)
    Ring W. Lardner. World. May 10. (1 M.)
    Booth Tarkington. World. Jun. 21. (1 M.)
    Mary Heaton Vorse. World. Jul. 12. (5 M.)
Merz, Charles.
    By Margery Latimer. Books. Nov. 2, '24. (2.)
    By Johan J. Smertenko. Nat. (N. Y.) Apr. 22. (120:469.)
Meynell, Viola.
    By Louise Bogan. Sat. R. (N. Y.) Apr. 25. (1:703.)
    By Louise Maunsell Field. L. Rev. May 29. (3.)
    By Clarence H. Garnier. N. A. Rev. Sept.–Nov. (222:163.)
    By Lewis Mumford. N. Rep. Jun. 24. (43:132.)
    By Mary Ross. Books. Apr. 12. (4.)
MITCHELL, JOHN E.
    Russian Short Stories. World. Mar. 29. (7 M.)
    Short Stories. World. May 3. (7 M.)
Montague, C. E.
    By Stephen Gwynn. Yale. Jul. (14:811.)
MONTGOMERY, JOHN.
    Katherine Mansfield. D. D. Nov.–Dec., '24. (7:73.)
Moore, George.
    By Virginia Rice. Book. (N. Y.) Jun. (61:431.)
MORAND, PAUL.
    Short Story. Dial. Jan. (78:51.)
Morand, Paul.
    By Ernest Boyd. Ind. Aug. 1. (115:135.)
    By John Mosher. Pear. (Am.) Feb. (51:52.)
    By Paul Souday. N. Y. Times. Jul. 5. (16.)
MORISON, SAMUEL ELIOT.
    Lincoln Colcord. Yale. Oct., '24. (14:195.)
MORLEY, CHRISTOPHER.
    Sherwood Anderson. Sat. R. (N. Y.) Aug. 15. (2:43.)
    Joseph Conrad. Sat. R. (N. Y.) Dec. 27, '24. (1:415.)
        Apr. 25. (1:707.)

MORLEY, FRANK V.
  H. M. Tomlinson. Sat. R. (N. Y.) Dec. 27, '24. (1:409.)
MORRIS, LLOYD.
  American Short Story. N. Y. Times. Jan. 18. (6.)
  Sherwood Anderson. N. Y. Times. Oct. 12, '24. (6.)
  Washington Irving. N. Y. Times. Apr. 26. (3.)
  James Joyce. Int. Apr. (3:321.)
MOSHER, JOHN.
  Paul Morand. Pear. (Am.) Feb. (51:52.)
MOTT, FRANK LUTHER.
  Sherwood Anderson. Mid. Jan. 15. (11:54.)
MOULT, THOMAS.
  Joseph Conrad. Yale. Jan. (14:295.)
  Anatole France. Book. (N. Y.) Dec., '24. (60:465.)
MUIR, EDWIN.
  D. H. Lawrence. Nat. (N. Y.) Feb. 11. (120:148.)
MULKINS, DORA.
  Julia Peterkin. Int. Jan. (3:138.)
MUMFORD, LEWIS.
  Sylvia Lynd. N. Rep. Jun. 24. (43:132.)
  Viola Meynell. N. Rep. Jun. 24. (43:132.)
MUNSON, GORHAM B.
  Kenneth Burke. L. Rev. Oct. 11, '24. (3.)
  Jean Toomer. Opp. Sept. (3:262.)
Musset, Alfred de.
  By John Ellingston. N. Y. Times. Aug. 2. (5.)

N

NAZAROFF, ALEXANDER I.
  Ivan Bunin. Sat. R. (N. Y.) Feb. 7. (1:512.)
  Fyodor Dostoevsky. Sat. R. (N. Y.) Aug. 8. (2:30.) N. Y.
    Times. Jul. 19. (9.)
  Maxim Gorky. N. Y. Times. Jan. 4. (11.)
  Alexander Pushkin. Int. Nov., '24. (2:864.)
  Lyof Tolstoy. N. Y. Times. Aug. 16. (1.)
NEVINS, ALLAN.
  Vicente Blasco Ibáñez. Sat. R. (N. Y.) Jul. 4. (1:871.)
NEWMAN, C. A.
  Charles J. Finger. Dear. Ind. May 21. (14.)
NILES, ABBIE.
  Russian Short Stories. Sat. R. (N. Y.) Mar. 28. (1:627.)
NILES, E. A.
  Aldous Huxley. Ind. Oct. 25, '24. (113:318.)
Norris, Kathleen.
  By Patrick Arnold. Book. (N. Y.) Jul. (61:563.)
Noyes, Alfred.
  By Stella Heilbrunn. Int. Mar. (3:287.)
O'BRIEN, EDWARD J.
  American Short Story. L. Rev. Apr. 11. (2.)
Ogawa, Mimei.
  By John Carter. N. Y. Times. Jul. 26. (1.)

O'Higgins, Harvey.
   Fictionist's Problem. Sat. R. (N. Y.)   Oct. 11, '24.   (177.)
Olgin, Moissaye J.
   Russian Short Stories. Work. May.   (325.)
Orage, A. R.
   Katherine Mansfield. Cen. Nov., '24.   (109:36.)
O'Sheel, Shaemas.
   Aldous Huxley. Sat. R. (N. Y.)   Oct. 18, '24.   (1:197.)
Overton, Grant.
   Ellen Glasgow. Book. (N. Y.)   May.   (61:291.)
   Rudyard Kipling. Book. (N. Y.)   Mar.   (61:65.)
   Ring W. Lardner. Book. (N. Y.)   Sept.   (62:44.)
   W. B. Maxwell. Book. (N. Y.)   Jan.   (60:611.)
   Rafael Sabatini. Book. (N. Y.)   Feb.   (60:728.)
   Albert Payson Terhune. Book. (N. Y.)   Jun.   (61:445.)

P

Page, Thomas Nelson.
   By Arthur H. Quinn. Sat. R. (N. Y.)   Mar. 21.   (1:609.)
Palmer, Vance.
   D. H. Lawrence. Ind. Apr. 11.   (114:414.)
Paterson, Isabel.
   Short Story. Books. Jan. 4.   (12.)
Patrick, Arnold.
   Edna Ferber. Book. (N. Y.)   Apr.   (61:164.)
   Joseph C. Lincoln. Book. (N. Y.)   Jan.   (60:593.)
   Kathleen Norris. Book. (N. Y.)   Jul.   (61:563.)
Pattee, Fred Lewis.
   Sarah Orne Jewett. N. Y. Sun. Apr. 18.   (6.)
Pearson, Edmund Lester.
   Michael Arlen. Outl. (N. Y.)   Jun. 10.   (140:221.)
Pennington, Edgar Legare.
   Augustus B. Lonstreet. Int. Oct., '24.   (2:788.)
Pentifer, John.
   American Short Story. A. Merc. Jan.   (4:90.)
Peterkin, Julia.
   By Margery Latimer. Books. Dec. 14, '24.   (8.)
   By Dora-Mulkins. Int. Jan.   (3:138.)
Phelps, William Lyon.
   Anatole France. Scr. Feb.   (77:210.)
   Thomas Hardy. Sat. R. (N. Y.)   Jun. 6.   (1:808.)
   Henry James. Int. Jul.   (3:521.)
Pickens, Vinton Liddell.
   Maxim Gorky. Rev. Jul.   (5:109.)
Pilniak, Boris.
   By Herschel Brickell. L. Rev. Jan. 17.   (6.)
   By William A. Drake. Books. Mar. 8.   (7.)
   By Joseph Wood Krutch. Nat. (N. Y.)   Feb. 11.   (120:163.)
   By Arthur Ruhl. Sat. R. (N. Y.)   Mar. 14.   (1:595.)
   By Avrahm Yarmolinsky. Books. Mar. 15.   (11.)

Pirandello, Luigi.
    By F. Vinci Roman. Pear. (Am.) Feb. (51:36.)
Poe, Edgar Allan.
    By Edwin A. Alderman. Va. Apr. (1:78.)
    Anonymous. Nat. (N. Y.) Dec. 10, '24. (119:615.)
    By John Jay Chapman. N. Y. Times. Nov. 2, '24. (2.)
    By George De Mille. A. Merc. Apr. (4:433.)
    By H. L. Mencken. World. Aug. 16. (3 M.)
    By Paul Souday. N. Y. Times. Feb. 22. (11.)
    Stanley T. Williams. Yale. Jul. (14:756.)
Poole, Ernest.
    By Dorothy Bacon Woolsey. N. Rep. Sept. 23. (44:129.)
POPE, ELFRIDA H.
    Henry James. Sat. R. (N. Y.) Jul. 11. (1:902.)
POWELL, DAWN.
    Stephen McKenna. L. Rev. Sept. 20. (30.)
POWYS, JOHN COWPER.
    Llewellyn Powys. Cen. Sept. (110:553.)
    T. F. Powys. Cen. Sept. (110:553.)
POWYS, LLEWELLYN.
    Sherwood Anderson. Dial. Apr. (78:330.)
    E. L. Grant Watson. Books. Feb. 15. (4.)
    Pauline Smith. Books. Apr. 19. (6.)
Powys, Llewellyn.
    Anonymous. Books. Aug. 30. (5 V.)
    By John Cowper Powys. Cen. Sept. (110:553.)
Powys, T. F.
    By John Cowper Powys. Cen. Sept. (110:553.)
PRESTON, JOHN HYDE.
    Joseph Conrad. Int. Jan. (3:137.)
Puccini, Mario.
    By William Bolitho. World. Feb. 15. (6.)
PUCKETTE, C. McD.
    R. Emmet Kennedy. Sat. R. (N. Y.) Jan. 3. (1:427.)
Pushkin, Alexander.

    By Alexander I. Nazaroff. Int. Nov., '24. (2:864.)
QUICK, MARETTE.   Q
    George Gissing. Guar. (Am.) Apr. (1:274.)
QUINN, ARTHUR H.
    George W. Cable. Sat. R. (N. Y.) Mar. 21. (1:609.)
    Thomas Nelson Page. Sat. R. (N. Y.) Mar. 21. (1:609.)
    F. Hopkinson Smith. Sat. R. (N. Y.) Mar. 21. (1:609.)

R., D.   R
    Ring W. Lardner. Ind. May 23. (114:590.)
RADZIWILL, PRINCESS.
    Leonid Andreyev. Sat. R. (N. Y.) Oct. 4, '24. (1:164.)
    Honoré de Balzac. For. Jan. (73:40.) Feb. (73:189.)
    Anatole France. For. Dec., '24. (72:827.)

RAMSAY, JANET.
    American Short Story. Books. Aug. 16. (10.)
RAMSAY, R. L.
    American Short Story. L. Rev. May 9. (14.)
RASCOE, BURTON.
    James Branch Cabell. Nat. (N. Y.) Apr. 29. (120:494.)
    Anatole France. Book. (N. Y.) Nov., '24. (60:337.)
    Waldo Frank. A. D. Oct., '24. (41.)
    Glenway Wescott. A. D. Oct., '24. (41.)
REDMAN, BEN RAY.
    James Branch Cabell. Int. Nov., '24. (2:860.)
    Henry James. World. Apr. 19. (6 M.)
Rejmont, Ladislas.
    Annonymous. Liv. A. Jan. 17. (324:176.)
    By Ernest Boyd. Sat. R. (N. Y.) Nov. 29, '24. (1:317.)
    By Rupert Hughes. Int. Feb. (3:170.)
    By Stender-Petersen. Liv. A. Jan. 17. (324:165.)
Remizov, Aleksei.
    By Herschel Brickell. L. Rev. Jan. 17. (6.)
    By William A. Drake. Books. Mar. 8. (7.)
    By Joseph Wood Krutch. Nat. (N. Y.) Feb. 11. (120:163.)
    By Avrahm Yarmolinsky. Books. Mar. 15. (11.)
REUTER, GABRIELE.
    Albrecht Schaffer. N. Y. Times. Jun. 14. (20.)
    Frank Theiss. N. Y. Times. Jun. 14. (20.)
    Jakob Wassermann. N. Y. Times. Jun. 14. (20.)
RICE, VIRGINIA.
    George Moore. Book. (N. Y.) Jun. (61:431.)
RICKERT, EDITH.
    James Joyce. N. Rep. Jan. 7. (41:181.)
    D. H. Lawrence. N. Rep. Jan. 7. (41:181.)
ROBERTS, CECIL.
    Joseph Conrad. Book. (N. Y.) Jul. (61:536.)
ROMAN, F. VINCI.
    Luigi Pirandello. Pear. (Am.) Feb. (51:36.)
ROSCOE, E. S.
    Henry James. Book. (N. Y.) Jan. (60:584.)
ROSS, MARY.
    Katharine Mansfield. Books. Oct. 19, '24. (3.)
    Viola Meynell. Books. Apr. 12. (4.)
    Osbert Sitwell. Books. Mar. 22. (11.)
RUHL, ARTHUR.
    Fyodor Dostoevsky. L. Rev. Oct. 11, '24. (2.)
    Boris Pilniak. Sat. R. (N. Y.) Mar. 14. (1:595.)
RUSSELL, OLAND D.
    Pauline Smith. L. Rev. Mar. 28. (12.)
Russian Short Stories.
    By Eva Goldbeck. L. Rev. Apr. 11. (3.)
    By Betsy Greenebaum. N. Rep. May 27. (43:25.)
    By John E. Mitchell. World. Mar. 29. (7 M.)

SHORE, W. TEIGNMOUTH.
> G. K. Chesterton. Dear. Ind. May 2. (2.)

Short Story.
> Anonymous. Sat. R. (N. Y.) Dec. 27, '24. (1:409.) N. Y.
> Times. Dec. 28, '24. (12.)
> By Hansell Baugh. Rev. Jul. (5:105.)
> By Gerald Hewes Carson. Book. (N. Y.) Feb. (60:769.)
> By John Cournos. L. Rev. Oct. 11, '24. (1.)
> By N. Bryllion Fagin. D. D. Jan.–Feb. (7:116.) Int. Apr.
> (3:301.)
> By Henry L. Mencken. World. Feb. 22. (3 E.)
> By John E. Mitchell. World. May 3. (7 M.)
> By Paul Morand. Dial. Jan. (78:51.)
> By Isabel Paterson. Books. Jan. 4. (11.)
> By Carl Van Doren. Nat. (N. Y.) Dec. 24, '24. (119:711.)
> By Edith Wharton. Scr. Apr. (77:344.)

SHUSTER, GEORGE N.
> Robert Louis Stevenson. Cath. W. Oct., '24. (120:89.)

SIFTON, PAUL F.
> American Short Story. World. Feb. 22. (7.)

Sitwell, Osbert.
> Anonymous. N. Y. Times. Mar. 1. (6.)
> By Joseph Wood Krutch. Nat. (N. Y.) Apr. 29. (120:496.)
> By Mary Ross. Books. Mar. 22. (11.)
> By Lawrence Stallings. World. Mar. 27. (13.)
> By Allan Updegraff. N. Y. Sun. Mar. 28. (7.)
> By Glenway Wescott. Dial. Jun. (78:507.)

SMERTENKO, JOHAN J.
> American Short Story. Nat. (N. Y.) Apr. 22. (120:469.)
> British Short Story. Nat. (N. Y.) Apr. 22. (120:469.)
> George F. Hummel. Nat. (N. Y.) Apr. 22. (120:469.)
> Charles Merz. Nat. (N. Y.) Apr. 22. (120:469.)
> Russian Short Stories. Nat. (N. Y.) Apr. 22. (120:469.)
> Giovanni Verga. Nat. (N. Y.) Apr. 22. (120:469.)
> Emile Verhaeren. Nat. (N. Y.) Apr. 22. (120:469.)
> Stefan Zweig. Books. Aug. 16. (5 V.)

Smith, F. Hopkinson.
> By Arthur H. Quinn. Sat. R. (N. Y.) Mar. 21. (1:609.)

SMITH, HARRISON.
> Thomas Boyd. Books. Apr. 26. (11.)

SMITH, NORA ARCHIBALD.
> Kate Douglas Wiggin. Book. (N. Y.) May. (61:281.)

Smith, Pauline.
> By Llewellyn Powys. Books. Apr. 19. (6.)
> By Oland D. Russell. L. Rev. Mar. 28. (12.)
> By Brooks Shepard. Sat. R. (N. Y.) Apr. 25. (1:703.)

SORANI, ALDO.
> Thomas Mann. Sat. R. (N. Y.) Aug. 1. (2:13.)

Souday, Paul.
    Jules Barbey d'Aurevilly. N. Y. Times. Jul. 19. (12.)
    Paul Bourget. N. Y. Times. Apr. 5. (10.)
    Anatole France. N. Y Times. Dec. 14, '24. (8.)
    Pierre Loüys. N. Y. Times. May 17. (16.)
    Guy de Maupassant. N. Y. Times. Sept. 13. (7.)
    Paul Morand. N. Y. Times. Jul. 5. (16.)
    Edgar Allan Poe. N. Y. Times. Feb. 22. (11.)
    Jules Tellier. N. Y. Times. Sept. 20. (11.)
Sparling, E. Earl.
    By Grace King. L. Rev. Mar. 14. (12.)
    By Lawrence Lee. Int. May. (3:427.)
Squire, J. C.
    By Lisle Bell. Books. Mar. 8. (11.)
    By H. W. Boynton. N. Y. Sun. Feb. 2.
    By E. V. N. Rep. Apr. 22. (42:246.)
Stagg, Hunter.
    Edith Wharton. Rev. Jul. (5:98.)
Stallings, Lawrence.
    Ring W. Lardner. World. Apr. 13. (11.)
    Osbert Sitwell. World. Mar. 27. (13.)
Starrett, Vincent.
    Richard Harding Davis. Rev. Oct., '24. (4:352.)
Stedman, Nathan P.
    Maxim Gorky. Int. Feb. (3:203.)
Stein, Gertrude.
    By Mary Crockett. Mod. Q. Feb. (2:233.)
Stephens, James.
    By Charles E. Aiken. Cath. W. Apr. (121:132.)
Sterling, George.
    Ambrose Bierce. A. Merc. Sept., '25. (6:10.)
Sternheim, Carl.
    By William A. Drake. Books. Aug. 23. (7.)
Steuart, John A.
    Robert Louis Stevenson. Sat. R. (N. Y.) Jan. 24. (1:486.)
Stevenson, Robert Louis.
    Anonymous. Sat. R. (N. Y). Dec. 6, '24. (1:339.)
    By Ernest Boyd. Ind. Dec. 13, '24. (13:520.)
    By Clarence H. Gaines. N. A. Rev. Mar. (221:567.)
    By Clayton Hamilton. Int. Jan. (3:110.)
    By George S. Hellman. Book. (N. Y.) Jan. (60:575.)
    By A. B. de M. C. S. M. Oct. 25, '24. (9.)
    By H. L. Mencken. A. Merc. Nov., '24. (3:378.) Jan. (4: 125.)
    By George N. Schuster. Cath. W. Oct., '24. (120:89.)
    By Stuart P. Sherman. Books. Nov. 23, '24. (1.)
    By John A. Steuart. Sat. R. (N. Y.) Jan. 24. (1:486.)
    By Frank Swinnerton. Sat. R. (N. Y.) Dec. 6, '24. (:344.)
    By Frederic F. Van de Water. N. Y. Trib. Jan. 27. (18.)
Stewart, Alexander G.
    Rudyard Kipling. Int. Jan. (3:100.)

Stone, Melville E.
   A. Conan Doyle. L. Rev. Oct. 18, '24. (1.)
Stork, Charles Wharton.
   Arnold Bennett. L. Rev. Jan. 3. (3.)
Street, Julian.
   By Markey Morris. Int. Aug. (3:618.)
Strong, L. A. G.
   By John Cournos. L. Rev. Sept. 5. (2.)
Stuart, Henry Longan.
   Vicente Blasco Ibáñez. N. Y. Times. May 31. (9.)
   Thomas Hardy. N. Y. Sun. Jan. 19. (14.)
   Ring W. Lardner. N. Y. Times. Apr. 19. (1.)
   Guy de Maupassant. N. Y. Sun. Jan. 17. (6.)
Sung-Ling, P'u.
   By John Carter. N. Y. Times. Mar. 29. (6.)
Swinnerton, Frank.
   Robert Louis Stevenson. Sat. R. (N. Y.) Dec. 6, '24. (1:344.)

T

Tarkington, Booth.
   By Flora Merrill. World. Jun. 21. (1 M.)
Tartak, Elias L.
   Anton Chekhov. J. T. Jan. 2. (16.)
Tellier, Jules.
   By Paul Souday. N. Y. Times. Sept. 20. (11.)
Terhune, Albert Payson.
   By Grant Overton. Book. (N. Y.) Jun. (61:445.)
Theiss, Frank.
   By Gabriele Reuter. N. Y. Times. Jun. 14. (20.)
Thérive, André.
   Georges Duhamel. Liv. A. Sept. 12. (326:587.)
Thompson, Dorothy.
   Fyodor Dostoevsky. L. Rev. Jan. 3. (7.)
Thompson, Ruth Willis.
   Pierre Louys. L. Rev. Sept. 12. (5.)
Tinker, Edward Larocque.
   "O. Henry." Book. (N. Y.) Jun. (61:436.)
Tittle, Walter.
   Willa Cather. Cen. Jul. (110·305.)
   Joseph Conrad. N. Y. Times. May 17. (2.) Outl. (N. Y.)
      Jul. 1. (140:333.) Jul. 8. (140:361.)
   Theodore Dreiser. Cen. Aug. (110:441.)
   Ring W. Lardner. Cen. Jul. (110:305.)
   Israel Zangwill. Cen. Oct., '24. (108:798.)
Tolstoy, Count Lyof.
   By Ernest Boyd. Ind. Jul. 4. (115:22.)
   By V. Bulgakov. McC. Aug. (1:538.)
   By John Cournos. L. Rev. Sept. 19. (2.)
   By Maxim Gorky. Dial. Feb. (78:96.)
   By Alexander I. Nazaroff. N. Y. Times. Aug. 16. (1.)

Tomlinson, H. M.
> By Frank V. Morley. Sat. R. (N. Y.) Dec. 27, '24. (1:409.)

Toomer, Jean.
> By Gorham B. Munson. Opp. Sept. (3:262.)

Townsend, R. B.
> John Galsworthy. Outl. (N. Y.) Sept. 16. (114:98.)

Tsunoda, Rinsaku.
> Japanese Short Stories. W. T. Jun. (8:189.)

Tully, Jim.
> Olive Schreiner. Int. Sept. (3:653.)

U

Updegraff, Allan.
> Osbert Sitwell. N. Y. Sun. Mar. 28. (7.)

V

Vaillant-Couturier, Paul.
> Anatole France. Nat. (N. Y.) Apr. 15. (120:406.)

Van De Water, Frederic F.
> Robert Louis Stevenson. N. Y. Trib. Jan. 27. (18.)

Van Doren, Carl.
> Sherwood Anderson. Cen. Jul. (110:362.)
> James Branch Cabell. Int. Dec., '24. (3:12.) Cen. Nov., '24. (109:129.)
> Anatole France. Cen. Dec., '24. (109:418.) Aug. (110:510.)
> Thomas Hardy. Cen. Jan. (109:418.)
> Henry James. Cen. Sept. (110:637.)
> D. H. Lawrence. Cen. Sept. (110:639.)
> Short Story. Nat. (N. Y.) Dec. 24, '24. (119:711.)

Van Doren, Mark.
> Joseph Conrad. Nat. (N. Y.) Jan. 14. (120:45.)
> Anatole France. Nat. (N. Y.) Nov. 5, '24. (119:497.)
> John Galsworthy. Nat. (N. Y.) Sept. 2. (121:258.)

Venezuelan Short Stories.
> By Harriet V. Wishnieff. Sat. R. (N. Y.) Nov. 8, '24. (1:271.)

Verga, Giovanni.
> By Johan J. Smertenko. Nat. (N. Y.) Apr. 22. (120:469.)
> By Domenico Vittonini. Guar. (Am.) Aug. (1:405.)
> By Eliseo Vivas. Books. Apr. 19. (15.)

Verhaeren, Emile.
> By John Herrmann. Books. Feb. 22. (3.)
> By Johan J. Smertenko. Nat. (N. Y.) Apr. 22. (120:469.)

Vincent, Elizabeth.
> Maxim Gorky. N. Rep. Feb. 25. (42:22.)

Vittonini, Domenico.
> Giovanni Verga. Guar. (Am.) Aug. (1:405.)

Vivas, Eliseo.
> D. H. Lawrence. Guar. (Am.) Apr. (1:267.)
> Giovanni Verga. Books. Apr. 19. (15.)

Vorse, Mary Heaton.
    By Flora Merrill. World. Jul. 12. (5 M.)

W

WALKER, CHARLES R.
    Joseph Conrad. Ind. Feb. 7. (114:161.)
WASSERMANN, EDWARD.
    Anatole France. Book. (N. Y.) Apr. (61:197.)
Wassermann, Jakob.
    By Gabriele Reuter. N. Y. Times. Jun. 14. (20.)
WEAVER, RAYMOND.
    Aldous Huxley. Book. (N. Y.) Nov., '24. (60:262.)
WEITZENHORN, LOUIS.
    Anatole France. World. Jun. 21. (4 M.)
    Thomas Hardy. World. Apr. 12. (6 M.)
Wells, H. G.
    By Llewellyn Jones. C. E. P. Oct. 24, '24. (1.)
WESCOTT, GLENWAY.
    Kenneth Burke. Tr. Oct., '24. (2:446.)
    Osbert Sitwell. Dial. Jun. (78:507.)
Wescott, Glenway.
    By Burton Roscoe. A. D. Oct., '24. (41.)
WESTERGAARD, WALDEMAR.
    Jeppe Aakjaer. Scan. Nov., '24. (12:665.)
WHARTON, EDITH.
    Short Story. Scr. Apr. (77:344.)
Wharton, Edith.
    By James L. Ford. Int. Oct., '24. (2:785.)
    By Hunter Stagg. Rev. Jul. (5:98.)
WHIPPLE, T. K.
    Katherine Mansfield. Sat. R. (N. Y.) Dec. 6, '24. (1:342.)
WIENER, LEO.
    Anton Chekhov. Sat. R. (N. Y.) Apr. 4. (1:646.)
Wiggin, Kate Douglas.
    By Nora Archibald Smith. Book. (N. Y.) May. (61:281.)
WILLIAMS, BLANCHE COLTON.
    American Short Story. N. Y. Sun. Jan. 31. (7.)
    Richard Washburn Child. N. Y. Sun. April. 18. (7.)
WILLIAMS, STANLEY T.
    Stephen Crane. Yale. Oct., '24. (14:172.)
    Edgar Allan Poe. Yale. Jul. (14:756.)
WILSON, EDMUND.
    Anatole France. N. Rep. Feb. 11. (41:308.)
    Ernest Hemingway. Dial. Oct., '24. (77:340.)
    James Joyce. Dial. Nov., '24. (77:430.)
Wilson, Harry Leon.
    By Myla Jo Closser. Book. (N. Y.) Jun. (61:458.)
WILSON, JAMES SOUTHALL.
    James Branch Cabell. Va. Apr. (1:150.)

INDEX OF SHORT STORIES IN BOOKS

OCTOBER, 1924, TO SEPTEMBER, 1925

I. AMERICAN AUTHORS

A

ADAMS, SAMUEL HOPKINS. (1871– .)
(See 1923.)
Such as Walk in Darkness. Gray. 227.

ADE, GEORGE. (1866– .) (See 1920.)
The Feud. Aces, B. 3.

AIKEN, CONRAD POTTER. (1889– .)
(See 1924.)
Anniversary. Aiken. 211.
Bring! Bring! Aiken. 11.
By my Troth, Nerissa! Aiken. 93.
Dark City. Aiken. 144.
Disciple. Aiken. 56. Harper. 325.
Escape from Fatuity. Aiken. 120.
Hey, Taxi! Aiken. 132.
Last Visit. Aiken. 171.
Letter. Aiken. 186.
Orange Moth. Aiken. 158.
Smith and Jones. Aiken. 104.
Soliloquy on a Park Bench. Aiken. 232.
Strange Moonlight. Aiken. 37.

ALEXANDER, CHARLES. (See 1923.)
As a Dog Should. Gray. 3.

ANDERSON, SHERWOOD. (1876– .)
(See 1924.)
I'm a Fool. Newman. 246.
Mother. Robinson. 1.

ANTIN, MARY (MARY ANTIN GRABAU).
(1881– .)
Malinka's Atonement. Aces B. 7.

ASCH, NATHAN. (1902– .)
Gertrude Donovan. Humphrey A. 227.

AUSTIN, WILLIAM. (1778–1841). (See
1923.)
Late Joseph Natterstrom. Austin C.
242.
Man With the Cloaks. Austin C. 270.
Martha Gardner, or Moral Reaction.
Austin C. 257.
Peter Rugg, the Missing Man. Austin
C. 207.

B

BABCOCK, EDWINA STANTON.
Wavering Gold. Harper. 188.

BANNING, MARGARET CULKIN.
Women Come to Judgment. Harper.
135.

BARENTS, WILLIAM.
Early Arctic Adventure. French K. 28.

BARNES, DJUNA. (1892– .) (See 1920.)
Little Girl Tells a Story to a Lady.
Contact. 1.

BARTLETT, FREDERIC ORIN. (1876– .)
(See 1920.)
Trap. Humphrey A. 3.

BASSETT, FLETCHER S.
Phantom Ship. French K. 276.

BENET, STEPHEN VINCENT. (1898– .)
Uriah's Son. Prize F. 53.

BERCOVICI, KONRAD. (1882– .) (See
1924.)
Drought. Aces B. 48.

BIERCE, AMBROSE. (1842–1914?) (See
1924.)
Monk and the Hangman's Daughter.
Bierce C. 19.

BIGGERS, EARL DERR. (1884– .)
Apron of Genius. Fox. 166.

BOURKE, S. TEN EYCK.
"Will of the Gods." Fox. 126.

BOYD, THOMAS.
Kentucky Boy. Boyd B. 33.
Little Gall. Boyd B. 165.
Long Shot. Boyd B. 249.
Nine Days' Kitten. Boyd B. 219.
Responsibility. Boyd B. 65.
Ribbon Counter. Boyd B. 191.
Rintintin. Boyd B. 131.
Semper Fidelis. Boyd B. 317.
"Sound Adjutant's Call." Boyd B. 97.
Unadorned. Boyd B. 1.
Uninvited. Boyd B. 299.

BRADY, MARIEL.
Autograph Album. Copy B. 25.

BRAND, MAX.
Bulldog. Gray. 37.

BROWN, ALICE.
Girl in the Tree. Harper. 160.

BROWNE, PORTER EMERSON. (1879– .)
Courtship of Miles Sheehan. Fox. 263.

BRYSON, LYMAN LLOYD. (1888– .)
Cyprian. Humphrey A. 214.

BUCK, MITCHELL S.
Courtesan. Buck 42.
Greek. Buck. 66.
Pharoah. Buck. 80.
Priest. Buck. 56.
Philosopher. Buck. 26.
Shepherdess. Buck. 90.

BUCKLEY, FREDERICK ROBERT WAKELIN.
Primitive Method. World. 118.

BUNNER, HENRY CUYLER. (1855–1896.)
(See 1923.)
Love-Letters of Smith. Hastings. 120.

P

PARADISE, VIOLA L.
Calabrian Goes Home. Humphrey A. 194.

PATTULLO, GEORGE. (1879– .)
Tie that Binds. Prize F. 142.

PETERKIN, JULIA M.
Ashes. Peterkin. 9.
Cat Fish. Peterkin. 123.
Finding Peace. Peterkin. 94.
Green Thursday. Peterkin. 26.
Meeting. Peterkin. 62.
Missie. Peterkin. 50.
Mount Pleasant. Peterkin. 79.
Plum Blossoms. Peterkin. 170.
Red Rooster. Peterkin. 103.
Son. Peterkin. 132.
Sunday. Peterkin. 143.
Teaching Jim. Peterkin. 115.

POE, EDGAR ALLAN. (1809–1849.) (See 1924.)
Fall of the House of Usher. Lynch. 264.
Masque of the Red Death. Hastings. 27.

POOLE, ERNEST. (1880– .)
Salvatore Schreider. Fox. 37.
Dormeuse. Poole B. 9.
Little Dark Man. Poole B. 41.
Mother Volga. Poole B. 103.
Stories that His Uncle Told. Poole B. 65.

PRICE, EDITH BALLINGER. (1897– .)
Boy from Beyant. Humphrey A. 67.

R

READ, FRANCES KAUTZ.
Engagement on the Rhine. Copy B. 113.

REESE, LIZETTE WOODWORTH. (1856– .)
Forgiveness. O'Brien N. 167.

RICE, ALICE CALDWELL (HEGAN). (MRS. CALE YOUNG RICE.) (1870– .)
Between Trains. Rice 185.
Day of Resurrection. Rice. 237.
Miss Gee. Rice. 61.
Mourning a la Mode. Rice. 133.
Phoebe. Rice. 3.

RICE, CALE YOUNG. (1872– .)
Commonwealth's Attorney. Rice. 103.
Environment. Rice. 157.
Gull's Nest. Rice. 271.
Heroes· Two Storiettes. Rice. 209.
Out of Darkness. Rice. 33.

RINEHART, MARY ROBERTS. (1876– .)
Twenty-Two. Aces. 164.

ROBERTSON, MORGAN. (1861–1915.)
Argonauts. Fox. 50.

RUNYON, ALFRED DAMON. (1840– .)
Breeze Kid's Big Tear-Off. Fox. 111.

S

SERGEL, ROGER L. (1894– .)
Nocturne: A Red Shawl. O'Brien N. 175.

SHELTON, RICHARD BARKER. See "OXFORD, JOHN BARTON."

SHER, BENJAMIN R.
Abe's Card. Aces. 224.
Rubber Heels. Aces B. 308.

SHIFFRIN, A. B. (1902– .)
Black Laugh. O'Brien N. 191.

SINGMASTER, ELSIE. (ELSIE SINGMASTER LEWARS.) (1879– .) (See 1920.)
Courier of the Czar. Prize F. 155.
November the Nineteenth. World. 331.
Pair of Lovers. Gray. 155.

SMITH, EDGAR VALENTINE. (1875– .) (See 1924.)
'Lijah. Prize F. 172.

SPEARS, RAYMOND SMILEY. (1850– .)
River Combine — Professional. Prize F. 190.

SPRINGER, FLETA CAMPBELL.
Legend. Harper. 108.

SQUIER, EMMA-LINDSAY. (MRS. GEORGE LLOYD MARK.) (1893– .)
Flower of Gold. Humphrey A. 37.
Soul of Caliban. Gray. 241.

STEELE, WILBUR DANIEL. (1886– .) (See 1923.)
Woman at Seven Brothers. Robinson. 382.
What Do You Mean — Americans? Prize F. 205.
When Hell Froze. Harper. 241.

STEIN, GERTRUDE.
Two Women. Contact. 303.

STOCKTON, FRANK RICHARD. (1834–1902.) (See 1924.)
Widow's Cruise. Hastings. 187.

STONE, ELINORE COWAN.
One Uses the Handkerchief. Prize F. 225.

STREET, JULIAN LEONARD. (1879– .) (See 1923.)
Mr. Bisbee's Princess. Street B. 1.
Speaking Likeness. Street B. 85.
Syringas. Street B. 159.

SUCKOW, RUTH. (1892– .) (See. 1924.)
Four Generations. O'Brien N. 198.

SWIFT, HELEN. (See 1924.)
Chicken-Woman and the Hen-Man. Freeman. 273.
Zachariah Jones. Freeman. 277.

T

TARKINGTON, NEWTON BOOTH. (1869– .). (See 1924.)
Big, Fat Lummox. Robinson. 406.
Fox Terrier or Something. Gray. 59.

TARLEAU, LISA YSAYE.
Loutré. World. 178. Harper 1.

TERHUNE, ALBERT PAYSON. (1872– .) (See 1923.)
Grudge. Gray. 65.

THOMPSON, MARY WOLFE. (See 1924.)
Turtle. Copy B. 182.

TRAIN, ARTHUR CHENEY. (1875– .)
Old Duke. Gray. 129.

TUTTLE, WORTH. (See 1923.)
Tree in the Forest. Copy B. 75.

II. BRITISH AND IRISH AUTHORS

III. Translations

A

AKURATERS, JANIS. (1876– .) (*Latvian.*)
Death. Eaton A. 239.

ANDERSEN, HANS CHRISTIAN. (1805–1875.) (*Danish.*)
Shepherdess and the Chimney Sweep. Newman. 61.

ANONYMOUS. (*French.*)
About the Peasant Who Got into Heaven by Pleading. Newman. 20.
Of the Churl Who Won Paradise. Hastings 1.

ANONYMOUS. (*Japanese.*)
Account of the Hari-Kiri Seitz. 280
Archery in the Olden Time. Seitz. 236.
Bell of Kawagoye. Seitz. 124.
Bitter for Sweet. Seitz. 219.
Carp in a Dream. Seitz. 106.
Confessions of Two Monks. Seitz. 240.
Doll Flowers. Seitz. 183.
Dream or No? Seitz. 231.
Fencing-Master's Story. Seitz. 132.
Forty-Seven Ronins. Seitz. 3.
Fowler. Seitz. 128.
Hangataro: The Faithful Dog. Seitz. 245.
Heroism of Torii Katsutaka. Seitz. 58.
Hidakagawa. Seitz. 254.
Holy Houses of Sleep. Seitz. 206.
Honest Kyusuke. Seitz. 35.
How to Meet Death. Seitz. 77.
Human Destiny. Seitz. 77.
Ichinotani. Seitz. 194.
Living-Field River. Seitz. 210.
Mecca of the Pilgrim. Seitz. 152.
My Lord Bag-o'-Rice. Hearn B. 47.
Old Man and the Mirror. Seitz. 227.
Ooka as a Matchmaker. Seitz. 164.
Oshichi of the Greengrocer. Seitz. 135.
Priest's Staff. Seitz. 201.
Rat Boy. Seitz. 177.
Shuzo's Wife — A Story of True Love. Seitz. 113.
Sundry Ghosts. Seitz. 170.
Sword. Seitz. 259.
True Story of Hidari Jingoro. Seitz. 79.
Ungo-yenji. Seitz. 265.
Vision of the Unseen. Seitz. 214.
Winning Without Hands. Seitz. 148.
Wrestling of a Damio. Seitz. 89.

AROSEV, A. (*Russian.*)
Lenin. Osip. 137.
Soldiers. Osip. 130.

B

BARBEY D'AUREVILLY, JULES. (1808–1889.) (*French.*)
At a Dinner of Atheists. Barbey. 181.
Beneath the Cards of a Game of Whist. Barbey. 127.
Crimson Curtain. Barbey. 3.
Greatest Love of Don Juan. Barbey. 51.
Happiness in Crime. Barbey. 77.
Woman's Revenge. Barbey. 239.

BLASCO IBANEZ, VINCENTE. (1867– .) (*See 1920.*) (*Spanish.*)
Cabure Feather. Ibáñez B. 221.
Four Sons of Eve. Ibáñez B 182.
General's Automobile. Ibáñez B. 280.
Hero. Ibáñex B. 35.
Life Sentence. Ibáñez B. 330.
Mad Virgins. Ibáñez B. 381.
Martinez's Insurrection. Ibáñez B. 305.
Monster. Ibáñez B. 350.
Old Woman of the Movies. Ibáñez B. 1.
Serbian Night. Ibáñez B. 341.
Serenade. Ibáñez B. 256.
Shot in the Night. Ibáñez B. 104.
Sleeping Car Porter. Ibáñez B. 369.
Sunset. Ibáñez B. 150. Eaton A. 362.
Widow's Loan. Ibáñez B. 63.

BOCCACCIO, GIOVANNI. (1313?–1375.) (*Italian.*)
Abraham Goes to the Court of Rome. Newman. 34.

BOULENGER, MARCEL. (1873– .) (*French.*)
Prodigal Child. Eaton B. 3.

BOURGET, PAUL. (1852– .) (*French.*)
Father and Son. Eaton B. 54.

BOUTET, FREDERIC. (*See 1922.*) (*French.*)
Quarter Pound. Eaton B. 74.

BRATESCU-VOINESTI, J. A. (1869– .) (*Rumanian.*)
Violoncello. Eaton A. 298.

BROCCHI, VIRGILIO. (*Italian.*)
Illusion. Eaton A. 158.

C

CAPEK, KAREL. (*Czechoslovak.*)
Imprint. Eaton A. 42.

CAPEK, KAREL. (1890– .) *and* CAPEK, JOSEF. (1887– .) (*Czechoslovak.*)
Island. Busch. 165.
Living Flame. Busch. 180.

CAPEK-CHOD, K. M. (1850– .) (*Czechoslovak.*)
At the Rotary Machine. Busch. 193.

CHEKHOV, ANTON PAVLOVITCH. (1861–1904.) (*See 1923.*) (*Russian.*)
Darling. Newman. 222.

"COLETTE." (MME. HENRI DE JOUVENEL.) (*French.*)
Ambulance Dogs. Colette. 151.
Autumn. Colette. 99.
For Sale: A Little Dog. Colette. 41.
Jealous Dog. Colette. 9.
Little Bulldog. Colette. 94.
"Lolu" — the White Borzoi. Colette. 59.
Man With the Fishes. Colette. 133.
Monsieur Maurice. Eaton B. 88.
Monsieur Rouzade's Little Pig. Colette. 140.
Mother Cat. Colette. 86.
Nonache — A Cat and a Kitten. Colette. 78.
Performing Dogs. Colette. 67.
Politicians, or The Old Lady and the Bear. Colette. 145.

MAGAZINE AVERAGES

OCTOBER, 1924, TO SEPTEMBER, 1925

The following table includes the averages of distinctive stories in twenty American periodicals published from October, 1924, to September, 1925, inclusive. One, two and three asterisks are employed to indicate relative distinction. "Three-asterisk stories" are considered worth reprinting in book form. The list excludes reprints.

PERIODICALS	No. of Stories Published	No. of Distinctive Stories Published			Percentage of Distinctive Stories Published		
		*	**	***	*	**	***
American Mercury	17	13	10	6	77	59	35
Atlantic Monthly	26	24	20	11	92	77	42
Catholic World	31	15	1	1	48	3	3
Century	26	26	20	14	100	77	54
Chicago Tribune (Syndicate Service)	52	14	8	2	27	15	4
Collier's Weekly (except September 19)	163	56	18	11	34	11	7
Cosmopolitan	128	46	20	8	36	16	6
Delineator	30	9	0	0	30	0	0
Designer	38	7	1	1	18	3	3
Dial	17	17	17	16	100	100	94
Everybody's Magazine . .	74	16	5	2	22	7	3
Good Housekeeping . . .	55	19	11	7	35	20	13
Harper's Magazine . . .	36	35	28	15	97	77	42
Ladies' Home Journal . .	52	17	9	1	33	18	2
Midland	23	21	8	0	91	35	0
Pictorial Review	49	33	21	13	66	42	26
Red Book Magazine . . .	119	28	15	5	24	13	4
Saturday Evening Post . .	396	67	14	5	16	4	1
Scribner's Magazine . . .	42	26	12	6	62	29	15
Woman's Home Companion . .	63	27	3	1	43	5	2

The following tables indicate the rank, during the period between October, 1924, and September, 1925, inclusive, by number and percentage of distinctive short stories published, of twenty periodicals coming within the scope of my examination which have published an average of 15 per cent or more of distinctive stories. The lists exclude reprints, but not translations.

By Percentage

1.	Century Magazine	100%
2.	Dial	100%
3.	Harper's Magazine	97%
4.	Atlantic Monthly	92%
5.	Midland	91%
6.	American Mercury	77%
7.	Pictorial Review	66%
8.	Scribner's Magazine	62%
9.	Catholic World	48%
10.	Woman's Home Companion	43%
11.	Cosmopolitan	36%
12.	Good Housekeeping	35%
13.	Collier's Weekly	34%
14.	Ladies' Home Journal	33%
15.	Delineator	30%
16.	Chicago Tribune (Syndicate Service)	27%
17.	Red Book Magazine	24%
18.	Everybody's Magazine	22%
19.	Designer	18%
20.	Saturday Evening Post	16%

By Number

1.	Saturday Evening Post	67
2.	Collier's Weekly	56
3.	Cosmopolitan	46
4.	Harper's Magazine	35
5.	Pictorial Review	33
6.	Red Book Magazine	28
7.	Woman's Home Companion	27
8.	Century Magazine	26
9.	Scribner's Magazine	26
10.	Atlantic Monthly	24
11.	Midland	21
12.	Good Housekeeping	19
13.	Dial	17
14.	Ladies' Home Journal	17
15.	Everybody's Magazine	16
16.	Catholic World	15
17.	Chicago Tribune (Syndicate Service)	14
18.	American Mercury	13
19.	Delineator	9
20.	Designer	7

The following periodicals have published during the same period ten or more "two-asterisk stories." The list excludes reprints, but not translations, Periodicals represented in this list during 1915, 1916, etc., to 1924 inclusive are represented by the prefixed letters a, b, etc., to j inclusive.

1.	abcdefghij	Harper's Magazine	28
2.	bcdefghij	Pictorial Review	21
3.	abcdefghij	Century Magazine	20
4.	cdef hij	Atlantic Monthly	20
5.	ij	Cosmopolitan	20
6.	abcde j	Collier's Weekly	18
7.	fghi	Dial	17
8.	i	Red Book Magazine	15
9.	abcdef j	Saturday Evening Post	14
10.	abcdef hij	Scribner's Magazine	12
11.		Good Housekeeping	11
12.		American Mercury	10
13.	i	Hearst's International	10

The following periodicals have published during the same period five or more "three-asterisk stories." The list excludes reprints, but not translations. The same signs are used as prefixes as in the previous list.

1.	fghij	Dial	16
2.	abcdefghij	Harper's Magazine	15
3.	abcdefghij	Century Magazine	14
4.	bcdefghij	Pictorial Review	13
5.	cdef hij	Atlantic Monthly	11
6.	ab d j	Collier's Weekly	11
7.	ij	Cosmopolitan	8
8.	j	Transatlantic Review	7
9.	c j	Good Housekeeping	7
10.		American Mercury	6
11.	a	Forum	6
12.	abcdef hij	Scribner's Magazine	6
13.	ij	Hearst's International	6
14.		Bookman (New York)	5
15.	i	Red Book Magazine	5
16.	abc ef i	Saturday Evening Post	5
17.		MacLean's Magazine	5

Ties in the above lists have been decided by taking relative rank in other lists into account.

INDEX OF SHORT STORIES PUBLISHED IN AMERICAN MAGAZINES

OCTOBER, 1924, TO SEPTEMBER, 1925

All short stories published in the following magazines are indexed:

All's Well
American Magazine
American Mercury
American-Scandinavian Review
Asia
Atlantic Monthly
Bookman (New York)
Books (New York Herald-Tribune)
Catholic World
Century
Chicago Tribune (Syndicate Service)
Collier's Weekly (except September 19)
Cosmopolitan
Delineator
Designer
Dial
Double Dealer
Echo
Everybody's Magazine
Forum
Golden Book
Good Housekeeping
Guardian (Philadelphia)
Harper's Bazar
Harper's Magazine
Hearst's International
Holland's Magazine
Independent
International Arts

Ladies' Home Journal
Leonardo
Liberty
Living Age (except April 18 to August 29)
Little Review
McCall's Magazine (except July to September)
Menorah Journal
Midland
Modern Quarterly
New Republic
New York Tribune (except September 13 and 20)
North American Review
Opportunity
Outlook (New York)
Pearson's Magazine (Chicago)
Pictorial Review
Red Book Magazine
Reviewer
Saturday Evening Post
Scribner's Magazine
Southwest Review
Stratford Monthly
Transatlantic Review
Vanity Fair
Wave
Woman's Home Companion
Workers' Monthly
World Tomorrow
Yale Review

Short stories of distinction only, published in the following magazines during the same period, are indexed. The list includes two British periodicals in which American stories were published which did not appear elsewhere.

Adventure
Ainslee's Magazine
American Boy
American Hebrew
Blue Book Magazine
B'nai B'rith Magazine
Calendar (London)
Canadian Forum
Cedar Rapids Republican
Charm
Commonweal
Country Gentleman
Day, The
Dearborn Independent
Elks Magazine
Farm and Fireside
Frontier
Golden Galleon
Hue and Cry
Inter-America

Iowa Literary Magazine
Jewish Forum
Jewish Tribune
London Mercury
McClure's Magazine
Macfadden Fiction-Lover's Magazine
MacLean's Magazine
Munsey's Magazine
New York Evening Post Literary Review
Open Road
Popular Magazine
Sea Stories Magazine
Short Stories
Sunset
Trident
Woman's World
Young Israel

I have considered many other magazines without finding any stories of distinction. One, two or three asterisks are prefixed to the titles of stories to indicate distinction. Three asterisks prefixed to a title indicate the fact that the story is listed in the "Roll of Honor." Cross references after an author's name refer to the last previous volume of this series in which his or her name appeared. (H) after the name of an author indicates that other stories by this author have been published in American periodicals between 1900 and 1914, and that these stories are listed in "The Standard Index of Short Stories" by Francis J. Hannigan, published by Small, Maynard and Company, 1918. The figures in parentheses after the title of a story refer to the volume and page number of the magazine. In cases where successive numbers of a magazine are not paged consecutively, the page number only is given in this index. As the reader will have noted, a few odd numbers of periodicals have been so far unprocurable for my purpose. I hope to report upon these next year. Those which I failed to obtain in time for last year's book are for the most part reported upon here.

I. AMERICAN AUTHORS

A

ABBOTT, ELEANOR HALLOWELL. (MRS. FORDYCE COBURN.) (1872–   .) (*See 1924.*) (*H.*)

Out of Nothing — and Roses. Del. May. (5.)

ABDULLAH, ACHMED. (ACHMED ABDULLAH NADIR KHAN EL-DURANI EL-IDRIS-SYEH.) ("A. A. NADIR".) (1881–   .) (*See 1924.*) (*H.*)

Affair of Honor. Hear. Jan. (58.)

*Ahee! Des. Aug. (5.)

First Hundred Thousand. Ev. June. (10.)

**Gates of Tamerlane. A. Merc. Aug., '24. (2:391.)

*Hound of the Wilderness. McCall. Feb. (14.)

*Magnificent Gesture. Elks. Mar. (5.)

BRACKETT, CHARLES. (1892–   .) (See
    1924.) Father's Day. S. E. P. July 4.
    (14.)
    Tenth-Word Love. S. E. P. Jan. 10.
    (6.)
BRADY, MARIEL. (See 1922.)
    Autograph Album. G. H. Oct., '24.
    (68.)
    Eyes of Argus. Hol. May. (16.)
BRECHT, HAROLD W.
    **Two Heroes. Harp. M. Sept. (151:
    478.)
BRENT, ROBERT WILLIAM.
    Doctor Winkleman. Oracle. March.
    (1: 9.)
BRETHERTON, VIVIEN R. (See 1924.)
    Wind Harp. McCall. Feb. (13.)
BRIGGS, ELLIS O. (See 1924.)
    Quiet Turkish Evening with Geral-
    dine. Col. Oct. 11, '24. (5.)
    *Shah is Dead: Checkmate. Ev. Jan.
    (43.)
BRINIG, MYRON.
    **Fear God and Take Your Own Part.
    Pict. R. June. (5.)
BRIRY, MALCOLM.
    Little Drops of Water. Ev. Sept. (25.)
BROOKS, GEORGE S. (See 1924.)
    Comedy Comet. McC. July.
    (1: 375.)
    *Pete Retires. Scr. Dec., '24. (76:
    645.)
BROOKS, JONATHAN. (See 1924.)
    Bright Work. Col. Oct. 18, '24.
    (8.)
    Brothers under the Pigskin. Col.
    Nov. 22, '24. (19.)
    Half-a-Stroke Heywood. Ev. Sept.
    (77.)
    His Son's Dad. Ev. Nov., '24.
    (47.)
    Jack O'Lantern. Ly. Aug. 15, (48.)
    Runnin' Fool. Am. Nov., '24. (52.)
    Three-Laigged Hoss. Ev. June.
    (59.)
    True Bills. Col. Dec. 6, '24. (17.)
    Water Bucket Baby. Am. Sept.
    (54.)
    Weep no Mo', Mah Lady. Col.
    Dec. 27, '24. (15.)
BROOKS, WINN.
    *Sixteen Fathoms Deep. Col. June
    27. (9.)
BROWN, ALICE. (1857–   .) (See
    1924.) (H.)
    *Piece of a Dream. W. H. C. Jan. (7.)
BROWN, BERNICE. (1890–   .) (See
    1924.)
    Letter. Red. Bk. Oct., '24. (77.)
    Persian Apple Sauce. L. H. J. Aug.
    (10.)
    Why Girls Leave Rome. L. H. J.
    March. (12.)
BROWN, KATHARINE HOLLAND. (See
    1924.) (H.)
    *Chivalry. Outlook. (N. Y.) Aug. 19.
    (140: 561.)
BROWN, KENNETH IRVING. (1896–   .)

***Christmas Guest. Atl. Dec., '24.
    (134: 797.)
BROWN, ROYAL. (See 1924.)
    All the Symptoms But One. Ly.
    Nov. 7, '24.
    Among the Idle Rich. Hear. Oct.,
    '24. (64.)
    Engagements are Like That. Des.
    Oct., '24. (5.)
    Everybody Lies. Des. May. (8.)
    Girl with the Pay-Roll. Cos. March.
    (81.)
    Inevitable Clinch. Cos. Aug. (68.)
    Love at First Sight. Hear. Nov.,
    '24. (40.)
    Love is Blind. Hear. Jan. (36.)
    Love Makes Gamblers of Us All. Cos.
    June. (62.)
    Should a Body Kiss a Body. Hear.
    Feb. (58.)
    So This is Love. Cos. July. (104.)
    When a Girl Needs a Friend. Cos.
    Sept. (104.)
BROWNE, R. K. G.
    Fruitful Visit. G. H. May. (54.)
BRUBAKER, HOWARD. (1892–   .) (See
    1922.) (H.)
    Connie Makes the Grade. Red Bk.
    Feb. (50.)
    Connie's Double Life. Red Bk. Mar.
    (76.)
    Conquering Connie. Red Bk. Jan.
    (74.)
    Soiled Wings. W. H. C. April. (13.)
BRYSON, LYMAN LLOYD. (1888–   .)
    (See 1918.)
    **Cyprian. Atl. Nov., '24. (134: 603.)
BUCHANAN, ROSEMARY.
    *Between Trains. Cath. W. Sept.
    (121: 768.)
BUNNER, HENRY CULVER. (1855–1896.)
    (See 1920.) (H.)
    **Hector. (R.) Gol. Jan. (1: 129.)
    **Zenobia's Infidelity. (R.) Gol. May.
    (1: 731.)
BURANELLI, PROSPER. (See 1924.)
    *White Pigeon. Ev. Mar. (150.)
BURKE, MORGAN. (1886–   .) (See
    1924.)
    Next Time a Lion. Ly. Oct. 25, '24.
    (37.)
BURLINGAME, ROGER.
    Bachelors on Horseback. Scr. April.
    (77: 405.)
BURNET, DANA. (1888–   .) (See 1924.)
    Breakfast with Bettina. S. E. P.
    June 20. (12.)
    Child. S. E. P. Aug. 8. (12.)
    Fine Feathers. Red Bk. March. (33.)
    Pinwheel Age. Cos. Oct., '24. (32.)
    Rose-covered Cottage. Col. June.
    13. (18.)
    *Technic. S. E. P. May 16. (14.)
    Those High-Society Blues. S. E. P.
    May 23. (8.)
    Underground Romance. Ly. Oct. 11,
    '24. (8.)
    Wings. Ly. Dec. 27, '24. (5.)

CHAPMAN, ELISABETH COBB.
  Drama for Lunch. Ly. May 16.
  (24.)
  Golf Bride. Ly. Oct. 25, '24. (59.)
  Mathilde is Different. Cos. July.
  (98.)
CHAPMAN, FREDERICK.
  One Cocker Spaniel Going North.
  W. H. C. Aug. (12.)
CHILD, MAUDE PARKER.
  Romance. S. E. P. Sept. 19. (18.)
CHILD, RICHARD WASHBURN (1881–   .)
  (See 1924.) (H.)
  *Cat. Des. Nov., '24. (5.)
  *Donna Quixote. Des. Dec., '24.
  (8.)
  For the Woman. Cos. Sept. (94.)
  Her Two Men. S. E. P. Jan. 24.
  (10.)
  *No Knowing Why. Des. Mar. (8.)
CHILDS, MARQUIS W.
  Roomer. I. L. M. May. (21.)
CHITTENDEN, GERALD. (H.)
  *Mrs. Riddle. Scr. Sept. (78: 243.)
CLARAGE, ELEANOR.
  Anniversary. A. Merc. June. (5:
  169.)
CLARK, EMILY. (MRS. EDWIN SWIFT
  BALCH.) (See 1924.)
  *Chocolate Sponge. A. Merc. June.
  5: 160.)
CLARK, VALMA. (See 1924.)
  **Devil's Third Horn. Col. Feb. 28.
  (18.)
  *Drive. Col. July 18. (17.)
  ***"Service." Scr. Oct., '24. (76: 356.)
  Substitute. Hol. Dec., '24. (12.)
  *Superstition. Hol. Oct., '24. (14.)
  **Woman of No Immagination. Scr.
  Aug. (78: 129.)
CLAUSEN, CARL. (See 1923.)
  Shelled. Chic. Trib. Jan. 18.
CLEMENS, SAMUEL LANGHORNE. See
  "TWAIN, MARK."
"CLOSE, UPTON." See HALL, JOSEPH W.
COATSWORTH, ELIZABETH J.
  *Man Who Loved Wild Animals.
  D. D. Nov.–Dec., '24. (7: 43.)
COBB, IRVIN SHREWSBURY. (1876–   .)
  (See 1924.) (H.)
  *Ace in the Hole. Cos. Aug. (40.)
  *Black Duck. Cos. July. (34.)
  *Button, Button . . . Cos. Dec., '24.
  (20.)
  **Coyote in Central Park. G. H.
  July. (22.)
  **Dead Line. Cos. Feb. (24.)
  *Hands Across the Sea. Harp. B.
  Aug. (45.)
  ***Nobody Sees the Waiter's Face.
  Cos. Jan. (26.)
  ***One Block from Fifth Avenue. (R.)
  Gol. May. (1: 629.)
  *Parker House Roll. Cos. May.
  (64.)
  *Power of the Press. Cos. June. (34.)
  ***Principle of the Thing. Cos. April.
  (68.) MacL. March 15. (2.)

***Standing Room Only. Cos. Oct.,
  '24. (16.)
**We of the Old South. Cos. Nov.,
  '24. (24.)
COHEN, BELLA. ("BELLA NEYO.") (1899–
  .) (See 1924.)
***Laugh. Calendar. July. (1: 387.)
***Yetta's Feller. Macf. Oct., '24.
  (21.)
COHEN, OCTAVUS ROY. (1891–   .)
  (See 1924.)
  Barberous. S. E. P. March 14. (22.)
  Bathing Booty. S. E. P. Oct. 4, '24.
  (10.)
  Blackmale. S. E. P. Jan. 17. (14.)
  Blue Steel. Red Bk. Aug. (56.)
  Bounce of Prevention. S. E. P.
  Sept. 19. (20.)
  **Case Ace. S. E. P. Feb. 28. (41.)
  Damaged Good. S. E. P. July 18.
  (14.)
  Fly and the Ointment. Chic. Trib.
  Nov. 23, '24.
  Inside Inflammation. S. E. P. Nov. 1,
  '24, (24.)
  Interlude. Ev. Nov., '24 (59.)
  Jazz You Like It. S. E. P. Aug.
  8. (14.)
  Lion and the Uniform. S. E. P.
  Jan. 31. (14.)
  Little Child. S. E. P. Oct. 18,
  '24. (24.)
  Miss Directed. S. E. P. Apr. 11.
  (20.)
  On With the Lance. S. E. P. May 2.
  (24.)
  Prologue. Des. May. (10.)
  Silent Call. G. H. May. (32.)
  To Love and to Honour. Col. Sept.
  12. (5.)
  Union Suit. Chic. Trib. May 24.
  White Lights and Amber. S. E. P.
  Dec. 20, '24. (33.)
  Write and Wrong. S. E. P., Mar. 7,
  (60.)
COLLINS, CHARLES. (See 1924.)
  Marvellous Marco. Chic. Trib.
  Nov. 30, '24.
COMFORT, MILDRED H.
  Water Gypsy. Ind. Jan. 3. (114:11.)
COMFORT, WILL LEVINGTON. (1878–   .)
  (See 1924.) (H.)
  Another's Man's Game. Ev. Sept.
  (9.)
  Damsel. Ev. June. (27.)
  Koot Hoomi. S. E. P. Jan. 10. (10.)
  Merv—. S. E. P. Aug. 29. (8.)
  Outside of a Horse. S. E. P. July 11.
  (12.)
  Thirty Years Late. S. E. P. April 18.
  (8.)
CONDON, FRANK. (See 1924.) (H.).
  Best Minds. S. E. P. May 2. (30.)
  Big Names. S. E. P. April 4, (28.)
  Brownie. S. E. P. Nov. 29, '24.
  (14.)
  Chronic and Incurable. Col. Nov. 1,
  '24. (5.)

CURTISS, PHILIP EVERETT. (1885–   .)
(See 1924.) (H.)
Penny in the Wide. L. H. J. Sept.
(16.)

D

DALE, VIRGINIA. (See 1924.)
Love Shy. Red Bk. Oct., '24. (68.)
Men are So Different. Red Bk. Mar.
(53.)
Some Men Stay Single. Cos. Sept.
(73.)
Things. Red Bk. Sept. (66.)
DALRYMPLE, C. LEONA. (See 1919.) (H.)
Age. Hol. Aug. (8.)
DANA, FRANCIS. (1866–   .) (See 1924.)
(H.)
Tripper Trap. S. E. P. July 25. (18.)
DARGAN, OLIVER TILFORD. (See 1924.)
*Serena Takes a Boarder. Rev. Apr.
(5: 10.)
DAVENPORT, WALTER.
Geoffrey John of Amiens. Ly. May
23. (33.)
Señor Roams with Rooney. Ly. Oct.
11 '24. (29.)
Society. Ly. Sept. 12. (25.)
Tough. Ly. Mar. 21. (37.)
DAVIES, OMA ALMONA. (See 1924.)
Bargain with Fate. G. H. Feb. (76.)
Eben and Ezer. S. E. P. June 13.
(18.)
Friend fur Apple Butter. S. E. P.
May 9. (18.)
Ground for Divorcement. S. E. P.
Apr. 11. (34.)
Hind End Frontmost. S. E. P. Sept.
12. (30.)
Just a Way to Go. G. H. Aug. (84.)
Kind fur Kind. S. E. P. Oct. 4, '24.
(20.)
Ten Cents a Cone Yet. S. E. P.
July 4. (8.)
Two Girls to Oncet. S. E. P. Dec. 6,
'24. (12.)
DAVIS, AARON. (See 1924.)
Bull of Bashan. S. E. P. May 9.
(24.)
Kitchen Cabinet. S. E. P. May 30.
(39.)
Opalescent Bore. S. E. P. Mar. 28.
(17.)
Polka-Dot Hounds. S. E. P. Oct. 25,
'24. (42.)
Simon Called Peter. S. E. P. Mar 7.
(20.)
DAVIS, ELMER HOLMES. (1890–   .)
(See 1924.)
Jeshurun. Col. Jan. 31. (10.)
No Girl. Col. Jan. 3. (8.)
DAVIS, LOUISE TAYLOR.
Hour at Tranquillity. Des. June.
(14.)
DAVIS, MARTHA KING.
Qualifying of Vivian. Hol. Feb.
(12.)
DAVIS, RICHARD HARDING. (1864–1916.)
(See 1918.) (H.)

**Consul. (R.) Ev. July. (111.)
***Walk Up the Avenue. (R.) Gol.
Jan. (1: 37.)
DAY, LILLIAN. (See 1923.)
Brief-Case Men. Hol. Feb. (22.)
DE BURGH, ELIZABETH.)
**Mrs. Buckle. Atl. Jan. (135: 105.)
DELAND, MARGARET WADE (CAMPBELL).
(1857–   .) (See 1915.) (H.)
**Third Volume. (R.) G. B. May.
(1: 702.)
DELANO, EDITH BARNARD. (See 1924.)
(See "H" under BARNARD and
DELANO.)
**Face of the Waters. L. H. J. May.
(12.)
**Resurrection. L. H. J. July. (14.)
Three Wise Men. L. H. J. Dec., '24.
(3.)
DE LEON, WALTER. (See 1924.)
Beautiful and the Dumb. Red Bk.
Nov., '24. (63.)
Claudia and the Fired Man. Red Bk.
Mar. (66.)
Green Complex. Red Bk. Sept. (82.)
Locke and Keyes. Hear. Dec., '24.
(32.)
Prof. B. B.'s Mary. Ly. May 31, '24.
(49.)
DELL, FLOYD. (1887–   .) (See 1924.)
(H.)
***Hallelujah, I'm a Bum! Cen. June.
(110: 137.)
Runaway. W. H. C. Oct., '24. (15.)
DERIEUX, SAMUEL A. (1881–1922.) (See
1924.)
Old Man Trouble. Col. Sept. 12.
(20.)
DETZER, KARL W. (See 1924.)
Red in the Devil's Hair. Ev. Dec.,
'24. (79.)
*Landman. Col. Aug. 15. (28.)
DEUTSCH, HERMANN BACHER. (See 1922.)
*Man who Did not Matter. Cos. July.
(40.)
Slunge. Col. Sept. 12. (7.)
*Queen of the Turf. Col. July 25. (5.)
Roughneck and the Lady. Cos. April.
(80.)
DE VOTO, BERNARD.
Lesion. Guar. Dec., '24. (4.)
DEXTER, GAYNE.
*Broadway Forever. Ev. Mar. (99.)
Fiddling Fool. Ly. Nov. 8, '24. (32.)
Lulu — She Steals the Show. Ev.
Feb. (72.)
*Serpent of Lies. Cos. Aug. (64.)
Shark Bait. Cos. Sept. (102.)
Society Stuff. Ev. April. (143.)
Star-Maker. Ev. Jan. (30.)
DIAMANT, GERTRUDE.
*Channa Makes Her Bed. Men. J.
Feb. (11: 1.)
DICKENSON, EDWIN COLE. (See 1918.)
Jonesy Gets His Swim. Scr. April.
(77: 385.)
DICKENSON, MAY FREUD. (See 1924.)
***Mouse. A. Merc. July, '24. (2: 357.)

ELLARD, GERALD.
Lady Miriam's Christmas Story.
Cath. W. Dec., '24. (120: 355.)
ELLERBE, ALMA MARTIN ESTABROOK.
(1871–   .), and ELLERBE, PAUL
LEE. (See 1924.) (See "H" under
ELLERBE, PAUL LEE.)
*Battle Axe. Col. Sept. 5. (20.)
*Doors. Del. Feb. (11.)
Pack Rat Springs the Trap. Col.
Oct. 4, '24. (16.)
**Services Rendered. Col. Aug. 8.
(12.)
Sunshine, Fresh Air, and a View.
W. H. C. Oct., '24. (27.)
**$2,000.00 Reward. Cos. Mar. (98.)
*Woman Nothing Ever Happened To.
W. W. Nov., '24. (5.)
ELLIOTT, JOHN L.
Yippy. Cen. July. (110: 292.)
ELMALEH, LEON H. See SOLIS-COHEN,
JUDITH and ELMALEH, LEON H.
EMERY, STEUART M. (See 1924.)
Homer Becomes Himself. Hol. June.
(14.)
Wild, Wild Child. Ly. Jan. 31. (13.)
With Interest to Date. Hol. May.
(5.)
EMMETT, ELIZABETH. (See 1924.)
Moon and Michael. Hol. July.
(14.)
ENGLAND, GEORGE ALLAN. (1877–   .)
(See 1923.) (H.)
Half a Brick. S. E. P. June 6. (22.)
ERSKINE, LAURIE YORK. (See 1924.)
Pictures. Ev. Nov., '24. (28.)
EVANS, IDA MAY. (See 1924.) (H.)
Achilles Always Has His Heel.
S. E. P. Nov. 8, '24. (22.)
Daughter of a Hawk. Red Bk. Sept.
(78.)
Little Devil. Red Bk. Aug. (52.)
Man's Money's Worth. S. E. P.
Nov. 29, '24. (36.)
Secret Room. Red Bk. June. (51.)
Spendthrift. Hear. Feb. (50.)
Su Sam Sa. Chic. Trib. July 19.
We Knew Him When——. Cos. Aug.
(72.)
EVERMAN, PAUL. (See 1924.)
*Ashen-Yellow. A. W. Oct., '24. (9.)

F

FAGIN, N. BRYLLION. (See 1924.)
***Buttoned Up. Pear. (Am.) Feb.
(48.)
FANLET, GEORGE.
Lie. Echo. Sept. (5.)
FARAGOH, FRANCIS EDWARDS. (See 1924.)
*Bessie Goes Steady. Pict. R. Oct.,
'24. (24.)
FARIS, PHOEBE O'NEALL. (See 1924.)
Moon's Laws. Des. April. (14.)
FARNHAM, W. I.
Professor Highbrow's Mule. Hol.
Sept. (14.)
FARRAR, JOHN CHIPMAN. (1896–   .)
(See 1922.)

Greatest Lover. Ev. Feb. (152.)
FERBER, EDNA. (1887–   .) (See 1924.)
(H.)
*Classified. Cos. Nov., '24. (16.)
**Mother Knows Best. Cos. April.
(28.)
FERNALD, CHESTER BAILEY. (1869–   .)
(See 1921.) (H.)
*Gentleman in the Barrel. (R.) Gol.
Mar. (1: 325.)
**Perhaps It Didn't Matter. (R.)
Gol. Sept. (2: 340.)
***Pot of Frightful Doom. (R.) Gol.
June. (1: 806.)
FIELD, EDWARD SALISBURY ("CHILDE
HAROLD.") (1878–   .) (H.)
Freedom First. S. E. P. May 30.
(14.)
Open Season. S. E. P. April 25.
(16.)
FINGER, CHARLES J. (1871–   .) (See
1924.)
*Count of St. Germain. Dearb. Ind.
May 30. (16.)
*Edward Wortley Montague. Dearb.
Ind. May 2. (16.)
*"Romeo" Coates. Dearb. Ind. May
16. (16.)
*Thomas Lodge. Dearb. Ind. June 27.
(16.)
*William Parsons, Esquire. Dearb.
Ind. June 13. (16.)
FISHER, DOROTHEA FRANCES CANFIELD.
See CANFIELD, DOROTHY.
FISHER, RUDOLPH. (1897–   .)
***City of Refuge. Atl. Feb. (135: 178.)
**Ringtail. Atl. May. (135: 652.)
FITZGERALD, FRANCIS SCOTT KEY. (1896–
    .) (See 1924.)
***Absolution. A. Merc. June, '24.
(2: 141.)
**Adjuster. Red Bk. Sept. (47.)
*Baby Party. Hear. Feb. (32.)
Love in the Night. S. E. P. Mar. 14.
(18.)
*One of My Oldest Friends. W. H. C.
Sept. (7.)
**Our Own Movie Queen. Chic. Trib.
June 7.
**Pusher-in-the-Face. W. H. C. Feb.
(27.)
Sensible Thing. Ly. July 5, '24.
(10.)
FITZGERALD, W. G. See "PHAYRE,
IGNATIUS."
FOLSOM, ELIZABETH IRONS. (1876–   .)
(See 1924.)
End of the World. Hol. Nov., '24.
(20.)
*Miracle of Love. Macf. Dec., '24.
(12.)
FORD, SEWELL. (1868–   .) (See 1924.)
(H.)
*Coots, S. E. P. Mar. 14. (16.)
*Easing In with Egbert. S. E. P.
Nov. 29, '24. (32.)
Enter Emil the Deuce. Ly. July 25.
(5.)

INDEX OF SHORT STORIES

KEMPTON, KENNETH PAYSON. (1891– .) (See 1923.)
Bale. Chic. Trib. Mar. 29.
Clear Havana. Col. Aug. 1. (15.)

KERR, SOPHIE. (1880– .) (See "H" under UNDERWOOD, SOPHIE KERR.)
And on the Other Hand —. Pict. R. Oct., '24. (14.)
Featherheads. S. E. P. Jan. 10. (42.)
Jeanne and Louise Were Friends. W. H. C. Jul. (14.)
Mary Could Cook. L. H. J. Jun. (32.)
No Man's Gift. Del. Apr. (6.)
Puddle Duck. S. E. P. Oct. 25, '24. (12.)
Tears. S. E. P. Mar. 21. (18.)
Tempered Peace. W. H. C. Oct., '24. (18.)
Something Good. S. E. P. Aug. 15. (18.)

KIELAR, WILLIAM J.
Getting Rid of Macklin. McC. Sept. (1: 720.)

KILBOURNE, FANNIE. ("MARY ALEX-ANDER.") (See 1924.)
*Battle of the Honeymoon. Am. Nov., '24. (39.)
Clinging Vine. Red Bk. Dec., '24. (68.)
Cynthia Comes Out. S. E. P. Apr. 4. (12.)
Dulcie Gets into the Rough. Am. Jan. (8.)
Education of Sally May. Col. May 23. (7.)
Gossip. Am. Mar. (13.)
Nancy Goes Romance Hunting. Am. Feb. (38.)
Kathleen's Mother. L. H. J. Aug. (8.)
Twins! Am. Dec., '24. (21.)
Will Deals With the Trouble-Maker. Am. Sept. (21.)
Will Keeps His Eye on the Ball. Am. Jul. (39.)
Woman's Place Is in the Home. S. E. P. Nov. 15, '24. (28.)

KILMAN, JULIAN. (1878– .) (See 1923.)
Fetters of Youth. Echo. Jul. (1.)
Old Fumble Fingers. Echo. Mar. (1.)

KING, WILLIAM BENJAMIN BASIL. (1850– .) (See 1918.) (H.)
*Heaven. Cos. Dec., '24. (82.)

KIRK, R. G. (See 1924.)
Air Hose. S. E. P. May 9. (16.)
Twenty-Third Degree. S. E. P. Oct. 18, '24. (14.)

KNAPP, ETHEL MARJORIE.
Temptation. Strat. Jan. (4: 12.)

KNOWLTON, CLARKE. (See 1924.)
***Bridegroom. Scr. Jun. (77: 629.)
***Lost Story. Scr. Aug. (78: 173.)

KOMROFF, MANUEL. (1890–.) (See 1924.)
***Beating of the Reeds. Guar. May-Jun. (1: 314.)

***Grace of Lambs. Atl. Mar. (135:376.)
***How Does It Feel to Be Free. Atl. Sept. (136: 329.)

KREBS, ROLAND.
Airy Adrienne Takes the Air. S. E. P. Sept. 5. (12.)
Go West, Young Woman. S. E. P. Sept. 26. (52.)

KUMMER, FREDERICK ARNOLD. (1873– .) (See 1924.) (H.)
Diamond Cut Diamond. Ly. Dec. 13, '24. (40.)
Transaction in Pearls. Ly. Nov. 22, '24.

KYNE, PETER BERNARD. (1880– . (See 1924.) (H.)
Bluebird. Cos. Feb. (16.)
Cappy Ricks and the Mystic Isles. Cos. Mar. (36.)
Lonely Man of Pahang. Cos. May. (50.)
Thoroughbreds. Cos. Sept. (50.)

L

LADD, FREDERIC P.
Mr. Bulltaker's Ladder. Hol. Apr. (15.)

LANE, D. R. (See 1924.)
Illegal Attachment. Sun. Nov., '24. (30.)

LANE, ROSE WILDER. (1877– .) (See 1924.)
*The Blue Bead. Harp. M. Jun. (150: 34.)

LAPE, FREDERICK H.
Mrs. McCumber. Col. May 9. (22.)

LARDNER, RING. W. (1885– .) (See 1923. (H.)
***Haircut. Ly. Mar. 28. (5.)
**Love Nest. Cos. Aug. (52.)
*Mr. and Mrs. Fix-It. Ly. May 9. (5.)
*Women. Ly. Jun. 20. (5.)
***Zone of Quiet. Cos. Jun. (44.)

LARSSON, GENEVIEVE. (See 1924.)
**Astrid and the Hill Folk. Pict. R. Dec., '24. (12.)

LATHROP, HARLEY P. (See 1923.)
Fightin' Heart of a Mick. Ly. Nov. 22, '24.

LATIMER, MARGERY. (See 1924.)
*Possession. Echo. Feb. (5.)

LAURISTON, VICTOR.
Not Black, nor White, but Gray. Hol. Apr. (22.)

LAWLOR, MARGRETTA SCOTT.
*John O'Keefe, the Blacksmith. D. D. Apr. (7:123.)

LAZARUS, SIDNEY F. (See 1924.)
Me and Hercules. S. E. P. Jul. 4. (18.)
That Patterson Girl. S. E. P. May 23. (24.)

LEA, FANNIE HEASLIP. (MRS. H. P. AGEE.) (1884– .) (See 1924.) (H.)
Bon Voyage. G. H. Oct., '24. (26.)
Dusk to Dawn. G. H. Jan. (26.)
Mr. Conway's Femme. S. E. P. May 16. (8.)

M

MABIE, LOUISE KENNEDY. (See 1924.)
(H.)
Prairie's Double Chin. L. H. J.
Feb. (16.)

MacALARNEY, ROBERT EMMET. (1873–
.) (See 1924.) (H.)
Gone to Glory. Col. Feb. 28. (5.)
Gunman's Widow. Ly. June 7,
'24. (12.)

McBLAIR, ROBERT. (See 1922.)
Miss DeGraff's Geranium. Pict. R.
May. (10.)

McCARDELL, ROY LARCOM. (1870– .)
Highboy and His Hannah. S. E. P.
Dec. 6, '24. (30.)

McCARTER, MARGARET HILL.
Candle in the Window. McCall.
Dec., '24. (10.)

McCLELLAND, MARION.
Not on the Bill. Col. Oct. 4, '24.
(14.)

McCLUNG, NELLIE LETITIA MOONEY.
(1873– .) (H.)
*Neutral Fuse. MacL. Dec. 1, '24.
(28.)

McCLURE, JOHN. (See 1924.)
*Grammarian. A. Merc. Dec., '24.
(3:399.)

McCoy, SAMUEL DUFF. (1882– .) (H.)
Prudence. Col. Oct. 18, '24. (10.)

McCULLUM, MELLA RUSSELL. (See 1924.)
Another Day. Col. Nov. 8, '24. (18.)
Roots. Col. Aug. 29. (28.)

MacDONALD, EDWINA LEVIN. (See 1924.)
Black and White Magic. Ev. May.
(14.)

MacDONALD, HAZEL CHRISTIE.
Husband for George-Anne. S. E. P.
Feb. 7. (16.)
Jo-Jo and the Marvelous Prince.
Hol. Dec., '24. (7.)

McDONALD, ROBERTA.
In the Tennessee Hills. McC. Jun.
(1:37.)

McFADDEN, MARION.
*Pescecani. Ind. May 9. (114:521.)

McGEEHAN, W. O. (1879– .) (See
1924.)
Barber of Broadway. Col. Nov. 1,
'24. (14.)
Nerve. Ly. Aug. 29. (12.)
Slide Trombone. Ly. May 23. (33.)
This Sporting Life. Col. Dec. 13,
'24. (5.)
Those Fearful Fillies. Ly. Jul. 4.
(44.)

MacGILL, CAROLINE E. (See 1924.)
Downfall of Sister Winefride. Cath.
W. Oct., '24. (120:81.)
Old Path. Cath. W. Jun. (121:334.)
Soul at the Crossroads. Cath. W.
Jan. (120:504.)
Way of Ethel Holroyd. Cath. W.
Jul. (121:503.)

MacGRATH, HAROLD. (1871– .) (See
1924.) (H.)
Cellini Plaque. S. E. P. Jan. 17. (5.)

Two Faces. Ly. Jan. 10. (32.)
Sporting Spinster. S. E. P. Feb. 7.
(8.)

McINTYRE, O. O.
That Glee-or-ious Fourth. Cos.
Jul. (60.)

MACKENDRICK, MARDA. (See 1919.)
Sunlight. Hol. Dec, '24. (18.)

McMORROW, THOMAS. (See 1924.)
All in the Family. S. E. P. Oct. 11,
'24. (12.)
And All Things Else. S. E. P. Jan. 3.
(20.)
Anything to Oblige. S. E. P. Feb. 21,
(30.)
Appointed Task. S. E. P. May 30.
(12.)
As It Was in the Beginning. S. E. P.
May 23. (40.)
Candidate. S. E. P. Oct. 25, '24.
(14.)
Counselor Ambrose Hinkle. S. E. P.
Jun. 6. (5.)
Found Money. S. E. P. Mar. 14.
(14.)
Give a Man Luck. S. E. P. Feb. 7.
(18.)
In Re Dollar-a-Step Company.
S. E. P. Jul. 18. (12.)
Joe Yorick Strives to Please. S. E. P.
Dec. 13, '24. (22.)
Mr. Pethick Meets the Check-
Grabbers. S. E. P. Feb. 28. (10.)
People Against Foleron. S. E. P.
Aug. 1. (12.)
People Against Hylebut. S. E. P.
Jun. 27. (12.)
People Against Joynes. S. E. P.
Sept. 26, '24. (22.)
Those Were the Happy Days. S. E. P.
Jan. 10. (14.)
Votes for Women. S. E. P. Nov. 8,
'24. (16.)

McNARY, HERBERT L.
Hail! Hail! the Gang's All Here. Col.
Jan. 17. (10.)

McNUTT, WILLIAM SLAVENS. (See 1924.)
(H.)
Boy from the Patch. Col. Nov. 29,
'24. (10.)
Buddy's One Idea. Ev. Aug. (75.)
Course of Blue Love. Col. Oct. 25,
'24. (10.)
Harbor Luck. Col. Aug. 22. (7.)
In Business for Himself. Col. Feb. 7.
(7.)
It's a Great Game. Ly. Apr. 11.
(35.)
Money Ain't Everything. Ly. Jul.
18. (15.)
Strong. Ly. Feb. 7. (16.)
Temporarily Out of Order. Ly.
May 17, '24. (7.)
Jazz Justice. Col. Dec. 27, '24.
(5.)

MARKET, CORINNE HARRIS. (See 1923.)
*Mystery of Room 513. Am. Dec.,
'24. (9.)

MITCHELL, RUTH COMFORT. (MRS. SANBORN YOUNG.) (See 1924.) (H.)
Blood and Tears. Red Bk. Feb. (43.)
Contempt of Families. W. H. C. Jul. (9.)
Crossroads. Red Bk. May. (84.)
Into Her Kingdom. Red Bk. Mar. (71.)
I Saw Three Ships Go Sailing By! W. H. C. Jan. (17.)
Little Sister. Red Bk. Jun. (80.)

MONTAGUE, MARGARET PRESCOTT. (1878– .) (See 1924.) (H.)
***Great Theme. N. A. Rev. Mar. (221: 522.)
***Roots. Atl. Aug. (136: 230.)

MONTGOMERY, LUCY MAUD. (MRS. EWEN MACDONALD.) (1874– .) (H.)
*Enter, Emily. Del. Jan. (10.)
*Her Dog Day. Del. Apr. (10.)
*Night Watch. Del. Mar. (10.)
*Too Few Cooks. Del. Feb. (10.)

MONTROSS, LOIS SEYSTER. (See 1924.)
Almost a Giant. G. H. Apr. (30.)
Boys in the House. Pict. R. May. (28.)
*Clever Accomplice. S. E. P. Apr. 18. (12.)
Georgy and the Dragon. Pict. R. Jul. (10.)
*Georgy Porgy, Prodigy. Pict. R. Jun. (12.)
Miss Ferry and Mr. Barge. Pict. R. Mar. (10.)

MOONE, LORNA. (See 1924.)
***Wantin' a Hand. Cen. Nov., '24. (109: 15.)

MOROSO, JOHN ANTONIO. (1874– .) (See 1924.) (H.)
*Ladders McLaughlin. Hol. Mar. (8.)

MORRIS, GOUVERNEUR. (1876– .) (See 1924.) (H.)
Wooing Without Words. Cos. Oct., '24. (52.)

MORRIS, HILDA. (See 1924.)
House That Waited. Hol. Jun. (17.)

MORRIS, LAWRENCE S. (1894– .) (See 1924.)
***Apples of Gold or Pictures of Silver. Scr. Jun. (77: 619.)

MORROW, HONORE MCCUE WILLSIE. (See 1924 and "H" under WILLSIE, HONORE.)
*Lost Speech. Del. Feb. (5.)

MORSE, STEARNS.
**Last House. Mid. Oct., '24. (10: 359.)

MORTON, LEIGH. (See 1924.)
Three Moments. Scr. Mar. (77: 290.)

MOSLEY, JEFFERSON.
***Secret at the Crossroads. For. Nov., '24. (72: 577.)

MULLEN, KATE. (See 1924.)
***Interval. For. Jan. (73: 79.)

MUNSTERBERG, MARGARETE.
*Aunt Minna. Strat. Nov., '24. (3: 171.)

MYGATT, GERALD. (See 1924.) (H.)
First Requisite. Col. Mar. 28. (15.)
Marjorie's Mirage. W. H. C. May. (23.)
Minus Romance. Col. Jan. 3. (15.)

N

NASON, LEONARD H.
Reward of Valor. Ly. Jul. 18. (5.)
Tank and the Doctor. Ly. Sept. 5. (21.)

NEALL, NOAH WEBSTER.
Innocent Husband. Hear. Nov., '24. (80.)

NEIDIG, WILLIAM JONATHAN. (1870– .) (See 1923.) (H.)
Blue Diamonds. S. E. P. Aug. 15. (8.)
Go to the Fire Ant. S. E. P. Mar. 7. (14.)
Walled Out. Red Bk. Jan. (85.)

NEWMAN, OLIVER PECK. (See 1922.)
Girl in the Cabinet. McCall. Apr. (14.)

"NEYO, BELLA." See COHEN, BELLA.

NICHOLL, LOUISE TOWNSEND. (See 1923.)
*Enchanted Kingdom. Cen. Nov., '24. (109: 41.)
***Green Ice. Cen. Mar. (109: 666.)

NORDHOFF, CHARLES B. (1887– .) (See 1922.)
*Man Who Was Laid on the Shelf. Hear. Feb. (16.)
*Thin Skin of Civilization. Hear. Oct., '24. (58.)

NORRIS, (BENJAMIN) FRANK(LIN). (1870–1902.) (H.)
***Grettir at Drangey. (R.) Gol. Jul. (2: 25.)

NORRIS, KATHLEEN. (1880– .) (See 1924.) (H.)
June Week. Cos. Dec., '24. (48.)
*Landslide. G. H. Jun. (22.)
***Masterpiece. Cos. Feb. (32.)

O

O'BRIEN, FITZJAMES. (1828–1862.)
***What Was It? (R.) Gol. Sept. (2: 365.)

O'BRIEN, JEAN.
Letters to Imaginary Mothers. Hol. Jun. (26.)

O'HAGAN, ANNE. (ANNE O'HAGAN SHINN.) (1869– .) (See 1923.) (H.)
Fire! Fire! Del. Jun. (14.)
Morey Wins His Heart's Desire. Chic. Trib. Feb. 15.

O'HARA, FRANK HURBURT. (See 1917.)
Story the Editor Didn't Want. W. H. C. Apr. (27.)

O'HIGGINS, HARVEY JERROLD. (1876– .) (See 1920.) (H.)
Burton Murder. Red Bk. Mar. (27.)
Forged Letter. Red Bk. Apr. (42.)

TRAIN, ETHEL KISSAM. (1875–   .)
(See 1923.) (H.)
Somebody Wants Me. Des. Oct., '24.
(12.)

TURNBULL, AGNES SLIGH. (See 1924.)
*False Barriers. Am. Feb. (8.)
Jessica Revives a Faded Petunia.
Am. Apr. (13.)
"So This is Life!" Am. Aug. (51.)

TURNBULL, ARCHIBALD DOUGLAS. (See
1924.)
Standing By. Hol. Nov., '24. (11.)

TURNER, GEORGE KIBBE. (1869–   .)
(See 1924.) (H.)
At the Murderer's Ball. Ly. May 16.
(5.)
Hen on Wheels. S. E. P. Feb. 14.
(24.)
No Questions Asked. Ly. Aug. 15.
(8.)
Street of the Forgotten Men. Ly.
Feb. 14. (17.)

TUTTLE, WORTH. (See 1924.)
*Color. Pear. (Am.) Oct., '24. (30.)
Yellow Seal. Ly. Jan. 10. (20.)

"TWAIN, MARK." (SAMUEL LANGHORNE
CLEMENS.) (1835–1910.) (See 1921.)
(H.)
***Mrs. McWilliams and the Lightning.
(R.) Gol. July. (2:61.)
***Notorious Jumping Frog of Calaveras
County. (R.) Gol. Jan. (1:105.)

U

UPSON, WILLIAM HAZLETT. (See 1924.)
Buzz Saw. Col. Jul. 11. (12.)
Charlie the Gloom Hound. S. E. P.
Jun. 13. (12.)
*Croix de Guerre. Col. Feb. 28. (11.)
Elephant. S. E. P. Apr. 25. (20.)
I'm in a Hurry. Col. May 2. (18.)
I Got a Swell Job, I Got a Peach of a
Girl. S. E. P. Aug. 29. (5.)
November 11, 1918. Col. Nov. 15,
'24. (10.)
Sun at St. Mihiel. S. E. P. May 2.
(28.)

V

VAN DE WATER, FREDERICK F. (See 1924.)
Dope. S. E. P. Feb. 14. (5.)
Faker. S. E. P. Apr. 11. (14.)
Horse Marine. S. E. P. Jan. 17.
(10.)
Three Minutes of Silent Prayer.
Scr. Dec., '24. (76:615.)

VAN DINE, WARREN L. (1902–   .)
(See 1924.)
*Prophet. I. L. M. Mar. (32.)

VAN DOREN, CARL.
**Boy on a Horse. Cen. Feb. (109:
561.)

VAN HISE, ALICE.
" 'Tis Better to Have Loved and
Lost —." Pict. R. Nov., '24. (30.)

VAN VORST, MARIE. (MRS. GAETANO
GAGIATI.) (See 1924.) (H.)
Who Follows—? Pict. R. May. (14.)

VANCE, LOUIS JOSEPH. (1879–   .) (H.)
Grey Flannels. McCall. Jan. (5.)
Gulp Stream. McCall. Oct., '24. (5.)
White Fire. Col. Aug. 1. (5.)

VANCE, LOUIS JOSEPH, and VERNEY,
FRANK E.
Base Methods. S. E. P. Jun. 6.
(16.)
Mad Dogs and the Minnow. S. E. P.
May 16. (20.)

VENABLE, EDWARD CARRINGTON. (1884–
    .) (See 1924.)
***Lines on the Portrait of a Lady.
Scr. Jun. (77:593.)
**Spur of the Moment. Atl. Jun.
(135:808.)

VERNEY, FRANK E. See also VANCE,
LOUIS JOSEPH and VERNEY, FRANK E.
**Man Between. Pict. R. Jun. (14.)

VITEZ, MIKLOS.
*Flunked. Am. H. Nov. 7, '24. (808.)

VORSE, MARY HEATON. (See 1924.) (H.)
**Big Fish. L. H. J. Dec., '24. (20.)
*Family. Col. Dec. 20, '24. (10.)
*First Stone. Red. Bk. Dec., '24. (56.)
***Sand. Pict. R. Jul. (14.)

VOTO, BERNARD DE. See DE VOTO,
BERNARD.

W

WALDMAN, MILTON. (1895–   .)
***Home Town. L. Merc. Dec., 24.
(11: 132.)

WALKER, HELEN. (See 1924.)
**Forbidden Disciple. Com. Apr. 8.
(1: 601.)

WALKER, ISABEL, and REDINGTON, HELEN.
Silver Shoon. Del. Jun. (10.)

WALMSLEY, STEPHEN M.
Reconstruction. Ev. Jan. (82.)

WALROND, ERIC.
Voodoo's Revenge. Opp. Jun.
(3: 209.)

WARD, FLORENCE BAIER.
Where the Road Forked. L. H. J.
Mar. (18.)

WATER, FREDERICK F. VAN DE. See
VAN DE WATER, FREDERICK F.

WATTS, CLAUDE SAMUEL. (1877–   .)
(See 1924.) (H.)
Deviled Crabs. McC. Sept. (1: 760.)
Good Bad Actor. S. E. P. Aug. 15.
(49.)

WEEKS, RAYMOND. (1863–   .) (See
1924.)
**On the Road to the Big Blue. Mid.
Jan. 1. (11: 19.)
*Fat Women of Boone. Mid. Jan. 1.
(11: 1.)
*Snakes of Boone. Mid. Jan. 1.
(11: 12.)
*Thou Canst Not Say I Didn't. Mid.
Jan. 1. (11: 27.)
**Two Gentlemen from Indiany. Mid.
Jan. 1. (11: 23.)

WEIMAN, RITA. (1889–   .) (See 1924.)
*Laughing Legacy. S. E. P. Aug. 15.
(5.)

WILLIAMS, JESSE LYNCH. (1871–　.)
(See 1924.) (H.)
　Actress and the Lady. Cos. Oct., '24.
　(24.)
WILLIAMS, MICHAEL. (1877–　.) (H.)
　*Coca Dope. Blue Bk. Apr. (47.)
　*False Face. Com. Dec. 3, '24. (1: 98.)
WILLIAMS, URSULA TRAINOR.
　Will Turner's Wife. For. Jul. (74:
　92.) (H.)
WILLIAMS, WILLIAM D. (H.)
　Last Choice of Crusty Dick. McC.
　Aug. (1: 568.)
WILLIAMS, WYTHE. (1881–　.)
　Splendid with Swords. S. E. P.
　Sept. 19. (26.)
WILLIS, WINIFRED.
　Clothes — or the Man. Col. Dec.
　20, '24. (22.)
WILLOUGHBY, BARRETT. (See 1924.)
　***Devil-Drum. Cen. Jan. (109: 393.)
WILLSIE, HONORE. See MORROW, HONORE
　WILLSIE.
WILSON, EDMUND.
　**Dandy Day. N. Rep. Aug. 19.
　(43: 348.)
WILSON, JOHN FLEMING. (1887–　.)
　(See 1920.) (H.)
　*Desert. Sh. St. Oct. 10, '24. (40.)
WILSON, MARY BADGER.
　Personal and Private. L. H. J. Nov.,
　'24. (12.)
WINSLOW, HORATIO. (See 1924.) (H.)
　Art Line. S. E. P. Aug. 29. (10.)
　Bimbo the Blood. S. E. P. Aug. 1.
　(8.)
　Cockatoo. S. E. P. Jul. 11. (8.)
　Confidential: Please Destroy. S. E. P.
　Oct. 18, '24. (18.)
　Didos: Official Report. S. E. P. Nov.
　22, '24. (8.)
　Grudge Fight. S. E. P. Sept. 26. (18.)
　Please Excuse Me. S. E. P. Apr. 4.
　(10.)
　Told to the Sporting Editor. S. E. P.
　Nov. 1, '24. (12.)
WINSMORE, ROBERT S. (See 1924.)
　Blind Spots. S. E. P. Mar. 14. (18.)
　Conover Crowd. S. E. P. Nov. 1, '24.
　(14.)
　Major's Monument. S. E. P. Jan. 3.
　(6.)
WISTER, OWEN. (1860–　.) (See 1924.)
　(H.)
　***La Tinaja Bonita. (R.) Gol. Jun.
　(1: 781.)
　***Second Missouri Compromise. (R.)
　Gol. Feb. (1: 178.)
　***Specimen Jones. (R.) Gol. Jan.
　(1: 109.)
WITWER, HARRY CHARLES. (1890–　.)
　(See 1924.)
　Charlotte's Ruse. Col. Nov. 15, '24.
　(5.)
　Chin He Loved to Touch. Cos. Aug.
　(93.)

5th Horseman of the Apocalypse.
　Cos. Feb. (59.)
Food for Scandal. Cos. Oct., '24.
　(46.)
Hood Riding Little Red. Cos. Apr.
　(94.)
Lady of Lyons, N. Y. Col. Jul. 18.
　(5.)
Love at First Fight. Cos. Jan. (54.)
Not So Big. Cos. Jun. (76.)
Pigskin He Loved to Touch. Cos.
　Dec., '24. (67.)
Scrambled Yeggs. Col. Oct. 4, '24.
　(5.)
So This is New York. Col. Aug. 8.
　(5.)
Survival of the Fattest. Cos. Nov.,
　'24. (339.)
Two Gentlemen of Verona, N. J.
　Cos. Sept. (85.)
WOLFF, WILLIAM ALMON. (1885–　.)
　(See 1924.) (H.)
　Dead Fall. Des. Dec., '24. (12.)
　Goddess of Chance. Des. Oct., '24.
　(14.)
　Little Upstart Brook. Ev. Aug.
　(60.)
　Rope That Wasn't Long Enough.
　Ly. May 10, '24. (37.)
　Thrift. Ly. Oct. 18, '24. (35.)
　Town Talk. Des. Jan. (14.)
　Tremper's Folly. Des. Nov., '24.
　(14.)
WOLFF, WILLIAM ALMON, and JOHNSON,
　AGNES C.
　Two Left Feet. Ly. Sept. 19. (48.)
WOOD, CLEMENT. (1888–　.) (See
　1924.)
　***Blue Circle. Int. Arts. Jun. (1: 17.)
　***Mother. Opp. Jul. (214.)
　***Trazan. Pict. R. Apr. (10.)
WOOD, JULIA FRANCES. (See 1924.) (H.)
　According to Code. Chic. Trib.
　Aug. 30.
WOODFORD, JACK.
　Kid's Old Lady. Echo. Aug. (12.)
　Only Beautiful Thing Left. Echo.
　May. (1.)
WOODROW, MRS. WILSON. (NANCY MANN
　WADDEL WOODROW.) (See 1924.)
　(H.)
　Heavy Sugar. Ly. Aug. 8. (17.)
WORCESTER, LUCY.
　Two Peters. Des. Aug. (14.)
WORTS, GEORGE FRANK. (1892–　.)
　(See 1923.)
　Message to the Maharajah. Col.
　Dec. 13, '24. (10.)
　When the Red Star Rises. Ev. Jul.
　(9.)
WYCKOFF, ELIZABETH PORTER. (See 1923.)
　Now Consider Theresa. W. H. C.
　Dec., '24. (32.)
WYLIE, ELINOR. (See 1924.)
　***Gideon's Revenge. Cen. Jan. (109:
　305.)

Y

YORE, CLEM.
Mile High Monte of the Bell Bar
Bell. Ev. Sept. (44.)
Tinker and Tick. C. G. Jul. 11. (10.)

YOUNG, EVERETT.
Diana and the House of Hate. Del.
Jul. (7.)
Exiles. W. H. C. Jun. (7.)

II. BRITISH AND IRISH AUTHORS

A

ANONYMOUS
Great Boar of Birkatheli (R.)
Liv. A. Mar. 7. (324:547.)
"ARLEN, MICHAEL." (DIKRAN KUYUM-
JIAN.) (See 1923.)
***Ace of Thirteens. Cen. Oct., '24.
(108: 733.)
**Battle of Berkeley Square. Red Bk.
Apr. (60.)
**Duke of Ladies. Red Bk. Jan. (34.)
**Hand and Flower. Red Bk. May.
(46.)
**Knife Thrower. Red Bk. Jul. (46.)
**Legend of Isolda. Red Bk. Mar.
(33.)
*Man from America. Red Bk. Jun.
(66.)
***One Gold Coin. Book. (N. Y.) Jan.
(60: 556.) Feb. (60: 699.)
*Owl on the Fountain. Harp. B. Mar.
(70.)
**Salute Mr. Lancelot. Red Bk. Dec.,
'24. (42.)
ATKEY, BERTRAM. (1880–   .) (See
1924.)
Dimity Gay, Daddy's Good Girl.
S. E. P. Apr. 18. (3.)
Winnie and the Shark. S. E. P.
Nov. 8, '24. (18.)
AUMONIER, STACY. (1887–   .) (See
1924.)
**Baby Grand. Mun. Dec., '24.
(83: 428.)
***Dark Red Roses. Ev. Oct., '24.
(29.)
**Juxtapositions. Pict. R. Nov., '24.
(12.)
***Source of Irritation. (R.) Gol.
Sept. (2: 293.)
AUSTIN, FREDERICK BRITTEN. (1885–
.) (See 1924.) (H.)
**Battle Piece: New Style. S. E. P.
Jul. 25. (8.)
***Battle Piece: Old Style. S. E. P.
Jul. 18. (3.)
Diamond Cut Diamond. Red Bk.
Feb. (80.)
Fourth Degree. Red Bk. Oct., '24.
(62.)
Great Mallett Case. Red Bk. Jan.
(78.)
***On the Flagship. S. E. P. Jun. 13.
(10.)
One-Eyed Moor. Red Bk. Nov., '24.
(57.)
Paris Frock. Red Bk. Dec., '24.
(50.)
*When the War God Walks Again.
S. E. P. Jan. 17. (3.)

B

BAILY, FRANCIS EVANS. (1887–   .)
(See 1924.)
Blessed Are the Shingled. S. E. P.
Aug. 1. (46.)
Thy Neighbor's Wife. Hear. Nov.,
'24. (58.)
BARRIE, SIR JAMES MATTHEW. (1860–
***Courting of T'nowhead's Bell. (R.)
Gol. Mar. (1: 445.)
BENNETT, ENOCH ARNOLD. (1867–   )
(See 1924.) (H.)
*Claribel. S. E. P. Aug. 22. (12.)
**Perfect Husband. Cos. Jan. (60.)
*Toreador. Col. Jan. 24. (7.)
***Umbrella. Col. Nov. 24, '24. (5.)
BENNETT, ROLF. (See 1922.)
***Bird of Fortune. Adv. Jul. 30.
(150.)
***Cask. Adv. Nov. 20, '24. (63.)
*Teeth of McClure. Adv. July 20.
(72.)
BENSON, EDWARD FREDERIC. (1867–
.) (See 1923.) (H.)
**Corstophine. Mun. Jan. (83: 623.)
BERESFORD, JOHN DAVYS. (1873–   .)
(See 1924.) (H.)
*Meeting Place. W. H. C. Feb. (12.)
*Three Cases. W. H. C. Nov., '24.
(7.)
BIBESCO, PRINCESS ELIZABETH. (See
1924.)
***"La Peronnière Letters." Chic. Trib.
Dec. 28, '24.
BOTTOME, PHYLLIS. (MRS. FORBES
DENNIS.) (See 1919.) (H.)
***Wonder-Child. Atl. Jan. (135: 48.)
BOWEN, ELIZABETH. (See 1924.)
*Parrot. Ev. Apr. (135.)
"BOWEN, MARJORIE." (GABRIEL MAR-
GARET VERE CAMPBELL COSTANZO
LONG.) (See 1924.) (H.)
Comfortable. Col. Mar. 14. (18.)
*Lady Who Lived in a Dream. MacL.
Oct. 15, '24. (19.)
Where Your Treasure Is. Chic. Trib.
Apr. 5.
BURDETT, OSBERT.
Perfect Host. (R.) Liv. A. Mar. 14.
(324: 614.)
BURKE, THOMAS. (1887–   .) (See
1924.)
***Spleen. (R.) Liv. A. Feb. 28. (324:
474.)

C

CHESTERTON, GILBERT KEITH. (1874–
.) (See 1924.) (H.)
***Arrow of Heaven. Col. Jul. 25. (12.)

CHESTERTON, GILBERT KEITH. (contd.)
***Asylum of Adventure. MacL. Nov.
   1, '24. (27.)
  **Chief Mourner of Marne. Harp. M.
   May. (150: 690.)
***Curse of the Golden Cross. Col.
   Jul. 11. (20.)
***Man with Two Beards. Harp. M.
   Apr. (150: 595.)
***Mirror of Death. Harp. M. Mar.
   (150: 394.)
***Oracle of the Dog. (R.) Gol. Sept.
   (2: 372.)
***Song of the Flying Fish. Harp. M.
   Jun. (150: 82.)
CHRISTIE, AGATHA.
   Mystery of the Spanish Shawl.
   Macf. Dec., '24. (38.)
CLIFFORD, SIR HUGH. (1866-   .) (See
   1917.)
***Further Side of Silence. (R.) Gol.
   Aug. (2: 159.)
***Lone-Hand Raid of Kûlop Sûmbing.
   Gol. Apr. (1: 485.)
COLLINS, DALE. (See 1924.)
  *God from Pennsylvania. Fron. Jun.
   (51.)
 **Good that is in the Worst of Us.
   Hear. Nov., '24. (32.)
  *Service to Science. Sun. Jan. (25.)
  *Surprise Island. Sun. Dec., '24. (20.)
COLUM, PADRAIC. (1881-   .) (See
   1924.)
***John Griggins — A Day in His Life.
   Com. Apr. 22, '25. (1: 657.)
  *Legend of Ys. Com. Sept. 23.
   (2:478.)
 **St. Martin and the Honest Man.
   Cen. Jun. (110: 238.)
  *Servitor. Com. Sept. 30. (2: 563.)
COPPARD, ALFRED EDGAR. (1878-   .)
   (See 1924.)
***Field of Mustard. Dial. Jul. (79: 47.)
COULDREY, OSWALD.
***Nandi in Pound. Atl. May. (135:602.)
COUTLER, GEOFFREY.
***Decoy. Tr. Oct., '24. (2: 365.)
COULTER, JOHN W.
 **Catholic Walks. (R.) Liv. A. Nov.
   22, '24. (323: 433.)
CUNNINGHAME GRAHAM, ROBERT BON-
   TINE. (1852-   .) (See 1920.)
***Convert. (R.) A. W. Aug.–Sept. (9.)

D

DATALLER, ROGER.
 **After-Meeting. (R.) Liv. A. Feb. 21.
   (324: 431.)
DAWSON, CONINGSBY (WILLIAM). (1883-
   .) (See 1922.) (H.)
  *Don's Garden. McCall. Mar. (11.)
DE LA MARE, WALTER JOHN. (1873-
   .) (See 1922.)
***Connoisseur. Yale. Jul. (14: 645.)
***Pigtails, Ltd. Atl. Aug. (136: 175.)
DELL, ETHEL M. (See 1924.) (H.)
   Full Measure. McCall. Jun. (5.)
   Master Key. McCall. Mar. (5.)

   Unknown Quantity. McCall. Oct.,
   '24. (22.)
DOUGLAS, NORMAN.
 **Queer! V. F. Jan. (46.)
DOYLE, SIR ARTHUR CONAN. (1859-   .)
   (See 1924.) (H.)
  *Billy Bones. G. H. Jun. (40.)
  *Adventure of the Three Garridebs.
   Col. Oct. 25, '24. (5.)
  *Adventure of the Illustrious Client.
   Col. Nov. 8, '24. (5.)
DUFFY, P. J. O'CONNOR. (See 1924.)
  *Boy from Gorthacaurnon. Cath. W.
   Jul. (121: 479.)
  *Colga MacCaffrey's Inheritance.
   Cath. W. Jan. (120: 477.)
 ·*Riches of the Poor Man. Cath. W.
   Nov., '24. (120: 203.)
  *Trenmore Jerningham. Cath. W.
   Mar. (120: 760.)
  *Woman of the Sea. Cath. W. May.
   (121: 208.)
DUKES, ASHLEY.
 *Listener. (R.) Liv. A. Oct. 11, '24.
   (323: 111.)
DUNSANY, EDWARD JOHN MORETON
   Drax Plunkett, 18th Baron. (1878-
) (See 1920.)
***Moral Little Tale. (R.) Gol. Sept.
   (2: 339.)

E

EDGINTON, MAY. (See 1924.) (H.)
   Love Reigneth Still. Pict.R. Aug. (10.)
  *This Happens Every Day. Pict. R.
   Feb. (12.)
   What Handsome People. S. E. P.
   Sept. 26. (24.)
   Why? Harp. B. Dec., '24. (76.)
EDWARDS, ETHEL ASHTON.
 *Clever Mr. Delavel. (R.) Liv. A.
   Mar. 28. (324: 708.)
ERTZ, SUSAN. (See 1924.)
  *Henry and the Muse. Pict. R. Aug.
   (15.)
ERVINE, ST. JOHN GREET. (1883-   .)
   (See 1915.) (H.)
***Mr. Peden Keeps His Cook. Cen.
   Dec., '24. (109: 195.)

F

FLETCHER, J. S. (See 1924.) (H.)
   Diamond Cut Diamond. Cos.Feb.(71.)
   Green Ink. Cos. Jan. (96.)

G

GALSWORTHY, JOHN. (1867-   .) (See
   1923.) (H.)
***Last Card. Red Bk. Feb. (48.)
***Mummy. Red Bk. Nov., '24. (68.)
***Water. Red Bk. Oct., '24. (43.)
GEORGE, WALTER LIONEL. (1882-
   (See 1922.)
  *Case of Olga Pennard. Ain. Dec.,
   '24. (129.)
  *Hand of Gladys Cockley. Pict. R.
   Sept. (7.)
   Last of His Line. Col. Oct.11,' 24. (15.)
  *Test. Charm. May. (11.)
  *Wedding of Ailie Fern. Col. Nov.
   22, '24. (5.)

WALPOLE, HUGH SEYMOUR. (contd.)
**Miss Finchley's Hour. G. H. Dec., '24. (14.)
***Old Elizabeth. G. H. Nov., '24. (46.)
WATSON, JOHN. See "MacLaren, Ian."
WELLS, CATHARINE. (MRS. H. G. WELLS.) (See 1924.) (H.)
*Dragon Fly. Tr. Nov., '24. (2: 511.)
WELLS, HERBERT GEORGE. (1866– .) (H.)
***Story of the Late Mr. Elvesham. (R.) Ev. Sept. (102.)
WETJEN, ALBERT RICHARD. (1900– .) (See 1924 under American Authors.)
*Admiral Jibbetts. Col. Mar. 14. (13.)
*Glory. Col. Sept. 26. (18.)
Heart of MacLoughlin. Ev. May. (55.)
*Mr. Atkins. Col. Mar. 28. (5.)
*North of the World. Sun. Mar. (22.)
**On the Coast Run. Col. Dec. 6, '24. (10.)
*'Ome Builder. Col. Feb. 21. (10.)
*Road of Adventure. Sh. St. Oct. 10, '24. (118.)
*Time. Col. Jan. 24. (14.)
*Tradition. Col. Apr. 18. (7.)
WHITECHURCH, VICTOR L. (H.)
*Adventure of Captain Ivan Koravitch. (R.) Gol. May. (1: 641.)
*In the House of the Mandarin. (R.) Liv. A. Nov. 1, '24. (323: 292.)
WILDRIDGE, OSWALD.
**Cotton Lord. Chic. Trib. Jul. 5.
WILLIAMS, I. A.
**Man Who Stole the Pelican. (R.) Liv. A. Dec. 6, '24. (323: 548.)
WILLIAMS, MARGERY. (MRS. FRANCESCO BIANCO.) (See 1924.)
*Nightingale Copse. H. C. Summer. (25.)
White Flower. Ev. Nov., '24. (172.)

WILLIAMSON, CHARLES NORRIS. (1859–?) and ALICE MURIEL LIVINGSTON. (1869– .) (See 1924.) (H.)
House of the Sun. Chic. Trib. Jan. 25.
WILLIAMSON, HENRY. (See 1924.)
***No Eel for Nog. Col. Apr. 11. (18.)
WODEHOUSE, PELHAM GRENVILLE. (1881– .) (See 1924.) (H.)
Awful Gladness of the Mater. S. E. P. Mar. 21. (10.)
Clustering Round Young Bingo. S. E. P. Feb. 21. (10.)
Custody of the Pumpkin. S. E. P. Nov. 29, '24. (5.)
High Stakes. S. E. P. Sept. 19. (8.)
Honeysuckle Cottage. S. E. P. Jan. 24. (8.)
Jane Gets Off the Fairway. S. E. P. Oct. 25, '24. (5.)
Purification of Rodney Spelvin. S. E. P. Aug. 22. (6.)
Something Squishy. S. E. P. Dec. 20, '24. (6.)
Without the Option. S. E. P. Jun. 27. (8.)
WOOLF, VIRGINIA. (See 1923.)
***Miss Ormerod. Dial. Dec., '24. (77: 466.)
WRYNN, ANTHONY.
Equinox. Dial. Sept. (79: 203.)
WYLIE, IDA ALENA ROSS. (1885– .) (See 1924.)
Exiles in Casserole. S. E. P. Feb. 21. (8.)
Mrs. Margrave Finds Her Children. G. H. Dec., '24. (70.)

Y

YATES, DORNFORD. (See 1924.)
Childish Things. S. E. P. Jun. 27. (43.)
Leading Strings. S. E. P. Nov. 22, '24. (18.)

III. TRANSLATIONS

A

ACREMANT, ALBERT. (See 1924.) (French.)
Assumed Name. N. Y. Trib. Apr. 12.
Sword Dancer of Montmartre. N. Y. Trib. Feb. 15.
ALARCON, PEDRO ANTONIO DE. (Spanish.)
***Captain Veneno's Proposal of Marriage. (R.) Gol. Jan. (1: 13.)
***Prophecy. (R.) Gol. Jun. (1: 812.)
ANDREYEV, LEONID NIKOLAEVICH. (1871–1919.) (See 1917.) (H.) (Russian.)
***Giant. Mod. Q. Fall, '24. (2: 119.)
ANNUNZIO, GABRIELE D'. (Italian.) See D'ANNUNZIO, GABRIELE.
ANONYMOUS. (German.)
*Mysterious Temple. (R.) Liv. A. Mar. 21. (324: 665.)
ARENNES, J. AD. (French.)
Purple Sweater. N. Y. Trib. Dec. 21, '24.

B

BACHELIN, HENRI. (See 1924.) (French.)
End of the Picture Auction. N. Y. Trib. Jun. 7.
BALZAC, HONORE DE. (1799–1850.) (See 1921.) (H.) (French.)
***El Verdugo. (R.) Gol. Apr. (1: 556.)
BARILLIER, BERTHE CARIANNE LE. See "BERTHEROY, JEAN."
BARJAC, CLAUDE. (See 1924.) (French.)
At the Season's End. N. Y. Trib. Oct. 19, '24.
"BERTHEROY, JEAN." (BERTHE CARIANNE LE BARILLIER.) (1860– .) (See 1924.) (French.)
*LeaningTower. N.Y. Trib. Oct. 5, '24.
Love Laughs Last and Best. N. Y. Trib. Jan. 18.
Wing Shot and Wounded Siren. N. Y. Trib. Nov. 3, '24.

"FRANCE, ANATOLE." *(contd.*
  ***Our Lady's Juggler. (*R.*) G. B.
    May. (1: 766.)
  ***Procurator of Judea. (*R.*) Gol. Aug.
    (2: 176.)
  ***Putois. (*R.*) Gol. Feb. (1: 189.)

G

GABORIAU, EMILE. (1835–1873.) *(See
  1921.) (French.)*
  **Accursed House. (*R.*) Gol. Mar.
    (1: 332.)
GARNIER, HUGUETTE. *(See 1924.)
  (French.)*
  Penny Ring. N. Y. Trib. Mar. 8.
GEIJERSTAM, GUSTAV A. F. *(Swedish.)*
  **Secret of the Forest. Scan. Oct., '24.
    (12: 612.)
GEVEL, CLAUDE. *(French.)*
  Message of the Wall. N. Y. Trib.
    Aug. 23.
GOGOL, NIKOLAI VASILIEVICH. (1809–
  1852.) *(See 1921.) (H.) (Russian.)*
  ***Diary of a Madman. Mod. Q.
    Winter, '24. (2: 177.)
GOMEZ JAIME, ALFREDO. *(Colombian.)*
  **I Come for a Soul. I. A. Oct., '24.
    (8: 55.)
"GORKY, MAXIM." (ALEXEI MAXIMO-
  VITCH PYESHKOV.) (1868 or 1869–
    .) *(See 1924.) (H.) (Russian.)*
  ***Gipsy: Makar Chudra. (*R.*) Gol.
    May. (1: 721.)
  ***Hermit. Col. May 16. (16.)
  ***Story of a Novel. S. W. Apr. (83.)
  ***Strange Murderer. Dial. Oct., '24.
    (77: 291.)
GOURMONT, REMY DE. (1858–1915.)
  (French.)
  Evening Chat. Guar. Mar. (1: 157.)
  Faun. Guar. Mar. (1: 160.)

H

HEIDENSTAMM, VERNER VON. *(Swedish.)*
  ***Clean White Shirt. (*R.*) Gol. Sept.
    (2: 363.)
  ***French Mons. (*R.*) Gol. Jan. (1: 5.)
  ***Mazeppa and His Ambassador. (*R.*)
    Gol. Feb. (1: 200.)
  ***Queen of the Marauders. (*R.*) Gol.
    Mar. (1: 430.)
  ***Sigrid the Haughty and Her Wooers.
    Scan. Dec., '24. (12: 722.)
HERFORT, PAUL. *(French.)*
  Four Pebbles. N. Y. Trib. Feb. 1.

I

IBANEZ, VICENTE BLASCO. *(Spanish.)*
  See BLASCO IBANEZ, VINCENTE.
IRETSKI. *(Russian.)*
  *Elusive Treasure. (*R.*) Liv. A.
    Sept. 12. (326: 590.)

J

JACOBSEN, JENS PETER. (1847–1885.)
  (Se e 1919.) (Danish.)
  ***Two Worlds. D. D. Jan.–Feb.
    (7: 86.)

K

KUPRIN, ALEXANDER. (1870– .) *(See
  1924.) (Russian.)*
  ***Winter Night's Tale. (*R.*) Liv. A.
    Jan. 24. (324: 213.)

L

"LEBLOND, MARIUS-ARY." *(French.)*
  **Little Brother of the Underbrush.
    Harp. M. Oct., '24. (149: 634.)
LECHE, MIA. *(Swedish.)*
  *Chiffons. (*R.*) Liv. A. Oct. 25, '24.
    (323: 208.)
LEMCHE, GYRITHE. *(Danish.)*
  **For Dear Life. Scan. Aug. (13: 467.)
LEVEL, MAURICE. *(See 1920.) (French.)*
  **Debt Collector. (*R.*) Gol. Feb.
    (1: 221.)

M

MARTORELLO, NOE S. *(Argentinian.)*
  ***Pedro. I. A. Apr. (8: 323.)
MAUPASSANT, HENRI-RENE-ALBERT-GUY
  DE. (1850–1893.) *(See 1922.) (H.)
  (French.)*
  ***Experiment in Love. (*R.*) Gol. Mar.
    (1: 439.)
  ***Night in Spring. (*R.*) Gol. May.
    (1: 678.)
  ***Sundays of a Parisian. (*R.*) Gol.
    Jan. (1: 124.) Feb. (1: 294.)
  **Toine. (*R.*) Gol. Sept. (2: 379.)
MERIMEE, PROSPER. (1803–1870.) *(H.)
  (French.)*
  ***Carmen. (*R.*) Ev. Jun. (97.)
  ***Djoumane. (*R.*) Gol. Jun. (1: 863.)
  **Game of Backgammon. (*R.*) Gol.
    Feb. (1: 282.)
  ***Lokis. (*R.*) Gol. Mar. (1: 361.)
  ***Tamango. (*R.*) Gol. Aug. (2: 245.)
METZGER, MADELEINE. *(French.)*
  *Hamond and the Horned Viper. N. Y.
    Trib. Aug. 30.
  *Manor-House Wedding. (*R.*) Liv. A.
    Dec. 13, '24. (323: 608.)
MUSSET, ALFRED DE. (1810–1857.)
  (French.)
  ***Story of a White Blackbird. (*R.*)
    Gol. Apr. (1: 499.)
  ***White Blackbird's Story. (*R.*) Pear.
    (Am.) Feb. (37.)

N

NAZOR, VLADIMIR. *(Croatian.)*
  **Angelo, the Stonecutter. (*R.*) Liv. A.
    Nov. 29, '24. (323: 483.)
NIETO, ALEJANDRO. *(Argentinian.)*
  ***Love's Labor Lost. (*R.*) Gol. June.
    (1: 881.)

P

PAYRO, ROBERTO J. *(Argentine.)*
  *Integrity. (*R.*) Liv. A. Oct. 18, '24.
    (323: 154.)
PEREZ, J. L. *(Yiddish.)*
  *Eighth Division Hell. Guar. Nov.,
    '24. (6.)
  *Miracle on the Sea. J. T. Sept. 18.
    (38.)